The Critics Acclaim
THE DEAN'S DECEMBER

"THE VITALITY, HUMANITY, ANGER AND WIT OF BELLOW ARE BACK . . . BELLOW, ALONG WITH UPDIKE, MALAMUD, CHEEVER . . . IS WHAT WE HAVE MOST TO CHERISH IN CONTEMPORARY AMERICAN LITERATURE."
—*Boston Sunday Globe*

"THE LATEST AND BEST . . . his fine, fictional instrument is perfectly tuned . . . two generations of Bellow fans should not be disappointed."
—*Time Magazine*

"Bellow is brilliant in this meticulously crafted novel."
—*Publishers Weekly*

"*THE DEAN'S DECEMBER* . . . is renewed testament to a grand career, our greatest since Faulkner's and Frost's . . . at an age when most writers are hopelessly repeating themselves, Bellow is still finding good new things to do."
—*Chicago Sun-Times*

SAUL BELLOW
THE DEAN'S DECEMBER

PUBLISHED BY POCKET BOOKS NEW YORK

Although portions of this novel are derived from real events, each character in it is fictional, a composite drawn from several individuals and from imagination. No reference to any living person is intended or should be inferred.

POCKET BOOKS, a Simon & Schuster division of
GULF & WESTERN CORPORATION
1230 Avenue of the Americas, New York, N Y 10020

Copyright © 1982 by Saul Bellow Limited

Published by arrangement with Harper & Row, Publishers, Inc
Library of Congress Catalog Card Number· 80-8705

ISBN: 0-671-45806-X

First Pocket Books printing January, 1983

10 9 8 7 6 5 4 3 2 1

POCKET and colophon are registered trademarks of Simon & Schuster

Printed in the U S.A

1

Corde, who led the life of an executive in America—wasn't a college dean a kind of executive?—found himself six or seven thousand miles from his base, in Bucharest, in winter, shut up in an old-fashioned apartment. Here everyone was kind—family and friends, warmhearted people—he liked them very much, to him they were "old Europe." But they had their own intense business. This was no ordinary visit. His wife's mother was dying. Corde had come to give support. But there was little he could do for Minna. Language was a problem. People spoke little French, less English. So Corde, the Dean, spent his days in Minna's old room sipping strong plum brandy, leafing through old books, staring out of the windows at earthquake-damaged buildings, winter skies, gray pigeons, pollarded trees, squalid orange-rusty trams hissing under trolley cables.

Corde's mother-in-law, who had had first a heart attack and then a stroke, was in the hospital. Only the Party hospital had the machines to keep her alive, but the rules were rigid there. She was in intensive care, and visits were forbidden. Corde and Minna had flown a day and a night to be with her but in five days had seen her only twice—the first time by special dispensation, the second without official permission. The hospital superintendent, a colonel in the secret police, was greatly offended because his rules had been broken. He was a tough bureaucrat. The staff lived in terror of him.

Minna and her aunt Gigi had decided (Corde took part in their discussions) that it would be polite to ask for an appointment. "Let's try to have a sensible talk with him."

On the telephone the Colonel had said, "Yes, come."

Minna, when she went to see him, brought her husband along—perhaps an American, a dean from Chicago, not quite elderly but getting there, would temper the Colonel's anger. No such thing happened. The Colonel was a lean, hollow-templed, tight-wrapped, braided-whip sort of man. Clearly, he wasn't going to give any satisfaction. An institution must keep its rules. Corde put in his two cents; he mentioned that he was an administrator himself—he had worked for many years on the Paris *Herald,* so he spoke French well enough. The Colonel politely let him speak his piece; he darkly, dryly listened, mouth compressed. He received, tolerated, the administrative comparison, despised it. He did not reply, and when the Dean was done he turned again to Minna.

There had been an impropriety. Under no circumstances could the administration tolerate that. Outraged, Minna was silent. What else could she be? Here only the Colonel had the right to be outraged. His high feeling—and he allowed it to go very high—was moderated in expression only by the depth of his voice. How sharp could a basso sound? Corde himself had a deep voice, deeper than the Colonel's, vibrating more. Where the Colonel was tight, Corde was inclined to be loose. The Colonel's sparse hair was slicked straight back, military style; Corde's baldness was more random, a broad bay, a straggling growth of back hair. From this enlarged face, the brown gaze of an intricate mind of an absent, probably dreamy tendency followed the conversation. You could not expect a Communist secret police colonel to take such a person seriously. He was only an American, a dean of students from somewhere in the middle of the country. Of these two visitors, Minna was by far the more distinguished. This beautiful woman, as the Colonel was sure to know, was a professor of astronomy, had an international reputation. A "hard" scientist. It was important for the Colonel to establish that he was not moved by such considerations. He was in as hard a field as she. Harder.

Minna spoke emotionally about her mother. She was an only child. The hearing the Colonel gave her was perfectly correct. A daughter who had come such a distance; a mother in intensive care, half paralyzed. Without knowing the language, Corde could understand all this easily enough, and interpreted the Colonel's position: Where you had hospitals, you had dying people, naturally. Because of the special circumstances an exception had been made for the *doamna* and her husband on their arrival. But there had been a second visit (here the incensed emphasis again), without permission.

Minna, in terse asides, translated for her husband. It wasn't really necessary. He loosely sat there in wrinkled woolen trousers and sports jacket, the image of the inappropriate American—in all circumstances inappropriate, incapable of learning the lessons of the twentieth century; spared, or scorned, by the forces of history or fate or whatever a European might want to call them. Corde was perfectly aware of this.

He nodded, his brown eyes, bulging somewhat, in communion with the speckled activity of the floor, uniformly speckled over the entire hospital. The director's office was tall but not much roomier than a good-sized closet—a walk-in closet at home. The desk, too, was small. Nothing was big except the Colonel's authority. The electric fixture was hung very high, remote. Here, as everywhere in Bucharest, the light was inadequate. They were short on energy in Rumania —something about subnormal rainfall and low water in the dams. That's right, blame nature. December brown set in at about three in the afternoon. By four it had climbed down the stucco of old walls, the gray of Communist residential blocks: brown darkness took over the pavements, and then came back again from the pavements more thickly and isolated the street lamps. These were feebly yellow in the impure melancholy winter effluence. Air-sadness, Corde called this. In the final stage of dusk, a brown sediment seemed to encircle the lamps. Then there was a livid death moment. Night began. Night was very difficult here, thought Albert Corde. He sat slumped and heavy-headed, his wide head seeking the support it could not get from its stem. This brought his moody eyes forward all the more, the joined brows, the bridge of his spectacles out of level. It was his wife with her fine back, her neck, her handsome look, who made the positive impression. But that was nothing to the whip-lash Colonel. Perhaps it only reminded him that this distinguished lady had defected twenty years ago, when she had been allowed out to study in the West, was here only because her mother was dying, arriving under the protection of her husband, this American dean; landing without a visa, met by a U.S. official (this meant a certain degree of influence). The Colonel would have all this information, of course. And Minna was not in a strong position; she had never formally renounced her Rumanian citizenship. If it had a mind to, the government could make trouble for her.

Valeria, the old woman, was not a Party member now, hadn't been one since, as Minister of Health, she fell in disgrace. That had happened thirty years ago. She was then denounced publicly by press and radio, expelled, threatened with prison, with death, too. Before he could come to trial, one of her colleagues who fell in the same shake-up had his head hacked off in his cell. This old militant who had survived Antonescu and also the Nazis was butchered with an ax or a meat cleaver. Dr. Valeria somehow came through. Dr. Valeria herself had founded this very hospital, the Party hospital. Three weeks ago, probably feeling the first touches of sickness (Corde thought of it as the advance death thrill, the final presage; each of us in peculiar communication with his own organs and their sick-signals), she began to make the rounds, out all day on the buses and trolley cars, said Gigi, calling on old acquaintances, arranging to be admitted. She had been rehabilitated late in the fifties, her pension restored, and she had quiet connections of her own among the old-timers of the bureaucracy.

So she was hooked in now to the respirator, scanner, monitor. The stroke had knocked out the respiratory center, her left side was paralyzed. She couldn't speak, couldn't open her eyes. She could hear, however, and work the fingers of her right hand. Her face was crisscrossed every which way with tapes, like the Union Jack. Or like windowpanes in cities under bombardment. Corde, an old journalist before he became a dean, knew these wartime scenes—sandbags, window tapes. Never saw the crisscross on a face like hers, though; too delicate for it. Still, the next step, a tracheotomy, was even worse. He was an experienced man. He knew the stages.

Before you were allowed to approach Valeria you had to put on a sterile gown and oversocks, huge and stiff. Also a surgical cap and mask. Valeria understood that her daughter had come, and her eyes moved under the lids. Minna was there. And protected by her husband—further proof of his dependability. When Corde spoke to her, she answered by pressing his fingers. Her son-in-law then noticed for the first time a deformity of one of her knuckles. Had it been broken once, was it arthritic? It was discolored. He had never before seen her hair down, only braided and pinned. He would never have guessed this fine white hair to be so long. There was also her big belly. Beneath it her thin legs. That, too, was painful to see. Every bit of it moved him—more than that, it worked him up; more than that, it made him wild, drove him into savage fantasies. He wanted to cry, as his wife was doing.

Tears did come, but also an eager violence, a kind of get-it-over ecstasy mingling pity and destructiveness. Part of him was a monster. What else could it be?

These reactions were caused by exhaustion, partly. They must have been. The trip had been long. He was fagged, dried out. His guts were strained. He felt plugged in the rear. Circulation to the face and scalp seemed insufficient. And a kind of demonic excitement rose up, for which no resolution seemed possible. Like evil forces, frantic, foul, working away. At the same time, his tears for the old woman were genuine, too. For the moment, he could suppress nothing, force nothing. Equally helpless before good and bad. On the electronic screen of the monitor, symbols and digits shimmied and whirled, he heard a faint scratching and ticking.

The Colonel, towards the last of the interview, put on a long, judicious look—cunning, twisting the knife —and said that if Valeria was removed from the intensive care unit, Minna might come as often as she liked. Unhooked from the machines, the old woman would die in fifteen minutes. This of course he did not spell out. But there was your choice, madam. This was the man's idea of a joke. You delivered it at the point of a knife.

That part of the conversation Corde had missed. Minna had told him about it. "My homecoming," she said after the interview, as they were going down the cement walk to the parking lot.

"Like tying a plastic bag over your face and telling you to breathe deep."

"I could kill him." Perhaps she could, from the set of her face—big eyes, intaken lips. "What should I do now, Albert? She'll be expecting us, waiting for us."

They were riding home in Petrescu's Russian compact, one of those strong dreary cars they drive in the satellite countries.

Mihai Petrescu had been *chef de cabinet* to Minna's father and to Valeria when she succeeded her late husband in the Ministry. He was attached to the family. Not himself a physician, he must have been the Party watchdog. He couldn't have had much to report. Dr. Raresh had been naively ideological, a Christian and moral Communist, praying for God's help before he opened a patient's skull. The country's first neurosurgeon, trained in Boston by the famous Cushing, he had been too emotional, too good, too much the high-principled doctor to make a Communist official. Minna said she could never understand how he could have been taken in so completely. In the thirties he had brushed aside as bourgeois propaganda what he had read in the world press about the Great Terror, Stalin's labor camps, the Communists in Spain, the pact with Hitler. Enthusiastic when Russian troops reached Bucharest, he went into the streets with roses for the soldiers. Within a week they had taken the watch from his wrist, put him out of his little Mercedes and driven it away. But he made no complaints. He did not move into a villa like other ministers. His colleagues disliked this. His austerity was too conspicuous. Before he died, the regime had already decided the man was a fool and kicked him upstairs. He was named ambassador to the U.S.A. They didn't want him around protesting the disappearance of his medical friends one after another. He didn't live to go to Washington. He lasted only a year.

When he died Valeria was offered the Ministry. She probably thought it might be dangerous to refuse. Minna was then a small girl. Petrescu stayed on as *chef de cabinet*. Lower-echelon KGB was how Corde figured him. Mihai seemed to have converted the official connection into familial intimacy. He told Corde when they had a schnapps together, *"Elle a été une mère, une consolatrice pour moi."* And for others, by the dozens. Valeria was a matriarch. Corde was well aware of that.

But sometimes Petrescu stayed away for years. He had not been seen for many months before Valeria's stroke. And even now he disappeared, reappeared unpredictably. Petrescu was squat, small-eyed; his fedora was unimpeded by hair so that the fuzz of the hat brim mingled with the growth of his ears in all-revealing daylight. In every conversation about Valeria his sentences had a way of creeping upwards, his pitch climbed as high as his voice could bring it, and then there was a steep drop, a crack of emotion. He was dramatically fervent about Valeria. Studying his face, Corde at the same time estimated that something like three-fourths of his creases were the creases of a very tough character, a man you could easily imagine slamming the table during an interrogation, capable perhaps of pulling a trigger. It wasn't just in Raymond Chandler novels that you met tough guys. All kinds of people are tough. But with the ladies Petrescu was wonderful, he behaved with gallantry, or else with saintly delicacy, he jumped up, moved chairs, tumbled out of the driver's seat to open the doors of his Soviet car. Today he was standing by, upstairs, with advice, telephoning, volunteering, murmuring, as silken with Minna and Tanti Gigi as the long fleshy lobes of his ears were silken. His underlip was full of a fervent desire to serve. Before he disappeared—for he soon did disappear—he played a leading part in the emotional composition whose theme was Valeria's last days. Great Valeria's end. For she was great—this was the conclusion Corde finally reached.

The apartment was shared by Valeria and Tanti Gigi. Corde and Minna were staying there. Visiting nieces, cousins, had to go to hotels. But under the special consanguinity regulations, the Cordes were permitted to move in with Gigi. Something of an invalid, Tanti Gigi managed the household with hysterical efficiency. She seemed to do it all in bathrobe and slippers and from her bed. When he knew the problems of the city better—the queues forming at daybreak, the aged women with oilcloth shopping bags waiting throughout the day—Corde was able to appreciate Gigi's virtuosity. The flat was as tentatively heated as it was electrically dim. Radiators turned cold after breakfast. The faucets went dry at 8 A.M. and did not run again until evening. The bathtub had no stopper. You flushed the toilet with buckets of water. Corde was not a man to demand comforts. He merely observed all this—a hungry observer. The parlor, once the brain surgeon's waiting room, was furnished with aging corpulent overstuffed chairs of bald, peeling leather. There were openwork brass lamps which resembled minarets. It was all quality stuff from the bourgeois days. The Biedermeier cabinets were probably despised in the twenties by young revolutionists, but in old age they clung to these things as relics of former happiness. Very odd, thought Corde, how much feeling went into these sofas, old orange brocade and frames with mother-of-pearl inlay; and the bric-a-brac and thin carpets, gilt-framed pictures, fat editions of Larousse, antiquated medical books in German and English. After her disgrace and loss of pension, during the period of ostracism, Valeria sold off the best of the silver and china. The last of the Baccarat had been smashed in the recent earthquake. While they were lying on the floor Tanti Gigi had heard the crystal minutely crumbling and tinkling, dancing on the floor, she said. The objects that remained were of no terrific value, but they were obviously consecrated—they were the family's old things: Dr. Raresh's worktable, Minna's bed, the pictures in her room, even her undergraduate notebooks.

Much better this old flat—it was a Balkan version of the Haussmann style—than the Intercontinental Hotel and the Plaza Athénée with their deluxe totalitarian comforts and the goings-on of the secret police—*securitate:* devices behind the draperies, tapes spinning in the insulated gloom. But you were bugged in the flat, too, probably with the latest American bugs. You name it, the manufacturing U.S. would sell it. Or else the French, the Japanese, the Italians would sell it. So if you wanted to talk privately you went outside, and in the streets, too, Minna would nudge you, directing

your attention to certain men lounging, walking slowly
or chatting. "Yup, I can spot 'em myself," said Corde.
The fat concierge, Ioanna, was in continual conversation with these loungers. She reported to them. But she
was also a friend of the family. That was how it went.
Valeria and Tanti Gigi had more than once explained
matters to him.

Corde knew the old girls very well. Valeria had
visited the States, and he and Minna had often met
them both abroad. When they were eligible for visas,
the old sisters flew to Paris, Frankfurt, London. Of
course they had to be sent for—no dollars, no passports
—and they came out of the country without a penny,
not even cab fare. Only last spring Valeria had joined
Corde and Minna in England.

Valeria studied people closely, but she may not have
been aware of the important place she held in Corde's
feelings. How could she be? The deep-voiced slouching
Dean would sit with his legs stretched out and his neck
resting on the back of his chair like a reporter on a
story, killing time patiently in a waiting room. His
nonchalant way of looking at you, the extruded brown
eyes, that drowned-in-dreams look, was probably the
source of his reputation as a swinger, a chaser. Minna
and Valeria had been warned against him. Erotic
instability, womanizing, was the charge. Judged by the
standards of perfect respectability, Corde had not been
a good prospect for marriage. "It's true he's been
married before, but so have I," said Minna to her
mother. Valeria's influence was great, but in this instance Minna made her own decision. It was a sound
decision. There was no instability. Corde proved to be
entirely straight. After several years of observation
Valeria gave him a clearance. She said to her daughter,
"You were perfectly right about Albert." She was not
after all one of your parochial Balkan ladies. She had
studied Freud, Ferenczi, she was a psychiatrist—Corde
forgave her the psychiatry; maybe psychiatry was dif-

ferent in the Balkans. He certainly wasn't kinky enough
to be written up as a case history.

So there they were, in Minna's old room. It was still a
schoolgirl's room. Valeria had kept it that way. There
were textbooks, diplomas, group photographs. This
was obviously Valeria's favorite place, where she read,
sewed, wrote letters. Corde was curious about the
books that crammed the shelves. Many were English
and French. He found an old collection of Oscar Wilde
published by some British reader's society in red cardboard, faded to weeping pink, and looked up some of
the poems he had learned by heart as an adolescent,
melodramatic pieces like "The Harlot's House," the
puppet prostitute and the clockwork lover, the scandals
of Greek love, the agonies of young men who had done
so well at school but woke up beside their murdered
mistresses in London with blood and wine upon their
hands. Why had they killed them? That's what love
does to you. An unsatisfactory proposition. Corde
particularly wanted to find the lines about the red hell
to which a man's sightless soul might stray. He found it,
it amused him—the earth reeling underfoot, and the
weary sunflowers—but not for long. He put down the
not-so-amusing book. He found the street more interesting.

Earthquake damage was still being repaired. A machine, a wheeled crane, worked its way down the block.
A crew of two stood in the large bucket to patch cracks
in stucco, working around the open porches. Women in
kerchiefs whacked their carpets in the morning. From
all sides one heard the percussion of carpet beaters.
Give it to them! The dust went off in the sunlight. A
dog barked, whined as if a beater had given him a
whack, then barked again. The barking of the dog, a
protest against the limits of dog experience (for God's
sake, open the universe a little more!)—so Corde felt,
being shut in. He might have gone rambling about the
city, but Minna was afraid the *securitate* would pick him

up. What if he were accused of selling dollars illegally?
She had heard stories about this. Friends warned her.
All right, she had worries enough, and he stayed put.

She was busy in the parlor. Friends she hadn't seen in
twenty years came to call—Viorica, Doina, Cornelia.
Corde was asked to present himself in the parlor, the
American husband. The telephone rang all the time.
As soon as possible he went back to the room, his
retreat. For three days he thought how much good it
would do him to go out and walk off the tensions he had
brought from Chicago (cramps in his legs), then he
stopped thinking about it.

Back to the shelves. He pulled away the beds to see
what titles they concealed. Pedagogy was one of Valeria's interests. He found an unpublished primer with
pictures of cows, piglets, ponies. Curious about Minna's adolescence, he leafed through albums, studying
snapshots. In the drawers he turned up coins from
former regimes, embossed buttons, documents from
the time of the monarchy, stopped watches, Byzantine
crosses on thin silver chains, newspaper clippings,
letters from Dr. Cushing to Raresh, one of his best
pupils. There were also items about Corde—installed
as dean, receiving an honorary degree from Grinnell.
Minna had sent her mother a copy of the first installment of his long article on Chicago, the one that had
stirred up so much trouble. Trouble was still raging.
That was some of what he had brought with him.
Valeria had obviously read his piece closely, making
check marks in the margin where he had described the
crazy state of the prisoners in County Jail—the rule of
the barn bosses, the rackets, beatings, sodomizings and
stabbings in the worst of the tiers: in "Dodge City,"
"H-1"; the prisoners who tucked trouser bottoms into
socks to keep the rats from running up their legs in the
night. Now there *was* a red hell for the soul to stray
into.

Obviously it intrigued Valeria the psychiatrist to
study the personality of her son-in-law as it was re-

vealed in his choice of topics; his accounts of beatings and buggerings, of a murder with the sharp-honed metal of a bed leg, were underscored in red. He pored over these passages, hunched under his coat, noting how often he had mentioned the TV in each dayroom, the soaps and the sporting events, "society's alternatives continually in view," and "how strangely the mind of the criminal is stocked with images from that other anarchy, the legitimate one." Valeria had circled these sentences. She hadn't received the second installment. Mainly about the Rufus Ridpath scandal, the Spofford Mitchell case, it was filled with disobliging remarks about City Hall, the press, the sheriff, the governor. Corde had let himself go, indignant, cutting, reckless. He had made the college unhappy. One of its deans taking everybody on? A bad scene, an embarrassment. The administration behaved with restraint, but it was jittery. It was especially upset by Part Two. What would Valeria have thought of Part Two?

Valeria had never made Corde feel that she objected to the marriage; she had too much breeding for that, she was too tactful to antagonize him. She did study him, yes, but without apparent prejudice. Really, she was fair-minded. Although he hadn't much liked being under observation, he conceded that it wasn't unreasonable. "But Christ, do I need a parole officer?" Of course he was uncomfortable, and when he was uncomfortable he grew more silent, speaking only in a brief rumble. What was most distressing about being watched was that it made him see himself—a dish-faced man, long in the mouth. You could hardly blame him for being sensitive to close scrutiny. In giving his order to a waiter once, asking for an *omelette fines herbes,* he was pointedly corrected by Valeria. "The *s* is sounded—*feenzerbes.*" He was stunned, the abyss of pettiness opened. It *was* an abyss.

Nevertheless he was strongly drawn to the old woman. Last spring the three of them had stayed together at Durrants in George Street, and he was always in their company, didn't care to go off by himself. He tagged along to Liberty's, Jaeger's, Harrods. He enjoyed that. And last April great London had been wide open and the holiday gave him the kind of human "agreement" (he could find no other term for it) he very badly needed, was evidently looking for continually. He gladly followed the two ladies through Harrods ("Harrods of Jewry" to him, but now filled with Arabs). The parcels were heaped up in Valeria's room. He said to Minna, "Why not buy her something she can't give away, for herself only?"

"She doesn't seem to need . . ." Minna began. "It's enough for her to be with—with us. And especially here, in London. She adores London."

No one understood better than the English how to build coziness in a meager setting. You polished up old tables, you framed dinginess in margins of gilt; without apology, you dignified worn corners, brushed up the bald nap of your velours—these were the Dickensian touches that Corde approved. He wasn't quite sure how Valeria viewed this less than luxurious hotel. Couldn't her American son-in-law do better? Coming out of Bucharest, you probably would have preferred the Ritz. But he was a dean, merely, not the governor of Texas—no, the governor wouldn't have been good enough for Minna, nor a member of the board of Chase Manhattan. Still, the feeling of human "agreement" would not have been possible without the old woman's acceptance. She accepted him, soon enough. He was all right. They were both all right. If his manner was quiet (the parolee on good behavior), hers was undemonstratively accommodating. In the morning she went down early to buy the *Times* for Corde (by half past eight the porter was likely to tell him, "Sorry, sir, sold out"). She made sure that there was a copy of the paper on her son-in-law's chair. Then she sat in her neat suit, waiting in the breakfast room, the green silk scarf about her neck—lovely blue-green. Until Minna joined her, Valeria did not accept so much as a cup of tea from the

Spanish waiters. As breakfast drew to an end, Corde turned his chair aside slightly. The Dean, drawing back his head peculiarly—his neck was thin—focused his gaze on the *Times* (a foreign paper printed in his own language). Reading, he omitted no item of politics, the experienced newspaperman making his own swift observations. "I know these guys," was his attitude. As the ladies discussed their plans for the day, the Dean glanced also at the currency rates, the obituaries of civil servants and retired soldiers, the Court Calendar, items from Wimbledon—matters of minimal interest. He experienced alternate waves of bleakness and of warmth towards Valeria for her admirable control over such a diversity of factors—doubts (about him), love for her daughter, embarrassment at being without a penny of her own. Of course the daughter had a good income. But the son-in-law wanted very much to buy her coats, dresses, hats, purses, tickets, excursions, dinners, music, airline tickets. Then he would note her level look. She was wondering quietly about him. What sort of man is Albert—what is his quality? When he and Minna returned to their tight, small, neat Durrants room after breakfast, he said, "Here's a hundred pounds. Buy the old girl some kid gloves. Take her to Bond Street." Minna laughed at him.

Then he made an independent discovery, one it was impossible for Minna to make.

Minna, you see, had her astrophysical, mathematical preoccupations. Minna, in Corde's metaphor, was bringing together a needle from one end of the universe with a thread from the opposite end. Once this was accomplished, Corde couldn't say what there was to be sewn—this was his own way of concentrating his mind on the *mysterium tremendum*. Face it, the cosmos was beyond him. His own special ability was to put together for the general reader such pieces as this one from *Harper's*. Its topics (in Minna's schoolgirl room, he turned the pages) were the torments and wildness of black prisoners under the jurisdiction of the disabled sheriff of Cook County, who had himself broken his neck in a patriotic street brawl with rampaging Weathermen in the Loop, when he missed a flying tackle; and . . . no, there the Dean checked it, cooled it. He would stop with his ability to describe a scene for the common reader; or to deal with undergraduates—he did that fairly well, too. Or with his more important ability to engage (inexplicably) the affections of a woman like his wife, who had chosen him to share her planetary life. (Forgiving him his defects, his sins. But she would never regret it.) The county sheriff who campaigned from his wheelchair was, for the moment, set aside.

Corde's discovery in London was that Valeria no longer had the strength to travel, to fly back and forth. She was too old. The diagnosis was sudden but it was complete. "She can't hack it." She was sick, she doctored herself (he had seen pill bottles when she opened her pocketbook). Pushing eighty, she flew to England. Unless Minna formally renounced her Rumanian citizenship, she couldn't go to see her mother. It might not be safe. Hard to say why Minna balked at this formal renunciation. She found excuses. "I can't stand those people. I can't bear to correspond with them. Yes, I *will* go through with it. I've already got the forms filled in." True, she concentrated mostly on her science, couldn't be bothered with government papers, but that was a superficial explanation, considering the strength of her feeling for Valeria. But she preferred to assume that her mother was strong and well. That Valeria should be too sick to go abroad was inadmissible. As for Valeria, she would rather die in an airport than tell her daughter, "My dear, I'm too weak for suitcases, and I can't manage taxis, and I can't stand in line for customs, I'm too old for the jets." No, she came to London, her head full of lists—and every day she told Minna, "I have to bring dress material for Floara. I promised to get computer manuals for Ionel." And so with boots for Doina, tea from Fortnum's for Gigi. For herself she bought colored postcards of Westminster Abbey.

Corde was called upstairs to strap her boxy rawhide valises. To squeeze them shut took some doing. How did the old woman manage to haul these two fat trunks?—they *were* almost trunks.

"It must take plenty of wangling to get these damn things through customs."

"She's got what it takes," said Minna. She shrugged.

She had to read a paper before a scientific meeting in Copenhagen, and for two days Corde was in charge of Valeria. He entertained her at the Étoile on Charlotte Street. She loved the Étoile. He took her to a Rowlandson exhibition at Burlington House. That meant standing in a queue outside, and then making your way through crowded halls. The old woman smiled calmly at the stout, rosy, frilling ladies of fashion, at the fops, but Corde soon saw that the outing was too much for her. Strange to watch, troubling. He was upset for her. She couldn't keep her balance; she was tipping, listing, seemed unable to coordinate the movements of her feet. He said, "I've had enough Rowlandson, do you mind?" As he led her down the large staircase, the lightness and the largeness of her elbow surprised him. Why was the joint so big? It felt like dry sponge. She removed his hand. They emerged in the Piccadilly jam of vehicles and people. She said, "You have things to do, Albert. I'm going back to the hotel." He doubted even that she could hail a cab. He flagged one down and got in with her, saying, "I left my appointment book at the hotel; I don't remember where I'm supposed to go next." She made a place for him on the buttoned black leather seat and sat in the corner silent, even severe.

Corde's father had been an old-fashioned American, comfortable, calm, a "Pullman car type," his son called him. (The old guy had been a sort of playboy too, a man about town, but that was something else again.) Corde could reproduce his manner. That obtuse style

was helpful now. He gave Valeria no sign that he had
found her out. When he took her that night to a Turkish
dinner in Wardour Street, she seemed stronger, she
said how pleasant London was; she talked Communist
politics, reminisced about Ana Pauker, in whose government she had served. He told her a little about life
in Chicago. With red meat and a bottle of wine, she
picked up somewhat. She said she had been tired that
afternoon. Between three o'clock and five the body ran
out of blood sugar.

"Yes, I go into an afternoon slump myself. Often."

But he said quietly to Minna when they had seen
Valeria off at Heathrow, "Did the old girl say how good
a time she had? I don't think she can make the trip
again."

"You're not serious. Her only pleasure is coming out.
These holidays in a civilized place. And seeing us. She
lives for it."

He did not pursue the subject. He had gone on
record. Minna would have to follow up in her own way.

2

It was an instinct with Corde—maybe it was a weakness
—always to fix attention on certain particulars, in every
situation to grasp the details. If he took Valeria to dine
at the Étoile, he brought away with him a clear picture
of the wine waiter. That a bald man had triple creases
at the back of his skull could not be left out of account,
nor could the shape of his thumbs, the health of his
face, the spread of his nose, the strength of his stout
Italian body in the waiter's suit. Corde's eyes took in

also the dishes on the hors d'oeuvre cart, the slices of
champignons à la Grecque, the brown sauce, the
pattern of the table silver. With him, exclusively mental
acts seldom occurred. He was temperamentally an
image man. To observe so much was not practical,
sometimes it was disabling, often downright painful,
but actualities could not be left out.

So when he left Chicago, it had to be remembered
that he packed his dusty black zippered garment bag.
As he carried it, it rubbed against his leg with a
slithering sound (the synthetic material expressing itself). In the bag, his undistinguished clothing—shirts
spotted and scorched in the hand laundry, trousers that
should have gone to the cleaner (he could shut his eyes
and locate those spots exactly). Another item: in the
fever of departure, he saw the floating ice blocks in
Lake Michigan, gray-white and tan, the top layer of
snow stained with sand blown from the beaches by the
prevailing wind. Item: the red thermal undershirt he
removed from his luggage because he imagined that
Bucharest would be a Mediterranean sort of place, a
light city not a heavy one; rococo. Rococo! It was mass
after mass of socialist tenements and government office
buildings. Now he regretted that thermal shirt. Item:
the tube of salve he needed for the rash about his
ankles was squeezed dry, rolled up to the neck—he
should have ordered another before leaving. Item: his
pots of African violets. What good would it do to let the
rods of ultra-violet light burn on? A crisis—how to save
his plants! He had heard that if you put one end of a
rope in a bucket of water, the other end would deliver
sufficient moisture, but there was no time to set this up.
Item: the can of Earl Grey tea on the kitchen counter,
and the bananas. He took those with him to Europe.
Essential documents were left on his desk. He hadn't
been able to find his address book; he had most likely
hidden it from himself. He wouldn't be writing letters
anyway. His instinct was to cut, to drop everything and
fly away unencumbered. It was only the violets he

regretted leaving. Item: Minna packed her valise with
astronomical papers, giving them priority over dresses.
On the trip she couldn't be separated from these books
and reprints. They weren't checked through but had to
be carried as cabin luggage. Her eyes seemed to have
been displaced by stress; they looked like the fruit in an
eccentric still life. As soon as Gigi's wire came she
stopped eating. In a matter of hours she was looking
gaunt, and sallow; her face had a kind of negative
color. Her underlip was retracted, and her chin filled
with pressure marks. Corde was a close watcher of his
wife. Item: the cab to the airport ran between levees of
snow. Winter's first blizzard had struck Chicago. The
cab was overheated and stank of excrement. Of dogs?
Of people? It was torrid, also freezing; Arctic and
Sahara, mixed. Also, the driver was sloshed with eau
de cologne. The ribbed rubber floor was all filth and
grit. Corde said, "People have even stopped wiping
themselves." He took the precaution of saying this in
French, and there was something false about that—
raunchy gaiety (and disgust) in a foreign language.
Anyhow it fell flat, as Minna scarcely heard him.

More items were checked on the way to O'Hare. The
alarm system? The keys? The windows? Instructions to
the super to remove the mail from the box, the
newspapers from the front door? Had he gone to the
bank for dollars? Talked to de Prima, the lawyer? Left
Valeria's telephone number with Miss Porson at the
office? The college might need to reach them. Minna
was thinking not of the Dean's special problems but of
the time reserved for her on the telescope at Mount
Palomar. She had been due there Christmas week, but
that was now canceled, of course. "Yes, they know
where to find us," he said. With his dense eyebrows,
the plain length of his mouth, his low voice, his usual
posture was one of composure, and now and then
students told him that it was wonderful how "laid back"
he was. A handsome compliment but undeserved. He
was engaged in a sharp rearguard action against the

forces of agitation. When they took off from O'Hare, he felt that all the Chicago perplexities were injected into his nerves. Yet when he went into the lavatory of the Lufthansa 747 and the light went on, he seemed well enough to himself, with a mouth like a simple declarative sentence, although there were so many complex-compound things to be said.

Then, after making an air loop of thousands of miles, he found himself stuck. But alien as they were, his surroundings offered him intimacy, the instant intimacy of Minna's old room. For much of the day he lounged among Rumanian cushions on a divan, drinking peasant brandy and eating grapes, brownish green and heavy on the seeds, brought from the country by Tanti Gigi's far-flung agents. Because Gigi's heart was irregular, she was in bed much of the time, but women were coming and going all day, reporting to her, taking instructions. Corde was on her mind. He could drink only real coffee and, deprived of whiskey, he needed *pálinca,* at least. He was used to having meat (meat was virtually unobtainable), and a bottle of wine with it (you *could* get inferior wine on the black market). He had sacrificed his comforts to bring Minna here, and Gigi was therefore determined that he should have the best. ("What a rich, wonderful country we are," she said. "If only you could see the real Rumania.")

Despite doorbells and telephones, conferences, despite the developing struggle with the Colonel, despite the weight of a large totalitarian mass of life on the outside (the city was terrible!), he was quiet. No urgent calls, decisions, no hateful letters, no awkward conferences, infighting, or backbiting—people getting at him one way or another. After lunch he took off his clothing, pulled back the heavy gaudy bed cover (almost a rug) and went to sleep. Sometimes he did that after breakfast, too. He did not feel quite steady even in brilliant healthful weather; consciousness reeling as if he had been driving a car over endless plains and whole continents. He was eye-sick, head-sick, seat-sick, motion-sick, gut-sick, wheel-weary. So he rested after breakfast. The nights were not easy. Minna wasn't sleeping. She seemed to lie there rerunning in her mind all the worst sequences of the day. To these were added thoughts for which there hadn't been sufficient time. The room was cold, the nights unnaturally black—or was this Corde's own intensity working outward, blacker than night. He put out his fingers and fetched the covers over his bony shoulders, but when he heard Minna stirring he knew that he must get up and offer her comfort. Lying down with her usually helped. But not now.

She didn't turn when he entered her small bed and put his arms around her from behind. They held a whispered conversation.

Minna said, "What does she think? Days go by and I'm not there."

"What, she? She can't open her eyes, and in that room you couldn't tell days from nights anyway—besides, she understands why you're not there."

"Does she?"

"Are you kidding? With her experience? Inside the government? And/or private life? They've been under the Russians since 1945. That's a long, long time. She's got to know every wrinkle. You can be sure she thought it through even before we arrived."

"Yes, that may be."

He lowered his voice still more. "Even after a few days you feel them sitting on your face. And at this rate we may be looking at our own future."

"You shouldn't say that. . . ."

"It's not me that says it. *I* don't believe it, but it's what you hear and see. You should read what they say on the Russian New Right. Like, it's the weak democracies that produce dictatorships. Or that our decadence is heading full speed towards collapse. Of course, they overdo it. But you can't help thinking about it."

Minna let him go on, and he stopped himself. It wasn't exactly the time to develop such views. Evil

visions. The moronic inferno. He read too many articles and books. If the night hadn't been so black and
cold, none of this would have been said. The night
made you exaggerate. Between them on the pillow was
the float of her hair.

"They want to do a tracheotomy," she said.

"Do they have to?"

"Dr. Moldovanu said on the telephone that it had to
be done. He also told me that he wrote a report to the
Colonel about the visits. He suggested they were good
for my mother."

"They're all afraid of that bastard. He scares them to
death."

"Ileana told me that when Dr. Moldovanu's mother
had an infarct, he wasn't allowed to bring her to the
Party hospital. The request was refused."

"They call it an infarct here? There might be a way to
go over the man's head, if this were Chicago or
Honduras, or some such place."

"How can he not allow me . . . !"

It was Corde's habit to explain matters to his un-
worldly wife. It gave him pleasure and was sometimes
instructive even to himself. "This gives the man an
opportunity to test the efficiency of his controls. This is
fine tuning," said Corde. "Yesterday I sent a note to a
guy at the American embassy."

"Did you?"

"I asked Gigi to have it delivered for me. It's only a
couple of blocks, she said. You see, just before we left
Chicago I phoned my old friend Walter, in Washington,
and explained where we were going, told him about
this. He got back to me with some names here—
contacts. I don't expect great results, but I did tell this
guy in the information branch I wanted to visit him."

"Could he do us any good?"

"It's worth a try. I might suggest he ask the State
Department to put in its oar."

"No! Do you think they might . . . ?"

"There's an election coming, and this would be one

of those humane Christian things from the White
House. Make good copy."

"Do they do such things?"

"Those people are sweet, and mostly air, like
Nabisco wafers. Still, I did ask Walter to get to the right
desk in the State Department. I've been worried all
along about your dual citizenship."

"I should have attended to that long ago." She
changed the subject. In science she was scientific; in
other matters her methods were more magical, Corde
believed. By giving up the dual citizenship, she would
be admitting her mother's mortality, and that in itself
might have weakened the old woman. That kind of
primitive reasoning.

"Tanti Gigi wants me to get in touch with Dr.
Gherea," she said.

"Gherea?"

"You remember who he is? You *don't* remember."

"Yes, I do. I do so. Your father's pupil, the one he
trained in brain surgery."

"That's the man. He's the big neurosurgeon here,
practically the only one. My father made him. After my
father died he became a big shot."

"Is he good?"

"They say he's a genius."

"We'll have to think about it."

Her schoolgirl bed was too narrow for them both,
and he returned to the divan. Several times during the
night he got up to stroke her head or kiss her on the
shoulders. These remedies had always given Corde a
sense of useful power, but they were ineffectual now.
The night pangs were too bad. He had them himself.
He listened to Minna's breathing. She appeared to hold
her breath. He waited, listening until she exhaled. He
said at last, "Let's get out the bottle and have a shot or
two. No use lying here like dummies." He switched on
the light. They sat side by side in their coats, drinking
plum brandy. The stuff was slightly oily and rank, but

went down smooth and warm. Then up came the fermented fumes.

"It won't be easy to approach Gherea."

"Why not?" said Corde. "Don't you know him?"

"Thirty years ago he was like one of the family. But he's turned into a savage."

"In what way savage?"

"He knocks people down—assistants, anesthetists, nurses. He even hits his colleagues, doesn't give a damn for anybody. They have to take it from him. He punches and kicks them if they hand him the wrong instrument. And he won't operate without money. 'You don't give me five hundred thousand lei, I don't remove your brain tumor.'"

"A brute. You don't have to tell me about brutes. And the only game in town."

"That's it, Albert. Even the dictator's son, when he had a skull fracture and they brought him to Gherea, they say Gherea had him put in bed with another patient."

"Are they two to a bed here?"

"In lots of hospitals they are. This was Gherea's way of pointing out to *him* that he had to spend more on hospitals."

"So even the dictator has to put up with him. And what does Gherea do with the dough he squeezes from people—does he live it up?"

"I guess he must. But I don't see how—he never leaves the country. How do you live it up here? He doesn't have a second language. Maybe Russian. I think he comes from Bessarabia. He never goes abroad."

". . . Pictures, music?"

"They say he has no use for such stuff."

"Just himself and his knives and saws? Him and death? Only interested in the basic facts? What about sex?"

"That's just it; he has a lady friend and I happen to

know her. I met the woman in Zurich eight or ten years ago. She's very decent, divorced. They're together."

"And you want her to persuade him to examine Valeria?"

"What's your picture of Gherea?"

"Your people had class, and he was a boor. They took him up because he had a knack for surgery. He despised them. Thought it was idiotic that with all their advantages they should be Communists. A peasant mentality. He concentrated on learning the Cushing techniques from your father, and then to hell with him."

"That's about right," said Minna. Corde's speed in making connections never failed to please her. She counted on him to spell things out.

"Sure, I see him. He's the tough glory type who goes into people's heads with his tools and his fingers. The brain has got to be hell to work in. Save 'em or kill 'em. Hates sentiment, dramatizes himself as a beast . . . maybe there's a peasant mother who still pines for him out in the bush. He never sees her. There's only this devoted woman with access to his softer side."

"I'm going to talk to her. Tanti Gigi got the number for me."

"Can't hurt."

"You think I should?"

"Of course. Let Gherea look at the X-rays."

The X-rays would show a cloud over the brain of the sort Corde had once seen on a film. A smart microphotographer had managed to insert a tiny lens into the carotid artery and push it up to the skull, capturing a cerebral hemorrhage on his camera. What you saw was the blood beginning to fizz out. At first it wavered in a thick, black, woolly skein. Then it suddenly filled in, thickened, a black rush, the picture of death itself. The memory of this television documentary was something Corde preferred to avoid.

He thought, Sure, let Minna get this surgeon character to look at the clot, make his gesture. It won't do any good. But let her put up a fight. Valeria fought for her. Minna when she was brought back to earth could be a tigress. He had seen that. Fighting was quite unrealistic, of course. Under the circumstances it would get her nowhere. The Colonel had them all in chancery, like John L. Sullivan. But it was necessary emotionally to do battle.

Corde had heard anecdotes about Valeria's dignified refusal to rejoin the Party after she was "forgiven." She told the Central Committee that she had loved her late husband, and that if he had been unfaithful she would have loved him still but she would never have taken him back. In matters of self-respect she was the model for her daughter, her sister and all the ladies of her circle. Had she made serious trouble, it would have been easy enough for the regime to put her away, but this would have upset many old academicians and physicians and educators of her own dying generation. Why stir up the codgers? Besides, she had been a sensible old character, and circumspect, and knew exactly how far she could go, so they were letting her die in the best of their hospitals. But they weren't about to be agreeable to the daughter. The daughter came flying in from the U.S. trailing her streamers of scientific prestige, arriving with this dean of hers and demanding special treatment. She had forgotten how things were here. Maybe she had never known. They would give the daughter a few lumps. This was the score, as her brooding husband saw it. Naive Gigi considered herself to be next in line and came forward to carry on in her fallen sister's place. She was protecting Minna, too, as Valeria had done. All these fighters. Corde reviewed the situation as though he were browsing over it, but his conclusions were sharp enough. The ladies were getting nowhere. They couldn't get anywhere. But they were bound to try. He would try too.

"Let's drink up and get some sleep," he said.

"You haven't heard from Chicago?" she said. "Nothing from Miss Porson?"

"Not yet."

"Not from Vlada, or from Sam Beech?"

Minna took an interest in the Beech project. Beech
was a colleague at the college, a celebrated, a notable,
a pure scientist, very high in the pantheon, who had
asked the Dean for help in putting some of his ideas
before the general public. Vlada was a Serbian friend of
Minna's. They had been at Harvard graduate school
together. Lifelong students, both of them. Minna's old
lycée was nearby. You might see the shape of it up the
street even now if you could bear to open the door to
the stucco porch (it couldn't be much colder than the
room). That lycée had specialized in the "hard" disciplines, apparently. Behind the iron curtain, history and
literature were phony subjects, but mathematics and
the physical sciences were incorruptible.

Vlada was a member of Beech's research group, the
famous geologist's chief chemist. In Minna's view the
planet was a far better subject than slums, crimes and
prisons. Why bother with that sort of thing if you could
write instead about a geophysicist like Beech? She
confessed she couldn't understand why the *Harper's*
articles had disturbed so many people. What was in
them? Corde had watched her rattle through the glossy
pages, impatient, trying to do right by him. He doubted
that she had read them. She admitted that she found
the language hard, the spin he gave words was odd. She
was told that the Dean was a journalist of unusual
talent. That was good enough for her. The Dean said,
"Don't you believe it. There is no such thing. That's
just the way journalists pump, promote, gild and
bedizen themselves, and build up their profession,
which is basically a bad profession." The Cordes had a
language problem. When he let himself go she didn't
understand what he was saying. (What was *bedizen?*) In
all essentials, of course, he was perfectly straight with
her, an erratic person, a strange talker, but a secure
husband—a crystallized, not an accidental husband.

It meant a lot to her that Corde was approached by

Professor Beech after the first of his two articles in *Harper's*. The collaboration was Beech's idea. Corde then said to Minna, "You think this is the greatest, don't you? You look as if you just swallowed a double dose of delight." Yes, she was extremely pleased. Beech, you see, was a scientist. A joint article, when it was published, would remove Corde from the uproar he had somehow stirred up. "You think some of his class will rub off on me," said Corde.

When he understood what Beech was really after, he said that he might be willing to do the job. "Not so innocuous, either," he said to Minna, but she was too pleased to take this in.

Vlada herself was flying over from Chicago and was expected at Christmas. She had an only brother in Rumania whom she visited every year.

"If she actually *does* come," said Minna (there were often arbitrary delays over visas), "she'll bring a bundle of stuff for us from home. A mixed blessing. Bad as it is here, it's just as well for you to be away from Chicago."

"Yes," he said. "Quite a string of lesser evils."

"At least you haven't got that kid on your back."

He decided not to reply. He only said, "Better have some sleep. Drink up. I can always sack out for an hour, but you're on your feet all day."

3

The kid, Mason Zaehner, was the Dean's only nephew, the son of his widowed sister, Elfrida. Mason was a dropout, still connected with the college but drifting about the city. For a while he had taken special courses

in computer science. Those were only a cover,
apparently—but for what? More recently he had been a
busboy; and in the kitchen of the delicatessen-
restaurant that employed him, he became intimate with
a black dishwasher, a parolee. Corde had seen this
man's rap sheet. His crimes were the familiar ones—
theft, possession of stolen property, et cetera. He was
now charged with homicide. The young man he was
accused of killing was a student, Rickie Lester. The
Dean himself had had to identify the body. This was
unusual, but it was August; the college's top security
man was up in Eagle River, everybody was out of town.
It was Corde's impression that the young man's wife,
Lydia, was under sedation.

So the cops rang the Dean and at four o'clock in the
morning called for him in their blue-and-white car. It
was a rotten night. The air was heavy with the smell of
malting grain from the kilns of Falstaff beer, near
Calumet Harbor. This was better than the hot sulfur
and sewer gases vented by U.S. Steel. *That* acid stink
made you get out of bed to shut the windows. Through
an ectoplasmic darkness—night was lifting—the Dean
rode to the hospital. There he viewed the murdered
boy.

Rick Lester's face had the subtracted look of the just
dead. He had crashed through the window of his own
third-floor apartment, and his skull was broken on the
cement. His longish hair was damp (with blood?) and
hung backwards. His slender feet were dirty. The cops
said he had gone out barefoot earlier in the night.
Making the rounds of the bars, he had driven his car
without shoes. Many young people removed their shoes
in hot weather—as if they were surrounded by woods
and fields, not these broken-bottle, dog-fouled streets.
What did these charmed-life children think Chicago
was? The expression on Rick Lester's face suggested
that he would have given up this sort of caper if he had
lived. The folds of his mouth, his settled chin, gave him
a long white mature look of dignity. More adult, more

horsey, a different kind of human being altogether. Corde was inclined to think that his hurry-up death had taught him something. Since he had been subtracted once and for all from the active human sum, you could only try to guess when that lesson had been given. Illumination while falling? A ten-second review of his life?

An experienced man and far from young, Corde had not expected to feel this death so much. He couldn't see why. His feelings took him by surprise. Something seemed to be working its way upward, treading on his stomach and his guts. The pressure on his heart was especially heavy, unpleasantly hot and repulsively melting. He had no use for such sensations; he certainly didn't want the kid's death bristling over him like this. He had seen plenty of corpses. This one got to him, though. Corde believed that it was the evil that had overtaken the boy that did it. For he was a boy, with those slender feet curling apart. Corde didn't know him well enough to weep for him. So perhaps it wasn't the boy, entirely, but some other influence. After the identification was made and the face covered again, Corde's revulsion-depression, or whatever it was, took a different turn. He was unwilling to let the administration take over and follow its usual pattern, depending upon the homicide police, who would investigate at their own pace. It was beyond him to explain why he became so active in this case. He had had to handle student deaths before, mostly suicides, and to deal with parents. He wasn't particularly good at this, never saying what people expected of him although he chose his words with care. His pallor and the dish face and deep voice were not effectively combined into a manner. He wanted to say what he meant sensibly or warmly, but he was so unsuccessful with horrified families that he horrified himself—"I can't make sense of this senseless death," was what he tacitly confessed —and the odd phrases that came out only puzzled grieving parents and probably depressed them further.

What had happened? As yet the cops had little to
say. They told the Dean that Rick Lester had gone out
on the town that night. His wife was with him for a
while, but he took her home and then was too restless
to stay put. At two in the morning he turned up in a bar
they described as flaky. There "he made a pest of
himself, acted up, just about the only white person in
the place, making sex signals, according to the bartend-
er." The cops rumbled on, doing their heavy minimum
for this dean. It wasn't so much that they were cynical,
but their big-city-homicide outlook was summed up in
the thickness of their cheeks and bodies more than by
their words. The words were only a kind of stuffing.
Maybe this boy had hot pants, or drank more than he
could hold, or was freaked out on Quaaludes. Blood
tests would tell. He may have known the party or
parties who pushed him from the window. But although they sounded knowledgeable, the professional
work of the cops wasn't too good. They moved slowly,
indifferent. The mobile crime lab didn't do its job. And
then it turned out that the coroner's report was incom-
plete. It all became worse, not better, as summer
ended. The undertaker didn't do what he was supposed
to do. The young wife broke down. Then she said that
she must go away for a while at least.

One of the homicide cops had advised Corde to post
a reward, and Corde moved quickly to find the money.
He had run into trouble with the Provost about this.
They had never had trouble before. The Provost, Alec
Witt, was generally cooperative, and Corde had had a
good opinion of him; but Witt seemed to think that
Corde was moving too fast. This smooth man, Witt,
whose manner was ultraconsiderate and solicitous, all
mildness, wondered whether the college might not be
well advised to keep a low profile. There was a tricky
racial angle to the case, and no telling what disagreeable facts digging might bring out. But Corde persisted.
He had in his hand a list of funds from which money
could be taken. It was available, all right. He kept

bringing forward his wide head, sinking it so that the
glasses slipped away from his eyes and from his light-
haired, dense joined brows. He was low-keyed but
refused to accept a refusal. The college could afford it,
should do it. The Provost began to think the man would
resign if he couldn't have his way. Corde had gotten his
back up. For what reason? That the shrewd Provost
could not make out. He smiled one of his not-quite-
pleasant smiles of understanding gentleness, but he was
a rough Chicago man; his neck, his chest, told you that,
not big but brutal, definitely—charging linebacker's
strength packed into those muscles. Corde had never
had occasion to take this in before. The physical
Provost was revealed to him today. "I guess I can come
up with a few thousand bucks if you absolutely have to
offer money," Witt said at last.

"That's what it takes to get the information; the cops
are definite about it," Corde said.

As soon as the reward was announced, witnesses
came forward, sure enough, and within twenty-four
hours two suspects were arrested on their evidence.
One of these was Lucas Ebry, Mason's friend, and the
other a prostitute with a long criminal record. After
this, the case developed quickly. Student reaction was
also quick. That was Mason's doing. Immediately, he
organized something; Corde couldn't tell you what that
something was—a resistance movement, a defense
campaign. The radical student line was that the college
waged a secret war against blacks and that the Dean
was scheming with the prosecution, using the college's
clout to nail the black man. Resolutions were passed
and published in the student daily, which took up the
case in a big way.

Mason argued that there had been no murder. Rick
Lester hadn't been pushed from the window, he had
stumbled, he fell. Anyway, it was all his fault, he went
out that night looking for trouble, had been asking for
it. Campus militants developed the ideological aspects
of the case—the college was trying to restrict black

housing in the neighborhood, it refused to divest itself of South African investments, it was slow on Affirmative Action. Himself a campus radical forty years ago, the Dean saw how little things had changed. The same meetings, agitprop slogans, fanaticism, pressure methods the same. The Provost said, "This will die down by and by; it always does." What he really meant was, "See what you've stirred up." Corde's head came forward silently. His sober nod conceded nothing. He had Witt's number now—not that he knew what to do with it.

Mason had the nerve to drop in on his uncle. From her anteroom Corde's secretary, Miss Porson, said discreetly on the telephone—she was Corde's ally, but she loved the excitement, too—"Your nephew has just stopped by; wants a few minutes of your time."

"Tell him you're squeezing him in between appointments," said Corde.

His door was already opening, and there was his nephew, busy-minded, scheming Mason, in the usual youth drag—the worn narrow jeans, sprigged shirt, ponytail. What to make of Mason! Corde had always disliked puzzles and people who contrived to puzzle you. Did he dislike his nephew? No, but his feelings towards him were terribly mixed. Skinny, lanky, ambling, with pointed elbows, Mason gave himself graces, seemed even to fancy that there was a valuable kind of fragrance coming from him. What were his views? He was sometimes seen with the Workers' World International Marxist-Leninists, the ones who carried small red flags as they peddled their papers in the streets, but he wasn't one of them. A definite ideology would have made him easier to deal with, and Mason didn't intend to make anything easy. No, Corde couldn't identify the young man's position, if he had a position. Maybe there wasn't really any.

Mason came in with a light, bright Huckleberry Finn air. It made the Dean heavy-hearted. Behind the lightness there was supposed to be something dangerous, equivocal, what-have-you. Corde silently asked (and it was as much a prayer as a question), Must we go through this? Well, yes, we must. Accepting, he settled back in the Dean's chair and crossed his arms, his ankles. Leaning somewhat to the side, he composed himself. He said, "I've got somebody coming any minute, but sit down."

Mason when he sat was about as graceful as a driller's rig—a long frame, a remote head. You could see it going up and down rhythmically in a field of similar rigs. In time the boy would fill out, certainly, and the added weight might reduce his nervous intensity. His father had been bearish in build, anything but a nervous type. Mason senior, a high-powered Loop lawyer with connections in the Daley machine, had been tough, arrogant, a bulldozing type. Brutal people, those Chicago insiders, a special breed. Mason hadn't inherited his father's bulk—not yet. What had he inherited from him?

His nephew, as Corde saw him, was at an uncomfortable stage of development. Uncomfortable? Bright, light, he was also bristling, writhing. The young racket wasn't doing him a bit of good. Well, the field was very crowded; he was one of global millions. How to rise above the rest, grab the lead—that was the challenge, and he hadn't yet figured out how this was to be done. Hence the equivocal menace, a sort of announcement: "Watch this space." Corde looked down on these crowded fields packed with contenders; he was prepared to admit that. He was prepared to admit quite a lot about himself. For instance, you would not need to press hard to get him to concede that his patient air was only assumed, a pis aller and a burden. But it would have been a terrible mistake to try to discuss things with Mason frankly, or (still worse) on a theoretical level: youth, age, mass tendencies, self-presentation, demagogy. Corde had observed to Minna not long ago that although people talked to themselves all the time, never stopped communing with themselves, nobody had a good connection or knew what racket he was in—his *real* racket. Did Corde actually know? For most of his life he had had a bad connection himself. There was just a chance, however, that he might, at last, be headed in the right direction. Just a chance. He would have liked to tell his nephew that men and women were shadows, and shadows within shadows, to one another. Given encouragement, Corde would have liked being kindly, candid, affectionate, but Mason gave no encouragement, wasn't buying any kindly candor, and Corde was careful with him, never uncled him, never lectured. He was glad enough, *de minimis* (Mason senior used to say *de minimis;* he was fond of kidding—growling—in Latin), to make plain sense. Given the intricacy of these shadow-framed shadows, plain sense was plenty.

Corde was put off by puzzles, and here was Mason bent on puzzling him, and smiling at his uncle. It wasn't much of a smile. Mason's lips were set high across his face, they were puffy, they swelled, and between them were his ingenuous front teeth. His mother had darker coloring. Mason's hair was fair and brassy. Youthfully vital, it seemed also to have a mineral luster. In the length of his profile and the narrowness of his forehead, he resembled Elfrida. Corde was strongly attached to his sister, he loved her, so it was all the more painful to see the same features adapted to—well, to mischief, contrariness, contemporary expressions of face badly interpreted. This was tough luck—a pity. The pity took hold of Corde. It dragged his heart with sorrow—the skinny, ill-assembled, innerly weak kid taking the field against his uncle the Dean. But the sorrow was excessive, too. There was no call for heavy sorrow, it dragged him in the wrong direction. Corde put a stop to it.

The Dean's office was in a Brown Decade building. They had tried to move him to new quarters, but he fought that. The new rooms were too low, and the long modern lighting tubes hurt his eyes. Also, he preferred not to run into the Provost and other administrative personnel in the corridors or the men's room. The brownstone was more like his idea of a college building. He was not exactly deanlike in appearance. He wore a three-piece suit; the vest wasn't buttoned right somehow (no up-to-date official courting favor with undergraduates would dress in this style). He was something of a stand-in, a journalist passing for a dean. His wide face, a sphere enlarged by baldness, looked simple and calm but also a little dusty, with an on-the-shelf effect. There was something out of kilter in his look (the big glasses? the eyes themselves?). Long silky hairs at the base of his throat didn't sort well with the three-piece suit. The deep voice came from a man who after all didn't look very strong—a misleading appearance; he was strong enough.

"What's with your mother?" he said.

"I haven't see much of her lately . . . sorry about that. But how's your beautiful wife? I have to tell you, you really got lucky with this one, Uncle Albert."

Corde made no answer. It was not possible to misinterpret this silence. But Mason went on, "She's not only very smart, she's also warm and cheerful. You're livelier, too, with her. The other ladies must have depressed you. That's just about impossible with Minna. And she's got class. Mother loves her."

"What's on your mind, Mason?"

"You won't accept this as a social visit? You're busy? I'm making trouble for you?"

"I assume it's trouble you want to discuss."

"I wrote twice to you about it. You didn't answer."

"There was no way to answer those muddled, boiling, murky letters."

"You could have asked me to come in and have a talk."

"After you blasted me publicly, what was there to talk about?"

"The real facts of the case."

"I can tell you in short order just how I see those

facts. A student is dead. I'm dean of students. I had to take a hand in this. And I did. Two people were arrested, indicted, charged with homicide. That just about describes it."

"You put up a reward for information."

"Of course."

"Witnesses bought and paid for."

Corde absolutely refused to go along with this bright bitterness, the barrels-of-fun line that Mason tried to take with him. It was clearly rejected by his silence. He lowered his eyes to the simple gilt border of his desk—a straight line of stamped arabesques into which he would have liked to read sanity and order.

Mason said, "I have a special interest, too. Lucas Ebry is my friend."

"How close a friend is he?"

"You're suggesting that black street people don't have friendships? Especially with whites? Also, as soon as a reward was posted, 'friends' of Ebry and Riggie Hines came running with information? They wanted the money. Sure. As if white people from the bungalow belt wouldn't do the same for a buck."

"No doubt about it," said Corde.

"The blacks on food stamps, they're the *underclass*— that's what your sociologists around here call them. They're hoping that drugs and killings and prison will eliminate that lousy, trouble-making underclass."

"I'm not the sociologists. They're not my sociologists."

"No, you're my Uncle Albert, telling me not to put words in your mouth. Okay. But you're pushing for a conviction. You've made up your mind to get this one black man."

"Your friend Ebry is on trial for homicide. I didn't indict him, and I won't be trying him."

"You're buddy-buddy with all those Irish characters out of Notre Dame, Loyola and the Machine, the prosecutor, the State's Attorney's people."

"Naturally, I've talked to them."

Assume that there was nothing too rum to be true—could we say also that there was nobody too rum to be liked? The Dean and his nephew were family and so presumably liked or at least tried to like each other. The Dean would have made the effort (it would have been an effort), but liking was not what Mason wanted. He was here on a mature basis (to fight), meanwhile shuffling and grinning. His ultra-bright hey-presto look was insolent. Yes, he had a cause. But mostly he was eager to needle his uncle and he hoped—craved, longed—to drive his needle deep. He was here as a representative of the street people but he intended also to teach his ignorant uncle some lessons about Chicago's social reality. He had earned the right to speak for the oppressed because he and Lucas Ebry had worked together in the grease and garbage of the kitchen, sweat rags tied on their foreheads.

Mason was saying, "Week after week in that damn sewer. That's not a relationship an outside person can judge."

"Petty bourgeois and white, you mean."

"You said it."

There had been the army—mess halls, KP—but it would be foolish to bandy experiences with Mason. Corde let this pass. He waited while the second hand of the electric clock on the wall made one full cycle, like the long-legged fly. Mason's message was clear: Lucas Ebry was real, others (Uncle Albert, for instance) were not. Uncle Albert had no business to be messing with people who were wrapped up in an existence, in a reality that was completely beyond him. For those people the stakes were life and death. What did Uncle Albert stake? Let him stick to his fancy higher education—seminars in Plato and the Good. Those people of the *underclass,* dopers or muggers or whores: what were they, mice? To the "thinking population," to establishment intellectuals, they were nothing but mice! Thus Corde spelled out, parsed, his nephew's message. He even agreed, in part.

"But what about the boy who was killed?" he said.

"Who says he was killed!"

"Let's not quibble over words. He died. . . ."

"But you can't prove he was killed."

Steady in spite of the rise of unwanted anger, Corde said, "He was tied and gagged. He didn't first gag and then tie himself with strips from the drapes, did he? Or cut himself—slash his own ear with the kitchen knife? He went through the glass on the third floor with one of his arms still tied tight and the gag in his mouth. Then the police came . . . but what do we need to go over this for? There's the testimony of Mrs. Lester and the black woman."

"Are you going to put that whore in front of a jury? You never will. Her rap sheet goes back ten years. She's plea-bargaining. Her evidence isn't worth a damn. And the other lady, Lydia, what do you expect her to say? She and her husband went out that night looking for action. It was the kind of hot weather when people get raunchy, and that's what Lester was. He went to the bar and brought home Lucas Ebry and this black whore. Why do you think he did that?"

"Why do you think, if his wife was at home?"

"Lester went out twice, once with Lydia for a beer—at least that's what she said—and again after she went to bed. He took off alone in his car, no shoes on his feet. He went to this other bar, which is all black, and he didn't know how to behave. He got on everybody's nerves. He was damn loud, dumb and offensive. He tried to pick up Lucas Ebry and this black chick."

"It was they who picked him up."

The conversation here became painful to Corde for the motives it brought into question. He couldn't say what Lester had been looking for that night. Whatever the boy had done led, as if by prearranged stages, to his destruction and it was not impossible that all those wrong moves were made because they were wrong. An event had picked him to happen to. The gates of death were opening for the kid. Why shouldn't he himself have had some sense of this?

"You think he was just being nice and friendly," Mason said.

Corde conceded, "What he did that night seems out of character, but I don't believe it should have been punishable by death. Nothing he deserved to die for."

"I read what you said to the press about him, that he was a disciplined student and all that. He used to go to early mass."

"I didn't make it up," said Corde. "Two priests paid me a call. I didn't solicit the information. They told me he was religious. Why couldn't he have been?"

"No comment," said Mason, but the expression that worked about his mouth was nothing but comment. For a moment he was tough and mature in the manner of his late father, an artist in this sort of thing, an overbearing rude man. The late Zaehner had just such bulges in the lower cheek, and the identical bullying lusterless put-down stare. And Mason was still very young, only twenty-two. His brassy hair subsided on his jaws, towards the chin, in light streaks of down. You could almost see the pollen of adolescence over the bridge of his nose. Why did he have to be so very tall? His quiddity was overstretched.

"Whether he was religious is neither here nor there. His life was decently organized. He studied, worked, he was a married young man."

"Yeah? Well, let's continue with what happened. He acted like a loudmouth that night. He went up and down the bar, and forced people to shake hands with him. They could have cared less. A white student saying he understood their life and was *for* them. Big deal! They were turned off completely."

"This sounds like Ebry—the 'turned off.'"

"Never mind all the decent stuff," said Mason. "A nice clean boy and an Eagle Scout? You weren't born a dean, Uncle. Lester was as kinky as they come."

"Well, get to the point."

"He picked up Ebry and this Riggie Hines at the bar, and they went together to his apartment."

"That's from Ebry, too."

"Well, there were three people to begin with. One of them is dead. One is plea-bargaining—lying. What does that leave?"

Ebry, without bail money, was being held in County Jail. Riggie Hines was in prison, too.

Mason said, "How did they get into the apartment if Lester didn't invite them? So? Why did he?"

"For a sexual purpose? With his wife asleep? Why would he bring two people there? . . ."

"Riggie Hines is as tough as they come, and all whore. Ready for any damn thing. What's a white wife to her? You've seen her yourself. She goes around in a workshirt, wide open, and wears her jeans like a man. She spits on the floor like a trucker; and if a guy didn't pay her, she'd slug him. You don't bring home a broad like that at three in the morning to discuss academic subjects. She's a bad cunt."

Mason sketched all this for his uncle with an air of "You tell *me* how it happened, if not this way," and Corde had to agree that it wasn't easy to explain. It was like trying to see through a barrier of vapor or gas. Reconstruction was all the more problematic because of the emotional heaviness of all the circumstances, even time and weather. It had been one of those choking, peak-of-summer, urban-nightmare, sexual and obscene, running-bare times, and death panting behind the young man, closing in. But the evidence suggested that some unconscious choice had been made, some mixture, an emulsion of silliness and doom shaken up and running over. The younger generation didn't seem to understand who the people around them were, with whom they had to do.

Mason said, "He wanted Riggie Hines to go into the toilet with him."

"What for?"

"To go down on him while she was shitting."

Corde rejected this, hated it. He said violently, "Don't come to me with such talk. And you don't have to unload this kind of thing on that dead kid."

"Well, Uncle, I heard you saying to my mother once that we were living through some kind of sexual epidemic. You made quite a speech at the dinner table. Maybe you weren't aware that I was there. It happened about ten years ago, and I must have been about twelve, but I remember what you said. A kind of demon had ahold of us, was your idea. But here's an illustration and you don't accept it. You want him to be that dead kid, so nice, just an object of pity."

"According to the police, there was a dog shut up in the toilet."

"It was Lester's dog. He could have taken him to the kitchen."

"More Ebry. He's your one and only source."

"The woman says the same."

"I doubt that Lester had anything definite in mind," said Corde. "There was a melon in the icebox. He was going to entertain his visitors. He brought the melon and a carving knife into the parlor. Ebry grabbed the knife."

"That's not the way I heard it. That's Riggie's plea-bargaining. She's plenty familiar with knives. There's a stabbing on her rap sheet. Did she ever say how many people she cut? No, why should she?"

"I suppose," said Corde, "if you could get into that tight skull of hers you'd find it packed with grotesque ideas, deeds or pictures." It wasn't so much what he said that made Mason stare at him; it was the odd but characteristic lapse into abstruseness or into images by which grieving parents were also put off when the Dean was trying to console them.

"So he was just entertaining them with some nice cantaloupe."

"They held the knife on him," said Corde. "I suppose he put up some resistance, so they cut his ear to prove they meant business. They tore strips from the drapes and tied him up, they pushed a gag down his throat, and then they started to burglarize the apartment, which was what they had come for—hi-fi, tape recorder, earphones: those were stacked by the back door. Riggie pulled off Rick Lester's gold wedding band. That's in evidence, too, so we don't have to quibble about it. All right. Then Ebry dropped the TV set, and that woke up Mrs. Lester, and she came out in her short summer nightie. Till then she hadn't heard anything because of the noisy air conditioner in her bedroom. When his wife came in, Lester began to struggle. That's what seems to have happened. Riggie held him down, while Ebry jumped at Mrs. Lester from behind and forced her to the floor."

"Yes," said Mason. "So what have you got? A white woman, practically naked, and the black man on top of her with the knife. The classic rape fantasy."

"There was no rape."

"You bet not. What would he want that skinny broad for? He had his choice of women. At the restaurant they would come around to the kitchen and ask for him, plenty of white ones. And furthermore, Ebry wasn't the guy who was in Lester's apartment when the hassle started. He got disgusted long before, because Lester was patronizing the shit out of him."

"So he said in one of his statements. It was two other guys. Only Mrs. Lester picked him out in the lineup."

"How could she identify him if he was behind her? But all right, I'll go along with your reconstruction, Uncle. The husband saw the wife in her short nightie, on the floor, and he started to struggle. He got one arm free, and he managed to hop to his feet."

"Then he was pushed through the window, broke the glass and fell three stories. One arm was still tied and the gag was in his mouth. . . ."

"You really are hung up on that gag. Would it have been more humane if he wasn't gagged, so he could speak his last words? He fell, and he was killed. What else is there?" Mason scowled as he smiled.

"So that's your summary . . . what he had in mind was an orgy. Instead there was a fight, and if he was killed he had death coming to him."

"What do you want to add? 'Appalled'? 'Aghast'? 'All shook up'?"

For Corde this was the worst moment of their conversation. Strange interviews took place in a dean's office, stranger than you might think possible. Students who sought you out sometimes made curious requests or confessions, or boasts. But this interview, with the weight of his own family behind it, made his head ache, sent a pang through his eyeballs. Depressed, the Dean rose and opened the door to Miss Porson's outer office. Was there a student waiting? There was no one. The old girl's chair was empty. She was demonstratively sympathetic, his ally—she made a big thing of that— plenty of flourishes—but her instinct was to take off when the heat was on. She had gone to the ladies' room to smoke a cigarette and gossip with the other girls. So he was stuck with Mason. He saw no way to get rid of him. He longed to say, "I don't feel well. Beat it. Come back some other time." But that would have been weak. This was serious. It was crime and punishment, life and death for Ebry. Corde was furious with Miss Porson; gabby old bag, not worth a damn. But the real trouble, as he recognized, was that he was in a wrong relation to the sum of things—he himself. A sign of this was that he was in a useless debate—hopeless! all the premises were wrong—with this adolescent whose head was so remote. As he went back to his seat, Mason watched him.

The Dean understood only too well what the kid was transmitting when he said, "'Appalled'? 'All shook up'?" He was saying, Let's not fuck around with all these high sentiments and humane teachings and pieties and poetry, and the rest of that jazz. You keep going

back to the knife and the gag and the blood and the
corpse and the prostrated wife, and you do it to stir
yourself with horror. Stones advertising how "human"
they are.

The truth of this, even if it was not more than a
particle, was a poisonous particle.

The true voice of Chicago—the spirit of the age
speaking from its lowest register; the very bottom.

For Mason was never more like his father than when
he thought he had you dead to rights. There were no
two ways about Mason senior; he was either for you or
against. If he didn't approve, then he despised you.
Corde had long ago decided that Chicago was the
contempt center of the U.S.A. And he heard the
contempt note in his nephew's voice—the true, buzzing, bullying, braying La Salle Street brass. "Hold their
feet to the fire," Mason senior liked to say. Or, if it was
your own feet to the fire, "Got to bite the bullet." He
chose to speak in platitudes; but he interpreted them
powerfully, virile bruiser that he was. You were tough
or you were nothing. In realism and cunning these La
Salle Street characters were impressive because they
had the backing of the pragmatic culture of the city, the
state, the region, the country. In his brother-in-law's
view, the Dean had given up the real world to take
refuge with philosophy and art. Academics were hacks
and phonies. Old Mason could seem ponderously respectful, following polite protocol for liberals, but the
bottom line was this: he said, or growled, with nar-
rowed eyes, "I make my living by tipping over garbage
cans, but at least I go in the alley and tip them over
myself." Up in Lake Forest, Corde had been a subject
of jokes at the Zaehner dinner table: "the dud dean."
Elfrida didn't join in this fun, Corde was certain of
that. But she had married an extroverted, assertive
man, she preferred a husband who was altogether
different from her brother. Her brother, as she had
once told Corde, was strong-minded but at the same
time withdrawn, seemed to have a minimum of com-

mon ground with the people about him, and seldom "gave out" except on paper.

Seated again, and facing Mason, the Dean felt bleak—bleakest of all about himself. A gap had opened. No, a vacuum. A vacuum was there. He said, "Yes, when I looked at the boy's body in the morgue, it shook me up." He might have added: This one time, I *was* shaken.

Mason said, "I read the story in the *Trib*. The wife was in shock, and Dean Albert Corde identified the victim. . . . You probably swore you'd get the sons-ofbitches who did it."

"It's true I wanted them caught."

"You went to lots of trouble."

"It's also true that if they hadn't been found it would have upset me."

"What makes you so sure you got the right party? Okay, you made your own investigation. I know all about it. You went to the restaurant where we worked. You even went to see Toby Winthrop, that guy who runs the detoxification center, about Ebry."

"As a matter of fact, we didn't discuss him."

"You're like a mastermind nemesis when you get started. I bet if you had discussed him, Winthrop would have put Ebry down. Winthrop is one of these glamorous black types, a fund-raising personality."

Corde said, "Now I want to tell you something, Mason. I don't want you bothering Mrs. Lester. You paid her a visit to warn her not to push the case. You threatened that lots of ugly stuff would come out about her husband. Stay away from her. She's a good young woman."

"What does that mean, 'good young woman'?"

"It means that she has decent instincts. She feels, in earnest."

"Jesus-Cheesus," said Mason.

The Dean now had a swelling, pulsating, exorbitant headache. He had struck it rich this time. It was a beauty, right through the eyes. If he had been alone he would have gone to lie down. He kept an old aluminum lawn chair in the corner. Miss Porson had knitted an afghan for him. He often made use of this green and blue afghan, took comfort from it.

"Furthermore, Mason, you've been spreading stories on campus against the Lesters. No more of that, and knock off the threats."

"Does the relationship embarrass you—nephew against uncle?"

"It would surprise you how little that part of it affects me."

"Oh, this is just hysterical kid stuff?"

Corde, with swelling headache, a great balloon, but still patient, dropped his gaze to the desk. "Look, you came to have it out with me and settle all kinds of scores, put the whole mess on one square, like roulette. God knows what-all. It's too bad. . . ."

To Mason this earnestness was simply a ploy, Uncle Albert trying a softer approach. His smile said as much.

Corde now made a super effort to be fair, to reconsider. (Maybe he did have a blind spot.) He put his imagination to work once more on the circumstances of Rick Lester's death. For this purpose he had to absent himself briefly. He turned his swivel chair away from Mason and stared through the blue window and the fringe of autumn ivy. Let's try again. Begin by setting in place that boyish man's death. Begin with the crying ugliness of the Chicago night. Put that in the center. It had to be in the middle. Now then, who were the people involved? There was a business connection between Lucas Ebry and Riggie Hines. He pimped for her, steered students to her room. This information was from the cops. Very likely Mason knew it, too, if the friendship was as close as he claimed. But he'd see no special disgrace in pimping. It wasn't even pimping, only procuring. Those kids had to get themselves laid. So what? She didn't need Ebry's protection; she protected herself.

She had the build of a boxer and a boxer's compact tough head. Even the way she tucked back the mannish shirt to show the tops of her breasts was pugilistic—this must have worked sexually on the boy. Ebry! She could floor Ebry with a punch. He was a shrunken, twisting figure, burnt out; his small beard was twisted, too. He drooped at the knees, he was a sheared-off man. Those hands of his hung down looking gorged, and with loose skin. The orgy was another clumsy invention, like vice in the toilet, like Rick staggering around until he went through the window. Those were the people who had come to see Rickie Lester off. Now imagine this gang breaking into Lydia's bedroom to wake her with a proposition. She would have burst into tears.

No, the whole purpose was robbery. This was what Ebry had come for. When the two jumped Lester and grabbed the kitchen knife, they must have cut his ear only to make him lie still. Probably he stopped struggling then and they tied him up. Riggie must have yanked off his gold wedding band first thing. They weren't going to kill him. Neither had ever been booked for homicide, although Riggie was once an accessory. It was the dropped TV set (was Ebry too puny to lift it?) that set off the panic, when Lydia Lester ran from bed and Ebry threw her to the floor. Rick Lester struggled to his feet, and then either one or both of the robbers reached the murder point. Lucas Ebry was chaotic enough to do it, scared, desperate; the night hot enough, bad enough; Riggie Hines was tough enough. You saw women like that in police court for scalding a man with boiling grease, or for cutting him. So, to go to the evil conclusion, Lester was pushed. He couldn't have broken the window by staggering against it. The frames were old but they were wood, not cardboard. He would have had to be pushed.

As soon as he fell, Ebry began to run around wiping the fingerprints—from the TV, from the knife. But clean prints were found in Lester's Toyota. Experienced killers would have done something about Lydia

—she was a witness—but these two took off. They left
the loot and escaped down the back stairs. These were
ancient Chicago open back stairs and porches clapped
together of gray lumber, held up by crude cross-trusses.
There was a jumbled yard, a fence, and then the alley.
In the alley Riggie and Ebry split.

Corde's upper lip when he was reflecting turned
inward. His big open forehead rose bare towards the
crown, his Irish nose was short (he had Irish blood from
his mother), his eyes were large, his mouth plain and
wide. So, then, they split. After splitting, Riggie got rid
of the wedding ring. She passed it to a man, one of the
street people, and asked him to keep it for her. But as
soon as the reward was announced, this fellow went to
the police, made a statement, turned over the ring,
which was now in evidence, and claimed his dough. He
said he was willing to take the witness stand, but he
dropped out of sight later. Grady, the assistant State's
Attorney, had the cops looking for him. So there were
your facts. Corde wanted to be as impartial as possible,
severely, even passionately impartial, saying to himself
various things of characteristic oddity: Objectivity begins at home; harden yourself some more; it's no good
without a hard spirit; by telling yourself normal-
sounding stories, all you do is cling to nonexistent
normalcy; then life is no more than you're "inclined to
understand," and you're nowhere.

But the fact of facts was the body Corde had
identified at the hospital, the kid on the slab, the long
soiled feet, the face with the only-just-subtracted expression and the hint of mature knowledge. And then
the sequel (another set of facts, framed in fire): Grady
had ordered the body exhumed for further tests, but
these could not be made because the boy hadn't been
embalmed, and it was hot summer. However, the
family had been charged for embalming, and the bill
had been paid. But this was ordinary business practice,
built-in fraud, nothing to get worked up about (al-

though he was worked up). This last consideration, the decomposed body, was not mentioned by Corde. It would have given an opening for deeper nastiness.

Mason said, "Well, you've been sitting there for about five minutes without a word, only your lips moving. You want me to go. You're sore at me."

"Not exactly," said Corde in his low voice.

"I had a few things to say and wasn't sure you'd give me an appointment."

"Why not?"

"Maybe you don't want to see your antagonist face to face."

"What makes you think you're my antagonist?"

"Because if you aim to crucify this black dishwasher, you're going to have to fight me. Yes!" Corde was shaking his head. "If some black had fallen through the window, there wouldn't have been any damn reward or investigation or case. How many black people were killed in the same week? No big deals, no State's Attorney Grady, no press coverage."

"I'm sorry to say that's probably true. But it's my responsibility on this job to oversee the students. That's why we're discussing Rick Lester in the Dean's office, this nice autumn day." The nightmare fury of summer was behind them, and the (decomposing) heat had abated. As if the mad spell were over. But it had only been transposed. The same rotten music continued. This was its cooler key.

Corde understood very well what his nephew was saying to him. He said it to himself, and this was how it went: You meddle in things you have no sympathy with. These people do what they can in the space they've been confined to. Yes, they scrounge and they rob and they fuck; they drink and take drugs, they cut and shoot each other and die young. And what you, a man of routine, can't forgive is that they have no structure. They don't plan, and don't "do"; they only hang out. That's what disgusts you most.

He said to Mason, "It's odd how little you feel for Rick. He was a student like yourself."

"He wasn't like myself. He was your kind, not mine."

"He was a young man who went out on a hot night . . ."

"And ran into some blacks who murdered him. That's all you can see. You gave yourself away when you talked about the case to Mother. She told me how you described it. When the warrant went out for Riggie Hines, she was hiding out with a dope pusher in South Shore. The cops had to break down a door with baseball bats and drag her out from under the bed. That wasn't in the paper—she got it from you. You also said that witnesses came *running* to claim the dough. These people don't know what solidarity is. What's-his-name from Robert Taylor Homes, who described himself as a buddy, fingered Lucas Ebry and repeated what he claimed he heard. Those are my people, and you made them all seem subhuman to my mother—wild-ass savages from the Third World. And now I see that you are writing something about County Jail. It was advertised in the *Times*. Read Albert Corde in *Harper's* for November. With a complete Chicago background. You think *you* have anything to say about the people of this city?"

"The subject of those articles isn't the jail. There is—there happens to be—a description of the jail in them."

"Uncle Albert, you don't know a damn about what goes on."

"Because I haven't lived the life, like yourself?"

"You went to see County, and still you want to send people to prison? What the hell good is that?"

Corde agreed. "The prisons certainly are awful."

"Why, the Swedish government refused extradition in the case of one American because of the Attica riots and those other stinking places. We have one of the worst right next door in Pontiac." Mason had still more to say. "According to Mother, you got your angle on County Jail from Rufus Ridpath, whom they threw out of there."

"Ridpath is as straight as they come."

"Your kind of black man."

"He seems to me a decent, intelligent public servant."

"Public servant! What kind of civics shit is that? A sadist and a fink."

The conversation was leaking, sinking, capsizing. But here with a raging headache was steady Corde, still on the bridge, looking calm and responsible. Really, he was fed up now. He wanted to run Mason out by the seat of the pants.

Mason said, "A warden who beat up on prisoners."

"He was acquitted. You don't know damn-all about it. Acquitted but still disgraced. And there's a man who *genuinely* felt for the street people, worked to improve the prison. Until he took over, it was run by the criminals. . . ." Here Corde stopped and passed the edge of his hand over his forehead, shading his eyes from the overhead light. Mason was within easy reach of the switch, but he made no move towards it. If he rose from his seat, he would be on his way out. And Mason was going. Only he had more to say. Apparently he followed a prepared mental outline. Corde longed to be rid of him—an acute longing. No bum's rush; kicking him out was just a fantasy. Those greeny-blue eyes and long eyelashes, and the youth pollen sprinkled over the Huck Finn cheekbones, the cheerful pleasant conventions of his suburban upbringing, the ingenuous teeth representing ten thousand dollars' worth of orthodontia, the brassy hair pulled back, the sallow face, shaky pride, the distemper, infection, sepsis. You could almost smell the paste odor of fever. Corde's anger, when this odor reached him, began to pass off in pulsations. He sat there feeling sorry.

"You'll probably go back to Mother and raise hell with her because she repeated what you said."

"I won't do that."

"That's right. I gave you your favorite opening. I'm the one who makes her unhappy. You're the one that protects her. Love your sister."

Corde loved Elfrida. He did, in fact. And this, too, was held against him.

"I was always having you rubbed into me," Mason continued. "Uncle Albert this and Uncle Albert that. A big man, and smart, and a notable. Uncle Albert wrote those pieces on the Potsdam Conference in *The New Yorker*. Uncle Albert saw Harry Truman play poker, and came face to face with Joe Stalin."

"I sympathize with you there. You can get to hate the absent model. But still there was your father to keep the balance. . . ."

"Yes, he put you down some."

"He thought I was a jerk," said Corde, quite neutral.

"You don't seem very sore about that."

"I'm not, very. Your father never did things by halves. There were those he liked, all out, and those he despised, the same."

Mason said, "Off and on you tried to make like a good uncle. You took me fishing on the Cape once."

"I remember very well. We went to catch porgies in the channel, and I fell in."

"You arrived in the night, and then in the morning you put on shorts and you said we should go and fish off the rocks. I thought your legs were very ugly."

"I'm no ballet dancer—Bugayev or Nureyev or whatever. Well, I wasn't very graceful. I lost my footing on those slanting rock slabs. They were covered with seaweed. First thing I knew, I was falling."

"You took a flop and slid down your side over the barnacles."

"And was cut in about fifty slices. Those cuts were thin, but they were nasty."

"That's what it was. It left a nasty memory."

"I went into the drink, rod and all. There was quite a heavy swell." Corde smiled, almost as if it was a pleasant recollection.

He recalled the great weight of the dark green water, and the sky upside down, vast clouds, bottoms up, all white, and the fishing line curving on the current in a long fluid pleat. The rod was lost, like his eyeglasses. Then he couldn't get a grip in the slime of the breakwater, and the boy was too small to help. After Corde at last got himself out, he pulled off his sea-heavy shirt and wrapped it around his thigh. "Those barnacles were hard little bastards." The scars they made were like hash marks. "So that left an impression," he said.

"It was the first time I saw anybody bleed like that."

A porgy or a flounder, if they had managed to hook one in the channel, would have been less memorable, threshing and thrilling on the line, than Uncle Albert. Dumb and inept Uncle Albert, who wrote about Stalin and Churchill at Potsdam, didn't know how to fish. Distortion underfoot because of his big bifocals. The channel caught *him*. Nothing but a deep voice, a bulging eye, an opinionated manner, long hairs growing from his Adam's apple and, when he took off his pants, disgusting shanks. Plus the blood. Odd, I never thought my legs were so bad. Minna likes them well enough. The way I'm put together entertains her. But then she has a cosmic perspective. Not like this ornery kid—really, a cruel kid. He might have judged me with more charity if he had foreseen that he himself would grow up looking two-dimensional, like a drawing of a driller's rig. You had to study Mason to find the humanity in him. It was as hard to see as the thin line of mercury in some thermometers. But if you turned your thermometer in the light and found the lucky angle, you'd be sure to get a reading.

Miss Porson now looked in. Aware that she had stayed away too long (and you couldn't pry into the

secret feminine reasons for these irritating absences),
she put some melody into her voice, announcing,
"There's somebody waiting, Mr. Corde."

"One last thing," said Mason as he rose. "My mother
refused to underwrite a bond for Lucas Ebry. . . ."

"She didn't discuss it with me. I didn't advise her,"
said Corde.

4

Each of the long days in Minna's room was a succession
of curious states. The first was the state of rising,
pulling on your Chicago socks and sweaters (good
cashmere, but thinning at the heels and elbows), assem-
bling a dean who was less and less a dean within. The
room was dark, the cold mortifying. The toilet, located
in a small cell apart from the bathroom, was Gothic.
The toilet paper was rough. A long aeruginous pipe
only gave an empty croak when you pulled the chain.
No water above. You poured from one of the buckets
into the bowl. Corde himself now took charge and filled
them when the water was running. The buckets were
far too heavy for Gigi with her cardiac condition. The
bathtub might have been a reservoir if the stopper had
worked. All this was like old times in the States, before
the age of full convenience. It took you back.

On the dining room table, Turkish coffee was ready
in a long-handled brass pitcher, lots of chicory, together with boiled milk, grilled bread in place of toast,
brown marmalade with shreds of orange in it—ersatz,
but the best that conscientious Tanti Gigi could furnish.
Ladies with parcels reported to her. Her bed was a

command post. Kindly acquaintances did the errands. Aged women rose at four to stand in line for a few eggs, a small ration of sausages, three or four spotted pears. Corde had seen the shops and the produce, the gloomy queues—brown, gray, black, mud colors, and an atmosphere of compulsory exercise in the prison yard. The kindly ladies were certainly buying on the black market, since Corde and Minna gave Gigi all the lei, bought with dollars at the preposterous rate of exchange. Corde ate grapes and tangerines and other black market luxuries. From time to time he was served meat. It was the general opinion of the ladies that there should be good things in the house of death. Especially for people from the blessed world outside, foreigners who took steaks and tangerines for granted, who would feel the privation, who were as fastidious as dragons. It was outrageous what they devoured, in their innocence. Feeding an American must have diverted these elderly women. But they had forgotten, apparently, how to cook a steak. The meat was served dry, and even scorched. Maybe the cooking oil was no good. Anyway, the meat tasted of fire and suggested sacrifice. It carried a creaturely flavor; the smell of the stall, of the hide, was still there, and he had to suppress the unwanted feeling of animal intimacy that it gave him. But he ate his steak when it was served and told Gigi how good it was. He knew how much organization it took to get it. Gigi drove herself hard, knocked herself out. A physician cousin would come and put his stethoscope to her, and order her to stay in bed, but she got up to mix a cake for Corde because he had once said he liked her raisin cake, and when she wasn't baking she was otherwise busy. She dragged boxes from the shelves, looking for family records. She answered the telephone on the double. She put a shawl over her back and trotted downstairs to consult with Ioanna, the concierge. Concierges had police connections. You had to keep on the good side of them. If the elevator door had not been completely shut, you might see the top of

Gigi's head as she worked her way down step by step. Defensive magic was how Corde described these propitiatory calls Gigi went below to make. The staircase smelled of ancient plaster fallen from the gaps opened by the earthquake, and when you opened the door you were struck by the cold; it was like being thwacked with the flat of a saber.

Fifty years ago Gigi had been sent to study commercial English in London; and she spoke the language well enough, in the hoity-toity way of foreigners when they address Americans in *English* English. "See here, dear Albert, you will find the article you are seeking upon the buffet." But she wasn't being superior, only singing songs from a better time. She wouldn't have dreamed of putting the Dean down. "When this trouble is over," she promised him, "we will have to have a *taita tait.*"

Corde saw how it was. In this oppressive socialist wonderland she had depended on her sister to protect her. Now her sister was dying (although by saying "When this trouble is over" Gigi denied it) and she assumed the senior role. After years as an understudy she was trying to play it. She even took on Valeria's doubts about him. Corde became aware of this when he noticed that Gigi sometimes examined his face silently, dark, warm, brown eyes dilated with female speculation: Could he really, but *really,* be trusted? It was obvious that the question of his stability had been much discussed here. With his record of debauchery (something like Don Giovanni's 1,003 seductions), would he really settle down with their Minna? Corde no longer minded this. It was only fair that Gigi, too, should have a crack at him. American behavior *was* wild by the standards of these old-fashioned Eastern Europeans. Corde might have thrilled her by taking her into his confidence. "I *did* know some wild women, but that's over and done with. I wouldn't worry if I were you."

Tell it to the parole board!

Tanti Gigi in her seventies was still the little sister,

and willful, given to fits of goodness, tolerating no resistance to her sacrifices. Corde said to Minna, "Your aunt has all kinds of ideas."

"Yes, I know."

"I find it touching. These sisters."

"In the old days, when she was beautiful, she loved to dress. She was a marvelously fashionable dresser. I remember how people turned to look at her in the street. But then during the forties she began taking in the children of families who died in the war. There were about twenty orphans. My mother helped her. Then her husband died."

The apartment was in Valeria's name. Cousins discussed Gigi's future with Minna. What would she do when she was alone?

Just before Valeria's stroke, Gigi had had her hair done—bobbed, crimped, marcelled at the bottom (Corde didn't have the right word)—and now the whole arrangement was coming apart, standing out stiffly from her slender neck like the dry underfronds of a palmetto. She fussed over Corde at breakfast especially. "I wish we had a proper toaster, but there is not one. Can this coffee be drunk? It was clever of you to bring a tin of British tea from Chicago. Can we not obtain a foreign newspaper for you at the Intercontinental?" She also said, "What a pity that you cannot see what a beautiful country we have, instead of the dark side, and how frightfully dreary." She must have learned her English from Beatrix Potter's *Tale of Two Bad Mice.* It was pure nanny, in a Balkan version.

Corde said, "At the Intercontinental I saw nothing but *Pravda* and *Tribuna Ludu.* They don't seem to carry the *Herald Tribune.*" But he was really in two minds about the news. At home he read too many papers. He was better off without his daily dose of world botheration, sham happenings, without newspaper phrases. Nothing true—really true—could be said in the papers. In the dining room there was a huge shortwave radio which looked as if it could reach Java but gave only jamming squeals. The big TV with its wooden cowl was equally useless. On it you saw nobody but the dictator. He inspected, reviewed, greeted, presided; and there were fanfares, flowers and limousines. People were shown applauding. But if emigration were permitted, the country would be empty in less than a month.

The Dean began to take a special interest in the house plants. It was a good season for cyclamens. The shops were filled with pots of them. He looked up cyclamens in the big Larousse. Observing that Corde went about the apartment watering the plants, Tanti Gigi had her agents bring more flowers. He was glad to have their company. He believed they refreshed his head. The African violets he fussed over at home, those would all be dead by now.

After breakfast he went back to Minna's room, sat at Minna's student table with his coat over his shoulders, tried to write a letter or make a few notes for his new project in collaboration with Beech, read some of the documents Beech had given him; then he discovered that he was in a strange state. Presently he found himself staring at the cyclamens. And often he crept back into bed. The trial of Reggie Hines and Lucas Ebry was now in its second week. His office was supposed to keep him posted. Probably the jurors would be let out to do their Christmas shopping, and nothing would happen until after the holidays. As yet Miss Porson had sent no mail. They'd only been away eight days. So Corde slept a great deal, but not well. The restless ecstasy was what he had.

On some mornings the sun shone—clear winter blue. He looked through the ivy twigs on the porch side of the room. Small frozen berries, dark blue, fell from them. Pigeons descended. They must have been fed by the old ladies. But he was not greatly interested in the birds. It was the cyclamen plants that absorbed him hypnotically—the dark cores of the pink and the more purple circles of the white, the petals turned back, the leaves mottled in many shades of green. They were said by Larousse to belong to the primrose family. They grew from corms. Someone had once suggested to him that these green beings produced their leaves and flowers in a state of sleep, perfection devoid of consciousness, design without nerves. Put a handful of dirt in the pot, and they came up with this beauty. Who had said that, about the sleeping life of plants? Brooding over the cyclamens on the table, he often dozed; he felt too hazy to remember anything. He thought, if you had enough of these plants in a room and watered them with a Nembutal solution, they might cure insomnia, make a dream atmosphere.

His biological clock hadn't caught up. An abnormal sleepiness overtook him in the morning. He didn't fight it. He woke in the chair and found himself leaning back, his arms folded and his face turned upwards like a radar disk. The position made his neck ache. Giving in, he stripped and crawled naked under the covers. As he did this, he sometimes felt how long he had lived and how many, many times the naked creature had crept into its bedding. Minna would say nonsense to this, and that he was, like herself, younger than his years, but the coil in the person, so tight in early life, was certainly much looser. Not so loose as in his mother-in-law— Valeria, in intensive care, was always on his mind—but how could you deny the slippage?

Occasionally Minna woke him from his after-breakfast sleep. She came and asked him urgently (as if he would dream of refusing) to get up and greet special visitors. He heard names like Cousin Cornel, Badia Tich, Dr. Serbanescu, Dr. Voynich, Vlada's brother, relatives and colleagues of her parents. (The word "colleague" had far more weight here than in America. Americans now said "associate," as in "Ali Baba and the Forty Associates.") Most of the callers were elderly ailing people of breeding. They were aware how seedy they were, and seemed to shrug when shaking hands, as if to say, "You see how it is." To Corde they looked as if they were gotten up for a Depression party. They chatted in rusty French, for his sake, sparing him their worse English; and as they talked they tried of course to make out the American husband who sat there, hang-loose. He had pulled his clothing on half dazed, and felt insufficiently connected with his collar, socks, shoes, jacket. The Dean had not bought a new suit since getting married, five years ago. He no longer needed to make himself attractive, to divert attention from his thinning hair, long neck, circular face ("something like a sunflower in winter," were his own words). Still not awake, he answered polite inquiries with matching politeness, depending upon the measured bass voice to get him through. At least the Rareshes' only daughter had married an American who spoke some French. French was highly valued here, French was a delicious accomplishment. He explained that he had lived in Paris once, but his conversational powers were limited. He drank a glass of brandy (despite the dishcloth moldiness of the flavor, it had a clean, rousing effect); he ate a slice of Tanti's raisin cake, chased it with a cup of tea. He observed that everybody present was trying to tell him something, to convey by various signs what conditions here were. He gathered, moreover, that the colleagues and cousins were extremely proud of Min-na's scientific eminence. He was with them there. It warmed him to think how much there was also on the human side; if it had been appropriate to let himself go, he would have told them how rich she was in human qualities. The visitors would have been glad if the Dean had spoken intelligently about the United States in world politics. After all, he was from the blessed world outside. The West. He was free to speak. For them it was impossible. All conversations with foreigners had to be reported. Few people were bold enough to visit the American library. Those who sat in the reading room were probably secret agents. It was one of the greatest achievements of Communism to seal off so many millions of people. You wouldn't have thought it possible in this day and age that the techniques of censorship should equal the techniques of transmission. Of course, as in France under the Occupation, these captive millions were busy scrounging, keeping themselves alive. In the sadness of the afternoon, the subdued light of the curtailed day, the chill of the room (so disheartening!), the callers would have been grateful to hear something so exotic as an intelligent American; words of true interest, words of comfort, too—this dictatorship could not last forever. But he hadn't the heart to tell them things. Besides, Corde was not altogether with it. Not even the rousing brandy brought him into focus. It was not until Professor Voynich was leaving that mostly silent Corde identified him. Why, this was Vlada's brother. He rose to shake the doctor's hand a second time. "Do you expect Vlada for Christmas?"

"Definitely."

"I'm sorry . . . I'm a little vague today," said Corde. "I think she'll be bringing me news from Chicago."

Professor Voynich was elderly, wasted-looking. His sister was stout, pale, round; very unlike him. But then his sister hadn't been in prison for—for how many years was it? Much of the time the doctor had been in solitary confinement. Voynich said, as Corde was showing him out, "Your wife tells me you haven't seen much of the city. She is unfortunately busy. I should be happy one of these days to show you, before my sister arrives."

"I'd be grateful."

Corde, after he had closed the front door, didn't return to the parlor. He went back to the room and got into the sack again. A temperature of fifty-five degrees was ideal for cyclamens. He took his cue from them and gave up consciousness, he checked out. He was not sorry to feel himself going, surrendering his senses— sound, touch, closing his eyes—something like a swoon, he thought.

But next morning—and it was morning before he knew it—he was lively again. Someone telephoned from the American embassy. One of Corde's friends in Washington must have pulled an important wire. A car would be calling for Mr. Corde at half past ten. Corde shaved carefully, dressed neatly and went down. Ioanna, the concierge, watching from her *sous-sol* recess, had an event to report to the agents that day—a limousine with the American flag pulling up for Minna's husband.

Corde had sent a note to the cultural attaché. This was Milancey, a smooth-faced man who wore a fur hat; who had a hunched smile; who had seen to their visas when they arrived, had met them at the airport.

Milancey was expert in making the position clear: the U.S. Government had already done its duty by the Cordes and wasn't prepared to put itself out further. The limousine was a surprise, therefore. Milancey would never have sent this Bechstein-style automobile. Maybe the National Science Foundation, maybe a White House adviser familiar with Minna's work, had interceded, and word had come down to Milancey, who had passed it along to the First Secretary or the Minister. Someone at the top had dispatched the Lincoln Continental in which Corde was now riding, warmer than he had been in more than a week, resting his feet on a block of smooth felt that tumbled forward. In spite of these comforts, his eyes were those of a man under extreme pressure. Reaching the blocked, guarded street, the limousine turned into the embassy courtyard. Corde was met by a young woman, who guided him past the Marine sergeant's desk and up the circular marble staircase of the little palace to the Ambassador's office. In the anteroom a secretary rose and opened the door. The Ambassador was standing waiting behind his desk.

"Mr. Corde?"

Corde wondered just why he was being received by this discreet, soft-spoken, almost gentle, mysteriously earnest, handsome black man. Minna's astrophysics was not the explanation, not all of it. The Ambassador

said that he had served in the Paris embassy in the
mid-fifties, when Corde was writing for the *Herald
Tribune*. "I would turn to your pieces first thing." He
gestured towards a sofa. It would be an informal
conversation. It was possible that there wasn't much
official business to do in the holiday gap towards the
end of December, but it also occurred to Corde that the
Ambassador might have read the articles in *Harper's*.
Or perhaps *Time* or *Newsweek* had picked up the story
of the Ebry trial from the hometown papers, which
were none too friendly. Corde had accused the papers
of prejudicing the public against Rufus Ridpath, director of the County Jail, when he was being tried for
manhandling prisoners. They did a number on Ridpath. They printed damaging statements by informants
who weren't named. Grotesque front-page close-ups
made him look like a gorilla. To do this to the only man
who had the guts to go into the worst of the tiers and
recover control of the jail from the barn bosses and
their gangs was an outrage. "Somehow the media are
more comfortable with phonies, with unprincipled
men," was what Corde wrote. And now, in the Ebry
case, the media had a clear shot at him, and they were
banging away. A more experienced, craftier man would
have anticipated this. But moral excitement (was it
because it was so rare?) undermined your practical
judgment. Anyway, it was open season on Corde. The
papers reported Mason's friendship with Ebry and the
charges of the radical students. They hinted that Corde,
a racist, was carrying out the racist policies of the
college. There was an even more embarrassing compli-
cation. Corde's own cousin, Max Detillion, was defend-
ing Ebry. Mason had gotten him to take over the case
from the lawyer Ebry himself had retained. That was
wickedly shrewd of Mason. Oh, how misleading those
ingenuous teeth were, and the youth pollen, too, and
the long eyelashes! The kid was a devil. Cousin Max,
feuding with Corde, called a press conference immediately to announce that he wasn't taking a penny in fees

for representing this ghetto dishwasher. Maxie had a passion for publicity, and this time he was good copy. He owed that to his hated cousin, not to his legal talents. The source of Maxie's hatred was love gone sour, family wrangling. He was maddened with imaginary wrongs. Flashy, elderly, corrupt Maxie, with his bold eyes and his illiterate, furiously repetitious eloquence, had a moronic genius for getting attention. He needed the publicity; his practice was declining. The first lawyer was asked to withdraw.

But it was to no purpose that Corde worried himself about Mason and Max and the media in Chicago, for the Ambassador seemed to know nothing about any of it. He had prepared himself for difficulties this polite man had no thought of making. The Ambassador only wanted to talk about Paris in the fifties. "But you don't write for the papers anymore," he said.

"I gave that up. I still publish a piece now and then. There was one recently . . ."

"I must look that up." The Ambassador made a note with a silver ballpoint. "What sort of work have you been doing?"

"Professor of journalism back in my hometown. Even a dean. I'm not a real administrative type. I doubt that I can call myself a real professor, but I was curious to see what it was like."

It was calming to sit with the Ambassador. His office was beautifully furnished. The man was handsome and there was something about him—breeding, delicacy. Also, getting out of Minna's room was important, a change of scene. Corde had been shut in for too long.

"I suppose you had cultural inclinations you couldn't satisfy by journalism."

"Right you are. It would have to be a very special need to transfer you from Paris to Chicago. I had some reading to do, and wanted to find people to talk to. The right people to talk to—that's the hardest part of all."

"You must be interested in especially difficult things."

"I don't think they're all that difficult or esoteric. I was too busy in Paris. When busyness takes hold of you, then art, philosophy, poetry, those things go out the window. Just before I made the decision to move I was reading Rilke, especially his wartime letters."

"I don't know those."

On the leather sofa with the Ambassador, conversation seemed definitely possible. Mind you, it could never have been easy. When Rilke had complained about his inability to find an adequate attitude to the things and people about him, Corde had thought, Yes, that's very common—that's me, too. Odd that with such a temperament he should have become a newspaperman. A man of words? Yes, but words of the wrong kind. For some years, to cure himself of bad habits, bad usage, he had been mostly silent. And now it seemed he had even forgotten how to open his mouth. Corde's confinement in the silent room where Minna had done her lessons in astrophysics or mathematics, where Valeria kept her relics and wrote her letters, had made him rusty, had shrouded him in mute heart-aching numbness. There was a moment at the beginning of this chat with the Ambassador when he imagined that his face was surfacing, coming up from under like the face that Mason must have seen at the Cape, rising up from the green Atlantic, spectacles lost, back hair floating, big bare brow, French-Irish nose, blind eyes.

It wasn't that subjects were lacking. He was preparing to make an impassioned statement about Valeria. Together with this he wanted to try out on the Ambassador some of his notions about the mood of the West. Oh, he had lots of topics: the crazy state of the U.S., the outlook and psychology of officialdom in the Communist world, the peculiar psychoses of penitentiary societies like this one. The distinguished gentleness of the Ambassador was very encouraging. Corde actually wanted to open up. But he wisely decided to let the Ambassador direct the conversation.

The Ambassador asked for details of Valeria's case,

and Corde became more lively as he outlined it. A drink would have helped, but it wasn't a good idea to ask for one. The Ambassador said that he had read his note to Mr. Milancey very carefully. Corde had written slapdash, carelessly, never thinking that the attaché would show it around. Now he tried to remember what he had said.

"There are certain parallels," the Ambassador said. "I have a foreign wife, too. Mine is French. Her mother, an old French lady who lives with us, is very ill."

"I'm sorry to hear it. Yes, I see why you reacted. Can anything be done? We've been here for eight days—I think. I can't even keep track of the dates. My wife has seen her mother twice."

"Only twice . . . ?"

"About twenty minutes each time. For the second visit we didn't have permission from the Colonel—the hospital superintendent."

"How was it arranged, then?"

Corde glanced about. Even here, naming names might be a mistake. The embassy must certainly be bugged. "I don't know how. But my wife was accused of pulling a fast one. That would be completely out of character. She's an unusually . . ."

"She's an astronomer?"

"If we hadn't rushed here, we'd have been at Mount Palomar. The telescope would have been hers part of Christmas week. Now, well, she's never off the phone, trying to find help. You can imagine what a state she's in. She last saw her mother five days ago. She's grieving."

"Of course she is. What's the reason given?"

"Visits are out, no visiting in intensive care," said Corde.

"Yes, you wrote that in your letter. That is unusually rigid. Well, I'm on good terms with the Minister of Health. I'll call him this afternoon, shall I?"

"I assume he runs all the hospitals. He must be the

Colonel's superior. I'd be very grateful. Her mother won't live long. In times like these the whole thing may seem unimportant. I mean," Corde explained himself, "considering what one reads every day—terrorist acts, famine, genocide, events in Latin America, in Cambodia or in Uganda, where a hostage, an old lady at Entebbe who had to be taken to the hospital, was strangled by Amin's people. These brutal, horrible events. In Addis Ababa the regime has been murdering adolescents to crush the opposition, and they leave children's corpses on the parents' doorsteps. That's how things are done now. . . ."

"It's no trifle to Mrs. Corde, nevertheless, that she isn't allowed to see her mother."

"Nor to me. My wife is a simple person. No politics. Her mother wanted her out of it, brought her up that way. No politics, no history. Perhaps too much that way. Back home in Chicago, magazines arrive for her from civil rights organizations, and books by survivors of the camps, refugees. Because she's from Eastern Europe she's on the mailing lists. But she's too busy, so I'm the one that reads all this grim stuff. That's why I have a fairly complete idea of how things are in this part of the world—forced labor, mental hospitals for dissenters, censorship. I've gotten into the habit of reading this mail for her. She asks me to brief her. Anyway, here's the thing in outline: mother-in-law is in the Party hospital, and the superintendent is a colonel in the secret police. Not the type to respond to the humane appeal. I suspect, anyway, that he would like to teach my wife a lesson."

"Because she left the country?"

"That's part of it. Now the lady comes with an American passport and husband, flies in without a visa so that the embassy has to come to the rescue—by the way, she's still a dual citizen—and expects the Colonel to waive the regulations for her. What does she think this is? Besides, her mother was Minister of Health thirty years ago while this man was still very junior, learning his job in prison hospitals. According to the literature I've become addicted to, techniques are different now, according to Amnesty International they inject mind drugs in psychiatric hospitals, and who knows how many people are dying in those places. Electric shocks, sulfadiazine injections. And it was much rawer before, when the Colonel was an apprentice. One of my mother-in-law's colleagues, a Minister of Justice, had his head hacked off in his cell. They decided not to bring him to trial." Corde's excitement was running away with him. He couldn't say why. Well, yes, he could say approximately why. But it was certainly tactless, stupid, to lecture a high-ranking and experienced foreign service officer about atrocities. Tocqueville was dead right when he said that Americans (democrats everywhere) had no aptitude for conversation, they lectured. Bombast, clichés, chewed-up newsprint, naturally made the other party tune out. He had heard what you had heard, read what you had read. The Ambassador was too well bred to cut him off. He listened, he nodded, he waited. And Corde did after all have something to communicate. He tried again. "What I meant earlier when I spoke of trifles is that everybody now follows a scale: A is bad, but B is worse and C worse still. When you reach N, unspeakable evil, A becomes trivial. After thirty years in police work, and having seen whole regiments of corpses, the Colonel must have special views on suffering and death. So what's all the fuss about one old woman? You use the most extreme case to reduce all the rest. It's the same at home. . . . I can imagine what the Colonel would say about the ethical values of the West. So called."

He sensed that he had not altogether turned the Ambassador off by lecturing him. He was getting a polite hearing still. This man, quite black, very slender, had style, class, cultivation. He wore a light gray well-cut suit, and an Hermès necktie (Corde recognized the stirrup motif), and narrow black shoes which could only have come from Italy. Subtly considerate, he listened to Corde's explanations (or bombast), but obviously he didn't care to discuss Western humanism, civilized morality, nihilism East and West. He was a busy official.

"Let's see what the Minister of Health has to say."

"My wife thinks that her mother can't understand why she doesn't come."

"But that's not how you see it—you don't agree?"

"The old woman, with all her experience, must have it figured out."

"Is she fully conscious?"

"She was when we last saw her. They put a ballpoint in her fingers, and she wrote on a pad that she wanted to be taken home. That is, she wrote the word 'home.' But she can't be unhooked from the machines. The Colonel offered to do that."

"Ah, yes?"

"Yes, he said if she were moved out of intensive care she could be visited every day. But he was only kidding. The respiratory center is gone. She couldn't live ten minutes. This was just his way of sticking it to the daughter. A bonus."

The Ambassador was not altogether comfortable with these details. He was sympathetic, he was exquisitely decorous, but he didn't need to hear it all. But then Corde wasn't transmitting it all. Involuntary memory had passed through his head Goya's painting of Saturn—the naked squatting giant, open-mouthed, devouring. Death swallowing the old woman by the face. Again, the inability to find the adequate attitude. Corde *seemed* sober enough, but his controls were not in dependable working order.

Minna was always asking, "What's Mother thinking? What do you suppose goes through her mind?" And Corde often put it to himself: What would the old woman have felt if she had been able to open her eyes and had seen us standing there in those gowns and surgical masks? He was certain that she had laid her dying plans carefully, but she couldn't arrange Minna's future. There was still the one open question: Could he, Corde, this American, be trusted not to harm, or betray, or even ruin her daughter? The old woman was a very shrewd old woman, but she was a romantic old woman, too. She had loved her husband. When he died, all that was left of him was in their daughter. She sent her daughter directly into cosmic space. Nothing but particle physics, galaxies, equations. Minna had never read the *Communist Manifesto,* had never heard of Stalin's Great Terror. Now then, could Valeria entrust such a daughter to a man like Corde? Suppose Valeria had seen him staring down at her in intensive care, what sort of face did that gauze mask cover— sane, or what? A gentle soul, or a masked killer? Corde was always afraid that that deep old woman knew his worst thoughts, instability, weakness, vices. Oh, Jesus! So must I end up responsible for this life of maternal sacrifice, and the Roman matron purity, and the whole classic achievement! There's something crazy in this, too. There are people who find you out. And especially old women do. In Pushkin's *Queen of Spades,* maybe it wasn't so much gambler's lust that drove that wild plunger, Hermann; he may have hidden himself in the old woman's room because he needed to face her terrible gaze in a test of his soul. Well, Corde had his disorders, but his reply to Valeria was yes. Yes, she could trust him. He was stable. Yes, he had found his firm point. That was what he would have been ready to tell her. "Don't worry. Don't put me in your agonies. I love your daughter!"

No hint of these reflections (he hoped) was given; nor of what the nearness of death was doing to him, how wide open he was, how near to an emotional eruption.

The Ambassador must have been one of those patrician blacks from Washington or Philadelphia whose ancestors were manumitted slaves before the Civil War. Corde had met some of those before. They had summer homes in Edgartown. This was how, probably mistakenly, he placed him. "I can promise you some news later in the day, Mr. Corde," he said. "And if there's something else the embassy can help with . . ."

"Maybe the information library can let me have the *Tribune* for last week? Last papers I saw were on the plane flying over."

"I think we can find you some of those. There's a journalist in town, by the way, who spoke of you yesterday. Spangler, the columnist."

"What, is Dewey Spangler here?"

"He's on a swing through Eastern Europe. We had him in for a drink and he spoke of you warmly. You're old friends?"

"We were at school together. I haven't seen him in years—ten, maybe."

"May I give him your number?"

"Why, sure."

Spangler never looked him up in Chicago, but there was no need to tell this to the Ambassador. He had already said more than was strictly necessary. Too much comment altogether.

An old-boy reunion here in the Balkans would appeal to Dewey. What—two kids from the sidewalks of Chicago, and one of them now, forty years later, a syndicated bit-shot opinion-maker, and meeting in this heavy Communist and Byzantine capital? A great setting! Dewey had in fact become—what?—a public spokesman, a large-scale operator in D.C. For years he had kept his distance from Corde because he didn't like to be remembered as the kinky adolescent who had told preposterous lies, had screaming quarrels with his mother, and wrote violently revolutionary poems.

Corde didn't care greatly for Dewey's column. It was too statesmanlike and doughy. He was trying hard to be a Walter Lippmann. But Lippmann had been the pupil of Santayana and the protégé of potentates at an age when sharp-toothed Dewey in an undershirt was still shrieking and grimacing at his mother.

But we understood each other forty years ago, Corde thought. Of course it was Swinburne, Wilde, Nietzsche, Walt Whitman, in high school. Perfumed herbage, intoxicating lyricism and lamentation, rich music, nihilism and decadence had made them pals. The fat faded pink volume of Oscar Wilde that Corde had found on the lowest shelves, behind Valeria's bed, the pastryrich hyperboles of sightless souls and red hells, might have been an augury of this reunion. And there was still another connection (he would have thought of it if his wits had been working normally): Max Detillion, his cousin, once had shared their literary interests. He said he did, anyway. A showman even then, Maxie used to recite "The Ballad of Reading Gaol." "For each man kills the thing he loves . . . The poor dead woman whom he loved, and murdered in her bed." Dewey Spangler had made wicked fun of him. "Fat-ass lowbrow . . . gross and dainty . . . Arse Poetica"— these were some of the cracks he used to make. But later Dewey turned tolerant. He said that Maxie had after all shaped up and made something of himself. Dewey respected "achievers," if they didn't achieve too much. Corde's opinion had followed the reverse pattern. He believed that Maxie had lost track of himself altogether. Dewey had had no practical dealings with Max. Max had cost Corde tens of thousands. Even that might have been forgiven if only you had been able to talk openly and reasonably to the man. But the more harm he did you, the more harm he claimed you had done him. He grabbed everything for himself, even the injury. And then you were up against it—no rational judgment, you see, a kind of mystery in itself. Then there were other kinds of craziness, like the one about publicity. Mad for being in the papers, Max hung out with newspapermen, gossiping and buying them drinks. Naturally, he grabbed the Ebry case. It gave him a shot in the arm. And now Maxie, before the jury at Thirteenth and Michigan, swept the courtroom with bold Rooseveltian looks, the statesman-lion, a massive man but falling apart. The cause of the illness was neither virus nor bacteria, but erotic collapse. Maxie was in despair. Perhaps celebrity might be a remedy.

In a way Cousin Albert suffered with Cousin Max. There came to mind (Corde was a terrific reader; he had read far too much) Balzac's sex monsters in *Cousine Bette*, and the pitiable Baron Hulot, a feeble ancient man making passes at the woman who was nursing his dying wife. Corde had his reasons for these thoughts, for if he was going to see Dewey Spangler they would be discussing Cousin Max. Most likely Max had sent Spangler clippings from Chicago, where he was doing so wonderfully. Now they were celebrities, all three.

This was a burden on Corde: sorrow. Cousins, and once playmates, and affectionate, and Max had been a handsome young man, and now . . . some sort of blood trouble, so that Max needed not a literal dialysis but another kind of cleaning up. In his youth Max suffered from frequent nosebleeds; this was why Corde fixed on the corrupted blood.

The Ambassador had mentioned neither *Harper's* nor the Ebry trial, which meant that Spangler hadn't told him what was happening. It figured. Why should Dewey first claim him as an old pal and then louse him up? Corde and Spangler had been rivals thirty years ago. At first he, Corde, had been the more successful of the two. He was still in his early twenties when *The New Yorker* printed his personal account of the Potsdam Conference. The conference had been closed to the press, but Harry Vaughan, who was Truman's aide, had been a friend of Corde's father, and Corde, then a GI, most innocent-looking, with his goggles and cowlick, had wangled his way in. Vaughan was annoyed by the report, or was obliged to say that he was; but for jealous Spangler, who was then stuck in Chicago writing about Planned Parenthood and covering tenement fires for the City News Bureau, Corde's success was a terrible thing. It gave him a gruesome wound.

But he was combative, a fierce competitor and an ingenious politician; he made excellent use of his injury and his rage and soon shot ahead. Corde was much less ambitious than Spangler, wrote for a smaller public, seemed sometimes unnecessarily obscure (even, as one of his editors had said, "reclusive"). And when Corde became a professor (no big distinction; by now there were millions of professors), Spangler interpreted it as a victory ("I was too much for him, he's outclassed, no contest, hanging up his gloves") and became more tolerant, more friendly. He sympathized with Corde. Spangler was the worldly one, a shrewder man by far.

To the shrewder man those two articles in *Harper's* must have seemed unaccountable acts of self-destruction. Corde gave up his cover, ran out, swung wild at everyone, made enemies, riled the press most of all —treason to his own trade—virtually asking to be blown away. It was a hell of a strange development. Strangest of all was Corde's regression, for that was how Spangler would describe it. Corde had gone back to an earlier standard, to the days when he and Spangler were reading Shelley and Swinburne together in Lincoln Park. At the age of seventeen they would often quote to each other the line in which Shelley had described George III: "An old mad blind despised and dying king." The wonderful hard music of those words used to stir them. And it was this sort of music that Corde apparently wanted to work into his journalism. If indeed it *was* journalism. If indeed it was Shelley. If it wasn't, instead, Corde as George III himself, old, mad, blind, and sure to be despised in Chicago. Spangler when he had read him would first have been startled, then thrilled by the violence of his self-injury, and finally sorry for the poor guy. It was a wonder the editors of *Harper's* didn't try to restrain him. Here and there he just skirted libel. Crazy with rage, doing himself in.

All these conjectures (Max, Dewey, himself) Corde felt in his silent lips, with the buzzing, tickling sensation

one used to get as a kid by playing tunes through
cigarette paper on a comb. Wondering: Were these (the
personalities, articles, trials, etc.) his own portion of
the big-scale insanities of the twentieth century? Did
these present thoughts occur because he had been shut
up too long in Minna's old room? Or were they the
effects of Valeria's dying, or of the death of Rick
Lester? Did one turn aside the force of thousands of
declines or dooms or deaths and then decide, by some
process of selection too remote ever to be known, to fix
on certain ones? Yes, and then let those you have
chosen paint away in broad visceral strokes until the
fiery brushing undermined and overturned your judgment. And at last the superstructure (put together with
the protective cunning of the blind) began to totter?

The Ambassador walked out of the office with him to
the top of the delicate marble staircase. The embassy
must have been a boyar's palace once. The smooth
banisters were iridescent and curved again and again
like a nautilus shell. The black Ambassador from first
to last was very sympathetic: the sympathy may have
been no more than highly elaborated propriety, but
Corde somehow didn't think so. (No, it wasn't only
two, three, five chosen deaths being painted thickly, terribly, convulsively inside him, all over his guts,
liver, heart, over all his organs, but a large picture of
cities, crowds, peoples, an apocalypse, with images and
details supplied by his own disposition, observation, by
ideas, dreams, fantasies, his peculiar experience of
life.)

"It occurs to me," said Corde to the Ambassador,
"since my friend Spangler is here to interview big shots,
he may be able to put in a word for my wife."

"It's certainly a possibility. He must have contacts.
Yes, I'd ask him if I were you. He's staying at the
Intercontinental. I'll see to it that he gets your number.
He may be hard to reach."

The Ambassador's secretary had gathered up some
recent newspapers for Corde. After the good-bye

handshake—what Mencken once had called "the usual
hypocrisies"—Corde withdrew into a corner near the
desk of the Marine guard and shuffled through the
pages. He didn't, to tell the truth, want to find any
Chicago items. Some of the papers were held between
his knees. No, he didn't look too carefully. But Chicago
was nowhere mentioned. He must be nuts ("bubble
gum in the brain") to build such extensive and anxious
fantasies about the Ebry case. What he did find was one
of Dewey Spangler's syndicated columns. He didn't
read it, he only glanced through it. To take your oldest
friends seriously in their public character was not easy.
He generally put it to himself that Dewey had won a
brilliant victory over his own handicaps. You had to
bear in mind, moreover, that as a kid Dewey had had a
mass of handicaps. He had found the most advanta-
geous way of putting them together. You had to hand it
to him. He had come a long way, for sure.

Corde walked back from the embassy; he refused the
limousine. Minna would have been alarmed, but no
one was about to snatch him in the street. You couldn't
expect her to be rational now. Earth was strange
enough at the best of times. There was nothing too rum
to be true. That needed frequent emphasis. Nothing.
Under the looping brim of the fedora, as he walked, he
arranged the Ambassador's conversation, the promises
he had made, in phrases of maximum effectiveness.

He found a group of workmen busy in the lobby of
the apartment house, mixing tubs of cement and plaster. It was repair, not restoration. The marble panels
that had fallen from the walls during the earthquake
had all been stolen, said Gigi. There would be nothing
but stucco now. When Corde opened the street door, of
wrought iron and glass, Ioanna was on the watch
behind the fourfold window of her hutch. Her cheeks
were like cold-storage apples, a bandanna was knotted
under her chin, she had the shape of a bale. Although
she reported on a regular schedule to *securitate,* she
seemed nevertheless to consider herself one of the

Rareshes, a member of the family. She held on to that. Minna's husband was family, too, of course; but because he and Ioanna had no common language, she reserved a special look of pity for him, as if he were mentally retarded. As he passed her window, he stooped a little, lifting several of his gloved fingers to his hat brim. Idiot is as idiot does. She thought him idiotic? Somebody should.

Tanti Gigi had taken Corde down to Ioanna's quarters on a courtesy call (peculiar forms of protocol, in Eastern Europe), so he knew what was inside. On the walls of the tiny alcove above her head hung official portraits of the dictator and his wife. Nearby was a picture of the beautiful Nadia Comaneci, who didn't need the support of the solid earth and preferred to live in the air, like a Chagall bride. There was also an icon painted on glass with a full flowing brush—red, green and gilt. In this one, Elijah drove into heaven with two horses while saints and angels cried hosannah. By Ioanna's bedside, in the place of honor, was a photograph of Valeria, the Doamna Doctor. Thirty years ago, Ioanna had been the Doamna Doctor's housemaid. She was devoted to Valeria, no doubt about it, but she had to be paid off. Whenever Valeria went abroad, Ioanna's name was high on her shopping list. She was one of those for whom dress materials had to be bought, chocolates, bottles of Arpège, panty hose (the biggest size). All this was depicted as affection. And it *was* affection, who said it wasn't? It was both affection and payola. So there was Ioanna, big on emotion, loyal to the family, fully informed, very potent, dangerous to neglect. The bale figure, the scarlet pippin cheeks, the slow heaving of the big behind, the efficiency of her black-stockinged thick legs, the sincerely pitying face—Corde had taken full note of all of these. The concierge protected, loved and blackmailed the old sisters. How to interpret this? "They that have power to hurt and will do none . . . they are the lords and owners of their faces." No,

Shakespeare wasn't thinking of any Ioanna; he had
great souls in mind, nobility. But Gigi and Minna and
others had assured Corde that the concierge really
loved Valeria. He believed them ("I'll buy that"). She
was a blackmailer, but she also gave her heart. For
there was a love community of women here. The
matriarch was Valeria. Ioanna was a member in good
standing.

This apartment was the center of an extended feminine hierarchy. There was Tanti Gigi. She had gone to
London in the twenties and came back a Mayfair moth
in flapper dresses and costume jewelry, covered with
eye makeup and speaking Beatrix Potter English. She
was Little Sister, at Valeria's right hand. Then there
was Minna, in America, but figuring prominently;
distance made no difference, even Science didn't; she
was a full, willing member and a prominent one. Other
members were Viorica, Doina, Cornelia, even Serbian
Vlada in Chicago. Vlada in chemistry and Minna in
astronomy, both belonged to this emotional union. The
ladies consulted Valeria about their husbands, their
children, their careers, took her advice in matters of
love, education, religion. They made over clothing for
one another, raised and lowered hems, repaired zip-
pers, came to sickbeds, waited in queues. There was a
small male auxiliary, also. Mihai Petrescu, who had
been Valeria's *politruk* in the Ministry, the Party's
watchdog, was in it. He seemed, like Ioanna, to work
both sides of the street. No outsider could understand
these multiple roles and Chinese intricacies. It was
beyond Corde, certainly. It was not the American kind
of loyalty-duplicity; in America the emotions were
different somehow, perhaps thinner. Here you led a
crypto-emotional life in the shadow of the Party and
the State. You had no personal rights, but on the other
hand, the claims of feeling were more fully acknowledged.

He entered the elevator. The thing was made like a
china cabinet, and because it knocked when it was in

use, you heard a frail wooden echo inside. They had such elevators everywhere in Europe, in buildings of the Haussmann type, had them in Warsaw and in Belgrade, too, these (imitated) vestiges of bourgeois Paris.

He rose to the fifth floor. The talk with the genteel Ambassador, the American papers, the walk home, had stirred him through and through. It seemed to him that he had built up a life of strong mental excitement. Minna, who had been watching at the window, let him in and said, "Why did you walk? They should have sent you home in a car."

"No one thought of it."

"They've done a tracheotomy," said Minna.

"Who has? Oh, I see. I thought they would ask you."

"Dr. Moldovanu said last week that they probably would have to. Well, they did it. It went well, he said. It should help."

"Did he talk to you about a visit? What are the chances?"

"I couldn't discuss that with him on the phone. He recommended it to the Colonel, that I'm sure of. Speaking as her doctor, he said it would help my mother's chances of recovery if she could see me. . . ."

"The Colonel doesn't pay much attention to the doctors. I'd be surprised if Moldovanu mentioned it to him a second time."

"They're all scared. Yes, I think you're right."

Corde and Minna stood talking in the parlor. The peeling, swelling leather armchairs were uninviting. You didn't willingly sit down in them. Big medical volumes from Dr. Cushing's Boston were stacked on the shelves behind the telephone. Corde, too, felt out of date, like the chairs.

"What happened at the embassy? Did you talk to that man Milancey?"

"I was taken to the Ambassador."

"You are kidding! How unusual."

"He'd seen my letter."

"What's he like?"

"Well, he's black. He's handsome. He's a career diplomat. He thought it might help to talk to the Minister of Health. I suppose the M of H runs the hospitals," said Corde. "Well, they've done the tracheotomy. . . .'." They've peeled those big tapes from her face, he thought. Those were gone, anyway. To him they were especially oppressive.

"I'll have to ask my contacts about the Minister of Health. And write a note to the Ambassador. Albert, I talked to the lady who has a relationship with Dr. Gherea. I told you, didn't I, that I met her once in Switzerland? She remembered me. In fact, she knew all about my mother. Everybody is talking about it, all over town. I offered to go to Gherea's hospital myself to ask him to examine her. But do you know what the woman said? She said how much Gherea owed both my parents. She was very warm, she talked to me with real feeling. I think she'll arrange it all."

"Let her. She sounds like a good woman."

"Albert, I want to show you a photograph of Gherea. Tanti Gigi found it in a magazine. . . . What do you think?"

The man was stout, hairless. His mouth was set between determined swellings. He was immediately there: that's him.

"I'd say he was a very nice man to have in your corner. I wouldn't be happy to see him on the other fellow's side. There are plenty of pusses like that in Chicago. But if he's so big and important, maybe he can do something about the Colonel."

"Should I talk to him about that?"

"If I were you, I wouldn't go to this particular man with tears in my eyes. Skip the emotions, that's my hunch. If he's like the tough guys he reminds me of . . . It's his trade to scrape tumors out of people's brains."

"So was it my father's."

"From what I hear, your Communist surgeon father

got on his knees and prayed before he started cutting. Does this guy look like he sinks to his knees? Didn't you say he socks his anesthetist in the jaw if he crosses him?"

"I'll phone the woman back and ask whether Gherea might try with the Colonel. This is the sixth day I haven't seen my mother."

Without expecting Minna to follow what he was saying (she had too much on her mind; she only wanted to hear the sound of his voice, reassuring if only in the depth of its tones), Corde observed that here was another case of humane cooperation among women in a Communist society. Gigi insisted that Gherea loved his lady friend. Maybe he did. These tough guys always made exceptions. Hitler had had Eva Braun. People in reduced emotional circumstances set their affections on something or other. They were pitted against Eros— against the universe. Total misanthropes, true, absolute ones, were probably as rare as saints. He was trying to divert Minna. She wasn't listening, only staring. Concentration made her face severe. This happened also when she was doing science. With Corde Minna was often cheerful and childlike. When he pleased her, she might jump up and down and clap her hands like a small girl. But when she worked she was a different person entirely. She sat in her corner hours on end with a pad and pencil, writing symbols, her face turned downward, the upper lip lengthened, the chin compressed and dented. She was not an observer; if she had been one she might never have married a man with such a round bare crown and the stare of a Welsh prophet (his own image—it was the eyes he was thinking of). Until now she had had little interest in psychology. Her mother was the psychiatrist; she left all that to her. But now she was forced to study people. He wondered what her powerful intelligence would make of them—of him. He had said often enough that she'd have to come down to earth one day. Not much of a prediction. He was sorry for the satisfaction he had taken in making it. How often people had told *him* that sooner or later he'd have to come down to earth. Well, here she was, anyway, with everybody else, and fighting with childlike passion. "Why do I have to go to Gherea? He should have come to me."

She said this again. "He was a peasant kid with talent. Where would he have been without this family? Even his lady friend says it. My parents took him into the house. He lived right here. My father made him a neurosurgeon. Gherea has never trained anybody. He keeps his monopoly."

"Well, if the clot turns out to be operable, he may move Valeria to his hospital. If he should decide that it was medically necessary, how could the Colonel stop him?"

This was nothing but sophistry, clever comfort, holding the line. Surgery was unthinkable; you couldn't administer an anesthetic if the respiratory center was knocked out. If Gherea was coming to examine Valeria, he had almost certainly discussed the case with Dr. Moldovanu. Hopeless. Anyway, the brain surgeon would have a look at the X-rays, go through all the motions. He'd do that with King Kong delicacy, because his lady wanted the gestures made. It came under the heading of feminine boor-control. But it did Minna good to be angry. Corde himself was angry and trying to increase his anger with people in Chicago who were at this moment trying to do him in—with his cousin Max, for instance. Max was in the courtroom carrying on like John Barrymore in *Counsellor-at-Law*. You could almost see the old movies on which he had formed his character. Corde had studied the geology of his cousin's soul and identified the fossil remains.

Anger was better. In passivity you only deteriorated.

Minna said, "I've been so long in the States that I forgot how things are here. We made such fun of Valeria and her shopping lists, but look how people have to dress. The women are so depressed. They have no food, and there's nothing to wear. One year I washed and ironed the same blouse every night; it was all there was. Now I keep thinking of all the items I could have brought from Chicago. Like the navy dress with the white. I should have left a set of keys with Vlada."

"There was no time for keys. I'll leave my things here, except for this suit to fly back in."

"I'll ask Gigi if Professor Voynich will take your things."

"Better wait till Vlada arrives. She can't bring him to the States, I suppose."

"I'm not sure he wants to go."

"Start a new life? I suppose not. I'd hate it. It's time to stay put, for better or for worse. Voynich said he'd take me for a walk. I'd like to get out, see the city."

"Maybe his French is too rusty, and he feels awkward. He was a social democrat and had a bad time, not much pension. Wait a few days and Vlada will take you. She has to talk to you anyway about the article you're supposed to write with Sam Beech."

"I've by no means decided."

"Why not? Beech is brilliant. You shouldn't refuse. He's a great man."

Minna looked up to great men. She didn't look down on her husband; she didn't quite understand what he was after. But she preferred looking up, definitely. That Corde's articles were approved by an eminent man of science was important to Minna. Now she knew what to think of his critics. The articles themselves hadn't held her interest. Doing her best, she had rattled through the pages while he watched with a certain sympathy—even with envy. Why should slums, guns, drugs, jails, politics, intrigues, disorders matter? Leaving Hell, Dante saw the stars again. Minna saw them all the time. Mason had once said that his new aunt was charming but a little spacy. Uncle Albert was the worldly one, who was supposed to give guidance and support here below. He had come to Europe to interpose himself between Minna and this bughouse coun-

try. For clearly the guys in charge were psychopaths.
There were no rational grounds for what they did.

But Uncle Albert was not the worldly one, either.
Max and Mason were both agreed that he, Corde,
wasn't really with it, didn't know the score at all, and
that he deserved to be penalized for meddling, for
interfering with reality as the great majority of Americans experienced it—to which that majority actually
sacrificed itself. As if everybody were saying, "This is
life, this is what I give myself to. There is no other deal.
No holding back, go with the rest." Then a man like
Corde came haunting around. He would never put his
chips on the mortal roulette squares, good enough for
everybody else. Not on dollars, not on whiskey, not on
sexual embraces—but on what? On Swedenborg's angels, maybe? (Swedenborg was Uncle Albert's own
addition.) Then Corde remembered how in the office
he had wanted to open his heart to Mason, to tell him
that under the present manner of interpretation people
were shadows to one another, and shadows within
shadows, to suggest that these appalling shadows *con-
demned* our habitual manner of interpretation. Grant
this premise and . . . But the kid would never have
listened to this. In his opinion (his portion of the
prevailing chaos, but let's call it opinion), Uncle Albert
was flirting with a delusive philosophy and trying to
have an affair with nonexistent virtues. Mason's statement would have been, "Uncle, you're unreal, you're
out of it." And Corde, giving in to anger, might have
said, "I'm talking straight. Try to listen." But Mason
wouldn't—he couldn't. And now he was allied with a
longtime ill-wisher. He and Cousin Max would fix
Uncle Albert's wagon.

" . . . And in my opinion," Minna was saying, "it
would be excellent to work with a person like Beech.
Excellent."

To bring me within the bounds of higher sanity. Take
sanctuary with science.

Like Gigi, Minna was assuming her mother's tone

and some of her ways. Well, Valeria's was a role too
valuable to lose. It should be filled, no denying that.
Minna played it with greater authority than Gigi.

Corde had become attached to Gigi—her distracted,
flustered charm, her classic straight nose and full
Egyptian eyes. Even the permanent wave, gone wrong
at the back. He liked the old girl a lot. As for her, she
had noted how he tended the cyclamens. He watered
them from beneath, setting the pots in bowls of water.
She said to him, "There is not much to offer you. The
one thing we can be lavish of is these flowers." He
wondered what it might mean about him as a "serious
adult" that the flowers should claim so much of his
attention.

He mentioned to Minna that Dewey Spangler was in
town.

"I've forgotten who he is—remind me."

"You saw him on *Face the Nation,* don't you remember? My buddy from way back. The international
celebrity. The Washington columnist."

"He isn't one of the ones I've met."

"No."

"What's he doing here?"

"He's making one of his sweeps of Europe to gather
information. I suppose he'll write a series of pieces
about the Communist countries."

"Seeing him would make a change for you. You have
to sit here day after day."

"I've been thinking—he must have influence in high
places."

"Is he so important?"

"In his league, yes. The Ambassador thought so,
too. He'll probably have dinner with the dictator. The
dictator is another publicity genius, like my cousin
Maxie Detillion. Everybody says how progressive and
liberal he is."

Minna raised her eyes to the ceiling fixture to warn
against listening devices. But Corde had been whispering. She said, "Would your friend put in a word . . . ?"

"Who, Spangler? It can't hurt to ask. . . . Why don't we go to the room and have a drink. It feels like drink time."

"You have a packet of mail from Chicago. It's waiting on the table."

This gave him a start. He had fretted because there was no news from Chicago. Now it was here he wanted no part of it. He decided immediately to put off opening the packet. "From Miss Porson?"

"It looks like it."

"Well, let's have our drink."

He avoided looking too closely at his wife. The tubercular whiteness of her face upset him. Her big shocked eyes were immobile, her lower lip was indrawn, and she was gaunt, stiff. In a single week even her fingers had lost flesh, so that the joints and the nails stood out.

Shortly after they were married, one of Corde's academic friends had congratulated him, saying, "Do you remember that old piece of business from probability theory, that if a million monkeys jumped up and down on the keys of typewriters for a million years one of them would compose *Paradise Lost?* Well, you were like that with the ladies. You jumped up and down and you came up with a masterpiece."

Corde had a mild reflective way of looking at the ground between his feet, his hands gathered behind his back, when people took witty cuts at him. "More like *Paradise Regained,*" was his answer. Why was he supposed to have been a wild ladies' man? In others, much greater sexual irregularities weren't even noticed. It was his serious air that made him conspicuous. He looked moral, gazing Socratically at the ground with large eyes while people teased him about jumping monkeys. Well, he had only himself to blame. If he was going to look so earnest, let him be earnest in earnest. About Minna he *was* earnest.

"Christ! Miss Porson," he said.

"I thought you were waiting for mail."

"I *was* waiting. But facing it is something else."

"You can open it after lunch, if you aren't up to it."

He wasn't up to it at all. He had a stitch, a cramp, thinking about it. But now the telephone began to ring. There was a series of calls. The first was for him. On behalf of Dewey Spangler, the Ambassador's secretary inquired whether Mr. Corde was available to meet him at the Intercontinental. Mr. Spangler would send his car at three o'clock. For Minna's information, Corde repeated, "Mr. Spangler? Drinks at three? Just a moment, please." He covered the mouthpiece, waiting.

"Of course. Of course. Go," said Minna.

"Tell Mr. Spangler that I'll be waiting."

The next call was from Dr. Gherea's obliging lady friend. How decent of her! Her message (there were no short conversations in the Balkans) took twenty minutes to deliver; final arrangements had been made for the consultation. Dr. Moldovanu would phone her about it at ten o'clock tomorrow to report Gherea's opinion.

"That's what we wanted," said Corde, "your old man's protégé."

From the Chicago packet, which he opened with a sigh, he extracted a letter from his sister Elfrida. He galloped through it to see what it was about and then went back and studied it in detail. She was a subtle and tactful woman, good old Elfrida. She might have low tastes in men (that, unfortunately was common), but she was well-bred. First she wanted to know how Valeria was. She had great respect for Valeria. "That's a superior, dignified woman, not like us mixed hybrid Frenchies from the Midwest." Elfrida, too, had come to England last spring. In London one night, Corde had given all the ladies dinner at the Étoile—sometimes he thought he could live happily ever after on Charlotte Street. Elfrida's letter was particularly circumspect. She was damn careful with him. The word "fond" occurred several times. Why was that necessary? He and his sister loved each other; the "fond" was trivial.

Maybe it needed special emphasis because Corde had added lately to her burdens. He was temporarily—humiliatingly—in the Mason category, a troublemaker. So she wanted to assure him that (like Mason!) he had not lost her love. Elfrida had always been gentle with her brother. For his part, Corde had always tried to protect Elfrida, which aggravated Mason's resentment. Elfrida ought not to have had such a turbulent, fanatical son. She ought not to have married such a bully as Zaehner, either. That was her own vulgar streak. But of course Elfrida had no desire for her brother's protection. Nor for his critical analysis, thank you. Naturally, both father and son knew exactly what Corde thought of them. And now by his extreme queerness Mason made an exclusive claim on his mother—but Corde disliked all this psychology. Understanding was at bottom very tiresome.

Elfrida's letter was in part an offering. She wanted to convey affection and kindness to Minna. She did it with a sort of looping, rambling naive charm, not strictly literate, with feminine flourishes. Indirectly she appealed to her brother not to blame her for Mason's behavior, and spoke of "this admittedly difficult stage in Mason's maturing process." He didn't expect a mother to condemn her son. But what did she think existence was, dear girl? How she chose her tones was very odd. In one passage she was soft, in another inappropriately loud. Funny dynamics. She could be hardheaded enough when it was necessary. She was an excellent money manager. One of her paragraphs referred to the difficulties that Paine Webber was having with its computers. She was afraid that they might have lost track of her securities. "I never understood the printouts they sent. How could I? Electronics could make a beggar of me."

Zaehner had left her rich. He had had a big practice, and he used to enjoy quoting a famous Texas lawyer: "I'm just as interested in the poor and oppressed as

Clarence Darrow was. If they aren't poor when I meet them, they are when I'm through with 'em.''

A few days before the arrival of Gigi's wire, Corde had had a long talk with his sister.

Their meeting came before him now (the sun entered Minna's room, and its walls were relined with warm winter light). Like a colored picture, a carelessly inserted slide, Elfrida's parlor went back and forth, somewhat crooked, and then, right side up and better focused, he saw his sister Elfrida. If Corde's love for Elfrida had an extreme, almost exaggerated character, it was perhaps because she was curiously put together—very slender at the top, with a smooth dark head, and wide in the hips, a narrow profile combined with broad femininity. Her skin was imperfect, pitted on the cheekbones, but it was smooth in the hollows. She had the big mouth of a shouting comedienne and a talent for farcical gestures—she would make exaggerated gestures if she trusted you enough to let herself go. Her breath was acrid with tobacco, perfumed with lipstick; her teeth were irregular and spotty. Her air was that of a woman who had given in to disappointment and ruin. "Oh, to hell with it all!" This was conveyed, however, with a certain cleverness, ruefully amiable and warm. For of course she hadn't withdrawn the feminine claims of a younger woman. "American gals" seldom did. In their fifties they were still "dating." Corde didn't care to be well informed about these dates. She was seeing Stan Sorokin, Judge Sorokin, some years her junior. He courted her, pursued her, although since her husband's death three years ago she seemed to have become swarthier, more lined. But through all the transformations of middle age, the point of her upper lip, that strangely communicative tip, told you (told her brother, at least) what sort of woman she was—patient in disappointment, skeptical, practical, good access to her heart, if you knew where to look. It was all in the rising point of the lip.

Elfrida lived in an expensive hotel apartment near the "Magnificent Mile," just east of Water Tower Place. Corde disliked the commercial and promotional smoothness of the neighborhood, the showiness of the skyscrapers, the Bond Street and Rue de la Paix connections. "The Malignant Mammonism of the Magnificent Mile," he said to his sister. But Elfrida wouldn't acknowledge that it was the restaurants, the name hairdressers, the celebrities in the streets, that attracted her. She needed action, she insisted that she was happiest in a hotel apartment. Their father had been a hotel man. The Cordes had lived for years in a huge old apartment on Sheridan Road, but she preferred to remember the razzle-dazzle hotel life, the banquets, the big kitchens, the jazz bands, the bar gossip, and she told people, with a satisfaction her brother didn't share, "We were a pair of hotel brats." He was more apt to recall the drunks, freaks, noisemakers, check-kiters, the football deadheads, the salesmen and other business dumdums.

She and Zaehner had moved to the suburbs for Mason's sake. "You see how well *that* worked." She said to Corde, "When I'm out of sorts it comforts me that there are people down in the lobby. I don't have to face an empty lawn when my heart is troubled. Thank God I unloaded that big pretentious house."

This was her way of saying that living in Lake Forest had been Zaehner's idea. She seldom spoke frankly to Corde about her husband. The late Zaehner's attitude towards her brother had embarrassed her. She was still decently covering up—foolish wifeliness, Corde thought. There was too much there for tact to cover. Zaehner was tough. His face was charged with male strength in all the forms admired in Chicago. A big fellow, he was forceful, smart, cynical, political, rich, and he had no use for those who weren't. In the city that worked, he was one of those who gave people the works. So he despised his brother-in-law, a man large enough to be forceful, smart enough to be rich, proud enough to be contemptuous. To him Corde was a cop-out, a snob. From his side, Corde was careful to make no trouble for his sister. He let himself be baited, kept to his rule never to tangle with Zaehner. He held aloof, but of course there was tacit comment. The situation was complicated by the fact that in some respects Corde had liked his brother-in-law. He enjoyed his growling wit, his unpressed look, his practical jokes. (Zaehner would send call girls to visit his pals in the hospital, to cock-tease politicians and lawyers just out of the operating room.) Corde told Minna, "Zaehner was a Lyndon Johnson type of bully. When he turned away seven-eighths of his face but was still looking at you—watch out!" Lyndon Johnson was very remote from Minna. She gave Corde a dimpled smile, but he had learned that these smiles (affectionate, intimate, "steal your heart away") didn't signify understanding, only confidence that her husband, if she asked him to explain, could give her his grounds, would show why his remark deserved her smile. He would lay out the whole American scene, spelling out the similarities he saw between the late Zaehner and the late President: native sons, men of power, devoid of culture, lovers of money, fearlessly insolent. Spelling it all out was a labor. Moreover, none of this meant much to her. Besides, she had no time to listen; she was intensely elsewhere. Nevertheless, she sent him a delightful signal.

So Elfrida had asked him to come, largely because of Mason but also out of sisterly concern, and he was in her apartment, sinking into one of her slipcovered chairs. Her small rooms were over-decorated; she had brought too much stuff with her from the suburbs. On the wall over the sofa were three schlocky watercolors of the Place Vendôme. They belonged in a hospital thrift shop, but they were a Paris gift from Zaehner.

Elfrida wasted no time. Handing Corde a martini

and taking her English Ovals, the ashtray and matches into her lap, she began. "Let's see if we can get everything sorted, about you and Mason."

"And Max."

"Yes, Max. He's a nasty bastard. I always warned you about Cousin Detillion. I feel very sorry, Albert, for the heat you're getting."

"Although you'd say I brought it on myself, a good part of it."

"Well, I can't blame Mason on you. Nor Maxie. He always was repulsive. But there were things you could have avoided. You didn't need to publish those articles just before the trial. And then there's the trial itself."

"Well, there was a boy murdered. I didn't have much choice. There's also the young wife."

"But did you have to push so hard?"

"I didn't, not all that hard. The alternative was to accept the death. Just blame the urban situation—hot night, kid pushed out of a window. I could have let it all fade away, and be philosophical about it."

"We don't need to go into that. You had your reasons."

"Of course. You want me to explain why there's a warrant out for Mason's arrest."

"Yes, that's it. Why is there? Did you have anything to do with it?"

"Why would I? To stoke up the publicity fires for Cousin Maxie? I'm getting plenty of heat as it is. You just said it. The facts are in the papers—the real facts, for a change. Grady went before a grand jury and complained that Mason had raised hell with his witnesses. You can't expect a prosecutor to let the kid ruin his case. Hasn't he told you about this himself?"

"Mason?"

"He wouldn't have, naturally. But he threatened those street characters. He said he'd get 'em."

Elfrida said, "It's hard to imagine tough black street people being intimidated by skinny Mason. I can't picture that that Lake Forest schoolboy actually fired a gun at anybody. Do you believe that, Albert?"

"Not necessarily. But I don't necessarily disbelieve it. He's in real earnest about his pal Ebry. By working in the restaurant kitchen, he got to be an honorary black. He cornered those witnesses. . . ."

"They only came out of the woodwork to claim the reward."

Corde said, "One of them had the dead boy's wedding ring. The prostitute asked him to keep it for her. The other fellow put Ebry up that night, and Ebry told him he was in trouble. Mason warned those two. They took fright. . . ."

"Yes," said Elfrida. "That's what I read in the papers. They were shot at, got scared, and hid themselves."

"Without them, Grady had no case. He sent the plainclothesmen into the projects to flush them out, one from Cabrini Green, the other from Robert Taylor Homes. They were taken in custody. . . ."

"Can you see Mason sticking a gun in his pocket and going out at night to shoot anybody?"

"They're capable of making it all up, sure. *If* shots were fired—a doubtful proposition—somebody else might have fired them. There are enough guns around, and plenty of people out to get people. There's an armed population in the city with all kinds of weapons —not just Saturday night specials but machine guns, grenades. I wouldn't be surprised by rockets. Still, Mason did threaten the witnesses, gang style, that does seem to be a fact; and they didn't turn up at the trial, another fact."

Elfrida pulled back strands that had escaped from the tight black bonds of hair. Her brother almost imagined that the tightness helped her to keep her head in position. With a hint of strain or faintness, Elfrida confessed, "I don't follow. . . . He is a little bastard, isn't he."

"I wouldn't exaggerate," said Corde. "But what's he gone into hiding for? He's not exactly a hunted man. Obstructing justice isn't such a big deal in this case. He must be thrilled to pieces to be a fugitive. It's a terrific luxury for a kid like Mason. You corner two street people. You deliver a death threat. They take you *seriously*—that's a real thrill. It means you're pretty close to being black yourself. You don't have to be ashamed of your white skin."

"Ah, well, I don't have a corner on troubles. You've got your own, Albert."

Wrapped in his coat at Valeria's table, his chair tipped back, Corde reconstructed parts of this conversation. His memory was exceptionally clear. And he could see what a problem he had become to his sister. The last thing she wanted was the sort of "intelligent" discussion he specialized in. There were times when a humoring-the-mad look passed over her face. He knew his sister's mind as he knew her long neck, her characteristic dark female bittersweet fragrance. Mason might be playing a modern version of Tom Sawyer and Nigger Jim. It had an especially nasty twist now. Yes, but what game was Uncle Albert playing?

"You must have discussed this with somebody in the firm. I'd turn it over to Zaehner, Notkin and Delff if I were you."

"Yes, I've talked it over with Moe Delff. He says the indictment won't hold up, the court will dismiss it. But Mason has to surrender first, so I can put up a bond. Moe will go to the police with him. When it comes up for a hearing, Moe thinks the court will give your friend Grady hell for rushing to the grand jury."

"Is this all Delff?" Corde asked.

He was sounding her out about Judge Sorokin. He shouldn't have done this. It was not altogether brotherly amiability. She probably didn't like it. By the lowering of her eyes she confirmed his hunch. Nevertheless he went on. "I assume you've double-checked this with Sorokin."

Sorokin was a minor magistrate, a former precinct captain who owed his position to the Machine. There were officials in Chicago who didn't much mind being owned. Everybody had to be vetted by the Machine. You didn't get on the ballot unless the Machine put you there. Within the Machine, however, relations were hierarchical and feudal, not necessarily servile. Corde had dealt with this in his articles and Sorokin himself had been one of his informants. Corde liked him, on the whole. Alderman Siblish was said to have Sorokin in his pocket, yes, but the man was cheerful, boyishly good-natured. No really dirty work came his way; he wasn't important enough for that. He had risen from the North Side streets. Wounded at Omaha Beach (Purple Heart), he was far from disabled. For recreation he took Outward Bound survival trips, parachuting from helicopters into the trackless wild. Obviously Elfrida liked Sorokin, but she assumed that her brother, that great reader, journalist, highbrow professor, dean, and intellectual, took a dim view of the Judge, saw him as another Zaehner. Well, she preferred low Chicago male company, people like her own father, a man about town who used to take her to prizefights and nightclubs. Corde's tastes were different altogether. He'd been unwilling to go to the fights with Dad.

"Naturally, I talked it over with Stan Sorokin. Can you blame me? Every morning the papers are at the door. My heart races so, I can't swallow my coffee. It must be even worse for you, reading them."

"They seldom get anything right."

"But how irritating it must be. I'm sure your college isn't happy about it, either."

"So far they've been civilized. *I've* been the emotional party. They haven't much use for that. They'd prefer me to be cool. Anyway, they behave like gentlemen. No, they aren't happy—the circus it's turned into, with the Dean's nephew and the Dean's cousin Maxie, the student newspaper, the leftover Lefties of the sixties. Even the Spartacus Youth League from the thirties."

"But Mason, most of all."

Examining his behavior now, Corde thought he had done fairly well on the whole.

"You asked me to stop in on my way home, Elfrida. . . ."

"That's right."

"I didn't invite myself. In fact, I've stayed away deliberately. But I didn't come and complain about Mason. . . ."

"That's true, Albert. . . . I'm sure it is. I believe it. There is an emotional problem. I think Mason has been trying to get at you like this because he wasn't able to reach you otherwise."

So it was to be a session of suburban maternal psychology. He had no use at all for that stuff, but he saw no way to stop it. As he drank his martini, he tuned out, now and again. But if he paid little attention to her words, he listened closely to the sound of her voice, watched her face. She was warm of heart, naturally warm. She spoke of schools and teachers, of psychiatrists, of the loneliness of an only child and the problems of coping with a father like Zaehner, of Mason's lack of success with peer friendships and the effects of marijuana on the brain ("Recent studies show . . ."). Thank heavens Mason didn't have a serious drug problem. Composed, turning the stem of the martini glass, looking into the drink and again at Elfrida's imperfect skin, Corde felt the tidy parlor of the hotel apartment enclosing him—paneled white walls, white silk lampshades, upholstered restfulness, thick carpeting, porcelain cockatoos on the mantel, ornaments of Venetian glass and Meissen, the phony Place Vendôme watercolors, the enormous Hancock Tower with crossed trusses shutting off the westward view—and asked himself where the depth level was. Not in the ladies'-magazine pedagogy or the Lake Forest psychiatry, but in the natural warmth of his sister. In him it was represented if you liked by his feeling for Elfrida—for the length and smoothness of her head, the Vidal

Sassoon dye job, the damaged skin, the slender nose with its dark nostrils, the feminized tobacco flavor, her sweet-and-acrid fragrance. All these particulars, the apperceptive mass of a lifetime. Yes, she was heavy in the thighs, big in the hips. There was a perennially strange ultra-familiar contrast between the elongated upper body, the upstream, and the broad estuary of the lower half, the lower flow of womanliness. The depth level he was looking for was in the heat that came from her patchy face, from the art with which she was painted about the eyes, and even from the memories of odors, some of them undoubtedly sexual in origin— from an aching sort of personal history. Perhaps he loved the point of her upper lip most of all. He thought this to be a reading of true feelings and no mere projection. These times we live in give us foolish thoughts to think, dead categories of intellect and words that get us nowhere. It was just these words and categories that made the setting of a real depth level so important. I disagree with my misshapen old sister, we can't talk to each other, yet we have something palpable between us. Mason, somewhere, is aware of this and he doesn't like it. She loves him most, as is quite natural, but that's not enough for him. Maybe he's afraid that I may do him out of his legacy, if she's named me executor. But she's surely too smart to do that. My record with money is bad. I let Detillion swindle me. And I assume the Mason problem comes down to money, somewhere along the line. The form Mason's ambition has taken is downward, for the present. It's as that clever Frenchman said: there's positive transcendence and there's the negative kind. (Corde had stopped thirty years ago trying to discuss theories with Elfrida.) But when Mason's downward ambition stops—and where can it lead?—he'll want his dough. She'll die, he'll get it. He's waiting for that. Elfrida would not be shocked by these parricidal thoughts. Why should she be? If she hadn't read Proust's "Filial Sentiments of a Parricide," she had been married to Mason Zaehner, who had practiced law on La Salle Street for four decades. She had no need of Proust or Freud or Krafft-Ebing or Balzac or Aristophanes. Chicago had it all.

Zaehner the secretive lawyer was big on candor, in a showmanly way. He liked a bold statement over a drink, as when he told Corde that he lived by tipping over garbage cans. "Lived" was his euphemism for the crushing fees he charged. Sometimes he was more Darwinian—the struggle for existence in the Loop jungle. Some jungle! Who were the lions and tigers? It was more like the city dump. Rats were the principal fauna. And it wasn't Zaehner who struggled for existence; he arranged for others to do the struggling. And of course Zaehner sensed how mixed a view his brother-in-law took of him. He couldn't have missed it. You didn't have to be terribly deep for that. Corde had the trick, while keeping his mouth shut, of transmitting opinions. He looked at you with a newspaperman's silent irony. Well, Zaehner was affronted by those opinions. It was people like himself, Zaehner, who lived the life characteristic of the city and of the country, who were realistically connected with its operations, its historical position, its power—the actual American stuff. They were at the center. And who the fuck did this dud dean think *he* was!

Anyway, Zaehner died of heart failure on the expressway while driving back to Lake Forest, and he left a pile of money. And despite her fashionable address among gay bars and executive dining clubs, in these streets of canopies, marquees, doormen, Elfrida was not one of your big spenders. She didn't haunt the boutiques or wear designer dresses. She was increasing Zaehner's dollars, preserving them for Mason!

She was talking money to her brother now, saying that she had been trapped through bad advice with a conservative portfolio. Interest rates had shot up, the bonds declined by thirty percent; the gold hedge hadn't worked, either. About the Paine Webber computers she was rueful, giving him side glances with her slight, smiling dark face as if she were telling him that she had been abused physically, cornered and pinched by gross people. Corde in his polite way, but restive ("Okay, okay, enough!"), said, "SEC is watching this minor Paine Webber mixup, you can be sure. The *Wall Street Journal* said it was trivial." But in matters of money she didn't need his assurances. Sorokin, if she should decide to marry that virile, sleek-headed, nutria-bearded Marlboro Country judge from the North Side, would not come into any of the money. But to do him justice, it didn't appear that he was chasing Elfrida's dollars.

Holding together the ends of his coat collar against the chill in Minna's room and looking out now and then over the bleak Communist capital, or reaching out to the plum brandy, or feeling the soil under the cyclamens (as cyclamens loved low temperatures, they were in heaven here—*he* should be so beautiful at 48 degrees F!), Corde occasionally checked the time on his wrist. Dewey Spangler's car wasn't due yet, and Corde, Elfrida's letter filled with lady phrases before him, continued to reconstruct the last conversation he had had with her. It was important. And somehow he was better able to be objective here; the foreign setting made for more clarity. Or Valeria, dying.

When Elfrida was done with the money—and most of their meetings since she was widowed began like this (the foreground clutter of finance had to be swept away)—Corde claimed the equal time he was entitled to. It was inevitable that they should begin immediately to discuss Maxie Detillion.

Detillion: Why was it that there were people with whom he, Corde, was so tied that his perception of them amounted to a bondage? They were drawn together physically, so tightly that he was virtually absorbed by them. With Elfrida, this absorption was sweet and lucid. But it wasn't always sweet, and liking had nothing to do with it: he didn't *like* his cousin. A

kind of hypnotic coalescence was what occurred. Thus
he knew the pores of Detillion's face; the close serial
waves of his hair descending to a peak felt almost like
his own hair—as he remembered it. In action Max's
eyes were the eyes of a guru or a star of the German Expressionist movies. When Cousin Max rolled
them, Corde took the sensation into his own eyes.
Detillion had always had a tang of male acid about
him, but now he was beginning to smell like an old
man; you got a whiff of unaired clothes closets when
he passed by. He had grown side whiskers of macho
wool. Rouault would have wanted to paint Maxie—
had put other Maxies into his giant studies of corrupt
men.

In the courtroom, Maxie and Corde would occasionally look at each other without speaking. Corde's
presence may have made things harder for Lydia
Lester, whom he had come to protect and support. In
fact he saw that his being there aggravated Max's
sensationalism, made Max more melodramatic. He
sent continual eye messages to the two newspapermen
who covered the trial ("Don't miss this, hear?"). He
did not give the girl a hard time on the witness stand,
because juries sympathized with young women whose
husbands had been killed. Knowing this, he intended to
be tactful. He did not know that he oppressed her by
wooing her. He wasn't at all aware of it—simply didn't
know what he was doing. It would never have crossed
his mind that she was mourning, sick, shaky, frightened. The message he transmitted was that he was
doing his professional best to obtain testimony favorable to his client, but that when this ordeal was over he
would show her the other side of his nature, which was
tenderly erotic. He sent the same sexual message to all
females from a full heart. The innocence of it had in the
course of the years become clear to Corde—for it was
in a sense innocent—corrupt innocence. Before the
jury, Detillion came brandishing papers like Joe Mc-
Carthy. He was a brandishing man. What he really

flourished was his sex. His once handsome nose was beginning to look damaged, cartilages blasted, and as he aged and grew heavier his cheeks thickened, his color darkened; he looked leaden, he lost height, his pelvis widened, his courtroom pacing was slightly lame. Corde believed he was dying—the old mad blind despised and dying king.

What was it but intimacy to *see* Cousin Maxie Detillion like this? It made no difference that Max cut him, behaving with stupid, cold, waxen hauteur. To see someone like this was to enter into his life. Not necessarily a welcome experience.

Maxie was not a great observer, but it was impossible to remain unaware of so deep a lifetime interest. Detillion had always given this a sexual interpretation. "Albert admired the way I am with women. I was his role model."

Elfrida said, "It looks like you'll have Cousin Max with you at every stage of life."

Corde smiled. "If I die first, don't let him make my funeral arrangements."

"I used to knock myself out trying to understand why you went along with him till he thought he owned you. And when you broke away, he couldn't get it through his head. You betrayed him. *He's* the one with the grievance."

When Grandfather Detillion died, his property down in Joliet had been divided among his three grandchildren. Under the will, Max was executor of the estate. Elfrida had gotten her share of the money—Zaehner saw to that. Zaehner had said to Corde, "What's the matter with you, anyway; can't you see what's happening? The ground floor is rented to McDonald's hamburgers. Have you ever gotten a penny out of it?"

"I got tax write-offs."

"But cash, not one penny, right? He's swindling you. He's milking the property. The phony expenses he puts on the books, I spotted them in the first statement he sent out. When he bought us out he got a two-thirds

interest, so he controls it all—what else does he do for
you, in the way of business?"

Corde had in fact allowed Cousin Max to make
investments for him. Max had obtained from him various powers of attorney, as well as an authorization to
trade in securities through the Harris Trust in his name.
In his relations with Detillion (and not only Detillion),
Corde arranged somehow to persuade himself, however great the quirks of those he trusted, that he wasn't
going to be cheated. He had watched Maxie cheating
others—shifting and hiding assets, outfoxing creditors,
maneuvering to frustrate court orders, claiming preposterous tax deductions. For all his shenanigans he
was seldom liquid enough to pay his bills (he lived
high), he could never grab as much as he needed. But
not from *me,* Corde would tell himself. Max would
never cheat me.

"Let me put it on the line to you, brother-
in-law. . . ." Zaehner, masterly, prolonged his scowl,
silent. Lumps of severity formed at the corners of his
mouth. "Unless you hold your cousin's feet to the fire,
you'll never see a penny. You must have some idea how
much he screwed you out of."

Corde did have an idea, certainly, but he kept it
shrouded. It belonged to a group of shrouded objects
which he promised himself one day to examine. But on
that day a philosophical light would have to shine.
Otherwise it wouldn't do to remove the shrouds. He
guessed that Max had done him out of something
between two and three hundred thousand dollars. This
conservative estimate he kept to himself.

"Hold his feet to the fire—how?" Corde said.

"Demand an audit."

"Well, then there'd be an explosion. . . ."

"You wouldn't be *afraid* of that character, would
you?"

"I may be, a little. . . ."

"I think I understand. . . . It's not personal fear of
your creep cousin, but fear of what will have to come

to light about the relationship. Finding out . . . it wouldn't make you happy to look at the picture. Did Max draw your will? Is he going to be in charge when you kick off?"

"Yes, to both questions."

"Tear it up. Make a new will."

"I'd have to find another lawyer."

"A sobering thought, yes? Don't worry, I'll suggest a few safe names. . . . Since you came back to Chicago to be a perfesser, you and your cousin have used each other. He guided you around the Near North and Lincoln Avenue joints, access to the Playboy Mansion, and broads easy to get. Hard to get rid of, but that's a different subject. That's what he did for you. What you did for him was to give him some class. His reputation was really tacky. Not only that he was a rotten lawyer, but his dick was just plain hanging out. Then suddenly he turned into an intellectual. He started dropping intellectual names. People downtown wanted to punch him in the face. But that's no use. You want the bottom line? Detillion is bananas. All you have to do is watch him dancing, there's your proof."

In this Zaehner might have been right. On a dance floor, proud of his technique, Detillion would swing his wide buttocks with crazy grace, mincing out the Caribbean rhythms. In his cha-cha-cha, possessed, he had no eyes for his partner, whom he dominated as a matter of course, like the ringmaster's mare. It was the spectators he danced for. Since Corde was a great reader (who was now convinced that he had read too much, gathered too many associations, idled in too many picture galleries), he frequently saw his performing cousin's massive, ecstatic face in the Rouault version, a sexual oppressor of tragic multitudes of women (possibly also of men). But Detillion's own image when he was in action was of course quite different. He was anything but a screwer of girls. No, he was the agent or personification of Eros, all aflame, all gold, crimson, radiant, experiencing divine tumescence, bringing life.

The power to bless womankind was swelling in his pants. Zaehner said his dick was hanging out. His brother-in-law put the matter another way. But he had no intention of discussing Cousin Maxie extensively with Zaehner.

Corde credited Zaehner with high intelligence. He didn't feel superior to him. But Zaehner could not bear hearing Corde's thoughts, and whenever Corde tried to discuss his ideas, he shut him up. "You've lost me, Albert. Can't follow you there. Too mental for me." There was verbal deference, but furious contempt in the modulation of scowl into smile. Yes, this was another interesting relationship, no doubt about it. Another shrouded object in Corde's collection. If Cousin Maxie had affinities with Rouault, Zaehner was associated by Corde with Hermann Göring. This was sobering, severe, unfair—a crushing comparison, and never to be mentioned. Mason senior wore unpressed chalk-striped suits, his pants were low-slung in the seat, he had scuffed shoes. He was your informal Chicagoan. Göring had dressed himself in mountainous medieval velvet robes; he covered his face with pancake makeup; gems were his jelly beans. Still there seemed to be a similarity. Corde, at Valeria's table, tracing the Zaehner-Göring association to its origins, went back as far as a certain Mrs. Wooster, an American society lady in Paris (Rue de Rennes), who had altered her elderly, stern look when Göring's name was mentioned and said, "Why, he was nothing but a teddy bear. I knew him well." Until now inflexible, Mrs. Wooster had smiled with all the sweetness of a stern woman when she relents, and with this smile Göring was reconfirmed in Corde's mind as a great archetype of worldly evil. Zaehner was no great archetype, but to Elfrida, he also had been a teddy bear—anything but a beast of the Chicago jungle dumps.

At all events, Zaehner had kept after Corde and forced him at last, out of "self-respect," to take action against Detillion. It came to that. Detillion was exposed, was unshrouded.

And so Elfrida was saying to her brother in the overheated white rooms of Chicago (rooms which by the completeness of their furnishings, fullness of installation, and convenience, suggested that America had taken care of most outstanding human needs—what more did you want?)—was saying, "I should have told you, Albert, that when you and Cousin Max finally had your big legal hassle, Cousin Max came all the way out to Lake Forest to see me—a special trip. He told me he had to bare his heart to somebody in the family. He said he didn't deserve to be treated like this. He was being pushed too hard. Word was getting out. People were talking around town that he had rooked you, fucked you up with IRS, and he was incompetent. . . ."

"I didn't push him too hard. We settled out of court. What was he trying to get out of you?"

"He wanted me to arrange a conference with Mason, and Mason, as you remember, had just had his first coronary. Max called and left messages, but I wouldn't let Mason call back."

"It would have been worth ten thousand bucks to Max to have Zaehner get him off the hook with me."

"Max said, 'I'll never forgive what Albert did to my image.'"

"His image! And baring his heart! Poor Max. I get sore at him, but when I look closer or hear what he says, I turn sorry instead."

"You must have been. You let him off easy. What kind of settlement was that?"

"I dropped a lot of dough on him. Let's say I was paying tuition. I had to take a special course."

"Learning what, dear?"

"Things I should have known fifty years ago. A postgraduate seminar in boneheadedness and idiocy."

Corde was trying to get Elfrida to talk with him in *his* way. She was his sister, she ought to be able to do it. She ought to be willing.

"Maybe a quarter of a million wasn't tuition enough."

"I see what you mean. Losing that much dough didn't make me suffer enough. I'm still an idiot, and I haven't got the dough to enroll in another course."

Corde's intent was plain. He was sounding out his sister on the Chicago articles, trying to get her opinion. Did she see those disturbing pieces as his new venture in idiocy? He watched her very closely. When her face darkened, she was flushing. That made her look youthful. Then came tension and reticence and made her look elderly. She was perhaps as sorry for her brother as he was for Cousin Max. She believed he was a very strange man. His hang-ups were not like other people's —identifiable neuroses, alcoholism, bragging. Nothing normal. He had his own most original, incomprehensible way of screwing things up. No, she wasn't going to give an opinion on his articles. So there he had her judgment on them. He couldn't deny that it bothered him, but—he loved his sister just the same. She was actually miffed with him. She had much to say about those Chicago articles but she wouldn't talk. Her black eyes were critical, wistful, canny and angry. She seemed to ask why rock the boat—why push so hard, be so reckless, write so strangely? To Zaehner, Chicago had been the greatest city in the world, no place like it. And Corde's father had agreed with Zaehner, no place like Chicago—big, vital, new, the best! Old Corde, who had cut a figure here as a big hotel man and public personality, would have been bitterly annoyed with a son who knocked Chicago. Of course Elfrida *couldn't* approve.

She turned the discussion again to Cousin Max. "He made me a long speech, when he came out to see me. He walked up and down with his hands behind his back, spouting about a great evil all around him and drowning his soul, and how you of all people should turn up on the wicked side. All right, Albert—Max

mismanaged your money. But you let him do it. And
Mason was a devil to go to him with this case—I don't
blame you for being sore. But maybe you're being far
too sensitive. I doubt that anybody is really paying
much attention to Max. They can see what a ham he is.
Even if you're down on Chicago, give them *some*
credit."

"Did you happen to see him on Channel Two the
other night?"

On the tube, unexpectedly, Corde had switched on
his cousin. There was Maxie in full color with his
cumulus side whiskers and his face blazing with false
truthfulness. Corde had been astonished to hear his
own name spoken. "Dean Corde, who happens to be
my first cousin . . ." Corde had been greatly offended
by this. Hearing his name loudly spoken, he was
furious. Even now he was angry about it, aware of a
large area of atrocious anger very near. He could
almost touch it. Detillion made charges of racism, he
referred to the college as "a great institution. But its
relations with Affirmative Action are troubled." He
lied with his eyes and his brows even more than with
words. Corde had to admit that he spoke reasonably
well, in the unnatural style of the Chicago bar—Corde
had commented on this in *Harper's:* "The peculiar,
gentlemanly, high-toned illiteracy of lawyers before the
Bench . . ."

Corde said, "No, *I* shouldn't be so sensitive about
Max. But he comes every day and sprays the girl and
the family with untreated sewage. It was me that got
her involved, and I feel responsible . . . my family,
after all. Even a stronger person couldn't bear this
publicity circus, but this isn't a strong young woman.
She's inexperienced, she's dazed, and don't forget, the
boy's parents are sitting in the courtroom while Max
comes on, not with her but with Ebry and other
witnesses, about funny sexual practices, and suggesting
hadn't the young man gone out that night with a

lascivious purpose. Bringing in group sex and hinting at kinkiness with all kinds of esoteric kinks. It's too much."

"Too much for you, I see. You're very emotional about it."

"Well, of course I am, Elfrida. I'm *in* it. Mason knocked on her door last September, to tell her that she'd better not take the stand."

Elfrida said, "Yes, I think I heard that before." As she lowered her eyes, Corde dropped the subject. Elfrida then said, "I can see why she wants those people sent to jail. It's perfectly natural. She must feel she owes it to her husband."

"Grady says it's stupid of Max to push so hard, because if she were to break down in front of the jury it would do his case no good. I almost think Grady is hoping for it. But somehow she's toughing it out. I never thought she could."

"Sorokin's opinion is that Max is making a good defense, purely on the legal side."

Corde said, "Sometimes I think that if Detillion's prayers had been answered and he had become ultra-rich . . ."

"Yes . . . ?"

"Then all this psychopathic suffering of his would have been safely embalmed. He'd be a big giver, a patron of the opera and symphony, he'd be elected to all the boards. Nobody would notice how stupid or how cracked he was. But since he can't even pay his bills, he has to find a way to dress his disaster presentably. But this has to be done in public."

"I get what you're saying," said Elfrida. Her uneasiness was deep. *She* was herself ultra-rich, for one thing. Her moved and distracted brother might at any moment fall into one of his theorizing fits. He saw how it was. He would take off from his elevation, from his butte, in a mad flight of clarity—and heresy. His voice would be equable, deep, harmonious, not a sign of fanaticism, and he would say incomprehensible, ungraspable, glassy, slippery and, finally, terrible, harmful things—things that would have revolted their father and made the late Zaehner look grim. In Elfrida's opinion Albert didn't know what it was to be moderate, he exaggerated everything. But then his love for her also had an exaggerated character. If she was glad to have his love, why did she rule out his "exaggerated" theories? There was a certain amusement in his question. And then—honestly, now!—was it such a distorted theory? He was saying that you became an impregnable monster if you had money, so that if to begin with you felt yourself to be monstrous you could build impregnability by making a fortune. Because then you were a force of nature, although a psychopath. Or if you were without any persona, then you *bought* a persona. And underlying all of this—Corde had had to fly to Communist Europe and sit in his wife's schoolgirl room to understand it—underlying the whole of his recent phase of eccentricity (it wasn't at all eccentric from within) was his continuing dispute with Elfrida's husband, the late Zaehner. *Contra Zaehner* might have been the true title of those articles on Chicago. He hadn't been aware of this at first. The first conception was innocent. Originally period pieces, picturesque, charming, nostalgic, his essays somehow got out of hand. Naturally, he could not expect sympathy from his sister. She couldn't sympathize without disloyalty to Zaehner and to her son. Besides, she disagreed.

"Don't you worry, Elfrida," he had said to her before he left—meaning that he would not molest her, would not try to get her to talk *his* way.

She drew a long, thankful breath, and in her relief she said to him, "I think you ought to know, Albert, that Sorokin thinks you were right about Rufus Ridpath. Ridpath really did do his best at the County Jail. He was the only one who even tried to improve conditions and help the prisoners. And there were people who might have been out to get him. Sorokin agrees that he was basically honest. They not only ganged up to get rid of him but made sure that he had no future in politics around here."

"I don't think Ridpath would ever have run for office, that would be out of character. But did Sorokin tell you this? He was the one who sent me to Ridpath in the first place."

Elfrida made one of her faces. Corde understood exactly what it meant. She said, "You didn't have to go overboard and say that he was such a rare type of black man."

"That wasn't what I wrote. I said he was a rare type in any color. Black or white or ocher or green, there weren't many people in Chicago who bothered their minds with anything like justice. Puzzling, how few. You didn't even realize this until you met a person who did have it on his mind as a primary interest, and then it dawned on you how rare such a primary interest was. . . ."

"The phrase you used was 'a moral life.'"

"That was unfortunate. You've got to be careful about the big word. I realized even then that it would rub everybody the wrong way. This kind of abnormal, professorial Plato-and-Aristotle stuff is the kiss of death. I probably didn't do Ridpath much good, either. Definitely a mistake. . . ."

5

In the adjoining room, Minna was on the telephone. He had heard the ringing and now he became aware (he didn't often tune in) that this was an unusual call. Her voice went up sharply. He listened, and then went around through the corridor to the dining room. The Stambouli-work sofa was near the glass connecting door. He sat bent over, superattentive. The conversation was short. Minna tried to speak but the other party cut her off. Something bad was happening, that was certain. As soon as she rang off, she set out to find Corde. He heard her steps as she moved in the wrong direction, and called out, "Here." She couldn't answer when he asked what it was about, she only stared at him. "That wasn't intensive care?"

Valeria worse? Or dead? No, it hadn't been that sort of news, and it wasn't that sort of shock. Unlike Elfrida, Minna had no repertoire of faces. He had never seen her eyes so black or her skin so lined, so dry and white.

"Well, what was that?" he said.

"Albert, do you know who? It was the Colonel."

"Himself, in person?"

"It was the Colonel. I could murder him."

"What's he done? What did he say?"

"The Ambassador must have gone to work as soon as you left."

"I see. He called the Minister of Health, and the Minister called the Colonel? . . ."

"That's the way it must have been done."

"Well, all right, but what happened? Does the Minister of Health run the hospitals or doesn't he?"

"Not this hospital. The Colonel is in charge. He just told me in no uncertain way. He was terrible to me. Terrible, Albert!"

"I see. It's a power contest—a minister versus the secret police."

"It was no contest. He's the boss."

"That's becoming clear. I'm sorry, Minna. We shouldn't have tried to go over his head if we couldn't go high enough. The usual mistake, doing the thing by halves. Should have realized . . . a secret police colonel doesn't give a damn for a cabinet minister. I think this is why our old friend Petrescu keeps dropping from sight. He gave it a try but he was outranked, and now he stays away. It was the second visit, the one we didn't have permission for, that licked him. I shouldn't have fooled around with the Ambassador. I should have tried to get to the White House on it. A direct call, President to President. It might have been pulled off. Still might. These guys have a favored nation agreement with the U.S., a hell of an important thing to them. They wouldn't have refused."

"He said . . ."

"Yes, what did the Colonel tell you?"

"That I could see my mother one more time. Only once. That was what he said."

"Oh?" said Corde, as if he understood. He didn't understand at all. He had a sharp pang of eyestrain. "Give me that again: he said come and visit her?"

"Once, he said."

"And when?"

"He's going to leave that to me. I couldn't believe it. I tried to talk, but he cut me off. He said, 'Don't you understand Rumanian? I'm allowing you and your husband one visit.'"

Corde by now had taken this in. Come, once, and visit—it was the final visit. He said to Minna, "We started a fight with the Minister, and the Colonel won. I guess he took the dispute upstairs, and upstairs backed him. I should have given this more thought when the Ambassador offered. It was decent of him, but the usual result. You think you're priming the decency pump by pouring decency. It's never real. . . . Did he say, 'You and your husband'?"

"Yes, Albert. What will I tell him? I'm supposed to call back and say when we're coming."

"What about Tanti Gigi?" said Corde. "If this is the one and only visit? . . . No, you can't talk to him about Gigi."

"Albert, answer me: When shall we go? Tomorrow? When?"

"I'd go today—tonight," he said, rising from the settee.

"Are you   may die anytime?"

"Tomorrow we may think of more strings to pull. Maybe Gherea can move her. Maybe we can stir up somebody at the White House. We might wire Washington."

"He's waiting for my call."

"Then tell him tonight."

She went back to the telephone.

Corde fetched his coat over his shoulders. These were the shortest days. The afternoon light no sooner came in than it was on its way out. It was cold, too. Brittle scales began to show on the street puddles, a crystalline bitterness setting in. Where the light withdrew, the yellow-brown of the stucco was pocked with mild blue. (They could rub your face into that stucco if they liked.) On the open porches over the way— bottles, wet rags hung out to dry frozen at the points, and vine twigs. The glory of the day carried things easily when the sun shone; but when the sun passed, things seemed abandoned, they became dissociated, and you had to find a way to take them up yourself. Corde followed his wife's voice in the next room. Some languages are spoken, others sung. Even now, fighting the Colonel and the Communist state, she still sounded musical. As he—while pitying his wife; while hating the Colonel; while figuring why the Colonel had made such a decision; and what kind of ploys there had been; or what kind of deal the Colonel had cut with the Minister —still followed thought themes of his own. There was the Colonel in his tall broom-closet office, ruling on this, ruling on that, under a twenty-watt light. And there was personal humanity, a fringe receding before the worldwide process of consolidation. This process might seem too crude to be taken seriously, but don't kid yourself, it was shaping the future. And while this shaping went on, the inmost essence of the human being must be making its own, its necessary, its unique arrangements as it best could.

Now to move to Valeria and the life-support machines. Corde was convinced that the old woman was fully and probably even brilliantly conscious. The life supports were clicking and her mind was (he decided) exquisitely vivid—in a state of hypervividness. She wouldn't die until she had seen her daughter—seen her in a manner of speaking, since she couldn't open her eyes. They made scanning movements under the skin; they might be light-sensitive; they filled out the lids (an involuntary comparison) like ravioli. She was studying her death, that was for sure. Corde thought of her with extraordinary respect. Her personal humanity came from the old sources. Corde had become better informed about these sources in Paris and London. Amid eye pangs that made him pass his fingertips over his forehead from left to right (here in Eastern Europe he felt dehydrated and even conceived of his optic nerves as dry and frayed), he considered those old sources. He remembered that she had taken a serious interest in Structuralism, in Laing's psychiatry. Hell, what did she want to bother for? It must have been alien to her deeper life. In the deeper life she was traditional, even archaic. She had loved her husband, that was why she became a Communist militant: she had loved her husband, loved her daughter, her sister. Then for thirty years she had made up for the Marxism, for the sin of helping to bring in the new regime, by a private system of atonement, setting up her mutual-aid female network. Yet she kept up with sophisticated opinion; the Party had denounced her when she was expelled for "cosmopolitan psychologism," or Freudianism, but that was nothing. She was reading a book on the Hagia Sophia. It was on her desk. Corde was curious about it, but the language was beyond him. This same Valeria, when she visited her husband's grave, and her own burial place, lighted candles in front of the gravestone —there was a big granite stone out there. Gigi said,

"When she had to make an important decision, she went to the grave to talk to *him* about it." She brought food for the beggars in the cemetery. It wasn't only the mother-of-pearl inlay that was Stambouli-work. These were the Balkans. Here the deeper life was Byzantine, and even more archaic, never mind the Freud or the Laing—that was for the sophisticated, nervous public. There was no such sophistication here. She stood before the gates of death. And as a physician—but you didn't need to be a physician to know that you were dying. She even suspected perhaps that the authorities might decide to disconnect the life supports when they had had enough of her. Corde definitely thought that the Colonel might have this in mind. He had the authority, definitely. He could say, "Pull 'em," and that would be that. And at this, Corde (himself not so young, not so well) felt a curious affinity for the crystals of brittle ice whose glitter came up to his Balkan window. These badgering perplexities, intricacies of equilibrium, sick hopes, riddling evils, sadistic calculations—you might do worse than to return to that strict zero-blue and simple ice. In all this Corde felt singularly close to the old woman.

Minna when she came back said, "It's settled for tonight."

When Corde began to speak, she reminded him that the place was bugged by pointing to the light fixture.

"Let's walk around the block."

"When is the car coming for you?"

"Not just yet."

There were twenty minutes to spare. Spangler's driver was sure to be punctual. Drivers here, as elsewhere in Eastern Europe, reported to the secret police. For this reason they gave excellent service.

Corde and Minna descended together in the small elevator. He held the heavy wrought-iron-and-glass door for her as she stepped into the street. Towards midafternoon, the December sun was ready to check out. Below the winter beams there were violet shad-

ows; these were collected in the pitted surfaces of the
stucco walls, and made Corde think of choppy winter
water. A similar color gathered about the pollarded
trees. The pigeons afoot on the sidewalk had it, too,
with iridescent variations. In midstreet Corde noticed
the remains of small rats. They must have run for it
during the earthquake, got themselves conked by falling masonry and then rolled flat by trucks and cars.
That was how Corde figured them. They were as
two-dimensional as weather vanes. Here and there
amid the Balkan Haussmann blocks were earthquake
ruins or tumuli, and Corde assumed that they must also
be graves. The brick heaps exhaled decay. There were
unrecoverable bodies underneath. The smell was cold,
dank and bad. Coupled rusty-orange tramcars ran with
a slither of cables. Pale proletarian passengers looked
out. They wore caps, the women kerchiefs. Together
with cast-iron sinks and croaking pull-chain toilets,
these tramcars belonged to the old days. It was all like
looking backwards. You saw the decades in reverse.
Even the emotions belonged to an earlier time. The
issue of the struggle with the Colonel was human
sentiment—not accepted as an issue under the new
order. But the Colonel tacitly admitted it because it
gave pain. He knew it *was* an issue. It was Corde's
momentary fantasy that these ideas were gathered
about his head, as the light gathered, paler, around the
pruned trees, each one of which resembled a bouquet.

   Minna walked faster than usual. Back home you
could do nothing to quicken her pace. She had her own
notions of feminine poise, or the appropriate Raresh
dignity. But today she moved quickly. She held Corde's
arm, and when pedestrians approached, she gave it a
tug which meant "shut up." So he was silent, and she
looked sternly absentminded. Minna never came to the
dinner table, or got into bed at night, or went into the
street, without putting on fresh lipstick. But now her lip
was drawn thin and the red was hardly visible. She was
dry, pale; she looked very sick.

"You understand what the problem is, Albert," she said.

"Gigi."

"Yes, Tanti Gigi, and how we get her in."

"Of course," said Corde. "She has to see her sister. If there are passes for two at the gate, she can take my place."

"No, all three of us have to get in. We must all go. I wish we could turn to Petrescu. He's always been a good friend. You can be sure this is painful for him."

"We'll think about him some other time. He's in another strange branch of experience. We'll go into that later. Right now we have to make a plan."

"The first move is to get cigarettes. We'd better have plenty of them."

"Those I can buy at the Intercontinental valuta shop. King-sized Kents."

"Yes." They were walking through the reduced light and passed a triangular fenced park, palings leaning inward and green benches covered with frost. "There's my old school," she said. "And down that street lived families of boyars." Graceful buildings of the old regime were cut up into flats. In the dark shops where cans of peas and sauerkraut were stacked, you could see no customers. This was a once fashionable neighborhood. No more. The high apparatchiks had their villas elsewhere. "How can we even get to the hospital tonight?"

"You can't phone for a cab?" he said.

"You can phone, but you can't count on anything."

"Gigi says that Ioanna has a nephew who's a driver. You ought to talk to her about him."

"Yes; Traian is his name."

"I think you'd better try this Traian."

"I'll ask Ioanna," said Minna.

"Does he own an automobile?"

"I'll go into it right away."

"You can talk to Ioanna? I mean talk."

"Yes and no. Yes, if you approach it right. She has to

be treated like a relation. You don't mention money, but you have to give it to her by and by."

"Hire Traian to drive us. Do you remember the man?"

"Twenty years ago he wasn't a man. He was a fat boy, and he wasn't pleasant."

"Well, you'd better ask whether he can come."

"By seven."

"Once we're in the car—and I'll get a couple of cartons of Kents—you can explain what has to be done. They've got to be on the take here. Can't live on wages."

They turned the corner, and Minna said, "I think your friend's car is coming down the street."

"I should be standing by," said Corde. "I can change the appointment."

"No; you go for the cigarettes, and see your friend. There isn't anything you can do here. I'll go and talk to Ioanna."

She entered the building. Corde, his upper body braced against the cold, waited for the car. Three o'clock, and dusk already, tragic boredom coming with it. The forms of winter trees, the beauty of winter colors, were excepted from this. The trees made their tree gestures, but human beings were faced by the organized prevention of everything that came natural. The smooth limousine stopped and the driver came around and opened the door, let him into the warmth of the back seat. The privileged ride was short. Here was the American embassy again, the street cordoned off, sentries outside. And here was the Intercontinental.

The lobby was luxurious. You could sink deep into those long sofas—any of them; they were all unoccupied. The atmosphere was that of a mystery novel. From the restaurant came a smell of Turkish coffee. You realized that the Bosporus was just up the line, and that the Orient Express used to steam in here, with Mata Hari in the dining car and Levantine businessmen who were triple agents. In the opulent lobby there were two hard corners of totalitarian organization—a plywood booth where currencies were cashed and a newsstand which sold foreign newspapers. East German magazines hung from a wire by clips, and also *Pravda* and *l'Humanité*.

The valuta shop was on the second floor. Christmas was two days off. A little tree was surrounded by and powdered with cotton batting and mica snow. There were racks of peasant skirts, sheepskins, shelves with table linens and dolls in folk costume, carved wooden flasks, cameras, imported brandy. Among the shoppers were students from Africa. One of them, seeing Corde's passport in his hand, said to him in a crackling British accent, "The clarks here are insolent. They say any damned thing. They think we don't understand their damned language. The black-smocked women were sullen and tired, rushed. Corde thought himself lucky. The girl who sold him the Kents was smiling at him—peculiarly: as if she were about to puff at a dandelion to see what time it was. Nevertheless, it was a sort of smile. She slipped his cigarettes—two cartons of the king-sized—into a Christmas bag with plastic handles.

Was he in a mood for reunion with a high school friend? He felt as though he had been knocked over in the street by a motorcycle, bruised, taped around the chest. What he wanted was to go to the men's room, unbutton his shirt, pull off the adhesive bandages. But there were no bandages. He edged into the crowded restaurant and bar to find Dewey Spangler. Impatient, feeling hampered, feeling bruised, he *seemed* all right, only a little serious (nothing more than a dark mood). He looked about for Spangler. The meeting, the old-pal routine, would have to be brief. If Ioanna's nephew was unavailable, other arrangements would have to be made. Minna and Gigi needed him at home—his supportive presence, his suggestions. And the Kents, too; the Kents most of all, perhaps. The packed bar

intensified his caged mood (let me out of here!). Then
he saw Spangler, who had risen in his booth and was
beckoning with both arms, like an airlines employee
signaling a plane to its gate. Spangler's gestures had
always been inappropriate, erratic. Unexpectedly, this
was endearing. Bossy, fussing little bastard, in spite of
his world eminence he was still Screwy Dewey, the
starved alley-cat boy intellectual—the same Dewey
who had fought a two-hundred-pound Cubs fan in the
Wrigley Field bleachers, hitting him with a book of
poems. Spangler had been a frightful kid, but Corde
had loved him.

"Here, Albert, here," Dewey called.

What was it that made this meeting so rich? Thrilling
as hell, wasn't it? Spangler came to Chicago at least ten
times a year, a hundred times in the last decade, and he
never called Corde. But neither had Corde ever sent
him a note to say, "I liked your column of last
Wednesday." He liked few or none of the columns.
Dewey in the papers never surprised him. Start a
Dewey sentence and Corde, with his eyes closed, could
finish it for you. The system seldom varied. But in this
exotic café, all reservations, judgments, slights and
offenses were set aside. Here Spangler could measure
the distance he (or both of them) had come. He put an
arm about Corde. "Rah, rah, Lakeview!" His figure
had expanded and also grown compact. He was fleshy
now and dignified by his well-groomed beard. The fat
that had gathered in layers under his chin was disciplined, not slovenly, fat. These layers absorbed and
even dignified his ducking mannerism, gave it affirmative weight, positive gravity. But he still had that one
nervous habit. Although long years of psychoanalysis
actually seemed to have helped him. Spangler had been
recycled on the couch. He made no secret of it; on the
contrary, he frequently mentioned analysis in his column: he liked to reflect on the sense of human worth it
gave him, the distinct contribution it had made to his
appreciation of the Judeo-Christian value system.

"Wass willst du haben?" he said. "You remember that?"

"Yes, indeed. Louie and the Hungry Five, the comic German brass band from Old Heidelberg on Randolph Street, near the Oriental," said Corde.

"Right on."

Come to think of it, what could this meeting give Dewey but the pleasure of nostalgia? He had for many years avoided Corde. Corde embarrassed him: he knew his background, remembered his father and his mother, the Spangler household, its kitchen life, the leonine formation of Mrs. Spangler's face, the flimsy silk bells of her stockings, the thigh portion falling below the gartered knee. They were touching people, especially the father. Old Spangler was bald and ruddy but did not enjoy good health. "In the notions business," he said. But what notions were there late in the Depression? You went down to the wholesale outlets at Twelfth Street and Newberry and took goods "on approval" to peddle door to door—sun visors, for instance, or table runners or combinations or cotton socks. It was the ill-concealed fact that "notions" meant peddling that embarrassed Dewey, and the embarrassment was compounded by grandiose and exuberant fantasies. He used to tell all kinds of stories about his origins. His father had been in a La Salle Street brokerage firm, he sometimes said, and he himself had been educated in a military prep school. But Corde never gave him away. Why should he? He actively sympathized with him. Still he had been distrusted.

"The Heidelberg," said Dewey. "Your formidable memory."

"I'm glad to see you, pal."

Dewey wasted no time. "Albert, we were very close, weren't we, at fifteen and after?" said Dewey. "A consuming association. When you told me—and I told you—damn near everything. And now look at us. Not many peas left in the pod, perhaps, but what of it, since we've made something of ourselves? Consider the origins. . . ." This was a hinted offer of candor.

"I thought of you the other day when I came across a volume of Oscar Wilde in my mother-in-law's flat."

"Mad for Swinburne and Walter Pater. Mad for Wilde. What stuff!

> For, lo! with a little rod did I but touch the honey of
> romance,
> And must I lose a soul's inheritance?

Now we can guess what that little rod was. But we didn't guess then, in our innocence."

"No, we loved poetry."

"Odd, in Chicago, where the South Branch of the river, you remember, was Bubble Creek because the blood and tripes and tallow, the stockyards' shit, made it bubble in the summer. Doctors talk about an alcoholic dying of an *insult* to the brain. Well, that stink could have done it."

"Is it Chicago we're going to talk about?" said Corde.

"It is our native place, as you recently said in print."

The corpulence of his chin and throat, and perhaps also his worldly success, had made the down, down, downward pressure of his chin a movement of unshakable assertion. Like FDR's blinking. FDR's blink on Fox Movietone News meant: "Adversaries, beware." Then Dewey went on (it was predictable): "When you decided to go back, to me that was a sign of lifelong involvement. You were doing so well in Paris." (Was Spangler being patronizing? There was just the hint of a put-down in "doing well." He himself had become such a prodigy and hotshot.) "But when I read the first of your pieces in *Harper's*, I realized that you had scores to settle with the old town."

A waiter brought their drinks. Corde reclined in the booth, but his large hands were thrust deep into his trousers pockets, as far as to the wrists, a sure sign of tension. Dewey would not be taken in by his easy posture, or any of the old disguises. Dewey had the trick of making him an adolescent again. In adolescence Dewey had always had the upper hand. He had been precociously sharp.

Corde rumbled, "Not the old town anymore."

"I suppose it isn't. But you were your old self in your approach. You were eloquent, you were superexpressive. Just the way you used to be—you were metaphorical; you were emotional; you really let yourself go. I recognized lots of the old turns of phrase. Some of them still there."

"They probably are," said Corde.

"Made quite a stir, didn't you?"

Dewey's eyes, pale blue, now set in puffed and wrinkled lids, mocked him. Not unkindly. He was on first-name terms with Kissinger and Helmut Schmidt. Millions read him. In his recent swing through Europe and Asia, he had interviewed Sadat, Margaret Thatcher, Indira Gandhi. No reason to be mean with me, Corde was thinking, in the leisure of this personal nostalgic hour. Not so long as I admit his superiority. And I do admit it. Why shouldn't I? Corde now decided to make an open concession and to bring this chapter in Spangler's psychic history to a happy close. This syndicated columnist who was a sizable node in the relaying of the tensions that pulsated through the civilized world, made it tremble, saturated it with equivocation, covered its structural outlines with flourishes, filled it with anxieties, happened also to be an old friend. Yes, the same Dewey who at Lakeview had been so self-conscious about the size and shape of his ears that he would give them a nimble tuck under his cap when no one was looking, like an awkward girl; who even tried to fasten them to his head with tape. The Dewey who had tried to grow a mustache to resemble William Powell—William Powell had obsessed him. The pale vinegar worm he had been was now a pundit and an arbiter, his columns anxiously,

respectfully read in thirty countries. But it was the
original skinny, frantic, striving, screeching Dewey that
Corde had liked so much.

"You've been looking at the time, Albert."

"Yes, I'm sorry. I am uptight. There's a lot of trouble
here for us."

"So I've been told by the Ambassador. A good
fellow, the Ambassador. What's going on?"

"My wife's mother, dying . . ."

"Yes, yes, I remember now what he told me. Your
wife can't see her. That's too bad. It must work you up.
As your own mother's death did. I can remember
that."

"I thought you might," Corde said.

"The Ambassador mentioned that he was calling
somebody for you."

"So he did, but the result was negative—double
negative."

"Is that so: counterproductive? I wonder if I could
put in a word."

"I assume you're meeting the top people here."

"Yes, I am. I am," said Spangler. He drew his chin
inward swiftly, two, three, five times against the firm
fat of his throat.

"Then you might, if it's convenient. It's very late,
though."

"Yes, Albert, I'll try to find an opening. These
people have a stake in good relations with Washington.
Concerned about their commercial treaties. Besides,
they have a liberal image to sustain. Independence
from the Soviet bosses, voting against the bloc at the
U.N. now and then. All phony, of course."

"They'd like you to report them nicely."

"Correct."

"I've wondered about asking our own President to
make a personal call. Combined with Christmas, which
is now upon us, it might appeal to his PR people as a
pleasant item."

"You serious?" Rotund Spangler passed his hand

over his Shavian beard. It made a crisp sound. His hair was tight and vital; Corde envied him that.

"Is that too farfetched?"

"Whom have you got in Washington?"

"There's you for starters, Dewey."

It was much too late for White House intervention. Corde was being wicked, testing old Dewey. How would Dewey react? The reaction was just a little stiff. How could he refuse a humane request by an old friend? You renewed contacts sentimentally and there was an immediate push. You sent your car, made time available, and what did your pal do but ask you for a favor. A favor, what's more, that he'd never be able to reciprocate.

"You *are* troubled about your wife." Then Spangler said, as if abstractly, speculatively, "You must love her."

Corde said, "There's nothing too rum to be true."

"Ho, that's a beauty!" said Spangler. "Is it your own?"

"I heard it years ago on a Channel train from an old English gentleman. He was a lifelong atheist, but maybe God did exist, he said."

"Some Limey told you that? Yes, I think you love the woman. You're just rum enough to do it. You always wanted to love a woman. It's just when the whole world gives up on a thing that it turns you on. That's you." Spangler's pleasure at this meeting began to return. "We can feel out the White House if you like. It's a flaky administration, in case you haven't noticed. The chief executive is what the kids call a nerd. That's a very sanctimonious man. However, we might give it a try. I say might."

"I'd be very grateful."

"No need to be grateful. It gives me a chance to show how influential I've become."

"Still there is a sort of payola or payoff system, isn't there?"

"The quid pro quo? It's not what people usually

think. I'd make it seem an opportunity for the President, not ask him for a favor. But let's not make with the gratitude."

"You don't need anything at all from me."

"I always liked you, Albert. I was a little scarecrow. You were my special friend."

"You had others."

"I was a joke to them. The way I carried on, my fantasies—lies—and so on. You didn't twit me when you caught me in some bullshit."

"It was the poetry and the philosophy," said Corde. "I had to have you. It was the Spinoza and the Walt Whitman. It was the William Blake. Nobody else was interested. Besides, I loved the way you would carry on. You were extravagant. You'd holler and bawl at your poor mother, and call her a whore. . . . It gave me terrific pleasure. I never saw anything like it. You don't mind this reminiscence, do you?"

"Not a whole lot. It's true enough. And it's just you and me in this booth. No use pretending, between us. Anyway, she's been dead so long."

"She'd lose her temper and say, 'You're no kid of mine. You're a criminal's kid. They switched you on me in the hospital.' Lovable moments. I was fascinated. Nobody else like your people around the Lakeview neighborhood. Also, you loved your old man. You'd play checkers. He'd sit in his B.V.D.s, the sweat on his bald head, and study the board through his pop-bottle lenses. And his shaky knuckles with the fur on them. He gave us his streetcar transfers so we could bum around the city. He was a dear, unlucky man. . . . But I have to go, Dewey. I've enjoyed this. Are you taking off soon?"

"Just after Christmas. Don't run. The car will have you there in a few minutes."

"This is a terribly bad time for my wife."

Spangler said sympathetically but knowingly (superknowingly—that had always been a specialty with him): "I can just imagine. For you, too. All kinds of hell in Chicago. I'm damned if I can explain why you wrote those pieces. You might as well have stirred Bubble Creek with a ten-foot pole and forced the whole town to smell it. Then there's the trial you're mixed up in. The young man pushed from the window."

"You've been following that?"

"I always take the Chicago papers. My assistant forwards the clippings. Your fat-ass cousin is going to town on you, too. He's a bad actor."

"I thought you had changed your mind, and he was now okay by you."

"What are you talking about? You were the one who was nice to him in the old days. I didn't want him around. It was you who listened to his bogus poetry."

"Well, we needn't make a contest of it. I did say once that with a slot in his head Max would make a terrific piggy bank."

"Oh! Yes; you did, didn't you. What a gift you always had for those crushing one-liners. At the same time you were in dead earnest much too often. Moralistic. I think it's still there, too. Anyway, your cousin has a super hard-on for you. And what a performance he's giving."

"He gets plenty of help from the media. Ugly. Very hard for the young woman to take."

"What young woman is that? Oh, the girl, the young widow, you mean."

Dewey was not a good drinker. The double Chivas Regal made him talkative. He wanted a good long talk. He said, "What *was* this attack you made on the city!"

"I see no attack. I'm attached to Chicago—I'm speaking quite seriously."

"So am I serious, Albert. Aren't you aware of cutting loose with a lifetime of anger? How strange, for an intelligent man. You should have had some psychoanalysis, Albert. You pooh-poohed me when I recommended it, but you needed it. The Institute is right on Michigan Boulevard and you would have had your choice of the very best. *I* wasn't too good for it. With a little insight, you wouldn't be telling me now that you were *attached*. In *Harper's* you crossed and offended just about everybody. You might have gotten away with it if you had adopted the good old Mencken *Boobus Americanus* approach. Humor would have made a difference. But you lambasted them all. Really —you gave 'em hard cuts, straight across the muzzle. The obscurity of your language may have protected you somewhat—all the theorizing and the poetry. Lots of people must have been mystified and bogged down by it, and just gave up. All the better for you if they didn't read your message clearly. They're all happy, of course, to see you get your lumps. Ill will for ill will. *Harper's* came out of it okay, though. You were good for their circulation, which is pitiful at best. One of their guys in Washington was telling me you were doing yet another provocative piece on a different subject."

"With a man named Beech. But it isn't definite. I haven't decided."

"What's the field, biochemistry?"

"Geochemistry."

"Worse yet. What the hell do you, with your teeth cut on Shakespeare and Nietzsche, know about geochemistry? And you want to put in with the environmentalists? That's an extremely unattractive category of cranks. You're cranky enough already."

"Beech is no crank. There's a powerful scientific mind there."

"The best of them are diapered babies when they go public with a cause. Do you want me to name names? . . . Becoming a professor wasn't the right switch for you, Albert. You've lost some of your realism. You went from active to passive. Now you're tired of the passive and you've gone hyperactive, and gotten distorted and all tied in knots. Wrong for you. So you're a dean, and what next, boy?"

Dutch uncle had always been one of Dewey's favorite roles. And actually Corde didn't much mind; it was the old Dewey scolding away. It was agreeable because it was so characteristic. But Corde didn't have the time for it. He had to go. He downed his drink and collected his things. "Sorry, Dewey."

"Where are you going? I thought we'd have a talk."

"I haven't got the time I expected to have," said Corde. He began to edge out of the horseshoe booth with his sack of Kents. "I've got to go to the hospital with my wife, to see her mother."

"Why, I thought you couldn't."

"They've okayed one visit more."

"One? A last? They think she's dying?"

"They must. She is."

Very thoughtfully, Spangler spread both his hands stiffly on the table. They were braced by his short arms, so that his shoulders were lifted. Grimacing, he said, "Terrible. Terrible on your wife. Very bad. Punitive. Somebody's got it in for those ladies. I can understand why you'd think of taking it to the White House."

"It's too late. It was only a kind of fantasy, anyway. You're locked in, you're tense, and suddenly you remember that you're part of a proud superpower, and you say, 'I don't have to put up with this.' That's baloney, of course. It's from the good old days when an American abroad still got protection from his government. That went out with gunboat diplomacy. There's also the Chicago approach: 'I must know somebody who knows somebody.'"

"Somebody? That's me, for instance. I can still give it a try, if you like. I'm not really effective now. In the Kissinger days it was different. These new guys ain't much, Albert. You might as well talk to Bugs Bunny."

"There's actually nothing that would help now. But it's nice to see you, Dewey. I'll settle for just that. A touch of the old warmth—I'm grateful for it."

"Yes, this must be a hell of a place seen from inside. You're *in* it. I'm just another VIP, passing through. But my impression riding around the city is that it's got to be a miserable damn comfortless life, and scary as well as boring. I wish there were something I *could* do for

your missus. It's a shame she's being pushed around.
She's a distinguished scientist. These guys have no
class. Imagine what it takes to be in power here, the
types the Kremlin prefers to appoint. Real dogs. But
then"—recollection brightening Spangler's face—"how
does it go in *King Lear?* 'A dog's obeyed in office.' Or
else what we read in *Zarathustra:* 'Power stands on
crooked legs.' Nietzsche must have been thinking of
dogs, too. . . . Are there still kids who do that, get
together in Lincoln Park and read the way we used to
read—wallow in that glorious stuff: the *Zarathustra,*
the *Phaedrus,* that *Brigge* book by Rilke?"

Gruff, but looking into Corde's face with a steady
smile, Spangler was marveling (teasing) that this juve-
nilia should still be so influential. Spangler had put it
behind him; for some reason Corde had not. If Corde
suffered, smarted in this Eastern bloc capital, it was
because that glorious stuff made him vulnerable still,
because he had failed to put it aside at the proper time.
Wasn't that why he became a professor, and why he
fulminated in *Harper's?* It wasn't the fault of the
masterpieces. It was not knowing when to forget them
that was the mistake. A grown man allowing himself to
regress? At this moment when the nations, holding off
destruction, were convulsed with tensions; when a man
needed hardness, patience, maturity, circumspection,
craft, real knowledge of diplomacy, economics, science, history? Albert had lost his grip. Of course, it
was understandable, regrettable. It was forgivable. All
this shone out from Dewey's bearded, understanding,
patronizing, forgiving face.

A mysterious metamorphosis had occurred and skinny Dewey had become a bearded dwarf. The tones that
came from inside this broad, low figure hadn't changed.
He played on the same strings; it was the bowing that
was smoother. It was wonderful that the music, coming
from the places where the deep tones lived, should still
be what it had been forty years ago. He scoffed and he
scolded, but now he did it with affection and endear-

ment, soothing poor old nervous Albert. Albert returned his affection. But it was ungrateful in Dewey to depreciate the "glorious stuff." Without the *Zarathustra* and the *Lear*, what would have become of him? Would he ever have risen so high without the cultural capital he had accumulated in Lincoln Park; would he even have gotten out of Chicago? Dewey had never wasted anything in his life; he always got his money's worth. He had made the Shakespeare pay, just as he turned his years of psychoanalysis to use. His bookish adolescence had given him an edge over the guys at the City News Bureau and his competitors in Washington, so that now he could frame his columns in high-grade intellectual plush, passing easily from the President's budget message to John Stuart Mill, transmuting the rattle of the Chicago streetcars into the dark rich tones of political philosophy. Even the idea of filling the shoes of Walter Lippmann (a hell of a nasty ambition to suffer from, Corde thought) went back to the scrolled green benches of Lincoln Park. Corde didn't mean to put Dewey down. But origins were origins. You did the best you could with them. You couldn't turn them in for a better set.

There was something more. What did Dewey have in mind, that he was being so endearing: did he want to resume their vanished connection? Corde, holding his white plastic bag from the valuta shop, saw this possibility descending towards him from a past as remote as a former life on earth. It was, almost, a former life. Were these the boys who had mooched through Lincoln Park with poets and philosophers tucked under their sweaters; who bought caramel corn in the zoo and lounged against the replica of the Viking ship and made themselves at home with Socrates in the *Phaedrus* or with Rilke in Paris? Since then each of them had died at least three or four times. So it *was* a former earth life. Corde's feeling towards his friend was gentle but not particularly sentimental. Did Dewey still long for the old days of poetry and feeling? So did Corde, at times.

He reviewed the prospects for a revival of friendship with heartfelt objectivity. There was no question of rejecting Dewey. He'd never do that. But how far he'd admit him depended on his admissibility. They had diverged and diverged and diverged. Each of them had been spoilt, humanly, but in very different ways. Look at Dewey. Dewey grew up among warehouses, garages and taverns on Clark Street, not far from the site of the Valentine's Day massacre, but now he was a great figure in his profession, ten times more important than any U.S. senator you could name. When he discussed plutonium sales to the Third World or Russian natural gas or the diamonds the emperor Bokassa had given to Giscard, he did it with a flavor of art and high thought. He quoted Verlaine or Wittgenstein—in fact he quoted them too much. But those Rilke readings hadn't been wasted: the need for pure being, the fulfillment of the soul in art, *Weltinnenraum*. But then there was the *other* viewpoint, the La Salle Street one that you got from a man like Zaehner—it's a jungle out there. (Correction: a garbage dump!) Now, between these opposites, what ground had Dewey taken? The great public, the consumer of his views, didn't require him to take any ground. He needed only to keep talking. He lived (although Corde doubted that such tension should be called living) in a kind of event-glamour, among the deepest developments of the times, communicating what most concerned serious and responsible opinion. To Corde there was something bogus and grotesque about this. It was only "modern public consciousness." There was no real experience in it, none whatever. The forms that made true experience were corrupted. So Corde asked himself, "What would this wonderful palship of two old boys from Chicago look like if we brought it up to date?" The answer was that it could only look like Dewey's journalism. Dewey in his confident, comforting, but also peremptory way would tell him, "This is what we've got. Lucky us, to have such a bond." Their friendship revived, he would lay it all on you in his newspaper language, and strengthened by those Lincoln Park days, by books and poetry and friendship, by all that Corde had learned meantime, he might become an even more princely "communicator."

And now, with stormier objectivity, himself: How had Albert Corde been spoilt? Well, Albert Corde had illusions comparable to Dewey's, notwithstanding that they were in different fields. Look at him—an earnest, brooding, heart-struck, time-ravaged person (or boob), with his moral desires and taking up the burdens of mankind. He was, more or less in secret, serious about matters he couldn't even begin to discuss with Dewey. There was, for instance, the reunion of spirit and nature (divorced by science). Dewey (Corde happened to have caught this in one of his columns) was rough on writers who talked about "spirit," intellectuals in flight from the material realities of the present age. Corde could name you ten subjects on which they could never agree. And if he himself had been thoroughly clear in his mind, if the subjects had been cleanly thought out and resolved, there would be no difficulty in discussing them. So it was evident that Albert Corde was a spoilt case. Dewey pressed him about his motives for writing those *Harper's* articles. What was the real explanation? Again, the *high* intention—to prevent the American idea from being pounded into dust altogether. And here is our American idea: liberty, equality, justice, democracy, abundance. And here is what things are like today in a city like Chicago. Have a look! How does the public apprehend events? It doesn't apprehend them. It has been deprived of the capacity to experience them. Corde recognized how arrogant he had been. *His* patience was at an end. *He* had had enough. *He* was now opening his mouth to speak. And now, look out!

In the American moral crisis, the first requirement was to experience what was happening and to see what must be seen. The facts were covered from our perception. More than they had been in the past? Yes, because the changes, especially the increase in consciousness—and also in false consciousness—was accompanied by a peculiar kind of confusion. The increase of theories and discourse, itself a cause of new strange forms of blindness, the false representations of "communication," led to horrible distortions of public consciousness. Therefore the first act of morality was to disinter the reality, retrieve reality, dig it out from the trash, represent it anew as art would represent it. So when Dewey talked about the "poetry," pouring scorn on it, he was right insofar as Corde only made "poetic" gestures or passes, but not insofar as Corde was genuinely inspired. Insofar as he was inspired he had genuine political significance.

We were no longer talking about anything. The language of discourse had shut out experience altogether. Corde had accordingly spoken up—or attempted to speak up. I tried to make myself the moralist of seeing. I laid it on them. They mostly hated me for it. My own real consciousness had become intermittent over many years. That's what being spoilt means, in my case; it means fitfulness of vision. Now you have it, now you don't. That leads to exaggeration, also. Anyway, that was what I had in mind. Those Chicago guys may be right to hate me. I may deserve it. But not for this. I was speaking up for the noble ideas of the West in their American form. Which no one was asking me to do, and which I took upon myself without even thinking who the hell was I! A kind of natural effrontery. "This is your city—this is your American democracy. It's also my city. I have a right to picture it as I see it." Or else, "The public doesn't apprehend events which must be apprehended." And I intended to stick it to everybody.

"But you've got to go. Okay," said Dewey. "I'll walk you to the car."

Never again would the gesturing excited adolescent weedy Spangler be seen. There was now a stout dwarfish man awkwardly trying to get out of the booth, pushing on the table with his knuckles. His beard gave him an aspect of decent seniority. But he was half plastered. Corde, waiting for him, was also feeling the drink, for as his friend labored to rise, he looked to him like a kind of human plant—a short, fleshy trunk, and a spherical, overfull, overfructified face, rejoicing in itself. So go to it. Rejoice. Dewey moved him. Everything seemed to move him now.

"Never mind, pal. I can find my way."

"There's plenty of time. I wish this had been a longer drink. You were putting me on, about the White House, asking me to use my connections, and then it turns out to be too late."

"I guess I shouldn't have. Still, you passed the test."

"No big deal, I suppose. But you are a funny guy. You made a crisis for me with your scoop from Potsdam. I opened *The New Yorker* and was knocked over. My pal Albert, who used to dither about Blake and Yeats, writing a firsthand report about Stalin and Churchill, Truman. Stalin's demonic force. We had the Bomb. Uncle Joe's armies were used up—but he got what he wanted. How come? Anyhow, you hit the ground running. You were made by that piece. Then you turned around and *unmade* yourself. That's mighty peculiar. I can still remember how burned up I was, how I died of envy. It was a class connection that did it for you. You and I may have been intoxicated with the 'monuments of unaging intellect,' but you weren't too intoxicated to use your dad's pull. He had a drag with Harry Vaughan."

"Since, as you say, I unmade myself, you can forget about that now."

"I wanted to have a talk with you, Albert. Can we get together again?"

"You're the one with the busy schedule. I'll wait for a call."

"What about Christmas Day?"

"I can't tell you right now."

"Because you don't know when your mother-in-law will die? I see that."

"Most of the time, I'm at your disposal. Free. There's a friend of ours coming over from Chicago—a woman named Vlada. But she'll be here for quite a while. Look, when you talk to your Washington office, ask your staff about the Chicago trial."

Spangler said, "Yes, and I want to discuss that with you, too. It was on my agenda for today."

6

When Corde returned, Minna said, "Traian will drive us."

"All three?"

"Yes."

They sat down to a dinner of cold leftovers. Little was said at table. For a change, Tanti Gigi was silent. Tonight she was neither the kid sister nor the charming girl who had once lived in London, but a tense old woman, her strained neck with its bobbed hair bent over her plate.

Traian was punctual. He rapped at a pane of the curtained dining room door and asked permission to come in. Obese and Mexican-looking, he had long tufts of hair at the corners of his mouth. He wore his trousers close and tight, especially at the crotch. His many-zippered Hell's Angels leather jacket was reddish, his boots were black and highly polished. He was particularly attentive to Tanti Gigi. Of course, he had known her for most of his life. Probably she had often fed him in the little kitchen, when he was a small boy. They rose from the table and went into the vestibule. Orlon-Dacron fur coats hung there, purplish brown, but even

these synthetics were saturated with the fragrance of
the ladies, even (so Corde felt) with their personalities.
To the right was the primitive kitchen, to the left the
old-fashioned water closet. Above were closed cupboards containing boxes of family relics, documents.

Traian handed Gigi into the china-closet elevator,
aligned the swinging doors, pressed the button.
Squeezed into a corner, Corde lifted up his coat collar,
tied the muffler over it tightly, bracing himself for the
street. Minna looked sternly absentminded; gracefully
dissociated as well. By the small light, her white face
was dark under the eyes. The outward curve of her
upper lip, the pressure marks of her severe chin, almost
made a stranger of her. Corde was carrying the plastic
Christmas bag with the Kents in it. Minna got into the
front seat of the Dacia while Traian was hooking up the
windshield wipers—they would be stolen here if you
didn't lock them in the glove compartment. "Albert,
give me the cigarettes," she said. When Traian sat
behind the wheel, Minna spoke to him, handed him
one of the cartons. He opened it and filled the door
pocket with Kents. No surprise, no problem; he was
on. He drove to the hospital. Gigi, sitting beside Corde
in the back seat, seemed incapable of speaking.

Snow might have helped that night, brightened the
streets. It had begun to fall earlier but soon petered
out. No one went strolling in this blackness. There was
only an occasional car. Corde thought he had never
seen such street lamps before—something like phos-
phorescent humus inside the globes.

But at the hospital the porter's lodge was brightly
lighted. There were women from the country waiting
for passes, peasants in boots and kerchiefs. Then up
came Tanti Gigi in the draggled Orlon fur, her bent
back and bobbed gray hair, a splash of terror on her
face, her wide forehead pure white. She stood staring at
the ground. The porter had Minna and Corde on his
visitors list and handed them their passes. Traian got
him to come outside. The man carried a clipboard; he

was booted, a white smock came to his knees, he wore a woolen watch cap. His look was sulky. Primped to say no, thought Corde. Traian took the man by the arm and began to talk to him privately. Next to the porter's lodge there was an outer waiting room, shaped like a trolley car and well lighted. Gigi entered it and sat down.

As they went up the driveway together, Corde said to Minna, "Poor Gigi is scared. Do you think he'll get her in?"

"He seems to know his way around. . . ."

They entered the main building. Just inside the doors was a wide hall, a clerk behind a wicket, another long queue. Then two more spacious dark rooms, and then a door with frosted glass: Intensive Care. Corde recognized the woman who answered their knock; it was Dr. Drur, on duty tonight. Round-faced, speaking softly, she shook Minna's hand with particular warmth. That was significant, the sympathy. Again, Minna and Corde went through the robing routine—sterile gowns, caps, masks, the swelling white overshoes tied with tapes.

"Mammi!" said Minna. Corde followed slowly and stood in the door of the cubicle, but the doctor motioned him to come closer. Valeria's right hand stirred, as much as she could manage. The movement was slight. She knew what was happening, you could see that in the blind face. Also, the monitoring devices speeded up, briefly. Standing by the bed, Corde was much moved, but unsure what to do beyond signifying somehow that he would keep Minna from harm. He bent near and rumbled, "It's Albert, Valeria." She nodded.

Minna drew down the gauze mask to kiss Valeria. Then the quick, plump doctor came up with a pad of paper. She helped Valeria to close her fingers on a ballpoint pen, and the old woman tried to write. No control, thought Corde. Can't manage. She formed a few letters but ended in a big loose spiral that crossed the yellow page. Minna and the doctor tried to make out the word. Corde's guess was that she was asking still to be taken home. But a woman like Valeria would have made alternative preparations—plan A, plan B. Fully aware, and good and ready—that would be characteristic of her. He thought there was no other way to interpret the expression of her face; he derived it even from the posture of her legs and from the old woman's belly, which had risen higher than ever. On both sides of her face, the currents of hair were shining on the bed linen. Consciousness was as clear as it had ever been. No, more acute than ever, for when Minna signaled that he should take her hand (again he noted the blue splayed knuckle, and the blue kink of the vein there), she pressed his fingers promptly. He said, "We came as soon as possible." Then, as if he should not delay the essential message, he said in his deep voice, "I also love you, Valeria."

This had a violent effect. One of her knees came up, her eyes, very full under the skin of the lids, moved back and forth. She made an effort to force them to open. Her face was taken by a spasm. The monitors jumped simultaneously. All the numbers began to tumble and whirl. He might have killed her by saying that. Either because she believed him or because she did not. But she ought to have believed him. So far as he painfully knew, it was the truth. The doctor was startled by the speed of the flashing digits. She motioned to Corde and Minna to step back. No, to go.

They returned to the staff room. He took off his gown. He could hardly bear this. The light was very sharp in this doctors' room.

Minna said, "That was right, what you told her."

Corde was less sure of that.

Then Minna said, "Albert, what kind of state do you think she's in?"

He thought the soul was loosened in Valeria, ready to pull out, and that she could therefore know you for what you were. He answered nothing.

The doctor came in and the women spoke. Minna

said, "It's all right on the monitor again." She said she
would go out now and fetch her aunt. She was determined to get her in. She said, "Valeria was the big
sister; she always took care of her. Tonight I have to
do it." Gigi hadn't even asked to be brought. Corde figured that here in the Soviet bloc you learned to refrain
from asking. And then, too, Gigi depended on Minna
as she had done on Valeria. But it turned out that
Minna had promised her aunt—she would have told
her with severity: "I'm taking you. You'll see her!"

Minna folded and laid down the sterile gown and the
boots—she was even now thorough in her orderliness,
absentmindedly ritualistic. She told the doctor that she
was going out for a few minutes. She'd be right back.
The apprehensive doctor did not question her but
shook her head. This was wrong. The rules were being
broken. What if the Colonel should burst in?

As Corde helped Minna over the ice of the sloping
driveway, the evergreens made a chill sound above
them, as if things could simmer also below freezing.
Passive, stooped and silent, Gigi sat waiting to see
whether Minna would keep her promise. She would.
Traian's signal was that the cigarettes had worked, the
fix was in. So the two women now went up the slope to
the main building, while Corde took Gigi's place beside
Traian on the bench. Then the waiting room lights were
switched off. The porter, taking no chances, hid them
in darkness. As if the Colonel would care much. Now
that he had had his way, the matter was closed. The
doctors had probably told him that it was all over with
Valeria, and the deal with the Minister of Health was,
"Let them come."

Meanwhile, Valeria's mind was clear. This was what
impressed Corde most deeply. She could still hear and
understand everything, and respond. Probably Dr.
Drur with the soft face, and the intensive care staff,
talked with her, kept her informed. A physician herself
(the founder of this hospital), Valeria had seen plenty
of people go. The woman doctor seemed particularly

close to her. To have a woman in attendance was a good thing. She had probably said, "Your daughter has permission tonight." Valeria would understand what this signified. There again you saw the extent of the woman connection, its great importance.

Dr. Drur hadn't doped Valeria (professional courtesy) and she was dying in clear consciousness. And Corde contrasted this with the consciousness of that boy Rick Lester, when he realized that he had gone through the window and was falling. The young man had played a kind of game that night, assuming the usual safe conditions, but the conditions were missing —he had a gag in his throat and two or three seconds to recognize that he was finished. He, Corde, had more in common with that boy than with the old woman. She didn't have their sort of mind, the modern consciousness, that equivocal queer condition, working with a net of foolish assumptions, and so much absurd unwanted stuff lying on your heart. He was impressed with Valeria. (Couldn't he attribute it to his equivocal consciousness that he was so much impressed?) She and Dr. Raresh, Marxists, had gone into the streets with roses to greet the Russians, lived to see the prison state, repented. She went back to the old discipline, believed in the good, probably took it all seriously about the pure in heart seeing God, and the other beatitudes. (Nothing too rum?) Her ashes would be placed beside those of her husband.

Though it went against the grain, he suspected that his nephew may have been right, that on the night he was killed Rick Lester had been out for dirty sex, and it was this dirty sex momentum that had carried him through the window. Corde understood this far better than he understood the old woman's beliefs. So what was the pure-in-spirit bit? For an American who had been around, a man in his mid-fifties, this beatitude language was unreal. To use it betrayed him as a man wildly disturbed, a somehow crazy man. It was foreign, bookish—it was Dostoevsky stuff, that the vices of

Sodom coexisted with the adoration of the Holy Sophia, cynicism joined with purity in the heart of the paradoxical Russian. He was no Russian but Huguenot and Irish by descent, a Midwesterner flattened out by the prairies, a journalist and a lousy college dean. He suspected that the academic connection had been getting to him. He could feel, with Dr. Faustus, "O would that I had never seen Wittenberg, never read a book"; and it was no wonder that the classroom, the library environment, had driven him finally into the streets of Chicago, or that he had written—well, written that at the Cabrini Green black housing project, some man had butchered a hog in his apartment and had thrown the guts on the staircase, where a woman, slipping on them, had broken her arm, and screamed curses in the ambulance. She was smeared with pig's blood and shriller than the siren. It was illumination from a different side, Chicago light and color, not the Sermon on the Mount.

He was strongly agitated. He thought, Hadn't it been too easy, bribing the porter? Had he let Minna and Gigi walk into a trap, where the Colonel would swoop down on the deathbed and grab them? But what would he want to do that for—why arrest old Gigi? No, Corde saw that he was beginning to think like those women who imagined themselves locked in a mortal struggle with this police colonel, who, right now, must be dining in his luxurious villa, eating delicacies and drinking special vintages. The New Class, or new New Class, lived like Texas millionaires. Corde with his twenty-odd years in Europe understood this. Millions of Americans of his generation had gone out into the world. There were robustious theorists who maintained that this was one of the luckiest developments in history and had done humankind nothing but good. There was a very different point of view. Folks from Trenton, Topeka, Baton Rouge, who lived in Japan, Iran, Morocco, were, as he had read in a magazine, "representatives of the fantasmo imperium of corporate dollars." It was in his dentist's reception room that he had found this piece on American mercenaries and arms salesmen, "high-technology killers operating in Africa and Central America." He had picked up this magazine from the top of the lighted tropical fish tank.

He must ask Dewey Spangler about the "fantasmo imperium." It would amuse him. "Why would corporate dollars be spent on these twerps? Americans living abroad are always supposed to 'represent' something. But there's you, for instance, Albert—what would you be representing?"

That would be a good question. What *did* Corde represent? Who was this person sharing the bench with Ioanna's nephew Traian? He carried a U.S. passport and money and credit cards. He was dressed in coat, gloves, muffler and an encircling fedora over his radar-dish face, his somewhat swelling eyes and plain mouth. He seemed to be picking up signals from all over the universe, some from unseeable sources. His neck was long; his back, too, seemed to go on longer than was strictly necessary. He was a mid-American of mild appearance. He was aware of that. He called this "the Pullman car gentility" and believed he had inherited it from his Wilson-era grandfather. (Corde didn't admire Woodrow Wilson. Wilson had done great harm.) Anyway, he, Albert, was a Corde. Six generations in Joliet, Illinois, two in Chicago, and he had just told a dying old Macedonian woman in a Communist hospital that he loved her. This was the measure of the oddities life had compiled for him. "I also love you, Valeria." But although she must have been longing to hear this, and although it was true (it was, dammit, one hundred percent true!), she was nevertheless so shocked that the machines began to flash and yammer and the doctor was scared witless. Why had he upset her? He must have reminded her again of her fears, which she would carry into the life to come, or at least up to the gate of death. Perhaps there was no need to take this personally, or to compare himself, as he sometimes did, to a longtime sexual offender still on probation, though the most exacting parole officer would have been satisfied with him. Oh, those sexual offenses! He was by the strictest marital standards decent, mature, intelligent, responsible, an excellent husband. But within the historical currents he could not be viewed from a positive aspect because he was a representative of the rotten West, lacking ballast, the product of an undesirable historical development, a corrupted branch of humanity. One needn't go as far as the extremist Eastern dissidents who called Europe an incorrigible old whore and America her most degenerate descendant, in the stage of general paresis. That was going far. But it was possible to suspect him of being incapable of sustaining a serious relationship, as seriousness was defined by the older, indeed archaic, branch of humanity with its eternal fixtures. Valeria would therefore be thinking that the world Corde came from was the world in which her daughter must live out her life. She must depend now on that world and on this man. So Corde had been moved that in dying she should still be in torment over her daughter, and so Valeria heard his bass voice assuring her, and she was pierced with doubts. This "I also love you," which made her squeeze his hand, might be true, but it might be the truth merely of an agitated moment, no good within an hour. He could see that, yes. It was very painful to him, too.

If we could say what we meant, mean what we said! But we didn't seem to be set up for it. We were set up instead in a habitual state of hypnotic fixity, and this hypnotic fixity was the real fantasmo imperium. Well, never mind the philosophy. But on her deathbed an old woman hears the deep voice of her son-in-law, and it tells her that he loves her. Loves! With what! Nevertheless it *was* true, however queer. There *was* nothing too rum to be true. He depended on that now. Although Valeria—she wasn't going to have time to verify his declaration. She'd have to take his word for it, because for her this world of death was ending. World of death? He surprised himself when he put it that way. More of his poetry, Dewey Spangler would have said, and bared his teeth in a grin—Spangler still had those sharp and healthy teeth. Same dazzling teeth; the ginger marmalade beard was their new setting.

Still Dewey had asked him one really hot question: Why a professor in Chicago? Corde might have answered that the reason was coming, it was on its way. There were hidden and extensive fantasy ambitions and grand designs connected with it. At the moment of decision, it had been convenient that he should have no clear outline. He remembered how surprised his sister had been when he moved back. "Why a college, and why here?" Elfrida inquired.

He couldn't really answer, but he did say, "For me it's more like the front lines. Here is where the action is."

"I wouldn't have left Paris, not with an apartment on Rue Vaneau. Did you sell it for a fortune?"

"No fortune."

"Then getting away from some French broad or other?"

"No, that wasn't it, either, although there are plenty of broads that can inspire leaving—even going into hiding, or taking holy orders."

"Who said, 'When you're tired of Paris you're tired of life'?"

"It was said about London. And the same party said that no man of what he called 'intellectual enjoyment' would immerse himself and his posterity in American barbarism. But that was two hundred years ago."

"That's a real book answer," was Elfrida's comment. "You want to spend the rest of your life reading books in a college? Don't expect me to swallow that. I know you better. You're not a retirement type. You don't look it, but you're a combative type. You just said you were looking for action."

"When I was a kid I had martial instincts."

"You do still. I can't dope you out, Albert. What advantage do you see here?"

"There's the big advantage of backwardness. By the time the latest ideas reach Chicago, they're worn thin and easy to see through. You don't have to bother with them and it saves lots of trouble."

He stopped these thoughts and recollections, for he now caught sight of Minna and Gigi walking carefully, slow, down the slope under the pines. Corde went out to meet them. He asked no questions. No one spoke. It hadn't been a long visit. Maybe the doctor, frightened by Minna's boldness, had asked them to leave. The Colonel hadn't surprised them. No, the Colonel now cared nothing about any of them.

Traian opened the dark green doors of the tub-shaped Dacia. The interior was freezing.

At home, too, it was too cold to get into bed.

"Albert, I can't take my clothes off."

Corde poured from the *pálinca* bottle. "Let's swallow some of this."

They sat in their coats. When Corde removed his hat, he felt the cold on his bald crown. "You didn't stay long. . . ."

"Because of Dr. Drur. I took her completely by surprise with Gigi. I think there were watchers everywhere."

"And what did Gigi say?"

"She didn't say anything, just put her hand on Mother's arm. Lie down with me, Albert."

He pulled the heavy covers from his bed and piled them on hers. Then he turned off the tiny orange-tinted light bulb under the big parchment lampshade. Minna presently feel asleep. Corde, stretched beside her along the edge of the bed, went into a state of blankness for the rest of the night.

7

In the morning Minna was on the telephone again,
trying to reach Dr. Moldovanu, the passionate daughter still fighting for her mother. Corde thought, She
can't accept that it's over, the end, she saw Valeria for
the last time. But that was a lot to ask. He was being
too sensible. It was one of his persistent failings.

And so there he was, as usual. It was morning, and
he was sitting in the room. He had swallowed several
cups of Gigi's coffee. It was too weak to revive him
after his night of blankness. He frowned at the packet
of mail from his office. After his catatonic night on the
edge of the bed, under the burdensome stiff weight of
the Balkan rugs, he was too tired, felt too tender and
sore inside, to take on those letters from Chicago. He
opened his briefcase instead and looked for the Beech
documents. He must get them read before Vlada
Voynich arrived. To be idle this morning was a bad
idea. If he didn't pull himself together he'd suffer from
random thoughts. Those were the worst—they ate you
up. Clearing an efficient space on the desk, he set
himself to study Beech's scientific papers. He began
with Vlada's abstract. Immediately he found his antidote to the distress of random ideas. "Beech picked
you, on the basis of those articles in *Harper's,* to be his
interpreter," she wrote. "And since I have been part of
his team for some years, he requested that I give you a
little preliminary guidance. I am glad you had the
opportunity to meet him. His reactions to you were
very positive." (I liked him, too, thought Corde. Beech

was a terrific fellow. Also, to get an eminent man's positive reaction was pleasing.) "The situation is of the most urgent importance," he further read. "Beech wants his case stated not only to the general public but also to the Humanists." This gave Corde pause. Who were these Humanists, and why should Beech imagine that they were a group to whom any case could be stated? And if there was such a group, why should it be inclined to pay attention to Corde? He considered how to discuss this with a geologist like Beech. "You want to understand humanist intellectuals? Think of the Ruling Reptiles of the Mesozoic. . . ." Corde meantime read on. "I think you said that you listened to the tapes he gave you. In those he recorded his personal account of the research that led up to his discoveries and explained what they signified for the future of our species and, consequently, why they presented such an emotional problem for those who drew the inevitable logical conclusions." Yes, Corde had listened to the tapes. In the first minute, Beech said they had been made last summer in a Kansas barn. "Looking through the big open door over the summer wheat fields," the scientist had flatly intoned. "The Great Plains. My native grounds."

Vlada had told Corde in Chicago, "Albert, it was my doing, partly. I brought your articles to Beech's attention because I knew he was looking for somebody who had the necessary skills. Also the brains." Vlada spoke with the fully centered assurance of a stout woman. Her face was wide and pale, the brown Balkan eyes were large—no soft glances, but urgent business, shrewdness. She did not invite you to take part in dream enterprises; she was an extremely shrewd lady. (At moments her eyes did make personal confessions, too, painful ones. But never mind that now.) Beech himself had been more diffident. "After you've listened to these tapes and studied the materials, perhaps you'd consider further discussions leading to eventual collaboration. Naturally, I have a special point of view, as the man who directed the research—in the inside position, right in the middle." Beech's mildness had a special charm for Corde. What a nice man! And when you considered what a terrific charge he carried, the responsibility for such frightening findings (would the earth survive?), how gallant his mildness was. He said to Corde, "You, the author of those special articles, might—you just might—be able to blow the whistle. I want to stop everybody in their tracks and force them to follow. And you can be gripping. As with the blacks you described in public housing and in the jails . . ."

"I didn't please everybody."

"I would assume not. That's exactly it. And when I read your description of the inner city, I said, 'Here's a man who will want the real explanation of what goes on in those slums.'"

"And the explanation? What is the real explanation?"

"Millions of tons of intractable lead residues poisoning the children of the poor. They're the most exposed. The concentration is measurably heaviest in those old slum neighborhoods, piled up there for decades. It's the growing children who assimilate the lead fastest. The calcium takes it up. And if you watch the behavior of those kids with a clinical eye, you see the classic symptoms of chronic lead insult. I've asked Vlada Voynich to include Needleman's neuropsychiatric findings from the *New England Journal of Medicine* with the other papers. Crime and social disorganization in inner city populations can all be traced to the effects of lead. It comes down to the nerves, to brain damage."

Polite Corde, with silent lips, nodding, doubted this. He wore a look of quiet but high dubiety. Once more, a direct material cause? Everything had a direct material cause? If you gave people employment, money, clothing, shelter, food, protected them from infection and from poison, they wouldn't be criminal, they wouldn't be mad, they wouldn't despair? Sure, the right programs, rightly administered, would fix it. Direct material causes? Of course. Who could deny them? But what was odd was that no other causes were conceived of. "So it's lead, nothing but old lead?" he said.

"I would ask you to study the evidence."

And that was what Corde now began to do, reading through stapled documents, examining graphs.

You couldn't easily hide the sign of the crank from an experienced journalist, and as Spangler had said, these scientists were diapered babies when they went public with a cause. But Beech somehow inspired respect. There was a special seriousness about him. He was even physically, constitutionally serious. His head, for a body of such length, was small, his face devoid of personal vanity. Light hair, grizzled and cropped Marine style, gave him an old-fashioned hayseed look. His cheeks were austerely creased, his glance was dry. Corde had checked on his credentials. He was indeed an eminent man of science. That was unanimous. He had authoritatively dated the age of the earth, had analyzed the rocks brought back from the moon. Corde was beginning to think that with pure scientists, when they turned their eyes from their own disciplines, there were, occasionally, storms of convulsive clear consciousness; they suffered attacks of confusing lucidity.

Therefore Corde had listened closely to the tapes. In his small Chicago study he had switched off the lights, plugged in his headphones.

And here in Bucharest, too, he read with care. Consider: Eastern Europe as a place to read about endangered humanity. Corde was at Valeria's table and sore, rubbed raw within; he could feel the rawness as he bent over Beech's papers. He pressed his hands, for warmth, under his thighs.

What was the message? Three industrial centuries had vastly increased the mining and smelting of lead, and the unavoidable dispersal of lead in air, water, soil, was a danger too little understood. We had been "authoritatively assured" that lead levels were normal and tolerable. Far from it. Official standards are worse than incorrect; they are dangerously false. Investigations are conducted in laboratories themselves heavily contaminated. Only results obtained in ultra-clean sanctuary laboratories are dependable. These are few in number but only their evidence counts, and this evidence tells us that lead levels are about five hundredfold above natural prehistoric levels. The true levels have been established by fossil bone analysis, by the examination of the sediments of fresh and marine waters, of old tree-stem woods, of snow strata in the Antarctic, and of Greenland ice. The "emissions of forest foliage" have also been investigated, together with crustal components of silicate dusts, sea sprays and volcanic sulfurs. This mass of measurements and supporting data ("isotopic compositions") excited Corde, moved him. ("Is there something wrong, that I'm so liable to get agitated?") Radioactivity, of course, and also the depletion of the ozone layer by aerosols he was as familiar with as the next man. But on the midnight tapes recorded in the summer fields of Kansas, Corde had heard also of the chemical saturation of the soil by insecticides and fertilizers. This was why America was the world's greatest food producer. At what a cost! But the lead was far more dangerous than any of these. Beech's voice went on like the plains themselves.

Government agencies assigned the task of measurement and control were incompetent, said Beech. They lacked the necessary instruments and correct procedures. The true magnitude of this deadly poisoning of water, vegetation and air was discovered by the pure sciences of geochronology, cosmology and nuclear geochemistry. A truly accurate method of detecting tiny amounts of lead led to the discovery that the cycle of lead in the earth had been strongly perturbed. The conclusion: Chronic lead insult now affects all mankind. Biological dysfunctions, especially observable in the most advanced populations, must be considered among the causes of wars and revolutions. Mental disturbances resulting from lead poison are reflected in terrorism, barbarism, crime, cultural degradation. Visible everywhere are the irritability, emotional instability, general restlessness, reduced acuity of the reasoning powers, the difficulty of focusing, et cetera, which the practiced clinician can readily identify.

This irritability, this combination of inflammation and deadening—by God, I feel it myself! And I certainly observe it wherever I look! If he had been at home, Corde would have gone to the *Britannica* for more information. Fat medical books jutted from the shelves, within reach, but he was ignorant of Rumanian, weak in German. But for what Beech was getting at he needed no encyclopedia. We couldn't ourselves observe the dulling of consciousness since we were all its victims, and we would be dulled down into the abyss unaware that we were sinking. Tetraethyl fumes alone could do it—engine exhaust—and infants eating flaking lead paint in the slums became criminal morons. Without realizing it, Beech had become a burning moral visionary. He accused the engineers. Applied science, engineering technology, these were the powers of darkness which had poisoned land, air and water, the forests, the animals, the cities, and our own human cells.

Here was an apocalypse—yet another apocalypse to set before the public. It wouldn't be easy. The public was used to doom warnings; seasoned, hell—it was marinated in them. And there are evils, as someone has pointed out, that have the ability to survive identification and go on forever—money, for instance, or war. Those that are most determined to expose them can get no grip upon them. In the current language, that of the mass situation, nothing could be communicated. Nothing was harder to get hold of than the most potent, i.e., the most manifest evils. Here science itself, which was designed for deeper realization, experienced a singular failure. The genius of these evils was their ability

to create zones of incomprehension. It was because
they were so fully apparent that you couldn't see them.
Evidently Beech had begun to feel their power. He
couldn't pass through, couldn't get a hearing. He did
well to come to Albert Corde, therefore. It was a sound
instinct to ask the man who had written those *Harper's*
pieces to get him through the blockaded zones. If I
were convinced, I could do the job for him. And it
wouldn't be by the agitprop, demagogic, haranguing,
or the advertising or mystagogic methods; no fantasmo
imperium, nothing but unfaltering earnestness, like the
Ancient Mariner. You hold 'em with your glittering
eye. "The wedding guest he beat his breast, Yet he
cannot choose but hear." Beech was not another
environmentalist simply. If he had been "one more of
those," Corde would never have given him the time of
day. What he had learned by listening to his tapes with
the closest attention was that the geophysicist had
incorporated the planet itself into his deepest feelings,
as if it were a being which had given birth to life. Beech
was shocked by *Homo sapiens sapiens,* by its ingrati-
tude and impiety. *Homo sapiens sapiens* was incapable
of hearing earth's own poetry, or, now, its plea. Man
would degrade himself into an inferior hominid. (The
biological language was Beech's own.)

Corde felt that they had a lot in common, he and
Beech. There was even a physical affinity. Both were
plain-looking men from the Midwest, in their late
fifties, each with his own stratagem for keeping his
noble values out of sight until the moment of disclosure
(sometime before the end, and before, one hoped, it
was too late). And then to whom did you disclose?
Well, you went public, you printed in *Harper's,* or else
you chose a spokesman, a Corde, and approached him
with a proposition. This process (a scientist's discovery
and its sequel) was in itself, taken as an episode in the
evolution of the soul, a singularly moving thing. You
would never have divined that this dry, long, stooped
cactus, this scientific Beech, would at last cough up so

large and exquisite a flower. (The earth as a being;
earth's own poetry.) So, then, the problem: Deeper
realizations were accorded only to the sciences, and
there within strict limits. The same methods, the same
energies, could not be applied to the deeper questions
of existence. It was conceivable, even, that science had
drawn all the capacity for deeper realizations out of the
rest of mankind and monopolized it. This left everyone
else in a condition of great weakness. In this weakness
people did poetry, painting, humanism, fiddle-faddle—
idiocy.

Terribly moved, restless, clawed within, Corde could
not sit still. He heaved himself up from the table (with
its history of homework, its treasures of sentiment) and
went to look for Minna. He found her with Gigi in the
dining room. Of course they were talking about Valeria. He did not interrupt their conversation but stood
on the sidelines, in the background. His hands were
behind his back and he leaned against the doorframe.
Just looking, swell-eyed, through his goggles, and with
a silent mouth. Under the thick-legged dining room
table the vivid color had gone out of the Balkan carpet,
it was sere and wrinkled. The birds in the pattern could
scarcely fly. The cyclamens on the sideboard were also
worked with faint patterns—the dark leaves had a
whitish under-pattern, varied with gray, making a
smaller heart shape within the heart shape of the leaf.
The flowers were white.

"What's up?" said Corde at last. "What's the
latest?"

"They can't move her," said Minna. "Dr. Gherea
was very sorry."

"Did you talk to the lady friend? Is that who told
you?"

"I talked to Dr. Drur."

Gigi looked towards Corde, not directly at him. Her
eyes were deep dark brown and fluid. The work of the
beauty parlor was undone at the back, where her hair
came apart in white straws, like a whisk broom. But her

bangs were neatly combed out on her forehead. She had put on a dress today and high heels and lipstick. Maybe she didn't want the news of her sister's death to catch her in the brown dressing gown. This tragic old lady with the tarty, Frenchy name—if grief added weight to the body, it might come out in the curvature of her legs, for today she looked more bandy-legged. Corde also observed—perhaps it was the cut of the dress she wore—how strong her neck was. The neck muscles were heavy.

"Anyhow," said Minna, "surgery is out of the question."

Of course it was. No respiration, no anesthesia.

"Dear Albert! Shall I brew a pot of tea?"

"Thank you, no, Tanti Gigi. I'm doing a bit of paper work. I'll go back."

He was far too restless to sit with the women. He would as soon have had the tea poured over his head.

"There hasn't been any word from your friend Spangler?" said Minna.

"I wouldn't expect much from him."

"*Now* is when I should be with her," said Minna.

There was no answer to make. He muttered only that he would go back to his papers. Again, the room!

There was something in Corde's throat, some East European condensation, and it took East European brandy to clear it. He took two shots from the bottle while he reorganized the desk, putting aside the Beech documents. This mace of lead that was knocking our brains out . . . *Pálinca* left a kind of stale plum aftertaste. He sweetened his mouth with a few brown grapes, the last of them. Waiting for death, you see. There was very little he could do.

And now, at last, he took up the large manila envelope of mail from Chicago. Censorship had obviously unstuck the tapes. He had noticed that yesterday. Disgusted, he lifted the crisscrossed tapes with the point of Valeria's paper knife and shook them off. And Christ! all this stuff, these unwanted clippings and papers; nothing but trouble. Corde's posture was habitually relaxed, and as he went through his mail his body was turned three-fourths aside, askance, in "relaxed" avoidance. He held the sheaf unwillingly, passing paper after paper to the back.

On his own turf, he was at war. He couldn't say why it was necessary to be fighting there. But now, caught up in it, he had to see it through. Hadn't Elfrida told him that he was a combative type?

Miss Porson (or Ms., as she had taken to signing herself) had enclosed an elaborate memorandum, a bulletin from the front. She said she regretted sending him some of these items. He could do without them, where he was. "It must be a bad scene. My heart goes out to Minna." Towards Minna Miss Porson's female generosity and admiration were boundless. "Her wonderful style, the way she walks, her musical speaking voice, her perfect breeding," Miss Porson would say. This Miss Porson of his, Fay Porson, was an old slob (he was at present inclined to call her that) of no little charm. She couldn't have been much younger than Tanti Gigi, but she boasted that she turned on lovers half her age. In her late sixties, she was fleshy, but her bearing was jaunty. Her plump face, heavily made up, was whitish pink, as if washed in calamine lotion, and on some days she painted a raccoon band across her face in blue eye shadow—the mask of a burglar or a Venetian reveler. She kept up her pants with heavy silver-and-turquoise belts. The permanent Miss Porson, the Miss Porson of the deeper strata, turned out to be a bridge-playing Westchester matron. She had come to Chicago with her midlevel executive husband. Here she was widowed and here she preferred to remain. She could swing in Chicago. She was going to "put the sex into sexagenarian," she said. Corde had become fond of her. She was not the supersecretary and faultless organizer she claimed to be; she was overpaid. His dislike of administrative detail had made a hostage of him. Her erotic confidences and boasts set his teeth on edge. But he would not have been able now to replace her.

She wrote that there was only more of the same in the papers. As far as the press was concerned, Mr. Detillion could do no wrong, for the time being, anyway. As her late father would have said, they had Mr. Corde's head "in chancery" and they loved it. ("Chancery," Corde had learned, was a term from the days of John L. Sullivan: You caught your opponent's head under your arm and rubbed it with bare knuckles.) This, she continued, couldn't go on forever; the good guys would have their innings by and by. If the true facts could only be made known—how different it would look! The Dean was still struggling with financial and legal problems created by his cousin. Ms. Porson wished the details could be leaked to reporters. There was, for instance, the IRS matter, originally mishandled by Mr. Detillion when he signed a waiver on the statute of limitations because he was so confident that the government had no case. So now the IRS claim, with interest, was up to $23,000, and although the new lawyer, Mr. Gershenkorn, was doing his best, and would get an extension while the Dean was out of the country, he couldn't promise success. All this information, supplied in pure kindness, stuck in Corde's throat.

For his morale, she enclosed copies of fan letters from his readers. She admitted that some hate mail had also come in. She was saving it for his return. Most of the poison-pen notes were from the suburbs, where the diehard Chicago boosters all lived. Commuters who escaped from race problems and crime were indignant because he had told it as it was. She reported that the Provost had sent a note: The Dean was not to worry about the home front but to take care of Minna in this tragic moment. He expressed himself with great decency and delicacy, said Miss Porson.

There was one message for Minna, from the Mount Palomar Observatory. They would try to rearrange schedules in order to give her some telescope time in January. The rest of Miss Porson's memorandum itemized the notes and letters she was forwarding. He went through the memo again, for it was inconceivable that it should contain no mention of Lydia Lester. He had left Miss Porson in charge of that girl, and most of his last instructions had to do with her protection. He had spent the better part of an hour just before departure spelling it out on the telephone. Fay Porson had *seemed* to see the point. In fact, she had made remarks Corde had had no desire to hear, about the mixture of fatherly solicitude and guilt that motivated him. "Because it was you, Dean, that pushed for the trial? And the girl is so delicate? But she didn't have to go along, did she? In the end she decided that she wanted that pair to pay for what they did to the poor young husband—it was her *own* decision. You take too much on yourself, Dean." Corde had little liking for these psychological insights, but he had let himself in for them. You confided in people, you *had* to. From this came dependency, and then unwanted intimacy, and presently you discovered—horrifying!—that though Porson listened and nodded and looked as clever as Alexander Woollcott (whom she strikingly resembled) and as melting as a mother, that though you moved her to tears, she was an exasperating dumbhead, and a lustful old frump. "Not to worry!" was her last word to him, but obviously she hadn't even spoken to Lydia. He made yet another search. No, not a word about the girl. How could a beautiful young woman interest Fay Porson, who has just discovered her own youthfulness. She had her own sexual fat to fry. She wasn't going to give it to the grave. She was like that lascivious old woman in Aristophanes, claiming equal sexual rights with the other "girls," grabbing at all the handsome young men. And those young men wouldn't know what they were getting into until it was time to do the act. . . . But Corde went no further. He relented.

It occurred to him that Lydia Lester might have

complained to the Porson about him, said that he had dropped out at the worst moment, abandoned her. Corde had canceled all appointments during the trial. He had never missed a single session at Thirteenth and Michigan, the auxiliary Criminal Courts Building. He had laid on a car to call for Lydia each morning. He wouldn't allow her to take public transportation to that part of the city. Not even a cab was safe. Cabs were filthy and reckless, they stank. Cabbies hustled you, they were known to come on sexually with young women. Corde was taking no chances. Lydia was as delicate as she was tall. Everything possible must be done to protect her from shock. He was on hand well before court convened, sat with her before she was called to the stand, and tried to transmit waves of support while Maxie interrogated her. The Detillion caper had its own special interest. Maxie was taking no fee in this case. True, it was a PR gold mine for him, win or lose. Still, from habit, the legal-fee meter must have been clicking in his head, and he was desperately aware of what it was all costing him, of the drain, the sacrifice, of the outstanding bills he might have paid with a retainer. Yes, thought Corde, and because he conned me down in Joliet and screwed me up in Chicago, he is, by *his* logic, the injured party. That's how it works. You swindle a man and then grab even the sense of injury for yourself. A devouring man devours all there is.

So it was possible that Lydia Lester felt abandoned by the Dean. Maybe she, too, interpreted his solicitude as a proof of guilt. He had dragged her into this. It was the Dean's nephew who molested her and the Dean's cousin who afflicted her; it was the Dean who had published those articles of his at just the wrong moment, and then at the climax the Dean took off. She may well have burst out with this, and the Porson, too tactful to transmit tears and grievances at such a time, wouldn't even mention her name. But he was attributing far too much finesse to the old girl—the usual mistake. She had simply forgotten.

The Cordes had a spare room in Chicago, and Corde had suggested to Minna that Lydia should stay with them. Poor thing, she needed support. Corde had that sort of fervent pity in him. It was more than pity, however; it was also admiration. This girl, who looked as if she would crumble if some cabby propositioned her, if a derelict exhibited himself, who answered Detillion so faintly that he had to say, "Speak up . . . if the Court please, the witness is whispering"—this Lydia was punctual every morning, her blouse freshly ironed, her hair smoothly pinned. Corde said to Minna, "When I first urged her to do this she said absolutely not, she couldn't. Then I wondered whether it would be better not to start only to have her breaking down, but I misjudged her completely. It's like you get to the very limit of your weakness and then you come to a door, and if you have just enough strength to open that door you find all kinds of force inside. The girl found it. If I were still talking to Detillion—and you know how Detillion is with his sex business: if he should ever be elected to office, he wouldn't put his hand on a Bible to take the oath, he'd put it on his cock—if I were talking to that pig, I'd say, 'You're missing the whole point, Cousin.'"

Minna said, "There's one of your troubles. You still want to say things to any lost soul."

"Well, it's only 'just suppose.' I wouldn't think of talking to that meathead. And you're right, you've spotted one of my bad tendencies. I seem to carry this indignation load. But what I wanted to say about Lydia is that it's wonderful when a quality comes out you never would have expected. You look at the girl and she looks pale and ailing. She herself has a faint image—those long defenseless hands, the way she holds them. Lots of nice girls are brought up that way, with too faint an image of themselves. The family tells them they aren't strong. At lunchtime, when the court recesses, she has a small collapse. I drive her over to the Cantonese Chef on Wentworth Street so that she can rest her eyes in a dark booth. She has light-sensitive eye pains, like me. She gets a splitting headache in the courtroom. But after a few spoons of wonton soup she can go back and face Detillion again. Grady prays for her to faint—she *won't faint.*"

But Lydia Lester wasn't invited to sleep in the Cordes' guest room. Minna didn't like having a stranger in the house, opening drawers, reading mail and bank statements. She didn't put it that way. She said, "You mustn't forget, Albert, that we'd have to leave her here alone when we went to Mount Palomar." Corde yielded. He didn't share her sense of privacy, but he didn't argue; he let Minna have her way. He regretted it now. It would have been good for the girl. A protective atmosphere. Maybe another girl of compatible temperament would have been willing to stay with her. They would have looked after the place, watered the plants. (He still thought about his plants.) And if you didn't run the showers the seal dried out in the drains and you had sewer gas coming up. The arrangement would have been compassionate. Practical, too.

In the adjoining room, the women talked—they lived on the telephone. The instrument was warm with continual use. Corde kept his door ajar to hear what was going on. Ignorant of the language, he interpreted Minna's tones. And he was the man of the house. They counted on him. Now and then one of them looked in to tell him the latest; they didn't actually ask him for advice, but he gave them plenty of it, knowing that it would be disregarded for the most part. There was an additional telephone oddity. All calls were monitored. Somewhere in a burrow a man listened in. This agent made no effort to conceal his presence from these unimportant women. You heard him breathing, rattling papers, grumbling. Sometimes he even cut in: "That ain't what you said yesterday." Gigi said, "The man is obstreperous. I believe it possible that he is drinking."

Among the papers from Chicago Corde found a

letter from Rufus Ridpath. That pleased him. It was an important gesture, a sign of support. Corde had written passionately about the Ridpath case. No one else had stood up for Ridpath publicly. Of course Ridpath was not rehabilitated, but he had said to Corde, "At least you put the main facts on record." Mason junior dismissed Ridpath as *"your* kind of black man." There was too much of the freak or crank about Corde (liberal opinion's way of dismissing him). His own way of putting it: "If A. Corde is a man of strength, how come his hands are shaking?" Still the truth about Ridpath (or something like it) was now on record. No, it didn't signify much, unless it signified to make a friend. Corde achieved no practical result. Perhaps it was better for you not to have Corde take up your cause.

One of Corde's respected colleagues at the college, Sam Michaels, had observed, "There's less and less connection between blacks and whites. In the past, in spite of the silent war, there was a connection. Now the blacks don't want it, don't seem to care for white relationships." In Mason you saw an attempted reversal, a connection to be made on black terms. What terms were those? Lucas Ebry's terms? They didn't exist. Unreal! Young Mason's idea of boldness put him in the servile position. Besides, Corde wrote, the effective black "image" had been captured by the black gangs, the Rangers and the El Rukins, and the outlaw chieftains—black princes in their beautiful and elegant furs, boots, foreign cars. They controlled the drug trade. They ruled in the prisons. For young blacks, of all classes, even perhaps for young whites, they provided a powerful model. But Ridpath had nothing to do with images, image-making.

Removed from his post as director of the County Jail, Ridpath may have had to borrow money for his legal defense. He won his case but lost his reputation. People remembered the charges and forgot the acquittal—the usual pattern. Again, Sam Michaels—a supershrewd observer: "They couldn't prove the aggravated battery charge. That might mean that the prosecution was clumsy. Ill-prepared, didn't have the skill to prepare a case. Acquittal doesn't necessarily mean that Ridpath *was* innocent."

But Corde became convinced that powerful persons had been out to get the man. After repeated grand jury investigations—why so many? instigated by whom?—he had been indicted for brutalizing prisoners. Beatings in the cells! The newspapers and networks took out after him as if he had been Chicago's Idi Amin. Having a murdered general's head brought to the banquet table in a silver tureen? Shooting one of your own ministers between the eyes at a state banquet? You would have thought so. But the county couldn't make its charge stick. The defense was able to prove that deals had been arranged with the prosecution witnesses, who were promised shorter sentences. They had nothing to lose. Both were convicted murderers. Corde developed a particular, an intense interest in the Ridpath trial. He had long talks with Wolf Quitman, the defense lawyer. He interviewed people who had had professional dealings with Ridpath. He liked the man. And presently Corde found that he had linked himself with him. One seldom understands quite how such links are formed.

Ridpath wrote: "Hearing from your secretary that you had to leave the country suddenly because of your wife's mother, I thought I would go down to Thirteenth and Michigan and look at what was happening there. When the case broke in the papers, I seemed to remember the defendant. Sure enough, I recognized this man Ebry as soon as I saw him. Over the years he was in and out of County. Petty stuff, same over and over, he had a pattern, mainly street hustling. Not an outstanding sensational personality, in fact kind of a fuzzy outline. The evidence is pretty bad against him and I don't think your cousin will get him off, even acting the way he does in the courtroom. If it hadn't been for you it would have been the usual method of postponement after postponement by the lawyers until the witnesses moved away or died, and three, five, seven years later there would be no case. That's the most common. That's what your nephew hoped for. Where the press is concerned, you caused great resentment by your articles, implying they were lazy and cynical, and now you are their target of opportunity. Quitman and I both tipped you off to the danger when you were doing the research. Now they are in a position to do their number on you. As I look at it, the young man's wife probably couldn't see who pushed him out the window. It could have been either one. The prostitute is a tough gal, really fierce, and has a record of involvement in homicides. The man is low-key, even dull. There is no good way to appraise these people's actions, they all happen in fever-land. . . . I thought my impressions would be useful, knowing how much is riding on the case for you. . . ."

Corde had given a full description of Ridpath in *Harper's.* He was a man of hillocky build, short in the neck, with a powerful intelligent Negro head. His brief arms were widely separated by his cylinder chest; his eyes, also wide-set, measured you with extreme detachment. Under this waiting broad-gauged gaze you were to say why you had asked to see him. He was distrustful at first. Close-shaven, his scalp went into furrows when he raised his brows and began to speak. His ears were small and neat. Although he was completely dressed, coat and tie, nothing seemed in place. After several meetings, Corde concluded that he had no more than two suits, a gray and a brown. He also wore a belted plaid trench coat—if gray on gray could be described as a plaid. The hands, overlapped by shirt cuffs and coat sleeves, were also neat, not big. His arms were, so to speak, crowded apart by the high-breasted width of his body. And his hands were certainly not the hands of a "brutalizer." They couldn't have done much harm to the killers who testified against him—not the hands alone. But of course the indictment was for aggravated battery; bludgeon, blackjack—what weapon he was said to have used Corde couldn't remember.

Ridpath knew what "doing a number" was, because the papers had done a great one on him. Front-page close-ups made him look like Primo Carnera in black, and swelled and distorted his face as if he had acromegaly—they had thrown Ridpath into the distortion furnace.

Corde sometimes said about himself that he was often subject to fits of vividness. In ordinary contact there was a commonsense indifference or inertia in what you saw. But in a vividness fit you had the hillocky man, the obese breast, small hands, short neck, cannonball head—all of it. And then came what Dewey Spangler, tempering sarcasm with sympathy, called "poetry," "impressionism," "exaltation." Corde couldn't say whether this was set off by Ridpath alone or by the Chicago into which his investigation of Ridpath had led him. Whatever the cause, the result was highly nervous, ragged, wild, uncontrolled, turbulent. Corde had tried to clear Ridpath's reputation, but Ridpath's gratitude and loyalty may have been severely tested when he read what Corde had written about black Chicago. The Dean himself may then have seemed to be somewhere in fever-land. And downtown, in higher circles of influence, people may have been saying, "What's with this Professor? What's he talking? His pilot light is gone out."

In this emotional state, "investigative reporting" was utterly out of the question. Wolf Quitman, Ridpath's lawyer, must also have been puzzled by Corde. He couldn't possibly have foreseen—well, who can foresee exaltation? And Quitman wasn't, himself, an exaltation type. He was tough, a very tough man who practiced criminal law. His toughness, however, was not of the repellent downtown Chicago sort. He was a clear-faced, ruddy, muscular, active man. Even his face was muscular. His office was nothing at all like an office, more like a comfortable living room. A woolen shawl, presumably knitted by his wife, was folded on the chintz-and-maple sofa, and there were begonia plants all over the place. The begonias were set on glass shelves across the windows. (Corde was bound to take in the presence of plants.) Evidently Quitman didn't care to see City Hall over the way—a full block of ponderous limestone. Quitman said to Corde, "Professor, do you know what County Jail was like when Ridpath took it over?"

"Some idea."

"It was on the barn boss system. The gang chiefs ran it. Hard for you and me to imagine what went on there. Only by general terms, the catchwords. Damn rough scene. Drugs, rackets, homosexual rape. Plenty of money changing hands. Buy damn near anything you wanted. And people beaten and tortured. Lots of weapons. If you could work loose any piece of metal, you made yourself a knife. If you soaked a rolled newspaper in the toilet and hung it from the window in winter, it froze into a club. You could kill a man with it, and when it thawed where was the evidence? Not exactly the Montessori school. Excuse me if I offend, but professor-criminologists *were* brought in, and they were afraid to go into the tiers and put down the barn bosses, or even look at them. You can't blame them for it, but they sat in the office and wrote reports, or articles for criminology journals, while the suicide figures went up and up, and murders higher and higher. They didn't dare go into the tiers of the jail and they couldn't take charge."

"Ridpath went in?" said Corde.

"Of course. That's just what happened. He's a plain kind of a man. He goes by duty. The Mayor put him there, so it was his duty to take charge."

"Nobody really expected that?"

"Who could have expected it? He'd probably say he assumed it was the necessary thing to do. No, he wouldn't even say that much. And the barn bosses respected him. He grew up on the streets himself. . . . He's a thoughtful fellow."

Corde said, "Those are his people?"

"It's an attachment he lives for. There are plenty of hustlers around who live off the black crisis. You've met 'em, Professor, we've all met 'em. Now, I've been going almost daily to that jail for years. There's where my clients are, that's a joint I'm totally familiar with. For Ridpath it was a sixteen-hour day, seven days a week, and that's a place that leaves all the rest of them behind."

"So you say he was living in his office?"

"Like a cause, Professor, not like a job. He cut down murders and suicides. I don't think anybody could control the rackets, beatings, stabbings, torture, buggering. He gave it the best try anybody could give. But that didn't impress the political guys much. What do you expect? This is a damn tough city, and damn proud of being tough, and the County is the worst—what you'd expect of Chicago."

"And Ridpath's mission was to clean it up," said Corde.

"Out of the question completely," said Quitman.

"You must have some feeling for that—the savage, subsavage condition. Otherwise you wouldn't be in this kind of practice."

Quitman did not care for this remark. He turned it aside.

"You know what was wrong? The man didn't remember to play ball, and you have to play ball, sir—you have to play it. County Jail has a big budget. Suppliers and contractors came to the office (you understand who was sending 'em) and he wouldn't do business. He said, 'If I don't buy your meat boned I can save sixty cents a pound. I'm having it boned right here.' Too many savings. He saved a million dollars out of his budget and refunded it to the county. That money was supposed to be spent. What? Save dough by using the kitchen staff? Fuck the kitchen staff! Rufus got a bad name with the top guys. They thought he might become dangerous politically, too. Why else was he refunding from his budget? That's why they gave him the business."

"Who?"

Plainly, Quitman was startled by the naiveté of this question. He made no answer. Corde later obtained one from a Lakeview alumnus downtown—Silky Limpopo, who had been a star high-jumper ("over the bar like silk") and was now himself a criminal lawyer and a longtime City Hall Watcher. "You asked him who. Quitman wouldn't dream of telling you. Whoever thought Ridpath might be dangerous, that's who. Quitman would be nuts to tell you, and if he told you, you'd be bananas to print it. How do you think those big guys make their moves? They usually do it one on one, over a drink, or while going from the eighth green to the ninth tee. If any money has to change hands, it also is one on one, cash in an envelope which goes into a box at the bank. In Ridpath's case I doubt even if money had to change hands. He was in the way, that was enough. And just in case he did have political ambitions, the best thing was to dump on him. You'd like it very much if Quitman named names and you could take a good hefty cut at them evildoers. I can see that, Professor," said Silky. "You and me, Al, we'd never get anywhere with the politics. That's why I'm only a watcher. The hanky-panky is all going to be secret history, which nobody will ever write, not just because those guys aren't writers, but because they love the secrets. . . . They love 'em! Me, I deal professionally with deviants and sociopaths, like Quitman. *They*'ll confide in you, sometimes. But the secrets at the top in politics—never!"

"Oh, I won't be writing any exposé, Silky. No scoops," said Corde.

"What will you be doing?"

"Personalities, scenes, backgrounds, feelings, tones,

colors . . . Just between you and me, I wouldn't have been surprised if the strain of sixteen to eighteen hours a day in that place finally got to Ridpath. There must have been plenty of provocation, times when you'd want to lay violent hands on somebody." But Corde discovered that he was only speaking to himself.

Quitman himself would not talk too much. He and Corde had sat silently for a time in the bright office, figuring each other out. The garden of red begonias was now taking the warmth of the sun and the knitted shawl showed its red and iridescent fleece. What did such people make of Corde when he visited them? He was obviously a quiet dean type, no Watergate investigator. During his chat with Quitman, Corde remembered the close-mouthedness of G. O. O'Meara, whom he had interviewed at Meatcutters' Hall just last week. O'Meara, about ninety years old, wouldn't give Corde the time of day. And there had been no talk of the knife or the sledgehammer, the shambles, nor of strikes, nor of scabs, nor of company police. O'Meara was now a public man emeritus. Feeble, not quite with it, he still cut a figure among the big shots of Chicago. Beautifully respectful to the old guy, almost filial, they telephoned him in his meatcutters' palace. He went to board meetings, he attended banquets. There were testimonial plaques and scrolls and inscriptions on silver and bronze all over the place. The O'Meara who received the Dean was proud that he was a poet; full time, now. He presented Corde with a book of his verses—love sonnets to his wife. Yes! How the old boy had preened the last of his feathers. He made Corde listen to a poem he had recited on the Jack Paar show. His breath was perfumed with the penny candy he sucked continually. There were jars of jujubes in front of him. Not one of Corde's questions was answered, and when he got up to leave, the old man said to him, "So you wanted me to talk, but I didn't tell you a thing, did I?" Ancient O'Meara, packed with guile, terribly pleased with himself! Why should an important man in Chicago give information to any punk journalist who came along, calling himself a professor?

"They wouldn't let Ridpath be," said Quitman. "There were five grand jury investigations. One was federal, because he handled government money. There was nothing on him."

"But those people were persistent? . . ."

"His big automobile is about his only valuable asset. Grand juries being so easy to manipulate, it meant he was really clean. Somebody must've been real puzzled."

Corde had had frequent talks with Ridpath. Ridpath at first maintained an attitude of detachment, but presently became warmer. He seemed in the end to make Corde out to be some sort of delicate spirit. He couldn't quite see what he was after, but he said at last, "I might be able to help if I understood what you wanted to do."

"I can send you my notes. They're pretty full. If you have time to read them."

"Oh, plenty of time," said Ridpath.

They had been walking in a cold parking lot to Ridpath's giant automobile. Ridpath put his key, first, not into the door, but into a lock installed in the fender, which turned off the alarm system. The Cordes also had an alarm system. At home their doors and windows were wired.

8

Abruptly, Bucharest again—Minna burst into the room. All too plainly the news was bad.

"They phoned me from the hospital."

"They, who?"

"The women from intensive care. One of them. What she asked was, did I want them to light a candle."

"I see."

It was the end, then. A matter of hours.

"I told her, Of course! Please."

"Yes. Certainly you did."

"I didn't say anything to Gigi about this. You won't either, will you?"

"No. I'm staying put right here, going nowhere anyway."

Minna wore the maroon or mulberry-colored jersey pants suit. She had lost so much weight that the belt had slipped from the tunic down low on her hips. She gave no sign that she wanted comfort from Corde. She was right to keep her balance in her own way. If he had put an arm about her shoulders it would have been more for his own sake than for hers. Anyway, she went out, again abruptly, as he was preparing to rise, so he sat down again with a sudden sense that the chair cushion under him had been shaped to Valeria's figure. It was the same with the clothes in the armoire; they hung there with the shapes she had given them. If he got into bed for warmth, it would be her bed. All this combined to keep him fixed—stalled. He considered what to do. There seemed nothing to do but what he

173

had been doing. Perhaps more effectively. But what was there to be effective about? He didn't have it in him to conceive how he might do better. He put his fingertips under his glasses and rubbed his eyes. His dependency on these goggles made him recognize how much he was organized for observation and comprehension. The organization, however, was insufficient. The present moment brought this home to him. And just now his thoughts took their shape from Valeria, just as the cushion under him and the clothing in the armoire did. Corde's conjecture was that she was now unconscious. Vital signs must be diminishing, or the women wouldn't have lighted candles. Those must be burning in the outer room, away from the oxygen. Medical technicians offering to light a candle—imagine! And Minna, whose subject was astronomy, so badly wanting it. Please, do!

Despite the great weight of these conjectures, pictures, he leafed again through the papers spread over the desk.

To resume: The notes he had sent to Ridpath had gone into his articles with little revision, in the end. He didn't care to develop them much. They were painful. His motive had been to avoid playing up to readers, making it all too easy for them to say, "You see how bad we've become—all those appalling ghettos."

This was not what the Dean had really felt during the many days he spent in courtrooms and hospitals. Raising the indignation level—*that* easy satisfaction—was not his purpose. No, Dean Albert Corde, exercising his citizen's right to see how justice was administered in his native city—he recorded exotic scenes in the courtrooms at Harrison and Kedzie. However, all the exotics were as native as himself. On his own turf, which was also theirs, he found a wilderness wilder than the Guiana bush. The lawyers had let him sit in the front row with them. These were chicken-feed lawyers waiting for the Bench to assign them to a case. You could pick up a buck here. Some of these were elderly men, down on their luck. The younger ones were built like professional athletes, flashy dressers who went to hair stylists, not to barbers. Beautifully combed, like pretty ladies or dear small boys in Cruikshank's Dickens illustrations, they might have been either thugs or bouncers.

Called up by the court clerk, groups of defendants and lawyers formed and dissolved all day long from endless dockets—dope pushers, gun toters (everybody had a gun), child molesters, shoplifters, smackheads, purse snatchers, muggers, rapists, arsonists, wife beaters, car thieves, pimps bailing out their whores. People were all dressed up. Their glad rags were seldom clean. Young men wore high-waisted, flaring leatherette coats and high, puffed, long-billed caps; red-and-yellow wooden platform shoes, or Wild Bill Hickok dude boots; or crisscrossed their shins with candy-box ribbons. They wore dashikis, ponchos, cloaks, African amulets, rings and beads—symbolic ornaments symbolizing nothing. There were brash strong women, subtle black small women who had little to say. Their skulls sometimes were terraced, very curious; or else their hair was teased out, dyed, worked into small viper-tangle braids; put up in blue, pink, yellow plastic rollers. For all this gaiety of color, the gloom was very deep. No one seemed able to explain what he had done, who he was. It was all: "You brought us here, you tell us who we are, and what you want with us." Where did this gun come from? It was lying on a shelf. Where? In a burned-out abandoned house where somebody was selling liquor on a plank counter. How did you come to be there? I dunno.

You have before you an offender. This one is white, androgyne in outline, male in dress, open-mouthed, mute, idiotic, frightened, too old to be a boy (the hair is thin). The seat of his pants hangs down, full and dead, and his hands are lame at his sides. The bristles of his dewlaps are shaven in strips. He wears a turtleneck. His lawyer says he has no criminal record, Your Honor, never held a job but keeps house for his father and his brothers, factory workers. It's a motherless household, Your Honor. Regarding the packages of Tums he put in his pockets at the supermarket, he pleads guilty, but it was just one of those once-in-a-lifetime things. The lawyer says, in effect, Look at this poor slob forty-year-old adolescent with these fat tits in a dirty jersey; if you send him to County Jail they'll tear him to bits. They'll beat him, they'll burn him with cigarettes for the fun of it, they'll sodomize him day and night. He'll come out a cripple. Better just give him a scare and send him home. The judge nods, agrees and says, "What if I sentenced you—do you know what they'd do to you in jail?"

The next case is one of the sexual abuse of small children. Pictures are produced of screaming kids whose faces are spattered, covered with gobs of semen. Who would do this? And who had the presence of mind to take such pictures, waiting until the thing had been done? Some undercover-agent photographer?

In his articles, the Dean had had much to say about these "whirling lives." He was sorry now about that. He thought he had interrupted his accounts of County Jail, County Hospital and Robert Taylor Homes far too often with his unwanted and misplaced high-mindedness. On rereading, he himself passed quickly over the generalizing, philosophizing passages. They were irritating. He wouldn't, as a reader, have bothered to figure them out. Straight narrative was a relief and a consolation. "I go with Mr. Ridpath to the Taylor Homes." (Mr. Ridpath, bareheaded, is wearing his gray-within-gray plaid coat. Men who knew him at County Jail wave hello. There are snipers in the upper stories. Also, gangs are operating everywhere.) "He introduces me to Mr. Jones, one of the building engineers in the maintenance department. Vandalism here runs to more than a million dollars a year, one-third of the project's operating budget. 'We had ninety commodes in the warehouse last month, now we are down to two. How do they break the commodes at such a rate? Well, sir, being afraid to go at night to the incinerator drop on each floor, they flush their garbage down the toilet. The large bones stick in the pipes; your plumber tries to snake them out, and there goes your bowl, cracked. Then there're light bulbs. We don't use glass anymore, we use unbreakable plastic. Children hold newspaper torches to them and they melt away. The elevators—those are the biggest headaches of all. They are not built for such hard use or abuse. It's not just that people urinate in them. . . .'" They commit assault, robbery, rape in them. "'We have had young men getting on the top of elevator cabs, opening the hatch and threatening to pour in gas, to douse people with gasoline and set them afire. Project guards, trapped like this, have had to surrender their guns.'" Mr. Jones, black, a graduate of Tuskegee, is offered the protection of a pseudonym. His large sensitive eyes observe his fingertips on the edge of the desk as he speaks. Then he rearranges his documents. These are facts that should be known, and as Mr. Ridpath vouches for the Dean, Mr. Jones agrees to talk, but he doesn't feel quite safe.

Here in Eastern Europe, the morning's rain had turned to snow. The flakes were large—their shapes made Corde think of contact lenses—but as soon as they touched the pavements it was all over for them.

He turned again to the passages his mother-in-law had evidently read repeatedly. Some of these were items culled from the papers. Nine inmates of County Jail on November 25 sawed their way out of a segregated tier, handcuffed the guards, and then tried to climb down with a ladder of knotted bed sheets. Eight of them had been caught. The ninth, a man named Upshaw, escaped. This Upshaw had been confined to a state mental institution because psychiatrists had found him incompetent to stand trial in the decapitation murders of a man and a woman and the strangling of their young daughter. Escaping from the "mental facility," he had been apprehended and sent to County. Now he was at large. Six of the eight who were caught had been facing murder charges.

You see (Corde saw), you begin to lose contact with human beings and with the world. You experience spiritual loneliness. And of course there are the classics of this condition to study—or rather to mull over: Dostoevsky's apathy-with-intensity, and the rage for goodness so near to vileness and murderousness, and Nietzsche and the Existentialists, and all the rest of that. Then you tire of this preoccupation with the condition of being cut off and it seems better to go out and see at first hand the big manifestations of disorder and take a fresh reading from them. Not quite sufficient to say that at this moment of history the philosophical problems are identical with the political ones. This is true. It's okay. Only it's insufficient. You had better go see in detail exactly what is happening. But there I go again, and never mind that now. He turned the pages of the magazine and found that his mother-in-law had drawn double lines in the margins beside his account of the death of Gene Lewis at Twenty-sixth and California.

Brought from jail to the Criminal Courts Building for sentencing, Lewis was heavily but carelessly guarded by the sheriff's police, so that when his girl friend asked permission to give him a book—to divert him (the legal arguments would be long)—permission was granted, and she handed him a copy of *Ivanhoe*. This had been hollowed out, and there was a gun in it. As Lewis was handcuffed, the book was stuck under his arm. Corde had later been allowed to examine this copy of *Ivanhoe*. It was a boys' edition, with colored, glossy illustrations. The inside had been carved out with razor blades, but smoothly, a work of art, of love. The woman had been described by witnesses as "a high-style Twiggy-type chick with three-inch artificial eyelashes, and orange dust all over her cheeks. She was very slender, about six feet tall, she wore long skinny boots and was

gorgeous, out of this world." Why should the armed
guards, those Chicago payrollers, bother to open a
book—any book? Let the guy have his book. Once
seated, Lewis snapped off the rubber bands under the
defendant's table. The woman had also put in a key. He
unlocked the handcuffs and took out the magnum. He
lined up all five beerbellies against the wall and dis-
armed them. He didn't shoot anyone, but to prove to
Judge Makowski that the magnum was not a toy, he
fired a single shot into the floor. Then he raced out of
the courtroom. He dumped the guards' guns in a trash
basket and jumped into an elevator. But the elevator
was going up, not down. When he rushed out to change
on the next floor, he ran bang into a group of detectives
from Area Four. They shot him ten times in the head.
Paramedics from the Cermak Hospital came for the
corpse with a black plastic bag. The woman was never
identified. To look for her was a sheer waste of time.

Students at the college had objected, predictably, to
much that Corde had written. He had described broad-
daylight rapes and robberies, sexual acts in public
places, on the seats of CTA buses, on the floors of
public waiting rooms, men on Sheridan Road spraying
automobile fenders with their urine. So the students
called a meeting to denounce the Dean for writing such
things. Miss Porson had gone there, and sat in the hall
to take notes. She was pierced with excitement, afraid
(she might have been identified as a spy), and she was
indignant. But the militant students did not matter
much to Corde. He said to Miss Porson, "The usual
thing, looking for an issue, trying to catch me out. And
I brought it on myself for 'going public.' But by next
week I'll be forgotten." Miss Porson was wounded (so
deeply wounded, she said) for his sake. They had
misunderstood, they didn't know what a good man Mr.
Corde was. If you could trust her sympathetic heart,
the Dean was an angel. Well, you couldn't trust her
sympathetic heart—sorry, but she flattered him with
these flights of generous passion; she flattered herself,

too, in her dramatic declarations. The Dean had his
vanities. He could count the ways, if you asked. But he
was not, if his observations were true, exceptionally
vain. Besides, he had a thing about objectivity. Perhaps
impartiality was a more accurate term. As age, experience, and wear and tear reduced him physically, they
also revealed to him a strong preference for disinterest-
ed judgments. It was nothing like nonattachment, not
negative objectivity. He was objectivity (no, impartiality) intoxicated. The student militants, a small group
now, revolutionary Marxists (like the ones recently
murdered in Greensboro by Klan and Nazi riflemen),
passed a resolution declaring that the Dean was a racist
and that he owed a public apology "to Black, Puerto
Rican and Mexican toilers" for making them look "like
animals and savages."

Well, you wanted a lead apron and other protective
devices when you approached all this dangerous stuff.
It gave off deadly radiations and shocks of high voltage.
It wasn't as if Corde had been unaware of such dangers,
either, as if he had come out of his ivory tower after ten
years of seclusion unprepared, innocent, vulnerable,
discovering what monstrous destruction the gods had
unleashed. It was not like that at all. He had been
getting around, reading the papers, keeping up with the
criminologists, the economists, the social theorists, the
urban analysts, historians, yes, and the philosophers
and poets—he was one of our contemporaries, after all,
and a wide reader. Wider than most. But he thought he
would say something about this Chicago scene drawing
on his own experience, making fresh observations,
referring to his own feelings, and using his own language. The steps by which he reached this decision
were certainly peculiar. When you retraced them, they
took you back to sources like Baudelaire and Rilke,
even Montesquieu and Vico; also Machiavelli; also
Plato. Yes, why not? He had left the Paris *Herald* in
order to give more attention to these great sources. Did

he want to write about Chicago? For once, it would be done in style.

Without much success, he had tried to explain this to Minna. She wished him well. Her own interests were mainly astronomical. He was saying to her at breakfast about a year ago that he had been rereading the wartime letters of Rilke. He quoted to her: "Everything visible flung into the boiling abysses to be melted down . . . but hearts—shouldn't they have the power to hang suspended, to preserve themselves in a great cloud?" Minna seemed to be interested in this. But you couldn't be certain that you really had her attention. Still he continued. He said, "Rilke wouldn't discuss the war. He felt betrayed by his friends when they insisted on talking about it. Not just because the present was too brutal and too formless to be talked about, but because you could only talk about it in newspaper expressions. When you did that, he said, you felt disgust and horror at your own mouth. But then there was So-and-so, who said that you departed for the eternal only from Grand Central Station. This was in the day of the trains. What he meant, of course, is that the contemporary is your only point of departure. Hearts, sure, must have the power to hang suspended, but they can't do it indefinitely. Shouldn't . . ." He stopped. The morning must have been ill-chosen. For Minna was astrophysically removed from him. The signs were too plain to miss.

So he tested these truths of his against the blight of Chicago. By no means was it all blight. There was business Chicago sitting in its skyscrapers, monumental banking Chicago, corporate electronic computerized Chicago. There was historical Chicago, about which he wrote many curious things—speaking of the old neighborhoods, their atmosphere, their architecture, the trees, soil, water, the unexpectedly versatile light of the place. He surveyed the views of noteworthy visitors—Oscar Wilde, Rudyard Kipling, the famous Stead,

whose book *If Christ Came to Chicago* contained vivid
and valuable pages. It wasn't as if Corde had made a
beeline for the blight. Nor did he write about it because
of the opportunities it offered for romantic despair; nor
in a spirit of middle-class elegy or nostalgia. He was
even aware that the population moving away from
blighted areas had improved its condition in new
neighborhoods. But also it was fear that had made it
move. Also, it was desolation that was left behind,
endless square miles of ruin.

Occasionally he had tried at the breakfast table
before they went their separate ways to tell Minna what
he was up to. "Rufus Ridpath wants to help out. He
thinks it's important. He sends me lists of people to talk
to, and places that I should look at."

He should have known from the fixed look of his
wife's eyes not to talk to her now. Was he trying to
challenge the stars? She was concerned about her
husband (he was going into dangerous neighborhoods),
but it would have been wiser to postpone this discussion. She took a sharp tone with him. She said, "It's not
a good idea to get in so deep with this Ridpath. You
may look like two of a kind—out to get the establishment."

"Yes, he took a terrible beating. He's burnt up. He'd
like to get back at his enemies. I sympathize with him.
His feeling for his people is real. Are they part of
American society, or are they going to be eliminated
from it? To him this is not a theoretical question. If as
many as fifteen million people have already accepted to
be stoned out of their minds—and it isn't only the junk
use, but the anarchy, which is a sort of narcotic. And it
isn't just that he knows this—he *is* it himself, humanly."

"And why is he helping you—because he likes you?"

"Maybe he does. And maybe he has naive respect for
academics—thinks they are what they're supposed to
be. Morality and justice is their trade. After all, there
are libraries filled with marvelous books."

"Are you really talking about him, or about why you should take all this on?"

"Let me see if I can make it clear."

But that was absurd. He couldn't explain himself. It hadn't really been a matter of choice. Something had come over him. He went over the passages marked by Valeria to see whether they formed a pattern. She would have been more interested in his emotions, his character, than in Chicago.

There was, for instance, a long description of County Hospital.

Dr. Fulcher, the hospital's Negro chief, had suggested that Corde might find the kidney dialysis unit interesting. Valeria had heavily underlined his account of it.

The ancient County Hospital, yellow, broad and squat. The surrounding neighborhoods have decayed and fallen down. In the plain of collapse, this mass stands almost alone. Beyond the clearings the giant forms of the business district are gathered close. Between the antennae of the Sears Tower a rotating light blinks out. The weather is gray. The pulsating signal is fluid, evidently made of metals and crystals whose names only engineers might recognize.

I am guided by a Filipino nurse through old tunnels, baked dry by mammoth boilers. The pipes drip rusty water. By the door of the morgue, wheeled stretchers line the walls. The dried blood would be scraped from them if there were staff enough, but there is no money. In these subterranean passages there are alternating zones of heat and chill. Paleotechnic furnaces hugely branching out send warmth up into the ancient wards. The tiny Filipino woman brings me to a room in which reclining chairs are covered with clean sheets. Beside each chair is a complicated device, glass within glass, the inmost compartment filled with blood. We stand and watch the purification process. Hooked into a machine, a large black man in worn work clothes is only semiconscious. The seaman's watch cap has slipped from his head. His face is hairy, not bearded but unshaven, his big lips cannot close even when he tries to speak. The small woman whispers to me. Kidney patients seldom sleep well, and while their blood is being cleansed they sometimes fall into a stupor. The process takes four hours to complete. Some of the patients, their kidneys destroyed by a variety of diseases, are brought in several times a week. Lives have been extended for as long as ten years.

Kidney patients look puffy. The legs and arms of the veterans are disfigured by surgically produced fistulas. Blood vessels are fused to increase circulation and these conjoined or grafted veins and arteries make great painful lumps which have to be soaked daily. A woman is now brought in who can no longer be treated through the arms or the legs. Her fistula is on the chest. The cabdriver who picks up and returns all these dialysis patients is an enormous black woman in red jersey trousers. Her feet seem quite small. Her shoes have high heels. Her straightened hair hangs to her shoulders. She wears a cabby's cap and a quilted jacket. Solicitous, she supports the sufferer, settles her into her chair. These passenger-patients are her charges, her friends. She wheels forward the television set. The sick woman asks for Channel Two, and sighs and settles back and passes out.

Some of the patients are bald from chemotherapy. One old man has lost his black pigmentation. All that remains of his blackness is an astonishing mole here and there on his naked head, a strange man to see but decent, sensible, and his thoughts in good order. A retired plumber by trade, nonunion, he still takes an occasional job. But then an even older man is brought in who looks altogether senseless. The guide whispers to me: "Dementia—not with it." They seat this old man, and he waits, his jaw undershot, and his head, from which the hair appears to have been scorched, is hanging forward. The technician who takes care of him is a Chinese woman. She works with beautiful skill, washing the lumpy arm with disinfectants, then plugging in the tubes, light and quick, no sign of pain from the old man. But then she blunders. A valve has been left open on the tray, and immediately everything is covered with blood. The suddenness of this silent appearance and the volume of blood with which the tray fills makes my heart go faint. I am almost overcome by a thick and sweet nausea, as if my organs were melting like chocolate in hot weather. But the nurse, working under the blood, plugs the vent, stops the flow, gathers up the soaking napkins, spreads clean ones, wipes the tubes. This act of getting rid of the blood is performed with professional mastery, almost occult. I am astonished by the Chinese woman's lightness and speed. As for the old man, he has noticed nothing. The Filipino nurse says, "You are a little pale. Do you want to go?" As we walk away, she tells me about herself. She is a nun and belongs to a nursing order.

It wasn't just the blood. If it had been ordinary blood. But it was poisoned blood. It is said that these people pin their hopes on kidney transplants. But that will never happen. And these are dead men and women. The metabolic wastes obviously affect their brains. Nevertheless, these nurses and attendants are curiously emotional, extraordinarily tender towards these patients whom their machines keep alive, they manifest a wonderful but also amorphous pity, a powerful but somehow indiscriminate love for these people.

Dr. Fulcher, County's chief, wears a beige silk shirt of Oriental design, open at the throat, anything but negligent in style, and a fawn-colored suit. A big, graceful man, he is bald; the white hairs of his sideburns are wonderfully trimmed. About his neck hangs a pear-shaped pendant of brownish onyx, and his fingers display large, intricate silver rings. He has a great sense of what it means to be at the top. Vividly articulate, he is in command here, he has a presence. Where white men would be diffident, he is exuberant, a regal populist in style. After all, he is at the head of this vast (sinking) institution, and he acts it. He is a great politician, he bears himself like an artist.

No wonder *Harper's* lost millions of dollars, printing this sort of stuff. So Dewey Spangler would have said, much amused. And Corde would have answered—but he didn't answer, after all. The day was almost over, and he thought, I've spent too much time over this stuff. Why don't we go for a walk? There's still an hour of daylight.

He said to Minna, "What about a breath of fresh air?"

But there were cousins expected at four.

Gigi said, "Wouldn't you like a cup of the Twining's tea you brought from Chicago?"

9

The thing happened for which, after all, they had come. Well, Corde said to himself, they were here to see Valeria—no? Blunter, to see her off? In spite of the Colonel, the purpose was achieved—no?

The hospital called while they were at breakfast next morning. Old Cousin Dincutza answered the telephone. Corde also came into the small parlor. The old woman stood stooping, holding her lowered head to the phone. She wagged her arm as if to forbid him to come nearer. She made signals with her aged face. Yes, here it was, it had happened. She put down the instrument and said in a low voice, *"Elle est morte. Valeria est morte!"* Then she hurried past him to the dining room, where he heard her reporting to the women.

When he came in, Minna was looking sternly absent-minded. She did not seem to need comfort from her husband. She had made her preparations for this. She said, "You were right, Albert. If we hadn't gone that night I would never have seen her again. Just this morning I talked to Dr. Moldovanu. Mother died a little later, just before nine."

"I see. Well, what is there to do now? I suppose you've thought what to do."

"Yes, of course I have. Tonight is Christmas Eve."

"It is, isn't it. I've lost track."

"We'll try to set the funeral for the day after Christmas. We'll have to make the arrangements immediately. Traian will help. I discussed it with Ioanna last night. Petrescu came to the door just a while ago—before we sat down to breakfast. I talked to him for about five minutes. He already knew she was dead, I think."

"Petrescu?"

"He keeps in touch. He's always been like this. He watches from a distance. He made some suggestions about what to do."

"What needs to be done? Death certificate? Undertaker? I'll make the rounds with you today."

"Petrescu gave me a number where I can reach him during the morning. And there's Dincutza. Being over eighty, she knows a lot about such things. Whatever we have to do, cigarettes will make it easier."

"I must get more Kents."

"That's what I meant. Traian will drive you over to the Intercontinental. But will you see what Gigi's doing?"

Tanti Gigi was in the kitchen with Dincutza. Corde found them sobbing there. Then Gigi told Corde that she wanted to go below to see Ioanna, to tell her that it had happened. The elevator was stuck. On the cold staircase he put a shawl over Gigi's shoulders and helped her down to the concierge's lodge. It didn't make much sense that Gigi should go to Ioanna, whose job it was to tell the police everything. But why should sense be made? In the concierge's cavern, the two women sank to the small bed together, embracing and weeping in the alcove. Valeria's photograph was on the night table, and on the wall were pictures of the dictator and his wife. Corde passed again through the lobby, where workmen with hoes raised a dust, mixing cement for the cracked walls. He climbed back to the apartment. Minna, very thin and stern, staring past everyone, black beneath the eyes, was discussing details of the funeral with Dincutza.

Traian had come upstairs. He sat slumped in a straight-backed chair by the door, buckled up in his fancy multi-zippered leather jacket and being seemly— that is, decently downcast in the house of mourning. He was completely at Minna's disposal. He had plenty of time for her. It was no simple matter to obtain a death certificate. First you had to go to the hospital. You needed releases, authorizations, any number of official papers. "We'll have to drive all over town," said Minna. Corde was grateful to this Traian with the Mexican wisps at the corners of his conspicuous lips. He had taken the whole day off, Minna said. After Christmas he would be available, too.

More cigarettes were bought at the valuta shop. A pack or two of king-sized Kents saved dreary hours of waiting. From the Intercontinental they drove to the hospital, and after that to five or six government buildings—Corde, riding in the front seat of the Dacia, lost count. Traian knew what he was doing. Strange, what an expert he turned out to be. Traian in his leather cap and jacket, and his eyes like the green pulp of Concord grapes, was unbelievably effective. No waiting. He went to the head of the line. He presented himself at the desk boldly, making the essential signals, and putting down the cigarettes. He was a solid young man. His belly gave him more pull with gravitational forces than slighter people had, Corde thought. He took charge of all the papers. Minna paid the fees, signed the papers. She was firm, really very strong. Corde would never have guessed how strong she would turn out to be. She had no practical abilities, she had never needed them. Valeria had done all that. But now Valeria's powers had passed to her (hitherto) absentminded daughter. This is how she'll attend to me, too, Corde thought. It was an entirely commonsensical reflection; it hadn't the slightest emotional weight.

By early afternoon all the necessary documents had been collected. In record time, Corde would have said. Traian drove to the crematorium through a freezing rain. Workers' housing blocks and government buildings were covered with huge pictures of the President. His face, five stories tall, flapped and floated in gusts of rain. This must have been his way of resisting Christmas sentiment. He interposed himself.

Then the crematorium, standing on a hilltop, a huge domed building. Just as you would expect, the grounds were planted with small cypresses. Flanking the doors there were bas-relief figures of Graces in mourning, part Puvis de Chavannes, part socialist realism. Here as elsewhere, Traian seemed to know just what to do. Corde and Minna followed him to the desk (there was no office), where they began to make arrangements with the managing comrade. This man was dressed for the chill of the enormous circular place. He wore sweaters, shawls, an overcoat, an astrakhan hat. The astrakhan was a phony. He was not at all difficult, this official, not gloomy in the least, in fact he was more than normally cheerful, sociable—he was gabby. The paper work was done by his assistant, a young woman in the seventh or eighth month of pregnancy. Pregnancy was said to keep the body warm, the effect of double metabolism, or so Corde had heard. Anyway, she appeared unaffected by the cold—she alone. There was a green Nuremberg stove, but the comrade manager had it all to himself. Another mourner had already come up behind Corde. His coat was buttoned tightly across his belly; he was a stout man, very big, with a red, blustering face, but that was probably an effect of grief aggravated by the terrible cold. His blue bubble eyes were fixed on the tile stove. He reached over Corde's shoulders, trying to warm his distorted large fingers. Meantime the seated comrade manager was

receiving slips of paper from his assistant and using two
kinds of mucilage to stick them to the documents—
documents upon documents—and talking nonstop. He
asked whether a priest would perform a service. Priest?
Minna turned to Corde. No priest. Valeria was religious but there would be prayers at the cemetery when
her ashes were placed in the family headstone. All that
had been prepared by Valeria herself. Then did the
family want music? There were two choices, the Cho-
pin funeral march or, equally appropriate, Beethoven
—the slow movement from the Third Symphony. Four
minutes on tape. Minna chose the Beethoven. The
astrakhan hat nodded and nodded, writing on diligent-
ly, holding the pen in his thumb and two middle fingers,
the index pointing forward, riding above the papers.
Next, very courteous, anticipating baksheesh from the
American husband, he led the way to the center of the
hall. This was where services were held. There were
two single files of chairs for the principal mourners.
Under the center of the dome, in icy gloom, was
something that resembled a long metal barrel. It
opened longitudinally. This was the bier. When the
halves of the barrel closed, the body was mechanically
lowered for cremation—same mechanism in double
action. In this one spot, heat rose from below. Corde
and Minna drew away from it.

There were flowers here, all cyclamens. There wasn't
light enough to distinguish their colors. The plants had
been placed on the floor. Here they thrived like
anything—low temperatures; just what they wanted.
Above them, square containers of ashes were stacked
like canisters of Twining's tea. Each carried a photograph, and dates of birth and death, and an appropriate
legend: "Militant," "Engineer," "Teacher." So many
contemporary faces, like pedestrians snapped by a
sidewalk photographer. These must have been victims
of the earthquake. Witnesses said that tall new buildings had turned to powder as they collapsed. But why
were these tea boxes still here? Because there was no

consecrated ground prepared for them? Traian explained this to Minna. The regime was short of cemeteries. Graves were at a premium. But why should there be such congestion—wasn't there plenty of land beyond the suburbs? Trembling Dincutza had spoken of this at home. She criticized no one, of course. She only said that Valeria had bought graves in the year of Dr. Raresh's death, when she was still in the government. She had raised the granite monument and built two benches. She owned several other plots as well. One had been promised to Engineer Rioschi, who used to drive her quite often to the cemetery to tend the Doctor's grave. Dincutza stated shrilly (sometimes this kind old woman resembled Picasso's horse in *Guernica*), *"Nous savons combien elle aimait son mari."* Rioschi, you understand, didn't want to be stacked with these other cans in the crematorium when his time came, so he had been glad to drive Valeria. That had been their deal. He was a single man, you see.

The gray astrakhan now moved more quickly before them. Corde assumed that he was leading them to a chapel of some sort, a place where friends could view the body before the service. But no such thing. He brought them into a curved corridor where there were curtained recesses, tall and dim. Then Corde was astonished to see a pair of shoes sticking through the green-tinted transparent curtains. He was brushed by the soles, by the feet of a corpse. Next were a woman's feet, in high heels. In these cold recesses or cribs, corpses were laid out in their best clothes. Each one lay just visible in a shallow coffin shaped like a small punt and lined with dimity stuff, not much more than cheesecloth or insect netting. One tall corpse with a black Balkan mustache had his homburg set beside his head. He clasped his briefcase to his chest.

Lord, I am ignorant and a stranger to my fellow man. I had thought that I understood things pretty well. Not so.

The comrade manager said that he had wanted to

show Minna where Valeria might be brought from the hospital next day. "No, thank you, no," said Minna.

The hour for the service was fixed for ten o'clock on the morning of the twenty-sixth.

The funeral parlor was next. Coordination was the problem—the hearse to be sent to the hospital, the body to be ready for it.

In the dark shop, finished coffins were stacked against the walls. They were only half-coffins, really, lidless. An elderly workman had one on his trestle, tacking in the flimsy two-thread lining. Careful tucks made a simple ruffle along the top. Backed up against the tall tile stove, the place of privilege, an obese old woman in multiple sweaters and a circular fur hat repeated the order hoarsely as she wrote it out. The wisps of her hat matched the hairs of her whiskers. Her lips worked inwards continually. She was not chewing; she had no teeth. She seemed to be tasting her own mouth. She ordered the men about, growling and bullying, but she became happy when Minna paid her off and Traian gave her two packages of American cigarettes. As she shoved the money into the drawer she simultaneously heaved up her clumsy body to reach for the Kents.

Corde said, "Do we go home now?"

"Yes, there's nothing else to do today, except to see if I can place an announcement in the papers. That's the next thing. Then Gigi and I have to choose Valeria's clothes for the funeral. Traian will take them to the hospital."

They steered back through the freezing streets. The only heat he had felt all day came from under the bier. Yesterday he had suggested to Minna that they go out for fresh air. Now he wanted only to get back to his room.

Returning, they found the dining room table surrounded by old cousins. They came with small presents for the mourners. Gigi, wearing a black dress, was unwrapping cakes and bottles at the buffet. The cakes, like the old ladies who had baked them, were dimly spicy. Gigi told Corde, "You had two calls, one from overseas—I think your college in Chicago. They said they would call again." And the other? Dewey Spangler, thought Corde, reporting on his efforts with the White House.

He did not linger among the cousins. He felt used up; the round of offices, the crematorium, the coffin shop, had tired him deeply and the labor of French conversation was too much for him.

The cousins didn't really want to talk to him, anyway; they were only being polite. This was no time to swap French phrases. He went to his refuge, his sanctuary, his cell. He had his private bottle there, and his bed; the flowers also. Towards the flowers he felt slightly negative now, as if they had betrayed him by blooming at the crematorium. An effort of reconciliation might be necessary. The irrationality of this did not disturb him. If this was how he was, this was how he was.

The telephone rang and Minna looked in and said, "For you, my dear."

He picked up the instrument. "Albert? It's Dewey. So far, no luck with those Georgia yokels. I can keep trying. . . ."

"Thanks, Dewey. No point now. . . ."

"Oh? Sorry. When did she pass away?"

"Early this morning. Funeral the day after Christmas."

"You may not want to keep our date," said Dewey. "I'd understand."

"When are you leaving?"

"Evening of the twenty-sixth."

"Why not the same afternoon—after the funeral? I probably won't be needed then. There'll be lots of callers."

"Yes, that makes good sense. Not a bad idea to get away for a while and have a drink. It must all be completely foreign."

"Not completely."

"Not insofar as you liked that old woman."

"I did, yes."

"Foreign—I mean, to be an American in a foreign family. That I call an unusual experience. You didn't tell me that Minna's mother had been a friend of Ana Pauker, and knew Thorez and Tito. I found this out yesterday from an old-timer. He told me about her and that whole Stalinist generation."

"These people were no Stalinists. They were just unpolitical people who got into politics." Corde was beginning to wonder whether Dewey didn't scent a story in Valeria. After all, he owed his syndicate two columns a week.

"How is your wife taking it?" said Dewey.

"At the moment she's busy with arrangements. Doing fine."

"Yes," said Dewey. "It tends to hit one later."

"I've often heard that said."

"Poor girl. Say, before I forget, there's no news out of Chicago about your case. Unless you've heard from other sources."

"It's the holiday lull. Jurors would raise hell if they didn't get their Christmas."

"Well, Albert, I'll check back to see if it's convenient, after the funeral. I'm pretty busy here, but there's always a sort of gap before airport time."

Hanging up, Corde glanced into the dining room but didn't show himself. There were bowls of eggplant salad on the table. Dinner would be late, after the cousins went home. You didn't get much to eat here. Leftovers. But in the West everybody ate altogether too much and sometimes he imagined that overfeeding made people toxic, slowed their thinking. He was trying to account for the recent increase in his own mental acuity. It now seemed to him that he was thinking more clearly here. Evidently fasting and disruption of routine were beneficial. But if his ideas were more clear they were also much more singular. For example: Valeria was certainly dead. She had died, and she was dead, and last arrangements were being made. But he couldn't say that she was dead to him. It wouldn't have been an accurate statement. One might call this a comforting illusion, a common form of weakness, but in fact there was nothing at all comforting about it, he could take no comfort in it. Nor was it anything resembling an illusion. It was more like an internal fact of which he became conscious. He hadn't been looking for it. And he was not prompted to find a "rational" cause for this. Rationality of this sort left him cold. He owed it nothing. It was particularity that interested him. . . .

Again the phone sounded off, and Corde picked it up. He had a hunch that it would be Chicago, and he didn't want Minna to take it. He was right. The Provost was calling. "I wish you a Merry Christmas." He inquired how they were. Ah, bad! Very sorry indeed to hear the news. He asked to have his sincerest condolences conveyed. Corde rumbled, "Thanks. Very thoughtful of you, Alec."

One of the shrewdest operators that ever lived, the Provost was also very strong—the perfect, up-to-date American strongman. You felt his muscle the instant you engaged him. No one was more smooth, more plausible, long-headed, low-keyed than Witt. A man of masterly politeness, ultra-considerate, he had decided (elected in cold blood) to adopt the mild role. That was all right with Corde, by and large. Okay. He was willing to play any man's game and accommodate his needs, if he could, but he was beginning to find the Provost's highly perfected manner hard to take, especially hard since the onset of the troubles.

"I would so like to express my deepest sympathy to Minna. Is she there? I am so sorry to hear about her mother. . . ."

"I'm letting her sleep," said Corde.

"Ah, she must need the rest, poor thing." Minna's high standing, her academic importance, shielded

Corde from the Provost. He had never really grasped that, but he understood it fully now.

"I don't suppose there is any way to wire flowers to Eastern Europe," said the Provost.

"There may be; you can find out more easily at your end than I can here."

"Oh, for gosh sakes, I wouldn't dream of troubling you with that, Albert. You must have your hands full."

"Is there anything new on the legal side?"

The Provost said, "You may not have heard that you were subpoenaed by your cousin."

"Is that so?"

"Mr. Detillion wanted to put you on the stand to establish the heavy involvement of the college in this case. I've checked into that with our legal department. . . ."

"With some real lawyers . . ."

"Oh, there's no comparison," said the Provost. "I don't want to downgrade your cousin; you may have residual sentiments about him. But these are *crack* lawyers. Of course, you'd never have to get on the stand. The matter was gone into with the State's Attorney. But the newspapers gave the subpoena some play, which was what your cousin wanted. How come all the French names in your family, Albert?"

"The family explanation is that we were leftovers of the Louisiana Purchase. Napoleon sold us all to Thomas Jefferson so that he could pay for his invasion of Russia. . . . Well, I'm sorry to be a cause of so much trouble to the administration."

"Nonsense, Albert. There's no real trouble, just silliness."

Witt would concede him nothing. The likes of *you* can make us no trouble, was what he was saying. There was nevertheless real bitterness, and Corde could feel it. It came down from the communications satellite perfectly clear, pellucid. Corde was in an odd condition anyway, one that made it possible for him to see the Provost from all sides—the jut of his upper teeth, the gill-like creases under the ears, the continual play of deference and kindliness, command, pressure, threat—back and forth. No, he didn't like Corde. The Dean's appointment had been a mistake, and it was the Provost's job to clear up the mess. Corde was an outsider, he hadn't come up from the academic ranks, hadn't been shaped by the Ph.D. process. It wasn't even clear why he had wanted to become an academic, and even an administrator.

The Provost was still speaking. "Our people have met with Mr. Grady about this crazy subpoena. Since you're out of the country and can't be served, it's all in fun."

"And my nephew?"

"He came in, surrendered, and your sister posted a bond, so the young man is out. The grand jury's indictment probably won't stick, when it's reviewed, because the boy didn't have a preliminary hearing. But all the prosecution wanted was to establish that he had threatened the witnesses, which I'm afraid he really did."

"I doubt that he fired a pistol at them."

"Your guess is better than mine."

"Because I'm his uncle?"

"Oh, no," said Witt, suave again. "We can't be responsible for our relatives; we don't choose them."

"Only I seem to have more bad relatives than the normal person."

"We'll work it out, believe me," said the Provost.

Witt had from the first found it necessary to lead Corde step by step, rehearsing him, instructing him, making certain that he would interpret budgetary, educational, institutional policies appropriately. But (it was Corde himself saying all this for him) there was something unteachable about the Dean, an emotional block, a problem, a *fatum*. One of the permanent human problems, in every age of mankind (Corde saw it now), was the problem of not being a fool. This was truly terrible. Oh, that oppression, that fool-fear. It pierced your nose, blinded your eyes, split your heart with shame. And to Witt, a man of power, Corde was a fool. To conceal such an opinion was an operational necessity for a Witt. It was the sort of sacrifice (a sacrifice, not to let your opinion dart forth, and scream and mock) you had to make if you were to be a genuine administrator. That sort of thing you had to hold down. But then there was Witt's brutal infrastructure, which could not be covered up. Witt, thought Corde, had a brutal drive to let him know, to transmit by his perfected devices, what a fucking fool he was. The Dean had made Witt very angry. He had bollixed everything up with his muddled high seriousness. It was not so much the Lester case that angered the Provost. The real vexation was that he had published those magazine articles without a clearance from the college. Not to submit them for approval was out of line, unheard of, dangerous to the last degree—wild! Corde had attacked—whom hadn't he attacked: politicians, businessmen, the professions, and he had even loused up the Governor. Maybe suggestions had come to Witt from high places, by discreetest channels, that this was one highly expendable dean. For his part, Corde didn't want to hide behind Minna. But Minna was involved. For Witt there was a delicate tactical problem. But the Provost, Corde believed, took professional satisfaction in his maneuvers, in operations calling for an unusual degree of skill.

He heard the Provost saying, "Lester was one of our graduate students, and we couldn't have backed away from this case, it had to be followed up. I authorized the reward, you remember."

Corde did remember that. But he recalled also how plainly the Provost was put off by the Dean's emotionalism, his flushed face, his swollen eyes. "What verdict does the legal department predict?" Corde was asking, really, how the college hoped to come out of the case.

"Not pushing for a death sentence."

"I never had that in mind."

"Yes," said Witt. "You expressed your views in *Harper's* clearly enough. Capital punishment—according to you, nobody's hands are clean enough to throw the switch. What was your expression? Oh, yes, 'the official brutes'. . ."

What Corde had had in mind . . . as if the Provost cared what position Corde had taken. Witt despised him. Nor, to tell the whole truth, did Corde altogether blame him for it. He was able to admit to himself that he had been out of kilter when he wrote those articles. Dewey Spangler was right, in part. There was a sort of anarchy in the feelings with which those sketches were infused, an uncontrolled flow of "poetry," the truth-passion he had taken into his veins as an adolescent. Those sketches were raw, where was the control of deeper experience? There wasn't any. He had publicly given himself the fool test and he had flunked it. And now came a man like Alec Witt, Witt who represented power, qualified by the higher deviousness, as power usually was. Corde had challenged this "real-world" power without reflective preparation, without taking account of the higher deviousness. He had left himself wide open. And today of all days—Valeria lying in the hospital morgue!—this depressed the Dean fiercely. But oddly enough, when the wave of depression returned from its far low-down horizon it brought back the idea of having another go at the thing. Do it right next time!

But the Provost had not telephoned from the free world in order to discuss capital punishment with a high-principled idiot dean. Both parties now made a pause. Witt was about to disclose the true reason for his call. The deep Atlantic stream brimmed between them. They were—what—seven thousand miles apart? You weren't able to have conversations like this in the old days.

"When do you plan to be back?"

"For the new semester. Minna will have to settle up

her mother's affairs—the estate, such as it is. She also needs to get to Mount Palomar; she missed her telescope days."

"You haven't seen Vlada Voynich yet?" said the Provost.

"We've been expecting her. Her brother said she'd be here for Christmas."

"She's been telling what an interest you've developed in Beech's work."

"Purely amateur," said Corde.

"Of course it would be. In the nature of the case. Are you planning, actually, to write about it?"

Corde in his bass voice answered, "That was Beech's idea—*he* proposed it. He sent me the material."

"That's what Vlada told me. You haven't decided yet, though, have you?"

"It hasn't been on my mind much. I've put off thinking about it. I wouldn't want to jump into anything. If there's going to be more controversy . . . I need to be sure I've got a good grasp of the facts."

This should have reassured the Provost somewhat. Instead it made him press a little harder. "These environmental, ecological questions are very complex."

"I wouldn't do it if it were only that. I don't care to get mixed up in environmentalism. But I am interested in Beech himself. The personality of a scientist, his view of the modern world. But I'll have to wait until Minna's able to discuss it. I can't take it up with her now. I'll find out more from Vlada Voynich. She's bringing more material."

"So she told me, and I asked her also to give you copies of letters. . . ."

"What sort of letters?"

"Things that have come in—in connection with those *Harper's* pieces of yours."

"What, complaints to the college, objections?"

"Nothing to disturb you. Lots of curious items. Amazing how worked up people can become and what a variety of responses one can get. You'll find them really thought-provoking. I wouldn't think of upsetting you at a time like this. And you don't need to worry about things here; they're under control. I keep a careful eye on Lydia Lester. She was splendid on the witness stand. But you saw that yourself. So fragile, and turned out to have real guts."

Each of the Provost's final words touched an anxiety in Corde.

"It won't be a happy Christmas for poor Minna. Tell her at least that we think we can get another date for her at Mount Palomar. We'll be looking for you after the first of the year."

Corde explained to Minna under the dim chandelier of the dining room table—the taped black wires hung twisted from the broken plaster. "Alec Witt. Merry Christmas, and condolences. Don't worry about the telescope. And Vlada Voynich is on her way."

Gigi served an early dinner. It was eaten listlessly. For Christmas Eve the table had been laid with linens embroidered in red. Corde went to bed early. The twenty-fourth of December had lasted long enough.

On Christmas morning there were presents beside their coffee cups. The old girls saved gift-wrapping paper and ribbons from year to year. There were treasures of all kinds in the cupboards, boxes of pre-Communist ornaments. Gigi brought to the table the Christmas angels Minna remembered from childhood. They were designed to float slowly on wires radiating from a disk set in motion by the heat of a small candle. The toy would not work. "Valeria always could make it go," Gigi said. She wore deep mourning and her neck was strained as she bent to strike more matches. She had combed out the bobbed hair but at the back it still looked like a hayrick. "It may be the candles," she said. She went through the drawers of the buffet, looking for the right kind. She didn't know where Valeria had put them. Corde tinkered with the wires. Americans were supposed to be mechanically gifted, but he could get

nowhere with them. He only bent the toy badly. The
four angels hung motionless. That was the end of them.
Valeria had taken their secret with her.

"Then open your presents," said Gigi. She had given
Minna a peasant blouse. For Corde there was a large
gold pocket watch which had belonged to Dr. Raresh.
Surprised, he stared at it—graceful numerals, a shapely
swell to the tip of the hour hand. To set it you depressed
a tiny catch with your thumbnail. Gigi said, "This was
the present Valeria decided you should have this year."
He slipped it into the pocket of his cardigan and as he
bent to sip his coffee he felt the pull of the golden lump
near his waist. He reckoned that after London, and
especially after the Rowlandson exhibition and dinner at the Étoile, Valeria had accepted him as a full
member of the family. When he had tried to take her by
the elbow because she was listing, could no longer keep
her balance, when she pulled her arm away, it had
depressed him (something like the streak of a black
grease pencil over his feelings); he felt that she was
irritated with him. But that hadn't been what it meant.
On the contrary, it was then that his probation had
ended.

The morning was sunny. He studied the watch at
length in the bedroom. He read Vollard's memoirs and
reminiscences of painters—no boards, no back, nothing
but a bundle of stitched paper. Minna had no time for
him. She and Gigi spent most of the morning deciding
how to dress Valeria. Which dress or suit would she
have preferred, or shoes, or blouse or ornaments? They
decided that she should wear a greeny-blue silk suit
Minna had bought in London for her, and a green and
black paisley scarf, dark blue shoes. Traian took the
clothing to the hospital, together with a photograph to
show how Valeria put up her hair.

Gigi, who had been so passive while Valeria was
dying, turned assertive and militant, insisting that the
government must be "forced" to give her sister a public
funeral. She told this to Petrescu when he turned up on

Christmas Day. Petrescu surprised Corde by the genuineness of his grief. He carried himself (his swooping belly, his wide undercurves) with soldierly decorum but his eyes were red, tragic pouches under them. He was indulgent with Gigi, he sat sighing and let her talk. She told him (defying the listening devices) that the least the government could do was to acknowledge the fidelity of Dr. Raresh to the Party and the Revolution and the contributions made by this family to surgery, public health, and also astronomy. He answered patiently, his voice rising in spirals until it broke in the higher registers. Minna said to Corde how decent of him it was to come, and how loyal he was to the family. "I think he had no personal secrets from my mother."

Bound to have secrets, in his racket: Corde silently dissented. However, Petrescu's face certainly was ruined. If intensive care doctors could light candles for the dying, secret agents could mourn their adoptive mothers. There was sentiment all over the place. Petrescu had his family side, his soft side. He was delicately, even endearingly attentive to the ladies. He was thoughtful towards Corde, too, and brought him two green bottles of Chenin Blanc, unobtainable except in the commissaries for high-ranking bureaucrats.

Gigi explained to Corde what she was doing. "I am insisting that my sister should not have a commonplace funeral. She ought to be exposed publicly in the great lobby of the Medical School, as her husband was before her. It is only right and proper to give her official recognition."

"Will they give it?"

"We shall insist. I am requesting Mihai Petrescu to approach old members of the Politburo. They remember her. They are aware, as younger ones are not. There was typhus. There was starvation. Valeria asked Truman for supplies. He sent them. The Russians put their own labels on. Requesting drugs and food from America was one of her crimes."

Minna agreed with her aunt, while Corde was think-

ing that you saw eyes like his wife's in famine photographs. She was starving herself. It would take months
to restore her.

"If not the lobby of the Medical School, then the
Memorial Hall next door to the crematorium," said
Gigi.

Petrescu, downcast, much troubled, nodding, stroked
the fuzz of his fedora, stroked the dense hairs growing from his ears. In spite of its wide bottom, his
broad body sat uncomfortably. He often pressed his
palm over the thin hairs streaking backwards on
his skull. His fingers were actually trembling. His
pouchy eyes occasionally were lifted to carry silent
messages to Corde, to another man. These poor
women were *innocent* . . . they didn't *know,* couldn't
understand. Corde believed that Petrescu had tried to
make a stand against the Colonel, had been beaten
quickly, clobbered, forced to back off. Now, after
Valeria's death, he may have gotten official permission
to be helpful to the family. Petrescu's rank in the
security forces must have been fairly high. Whatever he
had to do in the line of duty (don't ask!) he atoned for
in this household by services, by emotional deeds,
tender attachments. He was an old-consciousness type
in a new-consciousness line of business. Gigi declared,
"I assure you, Albert, and I will even swear, that my
sister shall have her due. Until now my sister, who was
a figure in the history of our country, has been denied
notice in the national encyclopedia. But she shall have
it. I shall go to the greatest lengths. . . ."

But Minna privately told Corde, "Today I can't even
get the newspapers to print a notice of the funeral."

"Why do you suppose . . . ?"

"The obvious reasons. I ran away from them. And
my mother was expelled, then refused to rejoin the
Party. I think the funeral will be well attended, though.
Just word of mouth. The telephone doesn't stop ringing. My mother is a symbol. . . ."

"Of what?"

Minna whispered. "It isn't political, it's just the way life has to be lived, it's just people humanly disaffected." She covered his ear with cupped hands and said, "The government may be afraid of a demonstration at the Medical School."

Corde, who didn't believe this for a moment, nodded. He said, "Sure. I understand. But what would the demonstration be?"

"I told you. It would be sentiment. To approve what Valeria personally stood for. Just on human grounds. . . . Why don't you go and rest for a while, my dear. You're tired. This is hard on you. I can see. Vlada is coming later. She arrived this morning."

A clear Christmas Day. The room was surprisingly warm, the sun heating the windows. It made him feel how badly he needed a breather, "a few minutes of Paris," as he called it—some civilized *calme,* or *luxe.* He picked up the crumbling paperbound Vollard, his *Souvenirs d'un Marchand de Tableaux,* and read a few paragraphs about the testiness of Degas. "You'll see, Vollard, they'll raid the museums for Raphaels and Rembrandts and show them in the barracks and the prisons on the pretext that everybody has a right to beauty!" A crabby old bigot, and he looked so ferociously at a child who annoyed him in a restaurant that he scared the little girl into fits and she vomited on the table. But for this nastiness he gave full compensation in lovely painting and bronze. Whereas a fellow like the Provost . . . But the Provost was no genius-monster, he was only . . . And Corde now tried to protect his sunlit breather, the moment of peace, but he could not beat off Alec Witt and he presently surrendered to Chicago thoughts. The Provost's signal was easy to read: for the sake of the college, he was protecting Beech. Scientists were far too naive to protect themselves, and Corde was especially dangerous because he, too, was in a way an ingenu. Once a man like Witt decided that you were not a man to observe the discreet convention, that you talked out of turn, and that you

were a fool, nothing but trouble, you were out. He
would do everything possible to stop Corde from
writing a piece on Beech—"one of those pieces of his."
And you couldn't altogether blame the guy, thought
Corde. It's true, I was carried away. Hearts hanging in
the dark too long, and going bad, spoiling in suspen-
sion, and then having a seizure, an outburst. In most
things I don't hold with Dewey, he's too psychoanalyti-
cal, but he's clever enough in his own way or he
wouldn't have become such an eminence. Give him his
due. And he says I was settling scores with Chicago. I
must admit that I was retaliating on my brother-in-law,
on Max Detillion and on many another.

Tired of false opinions, and of his own distortions
most of all, Corde admitted that, yes, he had wanted to
give it to them (to a generalized Chicago), to stick it to
them. To stick it, and to make it stick so that they
couldn't shake it off. Now, a man in a position of real
responsibility, a Witt, for instance, he protects his
institution from everything immoderate. That's how
the silky style is justified. That's his method for dealing
with disruption: never lose your cool with the disrupt-
er, gag him with silk, tie him in knots with procedures.
Corde would class that as one of the hard, essential jobs
of democracy. I gave no sign that I was going to turn
disruptive. Dumb thoughtful sweet, was my type, mull-
ing things over. Then I turned out to be one of those
excessive, no-inner-gyroscope fellows he can't stand.
So he despises me; what of it? I detest him, too. That's
neither here nor there.

The publication of his articles had also given Corde a
profile of the country, a measure of its political opinions, a sample of its feelings. "I administered my own
Rorschach test to the U.S.," Corde said. Before leaving Chicago he had already received a batch of letters
forwarded by the editors of *Harper's*. "A flood of
mail," one of the assistants wrote. Liberals found him
reactionary. Conservatives called him crazy. Professional urbanologists said he was hasty. "Things have

always been like this in American cities, ugly and terrifying. Mr. Corde should have prepared himself by reading some history." "The author is a Brahmin. The Brahmins taught us to despise the cities, which accordingly became despicable." "Mr. Corde believes in gemütlichkeit more than in public welfare. And what makes him think that what it takes to save little black kids is to get them to read Shakespeare? Next he will suggest that we teach them Demosthenes and make speeches in Greek. The answer to juvenile crime is not in *King Lear* or *Macbeth*." "The Dean's opinion is that a moral revolution is required. His only heroes are two self-appointed possibly dubious benefactors." "You should be congratulated for opening up these lower depths of psychology to your readers, giving us an opportunity to look into the abysses of chaotic thinking, of anarchy and psychopathology."

Curious what people will pick on. About *Macbeth* Corde had only noted that in a class of black schoolchildren taught by a teacher "brave enough to ignore instructions from downtown," Shakespeare caused great excitement. The lines "And pity, like a naked newborn babe, Striding the blast" had pierced those pupils. You could see the power of the babe, how restlessness stopped. And Corde had written that perhaps only poetry had the strength "to rival the attractions of narcotics, the magnetism of TV, the excitements of sex, or the ecstasies of destruction."

It was certainly true that Corde had found himself in Chicago looking for examples of "moral initiative," and he had come up with two: Rufus Ridpath at County Jail; and Toby Winthrop, also black, an ex-hit man and heroin addict. He hadn't found his examples in any of the great universities, and there was a large academic population in Chicago. What Alec Witt probably would like to know was why Corde hadn't made his search for moral initiative in his own college. Why, thought Corde, I did look there, up and down, from end to end. Corde was not a subversive, no fifth columnist, nor had he become a professor with the secret motive of writing an exposé. He hadn't been joking when he quoted Milton to his sister Elfrida: "How charming is divine philosophy"—the mosaic motto on the ceiling of the library downtown. And the universities were where philosophy lived, or was supposed to be living. He had never forgotten the long, charmed years in a silent Dartmouth attic, where he had read Plato and Thucydides, Shakespeare. Wasn't it because of this Dartmouth reading that he gave up the *Trib* and came back from Europe? To continue his education, he said, after a twenty-year interruption by "news," by current human business.

It was Ridpath who had sent Corde to Toby Winthrop at Operation Contact. He drove to the South Side on a winter day streaky with snow. You could see the soot mingling with the drizzle. Corde hadn't come to this neighborhood in thirty years. It was then already decaying, now it was fully rotted. Only a few old brick bungalows remained, and a factory here and there. The expressway had cut across the east-west streets. The one remaining landmark was the abandoned Englewood Station—huge blocks of sandstone set deep, deep in the street, a kind of mortuary isolation, no travelers now, no passenger trains. A dirty snow brocade over the empty lots, and black men keeping warm at oil-drum bonfires. All this—low sky, wind, weed skeletons, ruin—went to Corde's nerves, his "Chicago wiring system," with peculiar effect. He found Operation Contact in a hidden half-block (ideal for muggings) between a warehouse and the expressway. Except on business, to make a sale, who would come to this place? He parked and got out of the car feeling the lack of almost everything you needed, humanly. Christ, the human curve had sunk down to base level, had gone beneath it. If there was another world, this was the time for it to show itself. The visible one didn't bear looking at.

Well, Corde entered the "detoxification center" and

climbed the stairs. Two landings, a wired-glass door where you showed your face and were buzzed in. You found yourself in a corridor, and then, unexpectedly, you came into a room furnished with umber and orange sofas. Philodendrons hung in all the corners. Here he met someone who encouraged him, a wiry, whiskery Negro who said, "Go on, man—go, go; you on the right track." The tentative, pale, blundering Dean amused him.

Winthrop's office window was heavily covered in flowered drapes of pink and green. The ex-hit man sat waiting for him. His trunk was enormous, his thighs were huge, his fingers thick. No business suit for him. He was dressed in matching shades of brown—a knitted shirt in beige, a carmel-colored suede jacket, chocolate trousers, tan cowboy boots. He wore a small brown cap with a visor, a boy's cap. His face curved inward like a saddle. He was bearded and, like Dr. Fulcher at County Hospital, he had pendants on his neck and big rings on his hands. He picked up the note Corde had sent him. In the lamplight the folded paper seemed no bigger than a white cabbage moth. "You a friend of Rufus Ridpath, Professor? He asked me to talk to you. Thinks we can do each other some good. Maybe he thinks you might be able to do something for him. Set the record straight."

"What do you think?"

"I think he was the best warden County ever had, and I was a prisoner before and during his time. . . ."

The body of this powerful man was significantly composed in the executive leather chair. If you had met him in the days when he was a paid executioner, if he had been waiting for you on a staircase, in an alley, you would never have escaped him. He would have killed you, easy.

"You can't do much for Ridpath. The guys who did the job on him don't have to worry about you or me, my friend. It's their town. Their names are in the paper every day. No trouble at all to get names. But that's *all*

you could get. Rufus doesn't really expect anything
from you. He just likes you. Now, what did he tell you
about me?"

"He said that you and your friend Smithers founded
this center to cure addiction without methadone, as you
cured yourself."

This man with the black nostrils, impressively staring
under the visor of the childish cap, interrupted him. He
said, "You bein' polite. He said I was a hit man, right? I
was, too, a hired killer working for very important
people in this city. I was tried three times for murder.
Those important people got me off. Ask me how, and I
identify you as a man who don't know this town."

How many people he had murdered, he didn't care
to say. But then he nearly killed himself with an
overdose of heroin. Someone should have warned him
how strong it was. After he took it he recognized it for
what it was. As it began to take effect, he saw that he
was dying. This happened in a hotel room near Sixty-
third and Stony Island, the end of the el tracks, the tip
of rat-shit Woodlawn. "I'm goin' to tell you just a little
about this."

A friend came and put him into a tub of cold water,
but he saw that Toby was dying and beat it. "No use
hangin' around. But after eighteen hours of death, I
came back."

He lifted himself from the tub, and just as he was, in
wet clothes, he went down into Sixty-third Street and
caught a cab to Billings Hospital, to the detoxification
unit. Because of his terrifying looks, the receptionist
signaled the police, who grabbed him in the lobby. But
they had nothing to hold him on at the station, only
vagrancy and loitering. "I bailed myself out. Always a
big bankroll in my pocket. I got another cab back to
Billings, but this time I stopped in an empty lot and tore
the leg off a table. I went in with it under my coat, and I
showed it to the receptionist. I said I'd beat her brains
out. That's how I got upstairs. They gave me the first
methadone shot. I was in a hospital gown, and I went to

the toilet and sat on the floor to wait for the reaction. I put my arms around the commode and held tight to it."

"But you didn't go through with the methadone treatment."

"No, sir. I did not. Something happened. When I came in I had the table leg, I was ready to kill. I would have killed the lady if she called the cops again. But in less than an hour I was called to stop a riot. I had to stop a man breaking up the joint. He was a black man, as big as me, and he had delirium tremens. He smashed the chairs in the patients' sitting room. He broke a coffee table, broke windows. The orderlies and nurses were like kindergarteners around him. He was like a buffalo. I had to take a hand, Professor. There was nothing else to do. I separated from the commode and went out and took control. I put my arms around the man. I got him to the floor and lay on the top of him. I don't say he was listening, but he wasn't so wild with me. They gave him a needle and we laid him on a cart and put him in bed."

"That was Smithers?"

"Smithers," said Winthrop. "I wish I could explain what it was all about. I've told this before. It's as if I kept after it till I could find out what happened that moment I took control of him. Maybe it was because I died twenty-four hours before. Maybe because my buddy left me in the bathtub in the hotel—that was all he knew how to do for me. But when they put Smithers in bed, I sat by him and minded him."

"This was when your own treatment stopped."

"I wouldn't leave him. They had to measure his body fluid. I held the man's Johnson for him. You understand what I'm saying? I held his dick for him to pee in the flask. He had a bad ulcer in his leg. I treated that, too. That was his cure, and it was my cure, at the same time. I was his mother, I was his daddy. And we stayed together since."

"And made this center."

"Built it ourselves in this old warehouse—the dormi-

tories, kitchen, shops downstairs to teach trades. We
bring in old people from the neighborhood—the old,
they're starving on food stamps, scavenging behind the
supermarkets. The markets post guards, they say they
don't want the old people to poison themselves on
spoiled fish. We need those old people here. They teach
upholstery, electrical work, cabinetmaking, dressmak-
ing. They teach respect to young hoodlums, too. But it
isn't only hoods. We get all kinds here. We take all the
kinds—white, black, Indians, whatever color they
come in. From the richest suburbs, from Lake
Forest . . ."

"You'd call this center a success?"

Winthrop stared at him a moment. Then he said,
"No, sir, I don't call it that. They come and go. It takes
with some. I could name you a many and a many it
never could save."

Until now Winthrop had sat immobile in his chair,
but now he turned and, to Corde's great surprise,
began to lower himself towards the floor. What was he
doing? He was on his knees, his big arm stretched
towards the floor, his fingers hooked upward. "You see
what we have to do? Those people are down in the
cesspool. We reach for them and try to get a hold.
Hang on—hang on! They'll drown in the shit if we can't
pull 'em out. Some of 'em we'll get out. Some of them
will go down. They'll drown and sink in the shit—never
make it." With an effort that caused one side of his face
to twitch, he labored to his feet and backed himself into
the chair again.

"You're telling me that the people who come
here . . ."

"I'm telling you, Professor, that the few who find us
and many hundred of thousand more who never do and
never will—they're marked out to be destroyed. Those
are people meant to die, sir. That's what we are looking
at."

10

It was at this point, out of earnestness and without seeing how it would be taken by the public, that Corde began to speak in his articles of "superfluous populations," "written off," "doomed peoples." That didn't go down well. You could use terms from sociology or Durkheim or Marx, you could speak of anomie or the lumpenproletariat, the black underclass, of economically redundant peasantries, the Third World, the effects of opium on the Chinese masses in the nineteenth century—as long as it was sufficiently theoretical it went over easily enough. You could discuss welfare politics, medical and social work bureaucracies, without objection. But when Corde began to make statements to the effect that in the wild, monstrous setting of half-demolished cities the choice that was offered was between a slow death and a sudden one, between attrition and quick destruction, he enraged a good many subscribers. Something went wrong. He wrote about whirling souls and became a whirling soul himself, lifted up, caught up, spinning, streaming with passions, compulsive protests, inspirations. He experienced, as he saw when he looked back, a kind of air anarchy. He began to use strange expressions. He wrote, for instance, that Toby Winthrop was a "reconstituted" human being, a "murderer-savior" type; that Winthrop was therefore an advanced modern case. Why? Because the advanced modern consciousness was a reduced consciousness inasmuch as it contained only the minimum of furniture that civilization was able to install (practical judgments, bare outlines of morality, sketches, cartoons instead of human beings); and this consciousness, because its equipment was humanly so meager, so abstract, was basically murderous. It was for this reason that murder was so easy to "understand" (or had he written "extenuate"? Thinness for thinness). He never did get around to explaining how we must reconstitute ourselves. Because of the incompleteness of his argument he confused many readers. Some wrote contemptuously, others were incensed. He hadn't meant to make such a stir. It took him by surprise.

But by far the most controversial part of his article was the interview with Sam Varennes. To this Varennes, the Public Defender in the Spofford Mitchell murder case, Corde had very nearly spoken his full mind. The results, in the lingo people were using nowadays, were "counterproductive."

Corde had gone to see Sam Varennes to discuss the case and to ask permission to interview Mitchell. Varennes was interested in publicity, but in the end he and his defense team decided that any pretrial media coverage would be prejudicial to their client. Corde had, however, reported his conversation with Varennes in full.

The Mitchell case was not exceptional. There were thousands of similar crimes in police files across the country. But there were special circumstances which made it important to Corde.

The victim was a young suburban housewife, the mother of two small children. She had just parked in a lot near the Loop when Mitchell approached and forced her at gunpoint into his own car. The time was about 2 P.M. Spofford Mitchell's Pontiac had been bought from a Clark Street dealer just after his recent release from prison. Corde didn't know how the purchase was financed. (The dealer wouldn't say.) In the front seat, Mitchell forced Mrs. Sathers to remove her slacks, to prevent escape. He drove to a remote alley and assaulted her sexually. Then he locked her into the trunk of his Pontiac. He took her out later in the day and raped her again. By his own testimony, this happened several times. At night he registered in a motel on the far South Side. He managed to get her from the trunk into the room without being seen. Possibly he was seen; it didn't seem to matter to those who saw. In the morning he led her out and locked her in the trunk again. At ten o'clock he was obliged to appear at a court hearing to answer an earlier rape charge. He parked the Pontiac, with Mrs. Sathers still in the trunk, in the official lot adjoining the court building. The rape hearing was inconclusive. When it ended he drove at random about the city. On the West Side that afternoon, passersby heard cries from the trunk of a parked car. No one thought to take down the license number; besides, the car pulled away quickly. Towards daybreak of the second day, for reasons not explained in the record, Spofford Mitchell let Mrs. Sathers go, warning her not to call the police. He watched from his car as she went down the street. This was in a white working-class neighborhood. She rang several doorbells, but no one would let her in. An incomprehensibly frantic woman at five in the morning —people wanted no part of her. They were afraid. As she turned away from the third or fourth closed door, Mitchell pulled up and reclaimed her. He drove to an empty lot, where he shot her in the head. He covered her body with trash.

She was soon discovered. Exceptionally prompt, the police descended on Mitchell. He was found in the garage behind his father's house, cleaning out the trunk of his Pontiac, hosing out the excrements. He confessed, then retracted, confessed again. He was being held in County Jail for trial. These were the facts Corde learned from the papers. He was then preparing his article. What might the real content of these facts be?

He made inquiries and was referred to the Public
Defender in charge of the case, Mr. Sam Varennes. In
Harper's he gave an account of his long conversation
with Varennes, whom he described as

> . . . a strong bald young man with prominent blond
> eyebrows and a wide throat, a college athlete in his
> time. The views we exchanged were enlightened, intel-
> ligent, liberal—did us both credit. To be appointed
> Defender you generally needed some sort of backup or
> sponsorship, still such appointees are often well-
> qualified conscientious public servants. Mr. Varennes
> is a scholarly lawyer, well nigh a Doctor of Jurispru-
> dence. I think he said Stanford.
>
> He asked first what feelings I had about the case. I
> admitted that I was subject to claustrophobia, and that
> I believed I might rather be killed than get into the
> trunk of a car at gunpoint, that sometimes I had
> fantasies in which I said, "You'll have to shoot me."
> But if I were pushed in and had the lid slammed on me I
> would hunt for a tire tool to hit the gunman with at the
> first opportunity. To lie in a trunk was like live burial. I
> could never endure it. I then said, "Only think how
> Mrs. Sathers must have begged the man every time he
> opened the lid."
>
> He seemed, to my own surprise, slightly surprised by
> this. "You think she prayed for her life?"
>
> "Begged or prayed—'Let me out!'"
>
> Mr. Varennes did not care for what I was telling him.
> He had put himself in a posture to make an effective
> argument for his client (a man, after all, a human being
> like the rest of us), so he was much disturbed. I think
> also that I myself—the interviewer—disturbed him. *I*
> was disturbed. He said, "You suppose? I hadn't
> thought about that. . . ."
>
> I said, "Oh, but she must have."
>
> "And he was indifferent, are you saying?"
>
> "I wouldn't say indifferent. I'm trying to guess
> whether he understood her emotions. If you say some-
> thing in all the earnestness of your heart, and wonder
> why this doesn't . . . with this earnestness it must—it

must get through. If he had understood her pleading he would have been a different kind of murderer."

"The kind who feeds on the victim's pain, like this mass killer Gacey, who specialized in boys? Part of his sexual kick? Subtler and more perverted . . . ?"

"Gacey seems to have tortured and mocked his victims."

"So you don't believe Mitchell was the same?"

"Classification of psychopaths is technically beyond me. My only guess about Mitchell is that he was just bound for death. If you've taken that fast direct track, you may be deaf and blind to something so exotic as the pleading of a woman whom you've locked in your car trunk."

"A more primitive person," said Varennes.

I saw that the Defender was examining me on my social views. Mr. Varennes is a muscular man. Even his throat has muscles, a pillar throat. I think he pumps iron. He said next, "As part of the defense we may argue that Mrs. Sathers accepted the situation."

"Does he say she did?"

"Some of the time she rode in the front seat with him. She was seen by witnesses when he stopped at a bar to buy a bottle of Seven-Up. When he went in to get the drink and left her, she sat and waited. She didn't run away. You might say he had tied her feet."

"I didn't. But it's probable that she was dazed."

"As dazed as all that?"

"Felt she was already destroyed. There must be a sense of complicity in rapes. The sex nerves can stream all by themselves. If people think they're going to be murdered anyway when it's over, they may desperately let go."

"Sexually?"

"Yes. In spite of themselves, spray it all out. They're going to die, you see. Good-bye to life."

"That's quite a theory."

"Maybe. But that's quite a situation," I said. "And with the special confused importance, the peculiar curse of sexuality or carnality we're under—we've placed it right in the center of life and connect it with savagery and criminality—it's not at all a wild conjec-

ture. The truth may even require a wilder interpretation. Our conception of physical life and of pleasure is
completely death-saturated. The full physical emphasis
is fatal. It cuts us off. The fullest physical joining may
always be flavored with death, therefore. This is why I
said Spofford Mitchell was on the fast track for death—
fast, clutching, dreamlike, orgastic. Grab it, do it, die."

I reminded myself that I was talking with a gymnast.
He had backed off his head as if to get a different slant,
and took me in again, extremely curious. So I resumed
the interviewer's role. "It may be wrong to pry into the
last hours of Mrs. Sathers. Well, we were discussing
why she didn't make a run for it when he went into the
bar. Is it a fact that witnesses saw her waiting
alone? . . ."

"I've taken the depositions."

"I'm trying to imagine the despair that kept her from
opening the door. And suppose he had chased her
down the street; would anybody have helped her?"

"Maybe not, against an armed man. Yes, when you
put it that way. I suppose that's what the prosecution
would say." His next comment was, "My team and I
are on these homicides year in year out. We can't get up
the same fervor as an outsider."

I made a particular effort now to recover my interviewer's detachment or professional cool. I am obliged
to admit that I never know why I say certain things
when I'm agitated. It was nice of him to call it "fervor";
it was far more insidious, a radical disturbance. But he
was a nice man. His looks appealed to me. I liked his
serious eyes and strong bald head. And this induced me
to talk more.

His examination continuing, for he was examining
me (as if there were something about me that was not
strictly speaking *contemporary*), he tried me on the
professional side and invited me to discuss the situation
in broader terms—the mood of the country, the inner
city, urban decay, political questions. He asked me to
describe the pieces I intended to write. Why was I
doing them, and what would they be like? I explained
that the Cordes had moved up to Chicago from Joliet
more than a century ago and that I had been born on

the North Side and thought it would be a good idea to describe the city as I had known it, and that my aim was more pictorial than analytical. I had looked up my high school zoology teacher, for instance, whom I had helped with the animals, feeding them and cleaning the cages. Also a self-educated Polish barber who used to lecture boys on Spengler's *Decline of the West* while he cut their hair. I had traced him to Poznan, where he was now living on his Social Security checks from America. I revisited the Larrabee Street YMCA. Also the Loop. The Loop's beaneries, handbooks, dinky dives and movie palaces were wiped out. Gigantic office towers had risen everywhere. Good-bye forever to the jazz musicians, and the boxing buffs who hung around the gymnasiums, to the billiard sharks from Bensinger's on Randolph Street. Then I mentioned a number of contemporary subjects, among them the new housing developments south of the Loop in the disused freight yards; and the mammoth Deep Tunnel engineering project, the Cloaca Maxima one hundred and thirty miles long and three hundred feet beneath the city. Not wishing to ruffle him, I made no reference to my interest in the abuse of "immunities" under federal law by U.S. attorneys (refractory witnesses who rejected the immunity offer were sentenced for contempt of court; judges had the right to send them to jail for a year). It would have done me no good to discuss this with Mr. Varennes. Nor did I mention my interest in the case of Rufus Ridpath, the same people who had dumped Ridpath having perhaps appointed Varennes.

Whether I could be trusted, what my angle was, why I wasn't somehow one hundred percent contemporary in my opinions—these were the Public Defender's questions. I came well accredited—journalist, professor, dean. But in spite of these credentials and the prospect of favorable publicity for his team, I was suspect, he smelled trouble.

He was right, too. A certain instability . . .

Corde laid aside Valeria's copy of *Harper's* and tried again, reframing the interview, as if he intended to write a new version, wider in perspective, closer to the real facts, taking bigger forces into account. The meeting with Varennes was one of those occasions when (if you are like Albert Corde) you are strongly tempted to say what is really on your mind. Very dangerous. In ordinary life you dig far below your real thoughts. But if you come soaring by, why shouldn't the fellow shoot you down? On the other hand, he may be the exceptional case, and perhaps he won't shoot. True, Varennes was running any number of dependability tests. Did I play by Chicago rules or would I cut some exotic caper and embarrass or damage him? For his part, the Provost had decided that I didn't accept the Chicago rules. He had trusted me, and I had brought tons of trouble down on him. But Varennes also buttered me up, you might say. He led me on. He said that on his first undergraduate holiday in Paris he had read my columns in the *Herald Tribune*. He asked whether I was familiar with Solzhenitsyn's Harvard Address. Yes, and here and there I agreed with it. I hedged a little.

Varennes was checking my papers, as it were, to see whether my liberal sympathies were in order. I said that liberalism had never accepted the Leninist premise that this was an age of wars and revolutions. Where the Communists saw class war, civil war, pictures of catastrophe, we only saw temporary aberrations. Capitalistic democracies could never be at home with the catastrophe outlook. We are used to peace and plenty, we are for everything nice and against cruelty, wickedness, craftiness, monstrousness. Worshipers of progress, its dependents, we are unwilling to reckon with villainy and misanthropy, we reject the *horrible*—the same as saying we are anti-philosophical. Our outlook requires the assumption that each of us is at heart trustworthy, each of us is naturally decent and wills the good. The English-speaking world is temperamentally like this. You see it in the novels of Dickens, clearly. In his world, there is suffering, there is evil, betrayal, corruption, savagery, sadism, but the ordeals end and decent people arrange a comfortable existence for themselves, making themselves cozy. You may say that was simply Victorianism, but it wasn't—isn't. Modern businessmen and politicians, if they're going to give billions in credit to the other side, don't want to think about an epoch of wars and revolutions. They need to think about contractual stability, and therefore assume the basic seriousness of the authorities in Communist countries—their counterparts, officials, practical people like themselves, but with different titles.

More of this real-sounding discussion, mutually comforting ideas. Those were the stillborn babies of intellect. Dead, really. I realized that long ago. They originate in the brain and die in the brain. Although it's true enough that a simple belief in progress goes with a deformed conception of human nature.

But Varennes got a bang out of this discussion. He didn't want all the time to be thinking about lousy rapes and murders. He knitted his fingers and said he had been reading a new study of the Munich mentality—Chamberlain's inability to dope out Hitler's designs. He asked me, "Where did you get your own catastrophe exposure?"

I said, "In Germany in the forties when I was young. But probably even more by what I read as a young kid in my father's library. He was an artilleryman in the First World War and collected books on the subject. I read a great deal at an impressionable age about trench warfare. In some sectors they paved trenches in winter with frozen bodies to protect the feet of the Tommies. You knew it was spring when the corpses began to cave in under your boots. I didn't stop with Remarque and Barbusse, or Kipling. I went into the memoirs of infantrymen and sappers. I recall an eyewitness account of rats eating their way into corpses, entering at the liver and gnawing their way upwards, getting so fat they had trouble squeezing out again at the mouth. There should be a shorthand for facts in that category.

Or maybe there ought to be a supplement to the Book of Common Prayer to cover them. They have rearranged our souls. This *is* Lenin's age of wars and revolutions. The idea has gotten around by now."

The Public Defender said, "Except the Americans? The last of the ideology-negative nations?"

Needing time to think over these propositions, Varennes turned his head to one side, looking out from the big but unopenable window of his air-conditioned office. He was a steady and strong man. He would be steady when he worked out at the gym; also steady and strong while he was cutting his medium-rare New York sirloin at Gene and Georgetti's; presumably he would be strong in the sack, a pillar of muscle on the bosom of some swelling, soft girl. I, instead, was folded skinny into my chair, hands clasped low in my lap (between my cambered thighs—the legs criticized by my nephew), with my swelled eyes, yoked goggles, whitening brow hairs, pale dish face and long, uncomplaisant (only complaisant-looking) mouth. Varennes went on, "Our catastrophe is these inner city slums? Or—tell me if I follow you—the Third World erupting all over?" And as well as I can remember, he went on to say I was suggesting that a man like Mitchell was an unconscious agent of world catastrophe, or an involuntary one. "Do you identify him with terrorists or Third World fanatics? Are you asking whether we—the bourgeois democracies—are capable of coming to grips with the catastrophe mentality?"

The thought I had then I can recall clearly. I said that America no more knew what to do with this black underclass than it knew what to do with its children. It was impossible for it to educate either, or to bind either to life. It was not itself securely attached to life just now. Sensing this, the children attached themselves to the black underclass, achieving a kind of coalescence with the demand-mass. It was not so much the inner city slum that threatened us as the slum of innermost being, of which the inner city was perhaps a material representation. As I spelled this out I felt that I looked ailing and sick. A kind of hot haze came over me. I felt my weakness as I approached the business of the soul—its true business in this age. Here a dean (or a writer of magazine articles) came to see a public defender to talk about a limited matter and their discussion became unlimited—their business was not being transacted. I was losing Mr. Varennes. Anguish beyond the bounds of human tolerance was not a subject a nice man like Mr. Varennes was ready for on an ordinary day. But I (damn!), starting to collect material for a review of life in my native city, and finding at once wounds, lesions, cancers, destructive fury, death, felt (and how quirkily) called upon for a special exertion—to interpret, to pity, to save! This was stupid. It was insane. But now the process was begun, how was I to stop it? I couldn't stop it.

Varennes seemed to glimpse this and he said, "It's still not clear to me what you have in mind, overall."

I took a different tack for the moment. I said, "You may have seen a long article in the paper recently. Fifty prominent people were interviewed on what Chicago needs to make it more exciting and dynamic."

"I think I saw that."

"Some of these people were lawyers, some were architects, one the owner of a ball club; also, business executives, advertising men, journalists and TV commentators, musicians, artistic directors, publishers, city planners, urbanologists, a famous linebacker, merchandising big shots, et cetera."

"The beautiful people," said Varennes.

"Well, now, some said we needed outdoor cafés like Paris or Venice, and others that we should have developments like Ghirardelli Square in San Francisco or Faneuil Hall in Boston. One wanted a gambling casino atop the Hancock Building; another that the banks of the Chicago River should be handsomely laid out. Or that there should be cultural meeting places; or more offbeat dining places, or discos. A twenty-four-hour deli. A better shake for the handicapped, especially those who use wheelchairs. But no one mentioned the terror. About the terrible wildness and dread in this huge place—nothing. About drugs, about guns . . ."

"Yes," Varennes said, "but that's hardly a serious matter, the opinions of those people, what the interior decorators are saying, what the feature editors print."

"Quite right, but it made me think it was high time to write a piece, since I grew up here. Several generations of Cordes . . ."

Varennes then said that we had had a very thoughtful exchange, he and I, and that was nice in its way (but what of it? by implication). I had to agree. We sat there explaining evils to each other, to pass them off somehow, redistribute the various monstrous elements, and compose something the well-disposed liberal democratic temperament could live with. Nobody actually said, "An evil has been done." No, it was rather, "An unfortunate crazed man destroyed a woman, true enough, but it would be wrong of us to constitute ourselves judges of this crime since its causes lie in certain human and social failures." A fine, broad-minded conclusion, and does us credit. Although real intelligence is too vigilant to accept this credit and suggests to us all (since it is universal, the common property of all human beings) that this is only a form, and a far from distinguished form, of mutual aid.

Varennes went on, "I don't know what you'd get out of talking with Spofford Mitchell. I'd have to take this up with my team, and I'd have to ask Spofford, too. I have to respect his rights. I guess you would find it interesting to see where he is. The more serious homicide cases are way down below. The officers don't even open their doors at mealtimes down there. They push their trays under the doors. Then the rats come along and lick the icing off the bars."

"Icing?"

Varennes said, "The kitchens bake cake. . . ."

The look we exchanged over the cake was singular.

But I broke it off, and backed down. I said, why not—cake and icing, why not? And it was too bad about the extra-security cells. I changed the subject. Of course I didn't want to get in the way, infringe on Mitchell's rights in any way or hamper his defense. He said he aimed to save Spofford Mitchell from the chair. I asked, was this a professional aim or a moral-legal one—was he speaking as a lawyer who didn't like to lose a case or did he have an obligation to save the man's life. He was not glad to hear this question. He was uptight as he said he saw no conflict, and what a bad gang the prosecution was. They kept a tally on their office wall. For a death sentence they chalked up a skull and crossbones.

Then he turned about and took the initiative from me. *He* became the questioner. He said I came down to inspect the Public Defender's office and put him on the defensive as a representative of the educated middle class as if I thought he held a sinecure, and was self-indulgent. At least this mass of trained muscle could speak honestly. The base of his big throat became charged with emotion. He wasn't angry yet, but a certain amount of indignation was developing, and he said that he didn't know yet where *I* stood, or from what point of view I was asking him whether he was being professional or moral.

Well, high feeling was—or might be—a true sign of earnestness. This was better than the first stage of conversation, in which we stated views that might begin to be serious—points for culture and serious concern earned on both sides.

In this phase of the talk I was quite happy, in a whirling disoriented way. I didn't expect him to let me interview Spofford Mitchell (I was a dangerous person), but it was in its way a satisfactory afternoon.

I said, "You're feeling out my racial views. No serious American can allow himself to be suspected of prejudice. This forces us to set aside the immediate data of experience. Because when we think concretely or preverbally, we do see a black skin or a white one, a broad nose or a thin one, just as we see a red apple on a green tree. These are percepts. They should not be under a taboo."

"Well, are they?"

"Yes, we try to stretch the taboo back to cover even these preverbal and concrete observations and simple identifications. Yes, you and I have been playing bad-minton with this subject for quite a while, with a shuttlecock flying back and forth over the taboo net."

Then he said, "Tell me, Dean, how do you see the two people in this case?"

"I see more than a white mask facing a black one. I see two pictures of the soul and spirit—if you will have it straight. In our flesh and blood existence I think we are pictures of something. So I see a picture, and a picture. Race has no bearing on it. I see Spofford Mitchell and Sally Sathers, two separatenesses, two separate and ignorant intelligences. One is staring at the other with terror, and the man is filled with a staggering passion to *break through,* in the only way he can conceive of breaking through—a sexual crash into release."

"Release! I see. From fever and delirium."

"From all the whirling. The horror is in the literalness—the genital literalness of the delusion. That's what gives the curse its finality. The literalness of bodies and their members—outsides without insides."

Sam Varennes seemed to give this some thought. He must actually have been thinking how to get rid of me. We're usually waiting for somebody to clear out and let us go on with the business of life (to cultivate the little obsessional garden). But my case was more special—I had just exposed myself as a nut, a crank in dean's clothing. That was our conversation seen from his side. Well, you never can tell what conclusions a man may reach when you try especially hard to talk straight to him. Neither party is good at it. No one is used to it. And all individual or true thoughts are essentially queer. But outsides without insides—what did that mean! Metaphysics? Epistemology? What?

We were sitting in his office in the Criminal Courts Building at Twenty-sixth and California. (Here Corde would have added to the printed version in *Harper's* that the sun was shining but even in broad daylight there was a touch of the violet hour. Maybe the architect had put a lavender tint into the glass to cut the glare. Maybe the atmosphere did it, or a metabolic derangement of the senses, a sudden increase of toxicity.) There had been many changes at Twenty-sixth and California since the old Bridewell days. New buildings had risen, a modern wing at County Jail, the achievement of Rufus Ridpath, for which his reward was disgrace, character assassination. Buses rolled up all day long. Prisoners brought from all the lockups in the city were unloaded here. The men hopped out by twos, handcuffed. As they went in pairs down the ramp to be processed in the jail, most were downcast or in a silent rage, but a few were having a hell of a time, reeling with homecoming spirits, yelling to the guards, "Hey, Mack! Look who's back!" They trooped in to be psyched, social-worked, assigned to cells.

Around the courts and prison buildings, viewed from the superb height of Varennes' office, lay huge rectangles, endless regions of the stunned city—many, many square miles of civil Passchendaele or Somme. Only at the center of the city, visible from all points over fields of demolition, the tall glamour of the skyscrapers. Around the towers, where the perpetual beacons mingled their flashes with open day, there was a turbulence of two kinds of light.

Varennes said, "When you talk about whirling you make it sound like the maelstrom—like Edgar Allan Poe."

"You mean apocalyptic. Once you start in with apocalypse you lose your dependable, constructive social frame of reference."

Now, here Corde would have added, in an improved

version of his article, that Varennes was healthy, a
normal person, with a preference for decent liberal
thought. The details of his appointment to the Public
Defender's job were normal in Cook County. It was
not easy to get in without sponsorship. But he was a
symbol, anyway, of the public demand for decency to
which even big Clout was obliged to make (limited)
concessions. Nevertheless he was an educated and a
decent man—jogged, pumped iron, his hobby was
fixing up classic cars. And he was interested in what the
Dean had to say. Dean Corde, sitting there, palms
upward in his lap, one leg flung over the other. The
Dean had an underbrow glance of swerving shrewdness. It seemed to interest Varennes in a theoretical
way to hear the Dean talk about turbulence and
whirling states, about subhuman incomprehension,
about a woman begging for life when the lid of the car
trunk was raised. Was his visitor trying to tell him (a
middle-class fear) that the country was falling apart or
something? Actually the Dean didn't seem to be that
sort of Nervous Nellie or commonplace hysteric. Some
part of him really was shrewd; at moments he was
acute, even hardheaded.

"What would you like?" said Varennes. "Would you
give the dead woman's husband a gun and let him take
shots at Mitchell through the bars of his cell?"

"Did I suggest anything like that?"

"No, you didn't, Dean. I suppose I'm only fishing."

The Dean said, "Let me make it clear to you what I
think. Your defendant belongs to that black underclass
everybody is openly talking about, which is economically 'redundant,' to use the term specialists now use,
falling farther and farther behind the rest of society,
locked into a culture of despair and crime—*I* wouldn't
say a culture, that's another specialists' word. There is
no culture there, it's only a wilderness, and damn
monstrous, too. We are talking about a people con-
signed to destruction, a doomed people. Compare
them to the last phase of the proletariat as pictured by

Marx. The proletariat, owning *nothing,* stripped utterly bare, would awaken at last from the nightmare of history. Entirely naked, it would have no illusions because there was nothing to support illusions and it would make a revolution without any scenario. It would need no historical script because of its merciless education in reality, and so forth. Well, here is a case of people denuded. And what's the effect of denudation, atomization? Of course, they aren't proletarians. They're just a lumpen population. We do not know how to approach this population. We haven't even conceived that reaching it may be a problem. So there's nothing but death before it. Maybe we've already made our decision. Those that can be advanced into the middle class, let them be advanced. The rest? Well, we do our best by them. We don't have to do any more. They kill some of us. Mostly they kill themselves. . . ."

Varennes asked, "Is this the conclusion you aim at in your article?"

"Oh, I haven't even begun to reach a conclusion. So far I'm only in the describing stage. What I'm telling you is simply what I see happening. The worst of it I haven't gotten around to at all—the slums we carry around inside us. Every man's *inner* inner city . . . Some other time we can talk about that."

That was the end of our conversation. The telephone rang. An important call. He excused himself (I was ready to leave) and got rid of me. He promised to discuss the matter with his colleagues. He was a very nice man. Almost talkable-to. Those are the worst. For a while you almost feel you're getting somewhere.

11

Vlada Voynich couldn't make it on Christmas Day. Travel had tired her, she explained to Minna on the telephone, but she would attend the funeral—of course she would be coming—and she'd visit them afterwards at home. Minna was busy with callers. It was Cousin Dincutza who brought this message to Corde. Corde was shut up in the room (by now it was his room). He had a bright winter day to look at. To mingle with visitors and make small talk was definitely beyond him. He didn't even try. Dincutza, replacing Gigi, who was very busy now, had assigned herself to look after him. She brought him a cup of tea occasionally, and she was his informant. He learned from her that Gigi's campaign to bring Valeria to the Medical School had failed—no lying in state. Petrescu had called just now to say that an announcement of the funeral had just appeared in the afternoon paper. It was to be held at the crematorium. No official honors.

In the morning Corde helped his ladies to organize themselves for the funeral. "It'll be cold as hell there," he said to Minna. "Remember what it was like the other day. That dome is a refrigerator." He urged her to wear her own American coat, but she wouldn't, she wrapped herself in her mother's synthetic fur. She had layers of sweaters underneath, so she'd be warm enough, she said. Gigi also wore an imitation fur. To Corde these coats were odd—the lusterless needles mingled brown and purple, they felt soft enough, they had a heavy look but no actual weight; it was up to the wearer to put life into them. Corde's motive, his theme today was to make sure that Minna had everything she might need. She didn't seem to want much. But if he hadn't offered, she would have noticed, abstracted though she was. Thankless work, but necessary.

For the funeral there was funeral weather. No more sun, that was gone, only linty clouds and a low cold horizon. At daybreak there had been frost over the pavements; patches of it remained. It was like the Chicago winter, which shrank your face and tightened your sphincters.

Cousin Dincutza was waiting with Traian beside the small Dacia. In the cold Traian's face was meaty, dense, the color of prosciutto. Under the zippered and belted leather jacket he was built like a small boiler. He wore the legs of his tight blue jeans tucked into his boot tops. At the corners of his mouth, the Mexican wisps, but when you saw him in profile the face turned Byzantine. It was the straight, long nose that did it, the full dark eye. Gigi, too, had this sort of nose, and unlike Traian, she had the classic long Byzantine neck. Age had made it muscular. Because she was so stooped now, the neck detached itself from the collar of the synthetic coat. Beneath her sadly intense brown eyes there were sallow circles. In her own setting Minna, too, looked like a Greek woman. This corner of Europe was after all Macedonian, Roman, Armenian, Turkish —the Eastern empire. If the cold reminded you of Chicago, the faces were from the ancient world. But then in Chicago you had something like a vast international refugee camp, and faces from all over. It was in Chicago after all that he, a Huguenot-Irish-Midwesterner and whatnot else, found the Macedonian-Armenian-Turkish-Slav woman who was exactly what he had been looking for.

Corde was put in the front seat. The three ladies were in the back. Dincutza, the poor relation, sat in a sort of padded Chinese jacket between the two synthetic furs. Traian's first stop was the hospital, where he

took a branching driveway to the side of the building.
Heavy but quick, a compact man in crunching boots, he
slammed the door and walked, efficient, to the service
entrance. They watched him go in. Traian, thank God,
knew what he was doing. When he returned, he spoke
to the bundled passengers through the driver's half-
open window. He said Valeria was dressed and ready,
and that the hearse was on its way, as arranged. He
would stand in the main driveway to wait for it. Then
he tipped his cap to Minna—or did he only resettle it on
his head?—and handed her a brown envelope containing Valeria's rings, two of them. Corde turned in his
seat as Minna shook them from the crumpled paper
into her hand. It had been necessary to saw through the
gold. They were clotted with blood. Corde drew back a
little at the sight of the red drops, but Minna did not
appear upset. She said, "This one with the stone was
my mother's engagement ring. She never took it off."
With her thumbnail she chipped off the dried blood and
wiped the rings with a paper tissue. She slipped off her
wedding band, put on the sawed rings, and then again
the wedding band. Keep them in place.

   The undertaker drove up in a panel truck. This was
not what Corde had expected—a sort of dry cleaner's
van, it would have been in the States. It backed up to
the loading platform. The body was put in, and then
Traian's little car followed the faded blue van-hearse
through the city. In the center of town traffic was
already heavy. The three ladies were silent, and Corde,
in the fedora, had nothing to say. He looked out,
noticing. What a man he was for noticing! Continually
attentive to his surroundings. As if he had been sent
down to *mind* the outer world, on a mission of observation and notation. The object of which was? To link up?
To classify? To penetrate? To follow a sprinting little
van-hearse over gloomy boulevards was the immediate
assignment.

   Around an uphill curve they came up to the mortuary chapel on its hilltop, trickling smoke from the dome

into gray air. The panel truck had just parked and
Traian pulled up behind it. The attendants were drawing out Valeria's lidless coffin. The technicians had seen
to her hair; it was carefully dressed, wouldn't be
exposed to the wind for long. Valeria was already being
carried up the long flight of stairs in her silk suit,
buttoned with silver Macedonian buttons, long in the
family. Italian high-heeled shoes. She had been wearing those shoes last spring in London when Corde had
noticed that she was stumbling, first in front of the hotel
and then at Burlington House. Those were the heels
that had gone crooked and tripped her up.

People stood waiting on the broad outer stairs, a
beggar's opera crowd of aged friends. Again, the suits
and coats, the Sunday-best outfits cut fifty years ago
from good prewar material. One old woman was
burdened by a real fur coat, so heavy she was hardly
strong enough to carry it. She seemed determined to
have a close look at Valeria. A ruined old husband
supported her as she labored down the stairs to the
coffin. They were just in time to see her as she passed.
Valeria carried up the stairs by two men looked very
much the Roman matron again, Corde thought, not the
old woman he had electrified on her deathbed.

Under the center of the dome the crowd was large.
The chairs on both sides of the bier were only in the
way, no one wanted to use them. They were pushed
back. Corde stood between Minna and Gigi; Cousin
Dincutza was directly behind him. Friends of the
family, coming up, understood only too well that
Minna might not be able to recognize them. She had
been gone more than twenty years. Some of them could
not easily raise their heads for identification, their neck
muscles had grown so stiff. Yes, many had the cervical
arthrosia. There were splashes of dark pigment on their
faces. Old mouths gaped up at you when they spoke.
These were "Papa's colleagues," or old Party com-
rades, busted journalists, onetime boyars, former
teachers, distant cousins. They came . . . well, they

had their reasons. They were there to signify, to testify. They came also to remind Minna of their existence. "Yes, we're still here, in case you wondered, and we could tell you plenty. And your mother, she got you away, it was one of her great successes. Good for you. And for her. Now it's over for her, and soon for us, too. And this is what turns us out, in this gloom." People had spent extravagantly on flowers. There were only carnations, and those were hard to come by. Dincutza said, *"En hiver on trouve très peu de fleurs. Ils coûtent les yeux de la tête."* She told Corde how many lei for a single carnation. Several times Valeria's face had to be cleared of flowers. Gigi, from the other side, told him that Petrescu alone was responsible for the wreaths. From official sources. There was a band of color also behind the crowd, on the perimeter. Along the curve of the wall were the square canisters of ashes, and pots of cyclamens with ribbons, lighted candles, burning speckles, fire grains, garnet points in the murk. There were candles, flowers, but it was freezing. Cold consumed Corde under his socks and sweaters. You could feel the fires below. Currents of heat flowed under the floor, but it wasn't the kind of heat you could be warmed by. It came from the openings at the edges of the raised bier, through the metal joints, from under the long bivalve barrel which would close when the coffin sank.

The speeches now began. Corde had lived long enough in Europe to be familiar with Communist oratory, the lame rhythms of rhetorical questions and answers. "Who was this woman? She was . . . a comrade, a militant . . ." Terrible stuff. Under the dome it sounded exceptionally heavy. He supposed that by now there was no other style of public speaking in any province of the Russian empire, and he blessed his ignorance of the language. The last speech—they were all short—was delivered by Mihai Petrescu, who proved to be by far the most emotional of them all. He could not finish, he broke down. As if to cover him, the slow movement of Beethoven's Third began to vibrate unevenly from loudspeakers. The tapes were frayed, thready, quavering. Minna brushed away the flowers on the step of the bier, knelt by the coffin and kissed Valeria. Next Tanti Gigi bent over her sister's face. The synthetic fur bristled over her back.

Cousin Dincutza just then began whispering to Corde from behind. There was a last formality to attend to. Still one document to be signed. Regulations required that a member of the family go below for final identification of the deceased before cremation.

"By me?"

"Or her sister, or her daughter."

"Not a cousin?"

A cousin was *pas assez proche*. Otherwise, wouldn't she have done it herself? She saw that he was rattled. The thought of going underneath bristled over him. He'd have to go. What alternative was there? The old woman took his arm soothingly, as if to tell him there was nothing to be afraid of. He put his faith in her mottled face, brown buck teeth, sparse hair, goodness of heart. He said okay. This was not the moment to speak to Minna. Quavering, the big Beethoven chords now concluded; the barrel cylinder was closing and simultaneously the coffin began to go down, flowers tumbling after into the gap. The action was quick. The heavy drum grated shut. Valeria had gone below.

Immediately, Minna and Gigi were surrounded by friends. Corde followed Dincutza through the crowd. Traian was waiting at the head of the stairs.

Corde went first, they made way for him. He took air like a diver and trotted down into the increasing heat. It thickened about him. When he reached the bottom he saw Ioanna beside the coffin, which had just arrived. She was kissing Valeria's hand, laying it to her cheek. She wept and spoke brokenly to the dead woman.

"What's she saying?"

"Asking to be forgiven," said Dincutza.

For being a police informer? Just as Petrescu, the only speaker who had choked up, was a member of the security forces? But it wasn't likely that Ioanna would blame herself for having a police connection. If you didn't have one you weren't a concierge, and what was wrong with being a concierge? And if she was going to protect the old sisters it was necessary to be in with the cops. And it wasn't the packets of money, it wasn't the presents from London that she did it for. She would have said, "The Doamna Doctor loved me; I loved her." When Ioanna, crouching by the coffin, lifted her eyes to Corde, the blue eyes burnt as if her tears were alcohol. Here was the heat he had felt underfoot in the hall. It was like a stokehold. It went into the tissues, drove all your moisture to the surface. Corde, who had come down shivering, now felt the hot weight of the fedora, his sweatband soaking. He tried by shallow breathing to keep out the corpse smoke, protect his lungs. The heat made you feel all your organs like paper, like the Christmas bell ornaments that used to unfold, all red cells inside and crackling when they were opened. His throat was drying out, and he began to cough. The punt coffin (with flowers) sat on a conveyor belt which moved forward a notch at a time. Weeping, Ioanna followed it. Again a stop. There were other bodies preceding Valeria's. Corde could only think of her as the dead, waiting to be burned. As between frost and flames, weren't flames better?

Traian was convincing the belowstairs official who sat at a high desk that this foreigner was qualified to sign for the family. His credentials had to be examined. He handed over the blue U.S. passport, still looking towards Ioanna. It was right that she should cry over the body, he even owed her something for it. Handed a ballpoint, Corde bent to the register and scrawled his name full across the page. Then he straightened, twitched off his glasses, groped in the inner pocket for the case—for the love of Christ, let's get out of here. There were sweat circles under his arms from the blasting heat. The people here weren't going to open those black steel doors and let them watch a coffin rattling over the rollers, entering, wouldn't show their fires to outsiders.

Dincutza now drew him towards the stairs again and Ioanna helped him as if he were a baby whose incompetence she pitied; but her bulk blocked his way. It was a tight fit in the staircase. Traian spoke sharply to her. On the first landing it was cold again. Corde felt cut in half by the extremes of heat and cold. So, again the freezing dome and the crowd surrounding Minna. Better this cold than that heat. Corde's breast, as narrow as a ladder, was crowded with emotions—fire, death, suffocation, put into an icy hold or, instead, crackling in a furnace. Your last options. They still appeared equally terrible. How to choose between them!

With Dincutza again making a way for him, he was brought back to stand beside Minna.

Ah, the American husband, the Dean. People had been looking for him. They had come to pay their respects, but they were here also to see this couple, the famous astronomer née Raresh and the man she had married. Old guys gave Corde rapid French handshakes, German bows. Gigi's interpretation of the large turnout was that people were telling the regime something. Well, maybe they were, but Corde did not see this as a demonstration. It wasn't because Valeria had fallen from grace, or because she had stood up to the Politburo or the Central Committee, or refused years later to rejoin the Party when they invited her. They came out with a sort of underfed dignity in what was left of their presocialist wardrobe, to affirm that there was a sort of life—and perhaps, as Communists or even Iron Guardists (it was conceivable), they had sinned against it—the old European life which at its most disgraceful was infinitely better than this present one. Most of them were too old to worry about reprisals, and in any case what had they done but dig their Vienna-made suits out of mothballs, put on the balding furs their backs were too weak to support, click heels, murmur French, pay respects to a leading member of their generation, et cetera?

Gigi said to Corde, "While you were away Vlada Voynich passed in the greetings line. But she said she would come later to the house. . . . Many important people are here. I have never seen such an occasion. I did not expect Dr. Gherea. He has had the decency, after all, and there he is in the line. Do you recognize him from the picture?"

Looking for the notorious neurosurgeon, Corde saw instead the heavy figure of his boyhood friend Dewey Spangler, the groomed beard, the full plum flush of his mature face. In moments of excitement he still executed the rapid double nod downward with his chin—a charming mannerism, come to think of it. Corde thought, Whattaya know. He took the trouble to come. I didn't realize I meant that much to him. . . . Maybe I don't.

Introduced to Minna, Dewey made an approving grimace to Corde, he gave his okay. Some things hadn't changed—Dewey's expressions of face, for instance. The essentials were what they had been, only more condensed. He said, "What about our drink, pal?"

"This afternoon?" said Corde.

"I'll rescue you at two o'clock. It's our last chance."

12

By noon, in clear, warmer weather, Corde welcomed the streets after the chill of the domed hall. It took hours to get the ice out of your system. Walking from the apartment with Vlada Voynich, he ventilated his lungs. All that day it felt to him as if he must make an effort to rewarm his blood and clear the smoke from his breathing tubes. He had had just time enough before leaving the house with Vlada to eat a slice of bread and butter and to swallow a large shot of Balkan plum brandy. Powerful stuff, but it went to his extremities rather than his brain; his hands and feet felt tighter, even the surface of his face was tingling as if a helpful pal had given him a few slaps for his own good. He was not entirely himself—the inward fever, ice in the system, he felt disarticulated. But why should he expect to be himself? At the crematorium he had gone through a death rehearsal. You couldn't rehearse death gratis. It had to cost something.

Vlada, glancing at him from the side, evidently saw that he didn't look well and said, "It's all been hard on you, hasn't it?" This was unacceptable, for some reason. He fended off her sympathy.

"You mean the whole December? Oh, I had some time to myself. I caught up on my sleep. The old apartment is very quiet, except for the telephone. Minna's room was a kind of sanctuary. It's Minna who's having it hard."

"Where shall we go for this talk?"

"If it isn't too cold, and the sun keeps shining, I'd prefer the open air to a café."

"There's a small park just up the street. There used to be."

"It's still there. Minna pointed it out the other day—near her old school."

Vlada was a woman in whom you could have confidence—solid. She was large, her face wide, middle-aged, calm, candid, her complexion very white, the whiteness thick, almost opaque. Because of the length of her smile, her brown eyes, she had something in common with Corde's sister Elfrida. Her hair, like Elfrida's, was unsuitably dyed, far too dark. He would have hesitated to touch it. Dyes and fixative sprays took the life out of hair. But Vlada must have considered this when she made her decision. She was a chemist, after all, she knew what manufacturers put into dyes and sprays.

They settled on a bench in the sun between two pollarded trees—dwarf branches knobbed, knuckled with sealed buds on the bunched twigs, and the trunks wrapped smooth in winter hides. "Ah, how nice." He bent his hat at the back to protect his neck from the chill. A poor park, badly kept; but he was glad to be here with Vlada. He trusted her, he took comfort in her. The large head of hair parted down the middle and coming down in two waves, the wide teeth, the reassuring feminine breath—to him these were elements of stability. She had been married once, many years ago. Her ex-husband had been, by her account, one of the world's permanent and growing population of educated lunatics. Too bad—she would make someone a dependable wife, a good warm embracer, and stable; she would be sympathetic, intelligent, decent. But above all she was stable. Corde often sized up marriageable women in this way, entertained notions about them —maybe illusions was the fitter word. "You haven't got any news for me about the Lucas Ebry trial, have you, Vlada?"

"Only more of the same in the newspapers."

"There ought to be a verdict soon. Did Alec Witt send some messages for me?"

"I brought you an envelope. It's back at the apartment. . . . My brother told me about the Colonel. So now you've had a taste of our country."

"Your country? I thought you were Serbian."

"We are. Voynich is a Serbian name. But my brother married a Rumanian woman. That's how I got here in my twenties."

"What did your brother tell you about the Colonel?"

"Firsthand he doesn't know, but people like this generally are trained in prison administration, sometimes in those so-called psychiatric institutions where they keep dissidents."

"They do everything Russian style. If you're a dissident who can't see the socialist paradise, you must be sick in the head. . . . This Colonel must have lots of clout."

"The decision on a case like this probably was made higher up."

"Because Minna defected? Valeria abhorred that word. The regime did have it in for Valeria. Was it some old class thing?"

"Valeria was not a boyar. The Party is still hard on old boyar families. She was a Communist, all right, but she couldn't get rid of the old distinguished-lady manner. Besides, she was a Dubcek sympathizer. Anyway, she's gone."

"Yes. It puzzled me that they should make so much trouble in a case like this, of no political importance—just a mother and her daughter. Only rubbing it in that nobody has any private rights. Which is not news. But as you say, she's gone. . . . I would have liked to talk to your brother. He said he'd come take me for a walk."

"Oh, he couldn't do that, Albert. He doesn't talk. If you have a conversation with a foreigner, you're supposed to report it to the authorities, and my brother has to be specially careful with the authorities. By the way,

if any of Minna's school friends wanted to invite her to
their homes they would have to go and get an official
clearance from something they call *Protocól*. Without
Protocól they couldn't give her a cup of tea."

"So your brother couldn't risk it?"

"My brother was in prison for ten years, as a social
democrat. Most of the time he was in solitary confinement. But then there was a mission of British Labor
Party people coming. They had met him in the old days.
When they were asked whom they would like to see,
they named him. So he was taken out of solitary. They
cleaned him up, shaved him, gave him a suit of clothes,
and he was taken to an apartment. He was supposed
to be giving a dinner to the British delegation. It
was about six in the evening. The guests were due at
seven. At about six-fifteen, they brought in his wife.
She had been in prison, too. Ten years. The one
didn't know whether the other was still living. She
was wearing a nice dress. No time to talk, the cook
was an agent, anyway. Any minute, the bell would
ring. . . ."

"Ah, what a thing. The visitors never caught on?
Like G. B. Shaw in Russia. Like Henry Wallace. The
old Potemkin Village trick . . . After which your brother and his wife weren't sent back?"

"They didn't send them back. . . . Last year his wife
died." (In the earthquake? I won't ask, Corde decided.
I may have passed her canister.) "And my brother lives
alone, very quietly. No promenades with foreigners,
though. He was sorry. He said you looked *sympa*. I told
him he was right. Beech also thinks you're *sympa-
thique*."

"I liked him, too."

"Have you had a chance to read the material I gave
you?"

"Oh, I've had nothing but time. I didn't often get out
of the house. Minna was afraid of letting me out alone.
She thought they might pick me up on some pretext,
and that would really complicate things. She may have

been exaggerating, but I didn't argue; it was better to stay put. Yes, I read the documents."

"I didn't give you any of the technical material."

"I see that. No point in loading me with chemical data I don't understand."

"How did you feel about it?"

"Let's see—how did I feel? I felt interested. I felt alarmed by the danger. Naturally, I'm a good concerned American. I want bad things to stop, good things to go forward. I want democracy to win, and civilization to survive, but I don't want to become an environmentalist. For me it would be a waste of time, and I haven't the time to waste."

"Beech would never call himself that. He thought you might not quite understand and he asked me to explain more fully. To begin with, he has confidence in you."

"How can he have? We met only twice—or was it three times? That's not enough."

"He's read you."

"It was you that made him."

"Yes, but he thinks you're an artist in your line, not the ordinary kind of journalist."

Corde put down his head to let this pass over. She was trying to calm him with flattery. Were there so many signs of nervousness? Enough, probably. And why shouldn't there be? "Well, if I'm some kind of artist, I must be busy with some kind of art. I wish I knew what it was."

In the wintry sunlight Vlada's face was densely white. She gave him a fully open look. But he didn't have the confidence he had once had in these open looks. It wasn't that he distrusted Vlada, but people were never as sincere as they revved themselves up to be. They couldn't guarantee that their purposes were fixed and constant. Yes, constancy. Love is not love which alters where it alteration finds. What did love have to do with it? She only wanted to show that he could really trust her. And what he thought was, I'm pale, I look unwell, I look rotten, I'm skittish and jumpy—I'm all over the place (quoting Shakespeare out of context). She wants to be nice to me. I had an especially blasting morning. It's still with me. All right, I trust you, Vlada, but you want to get me to take on this job. Probably she's somewhat surprised that I don't jump at the chance. It's an honor. One thing is that her eyes (the chestnut color, this open look) are very handsome. The dark contrast with the white complexion does it. And the eyes are supposed to take me into a proposition I suspect to be dubious. I am willing to yield to the *beaux yeux,* but not necessarily to the proposition. But she's all right, she's a good egg, and I'll hear her out if she'll hear me out. She's devoted to Beech. I envy him that. He's got beautiful support. If he weren't a good guy he wouldn't have won such devotion. No, that might not follow, either.

She said, "I've worked with him for years, and I can recommend him."

"I like the man's looks. He's one of those American hayseed farm types who turn out to be world geniuses. He looks like Ichabod Crane."

Vlada said, "Your looks are misleading, too."

Bass voice, mild manner, plain appearance—yes. He said, "In *Huckleberry Finn* there's a circus clown who falls over his own feet but turns out to be a marvelous equestrian and acrobat. Maybe that's the classic American model—look like a poor stick but turn somersaults on a galloping horse. Well, I won't fence around with you, Vlada, on a day like this."

At this very instant Valeria might be going into the fire, the roaring furnace which took off her hair, the silk scarf, grabbed away the green suit, melted the chased silver buttons, consumed the skin, flashed away the fat, blew up the organs, reached the bones, bore down on the skull—that refining fire, a ball of raging gold, a tiny sun, a star.

He had stopped talking.

"You were saying, a day like this?"

"Yes. I seem to have a headache, something like eyestrain. You wouldn't have a Tylenol in your purse? I can swallow it without water."

"No. Am I giving you a headache by putting pressure on you?"

"The Provost tried to tell me not to mix into this, that it might do Beech harm to associate with me. I shouldn't put Beech in the line of fire; he has troubles enough."

"Yes, the Provost had a chat with Beech."

"And suggested that he might come in for some of the heat I'm getting?"

"Well, are you really so hot as you think? It's just some local unpleasantness. Beech could say his findings affect all Homo sapiens, and the future of the entire species."

"I see that. He talks continually about *Homo sapiens sapiens,* and hominid evolution."

"What impressed him, and it's the word he used, is that you aren't contentious. You didn't look for trouble, but you're capable of fighting. But the antagonism of people in Chicago is insignificant. He has another ball game in mind altogether." (Corde enjoyed hearing slang from these foreign women.) "Besides, Beech and the Provost have never gotten along. Look, if you go to Washington and testify that the mining and smelting of lead have to stop and that the food and canning industries should be restrained and that the U.S. should lead a world campaign and start immediately to clean up the air and the waters, at a cost of billions . . ."

"It doesn't bring the college much financial support. It gets the FDA into the picture. And Witt would like to keep us apart—a wacko scientist and a cracked dean."

"Why worry about Witt?"

"It isn't worry. The college has been decent to me. Even Witt went out of his way."

"He put up the reward for information in the murder case. So if he feels you'd be bad for Beech you don't want to cross him. But this is merely administration

politics. You've got to look beyond that, much further.
Beech can't communicate. He says if he were to try to
do this himself he'd end up like Bucky Fuller, giving
incomprehensible lectures. I say nothing against Fuller
—he's wonderful. I only mean there's a special cult
public that loves high-minded kook specialists who
preach salvation through organic foods . . . how to
preserve the shrinking water reserves in a demographic
explosion. But try to understand what Beech is up
against. He has to start a world discussion at the highest
level. You have a gift for getting the attention of a
serious public."

"I'm good at sticking it to them, am I? That's
probably true, but true because I have my own ends. I
couldn't do it for other people. It wouldn't work. No
one would pay the slightest attention."

"I see that. I do. But if you understood his ends, they
might be yours, too. It wouldn't be a personal matter.
It's far from a personal matter with him."

"Yes, he made that clear to me. Liberal humanist
culture is weak because it lacks scientific knowledge.
He'd communicate some science to me and then we
could go forward. Minna also thinks it would *upgrade*
me to associate with a man of science. Better than
squalid Chicago, as a project."

"I can't really see why you're so skeptical. You're
making me argue, fight."

"I don't doubt the nobility of Beech's intentions."

"He's put together a masterpiece of research."

Corde said, "The sun is moving. I'm beginning to
feel cold again. Let's walk a little."

"I have enough layers so that I don't feel the frost,"
said Vlada. "When I'm about to come back to the old
country I always begin to eat more. Last year all I could
find in the shops here was boxes of salt, jars of garlic
pickles, some sauerkraut. Now and then chickens turn
up. You stand in line for eggs. Meat is hard to get even
on the black market. Fish, never. Other Eastern bloc
countries have changed from the original Stalin agricul-

tural plan. This one, never. You can't even buy potatoes. I always fly back slimmer."

They walked in the sun, on the crackling gravel path. "You carry the weight with class," said Corde.

"Among my Serbian family in Chicago, the women say, 'How do you expect to get a husband if you don't reduce?' But I tell them, 'I may not get one even if I stop eating, and then I'm a double loser.'"

"According to your own theory, the more you eat, the more you stupefy yourself with lead."

She laughed and said, "It doesn't build up as fast as that." Corde valued grace in fat women. Vlada walked well, she knew how to place her foot.

"You can't get inured or mithridated?"

She shook her head. That wasn't possible. "Only poisoned. The nervous system is permanently affected. Kids become behavior problems, restless, frantic, and intelligence is permanently impaired."

"Therefore this world—and no matter what we're like, it's a delicious world . . ."

"Yes, is the answer."

"So the bottom line is that we eat and drink lead, we breathe it. It accumulates in the seas, which are getting heavier by the day, and it's absorbed by plants and stockpiled in the calcium of the bones. Brains are being mineralized. The great reptiles with their small brains wore thick armor, but our big brains are being hardened from within?"

He amused Vlada with this survey. More widely smiling, lips large and long, and her white face vividly warm, she said, "I love it when you get going, Albert."

"That's all right," he said. "I'm only thinking aloud. I'm not talking myself into anything." Then he came near laughing, and when she asked him why, he said, "Well, you see what it's like here. We were at the crematorium just this morning and now we're discussing whether I should join Beech in his campaign to warn mankind against the greatest danger of all. At the moment I feel myself crawling between heaven and

earth, and it is a little funny to be offered a big role: the
rescuer. Christ, not me! The heart damn near jumped
out of my chest when I had to go below to identify
Valeria. I was dripping sweat and having fits and
convulsions in the guts. And now I'm strolling in this
park with you, I'm a gentleman again, taking the grand
survey of man's future, the fate of the earth."

"I see that," said Vlada. "It's a bad day to try to get
your attention for a project of this kind. Seems unreal
and far away in these circumstances."

"No, I admire Beech, and I'd like to go into some of
this with him. He probably feels he can't wait, pressed
for time. Asked you to sound me out, get me started."

"I never led him to think that because we're friends,
and I've been close to Minna since the Harvard days,
that I had you in my pocket."

"Of course you didn't. And I'm trying to look as
closely as I can at the whole proposition. Sometimes
these 'hard' scientists are far out, like a separate
species. It makes them especially interesting to me."

"You married one."

"I married one. That's different. That's love. It
brings Minna back from outer space. Some I've met
never do get back. Some are subject to storms of clear
consciousness—my homemade term. Like turbulence,
when the pilot asks you to fasten your seat belt. Then
there are the ones who have strong musical leanings or
are interested in poetry. Now that does appeal to me.
And as for those that are far, far out, absorbed in their
special complex games—I've often thought it possible
that one of them might turn out to be clairvoyant. Just a
little. But you have to be careful about this."

"Let me see if I'm following," said Vlada.

"Look at it this way: Lead as a mineral may or may
not be the threat that Beech warns us against, but being
'leaden' certainly is a characteristic. Sometimes I
say 'earthen'—we often experience this earthenness.
Sometimes I say 'sclerotic,' or 'blind,' 'eyes that see
not, ears that hear not'—and this leads up to 'the

general end of everything' heralded by sclerotic, blind and earthen. 'Lead' is more sinister, maybe because of its color, hue or weight. Lead communicates something special to us about matter, our existence in matter. At Lakeview there was a kid who wrote poems, Joey Hamil, and I remember one of his lines about 'Thy leaden mace flung upon my weathered brow.' He didn't have a weathered brow. He was only sixteen years old."

"So you wonder whether 'lead' is just what Professor Beech has fixed upon but stands for something else that we all sense."

"That's possible, isn't it? The man is in his supersterile lab built for the analysis of moon rocks when it strikes him from both sides that an imbalance in the mineral realm itself threatens mankind, all of life and the world itself. There's poetry in that, isn't there? Man's great technical works, looming over him, have coated him with deadly metal. We can't carry the weight. The blood is sobbing in us. Our brains grow feebler. This disaster also overtook the Roman Empire. It wasn't the barbarians, it wasn't the Christians, it wasn't moral corruption: his theory is that the real cause was the use of lead to prevent the souring of wine. Lead was the true source of the madness of the Caesars. Leaded wine brought the empire to ruin."

"Bones from Roman graves do show extreme concentrations of the metal," said Vlada. "I've examined those in my own lab."

"And that was only Rome. Now it's the whole world. And it isn't the Grand Inquisitor's universal anthill that we have to worry about after all, but something worse, more Titanic—universal stupefaction, a Saturnian, wild, gloomy murderousness, the raging of irritated nerves, and intelligence reduced by metal poison, so that the main ideas of mankind die out, including of course the idea of freedom."

Corde breathed sharply, still ridding himself of (imaginary) smoke inhalation. He drew in the blue icicle-

making air of the small park with its fallen fence of iron
stakes—collapsed on weeds and bushes.

"I wonder if Beech thinks as romantically as that,"
said Vlada.

"It's you that work with him—but who knows," said
Corde. "And I'm sure I'm overdrawing it, but if there
are mysterious forces around, only exaggeration can
help us to see them. We all sense that there are powers
that make the world—we see that when we look at
it—and other powers that unmake it. And when people
shed incomprehensible tears they feel that they're
expressing this truth, somehow, one that may be otherwise inexpressible in our present condition. But it's a
rare sense, and people aren't used to it, and it can't get
them anywhere. Tears may be intellectual, but they can
never be political. They save no man from being shot,
no child from being thrown alive into the furnace. My
late father-in-law would weep when he lost a patient.
At the same time he belonged to the Communist
underground. The Doctor would weep. I wonder if the
Communist ever did. . . ."

"This is an interesting talk," said Vlada. "But I'll
have to ask you to set me straight. . . ."

"Why, of course," said Corde. "I'm asking whether
certain impulses and feelings which play no part in the
scientific work of a man like Professor Beech and lie
ignored or undeveloped in his nature may not suddenly
have come to life. These resurrections can be gruesome. You can sometimes watch them—clumsy, absurd
heart stirrings after decades of atrophy. Sometimes it's
the most heartless people who are inspired after forty
years of reckoning and calculation and begin to accuse
everybody else of being heartless. But as I see Beech,
he's innocent of that. The news, let's call it that,
reaches him in his lab as he puts the results of his
research in order. Like, 'This earth which I've been
studying for a lifetime is a being, too. It gave birth to us
all, but we are ungrateful, greedy and evil. . . .'"

"And this is news to him—to continue your

argument—his feelings are untrained or undeveloped, and he gets carried away. I understand you better now. Even if he cried, which is not his way . . ."

"It wouldn't be a good approach to politics. You can see that I sympathize with him. And how I wish that clear, exquisite brains like his could resolve all our questions. They don't, though. It's endearing, however, that he looks like a hayseed, an Ichabod Crane, but that he's a man of feeling and even a visionary. He wants to protect and to bless. But then he begins to talk—and what neo-Darwinian stuff he expounds: the two-billion-year struggle by organisms in the biosphere. I'd rather eat a pound of dry starch with a demitasse spoon than read this. Truth should have some style."

"That's where you might be of help."

"What—if I tried to speak for him?"

"It would depend on how it was done."

"It depends upon what he would expect. There would be no difficulty in agreeing that inner city black kids should be saved from poisoning by lead or heroin or synthetic narcotics like the Tees and Blues. The doubtful part of his proposition is that human wickedness is absolutely a public health problem, and nothing but. No tragic density, no thickening of the substance of the soul, only chemistry or physiology. I can't bring myself to go with this medical point of view, whether it applies to murderers or to geniuses. At one end of the scale is Spofford Mitchell. Did he rape and murder a woman because he put flakes of lead paint in his mouth when he was an infant? At the other end, are Beethoven and Nietzsche great because they had syphilis? The twentieth-century Faustus believed this so completely that for the sake of his art he wouldn't have his lesions treated, and the spirochete gave him his awful masterpieces as a reward."

"You'd call that kind of medical interpretation itself 'sclerosis,' or 'lead.'" Vlada followed this.

"Where Beech sees poison lead I see poison thought

or poison theory. The view we hold of the material world may put us into a case as heavy as lead, a sarcophagus which nobody will even have the art to paint becomingly. The end of philosophy and of art will do to 'advanced' thought what flakes of lead paint or leaded exhaust fumes do to infants. Which of these do you think will bring us to the end of everything?"

"So that's how you understand this?"

"Real philosophy, not the groveling stuff the universities mainly do. Otherwise: I remember how I used to stare at Mendeleev's chart in the science class. There it all was—Fe, Cu, Na, He. That's what we were made of. I was so impressed! That's what everything was made of. But Pb is licking all the others. Pb is the Stalin of the elements, the boss. . . . Is it true that Beech has measured the age of the planet accurately?"

"Most geophysicists think so."

"I'm full of admiration. That in itself is wonderful—I listened over and over to the tapes he gave me. There are parts I can recall almost verbatim. He never meant to be a crusader. He was only investigating lead levels and this led him into horror chambers. Then he saw vast and terrible things all the way into the depths of hell, and so forth, and the material foundations of life on this earth being destroyed. And if pure scientists had really understood science they would have realized the morality and poetry implicit in its laws. They didn't. So it's all going to run down the drain, like blood in a Hitchcock movie. The Humanists also have flunked the course. They have no strength because they're ignorant of science. They're bound to be weak because they have no conception of what the main effort of the human mind has been for three centuries and what it has found. So Beech is offering me a trade. I must go back to the classroom and learn what it's all about— *really*. When I've understood the beauty and morality contained in the laws of science, I can take part in the decisive struggle—begin to restore the strength of Humanism."

"I see that doesn't sit very well with you."

"I gave up writing for the papers ten years ago because—well, because my modernity was all used up. I became a college professor in order to cure my ignorance. We made a trade. I teach young people to write for the papers and in return I have an opportunity to learn why my modernity was used up. At the college I had time to read scads of books. In Paris I was too busy doing art items and intellectual chitchat. I did have some interesting assignments. For instance, I wrote a few pieces on the poetess Tsvetayeva as she was remembered by the Russian colony in Paris. How her husband, whom she loved deeply, became a member of the GPU and was forced to take part in killings. But there I'm off the subject. I came back to Chicago to continue my education. And then I had to write those articles. There was no way to avoid it. The youngsters would say it was my karma. Well, there's low-down Chicago and there's high-up Chicago. There's Big Bill Thompson, and then there's Aristotle, who has also had a longtime association with the city, which amuses a great many people. Aristotle, believe it or not, became a great influence in certain parts of Chicago. Our great sister institution the University of Chicago revived him. A. N. Whitehead, you know, believed that Chicago had Athenian possibilities. Well, Big Bill, that crook, was a PR pioneer. His slogan was 'Put down your hammer, get a horn—Boost, don't knock!' And then there was Aristotle: A man without a city is either a beast or a god. Well, Chicago was the city. Or was it? *Where* was it, what had become of it? No cities? Then where was civilization? Or was the U.S.A. as a whole now my city? In that case I could move away from this chaos and live with Minna in a quiet place, and we could earn our bread somewhere in the woods, on a computer. The communications revolution could bypass Chicago or Detroit. Cities could be written off—dying generations, the blacks and Puerto Ricans, the aged too poor to move.

. . . Let them be ruined, decay, die and eliminate themselves. There are some who seem willing that this should happen. I'm not one of them. Not me."

Corde looked at his watch. It was half past one.

"Yes, you have an appointment at two o'clock," said Vlada. "We'd better start back. I'll try to explain to Beech why you haven't yet made up your mind. But now there's something else. I have another message from Chicago for you; this one is from your sister."

"Oh, you talked with Elfrida. How nice of you, Vlada, to call her."

"She called me. She sent a message. I suppose it's a message."

"What was it that Elfrida wanted you to tell me?"

"She was worried how you would take it, although I said I couldn't see why you would object. . . . She's gotten married."

"What—Elfrida married!" The unexpected news gave Corde a sharp pang. He gave no outward sign of this. He looked away and drew in his lips, thinking, Why should she do *that!* Well, that's Elfrida. He said, "I see. She married Sorokin?"

"Yes, the Judge. Are you surprised?"

He had stopped; his hands were deep in his pockets and his shoulders raised high. He looked sallow.

"You don't like that?"

"She didn't discuss it with me," he said. "But then why should she? She's a mature lady. Am I surprised? Only a little—Sorokin isn't so bad. He's good-natured, virile, he's a lively extrovert. I suppose she did the best she could. What I feel is more like sympathy for her. But among the Chicago types she had to choose from, she might have done worse."

"Isn't she a Chicago type herself?"

"He's a few years younger than Elfrida."

"Yes, she mentioned that."

"Well, there it is. Are they off on their honeymoon? They can't go, I suppose. Not while Mason is still in trouble."

"Mason is very angry with his mother."

"Is he? If he hadn't shaken her up so much she might not have jumped into this. Going it alone was too hard for her. Well, Elfrida . . . she remarried. I dearly love my sister."

"She said that. But she was worried you wouldn't approve."

"Maybe I was standoffish with Sorokin. I doubt that he took much notice. Anyway, I meant no real harm. But why is Mason so miffed? . . . A silly question, come to think of it. Mason came to her one day with a paperback from the drugstore and said she had to read it. It was a how-to book—how the middle-aged woman could manage by herself and be a well-adjusted widow. He put her on notice, she was supposed to keep a holding pattern. He brought her this manual as a Mother's Day present."

"At least she didn't take *that* from him."

"No. I think that clinched it. When I saw her studying this paperback on how to be happy while sad, I was sure she'd marry. And it's foolish to ask why she didn't discuss this match with me. My views are as obvious as Mason's."

"It seemed to me she did the smart thing."

"Well, of course. It was better not to let me put my prejudices on record. Then I'd have to stand by them, she'd feel hurt, et cetera, and she's too intelligent for that."

"So she is—attractive, also," said Vlada. "Well, there's nothing wrong with a husband like the Judge. You said it yourself. I wish I could find one of those. He's good-looking and amusing. He has a plan to ride a raft down a South American river."

"He told me about it. At the time, he planned to do it alone. I can't picture Elfrida rushing through the jungles downstream like the *African Queen,* hanging on to her Samsonite luggage. She's a little old for it. But then there's nobody too old to be young. That's the present outlook. Actually age has been on her mind, naturally it has, but the book Mason ordered her to read—she was supposed to go it alone like a brave modern mother—put her in a furious depression. She saw the handwriting on the nursing home wall."

"Say that she married in self-defense. She's not a young girl like Lydia Lester."

"No, I still think she *might* have talked it over with her only brother. But she and I never could find the common premise. And maybe she thought the Judge would make Mason a good role model—an extrovert who drops from helicopters. Not like an uncle who goes fishing for porgies and falls in the drink. She suspected me of being unsympathetic, of being put off by the boy's resemblance to his father. But I didn't dislike Mason senior. He was the special kind of highly intelligent top-grade barbarian I grew up with—people like my own father and my uncles. People to whom I was affectionately attached. Elfrida's opinion is that young Mason isn't as bad as other sons in her set. He thinks he's one of the black street people, but at least he doesn't burn out his veins with synthetic heroin, the stuff that has to be shot when it's scalding. The addicts become paralyzed. Mason will never really hurt himself. He's not a hijacker, kidnapper, terrorist. He's no Feltrinelli." Here, Corde paused. Then he said, "You can't even talk about your poor sister without getting into broad social questions. That's the worst of it. Now I suppose she'll sell the house on the Cape and invest it in parachutes."

13

The apartment was filled with callers. Some of them came with a second purpose: They wanted to get their children out of the country. You couldn't blame them for that. But how did one find sponsors, and where could you get dollars? You had to have the dollars.

Corde observed some of this. "Your mother was very fond of my daughter. She's an excellent student. She wants to do molecular biology . . ." then pulling a chair closer, urgently whispering, glancing significantly at the Dean. Minna listened in her solemn way. You never knew what she was hearing or whether her large eyes looked at you or through or past you. No, but she saw everything, felt it intensely, took it all to heart. Parents handed her term papers, manuscripts. She accepted them. Nobody was refused. She said she would ask the Dean to read some of them.

Corde said, "Spangler is expecting me."

"Yes, you should go out," she said. "When is the car coming? Yes, it'll be good for you to have a talk with your old pal. But don't stand waiting in the street. Promise you'll stay in the lobby. Please. . . ."

He took the packet from Alec Witt down with him, and had just time enough to see that it was stuffed with letters on his articles, mostly objecting, probably, alumni demanding that he be canned. Corde thought, I could do without crazy mail. Say what you liked about Miss Porson, she might be gross but her feminine instinct was to spare the Dean. You couldn't expect such delicacy from the Provost. But then (self-critical) why look to anyone to spare you? You didn't need to be spared at all, unless you believed that you had a very special and high calling and that right-minded ladies and gentlemen should temper the wind to you (a vocation left you shorn?). Some of the letters were addressed to him personally but Miss Porson had considered it necessary for the administration to see them. She had her own picture of the administration, a vision of the college hierarchy and of who owed what to whom. If you were Dean you reported to the Provost, who reported to the President, who went to the Board. . . .

Cremation or no cremation, a glistening day unfolded—business as usual for the weather. Corde, still bothered by smoke in his lungs, cleared his throat as he hurried into Spangler's limousine. Then the posh Intercontinental café and the big fragrance of the espresso machines. This time Dewey had taken a table by the window, warmed by the sun, an antidote to the horrible gloom of the crematorium. He was suavely solicitous—oh, what a smoothie Dewey had become in the great world! In the indoor sunlight he looked more corpulent—terraces of fat under his shirt, descending over the upswelling belly. He was belted beneath the sunny equator. There was only Corde to remember his skinny adolescence.

"Poor Albert. I'll order you a double Scotch. You were looking green in the mortuary."

"I had to go below and sign papers."

"Odd to see you in a foreign situation, so different from any other setting in the past."

"When you turned up, I had the opposite sensation. Familiarity. Do you remember after my mother's funeral—we were still at Lakeview—you came to the house?"

"No, my memory is dusty on this." (The little bastard. He was lying. But let him.)

"The living room was full of callers. You sat in a corner, behind everyone, and made faces at me."

Spangler was not pleased by this. "I don't remember that."

"Yes," said Corde. "You came to remind me of my duty as a nihilist not to give in to the middle-class hypocrisy of mourning, and the whole bourgeois sham."

"It sounds as though you hadn't forgiven me yet."

"I was angry with you, yes."

"I was an unpleasant kid, I admit. In those days I was the more eccentric one. Seriously, you couldn't hold it against me. This was back in the late thirties."

Skinny, wretched, weak, crowing, angry, Dewey in those days was eager to deal blows left and right. No, of course you couldn't hold it against him. "It's just a recollection—your grimacing and being so kinky when I was grieving so hard, just back from the cemetery. It was one of those winter days of cast-iron gloom, nothing but gray ice."

"It was Chicago winter, all right. But while you're remembering you might also remember that you were going off to Dartmouth that year. My family didn't have the money to send me even to the city college. And your father was sitting there, and he didn't like me."

"I don't think it was dislike. You puzzled my old man. When he found you in a dark corridor of the apartment on all fours, growling and being the wild beast, one of your special behaviors, he was mystified."

"Sure. But your people had money and connections. You got to Potsdam because of your father's pull. You wouldn't have been there if your dad hadn't been a crony of Harry Vaughan, who was one of Truman's guys. Same Harry Vaughan who accepted seven deep-freezers from lobbyists and a medal from Juan Perón."

"Well," said Corde, "all the better that you did it all on your own, without any Vaughans." He knew very well that Dewey had been a talented and tireless career politician. But how Dewey had made it to the top mattered little now. "And you were more eccentric than me."

"*Then* I was," Spangler said. "Okay, it wasn't your fault that your father was a fat cat hotel operator who drove a Packard and belonged to the country club. One thing I remember was that you took me to the family dentist and had him check my teeth and put it on your bill. The dentist was disgusted by all the tartar or plaque in my mouth—I never would brush. In spite of which there wasn't a single cavity. I was very proud."

Yes, a horribly vain and greedy child, Dewey. When he had two bits (on that day Corde was broke) he once ordered a sandwich for himself at the Woolworth counter on Washington Street—roast beef, a scoop of mashed potatoes, peas, a glazed flood of flour gravy or white sauce filling up the plate. Corde watched while Dewey ate it all by himself. He handled the knife and fork with jittering elegance and high breeding—a Chaplin couldn't have duplicated it. His wolfing sharp teeth and famished throat together with the hoity-toity, high-elbowed wielding of the dime store flatware. His ears were tucked under his cap. He offered his pal nothing. It may have been at that time that he shaved back his hairline to increase his resemblance to William Powell. Then the bristles came in, hence the cap. So it was extraordinary how he had civilized himself, somehow. Now he was a substantial public man, what cops in Chicago call "a notable," the companion of statesmen. He had made himself. And now this interesting reflection: Corde, too, had made himself. But then, deliberately, he had *un*made himself. Spangler reckoned that he had done this, that he had stopped writing for the papers, because he conceded Spangler's superiority and withdrew from competition. But this was not how Corde had unmade himself. He had a very different idea about the unmaking. And Spangler despite his theories and for all his world eminence was not entirely sure of himself with his old friend. Sitting with Corde, he felt himself still the squawking green kid, pushing too hard. Big-time deportment had not subdued the struggling punk.

"Yesterday I was received by Mr. and Mrs. President," said Dewey.

"What are they like?"

"He has a fine head of hair, but he looks like a Keystone Kop."

"Was anything said about my mother-in-law?"

"I said I had an old Chicago friend here, the husband of . . . the son-in-law of . . . Say, you are obsessed by those women. You *love* 'em. Mr. President made no comment."

"Still, with so much on your mind . . . Are you writing about the Warsaw Pact? And you remembered to mention it."

"Too late to help," said Spangler. He was modest when thanked, but he'd feel slighted, even outraged, if you failed to acknowledge his influence. Corde therefore acknowledged it. It wasn't flattery; more like charity. From Corde, Spangler needed the right signs. Corde's guess was that he had been a major theme in Spangler's lengthy analysis, the subject of countless groping hours on the couch. Their relationship, accepted at last, must have become an element of Spangler's maturity, his proof, bought with time and suffering effort, that he was indeed mature. In these meetings at the Intercontinental, Spangler was able to test the results of years of psychoanalytic therapy. He was all set now and the cure was firm. Still there was a certain uneasiness between them. Problems, once you conceive of them as problems, never let you alone, thought Corde. All occasions inform against you if you're problem-haunted. He was sorry for Dewey. Dewey still suspects that I know something he doesn't know, have something he just has to have.

His influence acknowledged, Dewey (turnabout) praised Minna. "Just as people said, Albert, your wife is a beauty. I also had a glimpse of the old lady in the coffin. She had quite a face—quite a face!"

Corde refrained from answering. He waited to see what subject Spangler proposed to discuss. Women, love, marriage? No, he'd want to talk about Chicago. Corde himself wanted that.

Dewey said, "That trial will be going to the jury in a few days. Did I hear that your cousin wanted to serve you with a subpoena?"

"That's correct."

"It would have been quite a trick—have a server grab you in the crematorium this morning."

"Maxie still amuses you."

"Not so much in person. I looked him up in Chicago a couple of weeks ago."

"What were you doing there?"

"Seeing my old dad, who's ninety-one years old. Max met me for a drink at the Drake. The cocktail waitress identified him. 'Aren't you the lawyer on that case? I seen you on TV.' Maxie preened. You made him a celebrity. He was just about to ask the girl what she was doing after work. He still has his lascivious hang-up. I remember his idea for sexual comfort stations—like public toilets. Drop four quarters in the slot and enter a private cubical. If you and your girl friend happen to be walking together and feel hot suddenly, you can get relief at the next corner."

Corde was not to be induced to talk about his cousin's peculiarities. Intermittently he still saw the panel truck hearse, and Ioanna on her knees by the coffin putting Valeria's hand to her cheek; and himself frowning with horror and scrawling his name on the register, freezing, sweating, frantic to escape; and on the stairs the extremes of heat and cold like two faces of an ax, splitting him in halves. He took a large swallow of whiskey. Spangler said, "This erotic stuff doesn't amuse you. . . . You don't believe your cousin can win the case?"

"Anything can happen in a Chicago court."

"You're very hard on the old toddling town. Are things so different elsewhere?"

"I suppose not. Among other discoveries, I found that Chicago wasn't Chicago anymore. Hundreds of thousands of people lived there who had no conception of a place. People *used* to be able to say . . ."

"Ah, yes," said Spangler. "I'm with you there. It's no longer a location, it's only a condition. South Bronx, Cleveland, Detroit, Saint Louis, from Newark to Watts —all the same noplace."

"Why do people decide to live here rather than there?" said Corde.

"Where's their inner reason? you're asking. But that's the modern condition," said Spangler. "That's all old hat. But I have to tell you, Albert. I read those pieces of yours with intense concentration, fascination. They may not have opened my eyes to Chicago, but I learned a lot about you. The old friend revealed. You wrote damn queer things I'm dying to ask you about."

"For example."

"You won't believe it, but I actually made notes. It was on the Concorde and I had a few hours. You said the setting was like the Gobi Desert." Spangler brought out his pocket notebook. "You said that Chicago was part of the habitable globe, of course, the laws of physics apply here as elsewhere, blood circulates in the veins, the same sky is above, but if you grew up in this place there were moments when you felt that it didn't meet nature's full earthly standard. And so on. A curious lack of final coherence, an environment not chosen to suit human needs . . . favorable to manufacture, shipping, construction. Now, I'm not going to argue with you about its charm, but you looked at everything as if the ophthalmologist had put drops in your eyes. I'm frankly surprised that the *Harper's* people let you go on as you did. The language you used from time to time . . ."

"Give me some instances."

"Oh, for example, 'the harsh things of the soul.' How one lives with them. Or, 'Politically is there any salvation for this order?' Many statements of this kind. That's why I said last time how lucky it would be for you if your readers would get impatient and drop the

magazine. But for me it's full of curiosities. I have my
own favorite passages. One of them is the long paragraph about the tunnel and reservoir project. I wish I
had copied it out—a mammoth sewer project costing
more than the Alaska pipeline, capacity forty billion
gallons, as wide as three locomotives side by side,
running for more than a hundred miles deep under the
city, maybe weakening the foundations of the skyscrapers. And all those tons of excrement, stunning to the
imagination. It won't be the face of Helen that topples
those great towers, it'll be you-know-what, and that's
the difference between Chicago and Ilium. Now tell
me, whom were you writing for? You pushed the
poetry too hard."

Corde said, "I don't think I forced poetry on Chicago. Maybe it was Chicago that forced the poetry on me.
But then there were also quiet, relaxed passages—
descriptions of residential streets. I did quite a lot with
domestic architecture."

"Yes, the interiors of the six-flats; that was quite
good, quite good. Neighborhood life in the thirties,
also. And the lakefront, and the Loop as it was before
the war. You had good touches on the parks. I liked the
bits about the parks. It's okay to be sentimental. Yes,
the good old days when Chicago was a city of immi-
grants who had found work, food and freedom and
a kind of friendly ugliness around them, and they
practiced their Old World trades—cabinetmakers,
tinsmiths, locksmiths, wurst-stuffers from Cracow,
confectioners from Sparta. Those passages had lots of
charm." Spangler here was noticeably condescending.
He himself faced the big public questions—the Persian
Gulf, Russian aims in East Africa, West European
neutralism and NATO, the resumption of SALT talks.
Such things were truly serious, questions with large,
permanent implications. It was after all Dewey the
plucked-chicken adolescent, the shrieker, the liar, the
problem child, who had attained world distinction.

What his blue eyes scanning Corde back and forth were saying was that the old Chicago was far away—Lincoln Park was far away and long ago, the thrills of Shakespeare and Plato, the recitations from "The Garden of Proserpine" and "Lapis Lazuli" and "The Waste Land," the disputes about *The Will to Power,* and what nihilism really meant, all of that, old pal, was boyhood, and one must detach oneself. (Corde hadn't detached himself.) Corde, still filled with feelings about Valeria, Minna, Elfrida (married!), was pleased to be here in the sunshine, however sad. Spangler was pleasant, mostly, garnished with so much beard and his hair in grizzled ginger waves. Why had he ever wanted to look like William Powell?

"One of your better ideas was to hunt up some of the Lakeview classmates. That part was all right. The guy from the central post office, the CPA, the probate court judge—I could take them or leave them. But you got lucky with guys like Billy Edrix, the Air Force Colonel whose wife tried to murder him. I didn't remember him."

"I happened to. From the track team."

"That was curious," said Spangler. "Even though she was convicted on the evidence of the two hit men she hired. And she tried to poison him, too, and once tried to beat his brains out with the telephone as he slept. With all this proven he still had to go on supporting her by court order and let her occupy the house while the conviction was on appeal What's *with* the judges?"

"Yes, and all the while Billy was still flying Air Force cargo planes between Germany and O'Hare."

When Corde went out to the far suburbs to talk to him, Billy said he only faintly recalled him. "Track, you say? Hell, I couldn't run across the lawn now."

Billy had built himself a new house, just finished, and they were standing in a raw hole in the ground ("This is gonna be landscaped") drinking beer out of cans.

Soldierly Billy wore hunting clothes, well stained. He didn't invite Corde indoors. The jeep was loaded. It was moving day. "Why'd she want to kill you, Billy?"

"You say you want to write about the case. Well, I'll tell you a few facts that weren't in the paper. She first made a deal with one of the neighbors' boys. I finally caught on. I took the boy for a ride in the jeep and said, 'Why are you following me around?' I put a gun to his head and said, 'Tell me why or I'll kill you this minute.' Then he told me. She promised him a thousand bucks to do me in. He told it in court, too." Billy was not deeply angry; he seemed reflective rather. He said, "She even told the Federal Narcotics people I was smuggling opium from Germany and investing the profits in a nightclub, a girlie joint. Every time I landed, they would search my plane. Search? They tore it apart. They must have seen *The French Connection*. Those guys will listen to any crazy broad who wants to put you under. And the court wouldn't let me divorce her even after she was convicted. Not until there was a complete financial fair settlement. Fucking courts are just as crazy as the fucking broads. You want to write about the lawyers and courts, that's what you want to do, Al."

Spangler said, "If she was out to kill him, why did he stay with her?"

"He couldn't bear to leave the children with a murderess, he said."

"Oh, I see, the children. You and I have no kids of our own. You have a nephew, however. Is he an only child?"

"Yes."

"Like myself. But my mother was too poor to spoil me."

"She spoiled you all she could, Dewey."

"You'll never understand about my parents. Your father drove a big Packard. My old man was a straphanger. Your old man didn't want us to be friends, but my mother approved. She hoped your dad would hire me in one of his hotels as a night clerk and then I could save money and go to Wright Junior College. Then you and my mother had trouble. Big trouble, Albert."

So Spangler remembered the trouble and was now capable of speaking about it.

At the age of sixteen the friends had written a book together. "A Death on the El," they had called it. They had finished it during the Christmas holiday and tossed a coin to see which of them would take the manuscript to New York to get it published. Spangler, who had won the toss, tucked the manuscript under his sweater and started immediately for New York. It took him three days, hitchhiking, to get there. Meanwhile Corde, covering for Dewey, had lied to his weeping mother. "I'm sorry, Mrs. Spangler, he didn't say where he was going." Uncle Harold Corde, who was living upstairs at the time, talked with Dewey's mother and took a hand in the matter. Together they forced Corde to go to police headquarters with them. They went there by streetcar. But even the Missing Persons Bureau was unable to break Albert down. He was already receiving letters from Dewey in New York. Dewey wrote, "The reader at Harcourt loves my part of the book, but says that you should go into the hotel business with your dad." Uncle Harold, forcing open the locked drawer of Corde's dresser, called everyone together and read Dewey's letters to the gathered family. Corde's mother was then dying.

Uncle Harold was a Republican politician, whose candidate, Alf Landon, had been defeated by Roosevelt. He was a shouting, bullying old man, not taken seriously by anyone. He called Corde "an aesthetic little sonofabitch" and said he was going to take his books down and burn 'em in the furnace. Corde's mother must have been in considerable pain then, the cancer being far advanced, her face mummified, unrecognizable, and her dark eyes sharp, looking angry. (It was death she was angry with, not her children.) It was impossible to tell what she was thinking when Uncle

Harold let Albert have it, but she must have been wounded. Corde remembered how heart-struck he was, and that he had carried his sore injured heart to Lincoln Park. That was always one of the peculiarities of Chicago: Where could you take your most passionate feelings? Carry them into what setting? It was exactly this time of year, Christmas week, getting on for January. The wind came down unchecked from the Arctic—white snow, black chain fences, trees bare, sky blue. Four decades and two continents didn't make much difference, for the present day was much like the other one—freezing blue, the sunlight, the women dying or dead.

Was it possible that Spangler was looking at him with large amusement? Fat face, plump hands, blue eyes, warm lids, brown, swelling and lacy—the sunlight revealed all their intricate puffiness and dark stain. Spangler tucked his laughter under his armpits, where his fingers were inserted, and crossed his smallish feet. Of course (Corde the persistent, almost fixated observer) Spangler now had a drum belly. His sharp teeth were clean, he had accepted the necessity to brush. Psychoanalysis and prestige had sobered him, cleaned him up, he no longer had the screaming-meemies. It was funny how fortunate a man could become, American style. Nietzsche had said that it was better to be a *monstre gai* than an *ennuyeux sentimental*. When Dewey told Miss Starr in the tenth grade that he was an orphan adopted by the cannibals who had eaten his parents and told of his escape on a raft from an African island, he was a *monstre gai*. Now, with Brezhnev and Kissinger and Indira Gandhi, he had still more thrilling real-life adventures. He had every reason to be pleased, therefore. But there was something that he wanted still from Corde. Could it be a heart-to-heart talk? No, not that. Could it be an edifying relationship? Maybe that was closer to the mark.

Spangler said, "You wrote mean things to me about my old lady."

"I felt mean about Uncle Harold."

"That old brute. He gave you a pretty good stab."

"He had your letter to stab me with."

"Yes, that must have been lousy for you, and I suppose your mother did take it hard. But it was just adolescent high jinks. Besides, Albert, that injury only put your back up, just as your Potsdam scoop put up mine. We're a pair of strong-willed and terrifically obstinate guys. For you the enemy was highlighted— Uncle Harold, the vulgar American mind. Wanted to burn your books of philosophy and poetry. It all came out in those *Harper's* sketches of yours. They really are queer work, and completely characteristic of you. I became so absorbed in them on the Concorde that I was in Paris before I knew it. Shortest flight I ever had. There were passages I can't say that I got—too cloudy, and even mystical. But still the old preoccupations. If I were you, I would have steered clear of guys like Vico and Hegel. Hegel saying that the spirit of the time is in us by nature. Where does that get us?"

"It gets us that this world as you experience it is your direct personal fate."

Dewey disliked being mystified. Aggressive and dogged, he made a movement of dismissal. "That doesn't tell me anything."

Corde weighed the matter. Shall I talk? . . . I'll talk. "I meant that we'd better deal with whatever it is that's in us by nature, and I don't see people being willing to do that. What I mainly see is the evasion. But this is a thing that works on the substance of the soul—the spirit of the time, in us by nature, working on every soul. We prefer to have such things served up to us as concepts. We'd rather have them abstract, stillborn, dead. But as long as they don't come to us with some kind of reality, as facts of experience, then all we can have instead of good and evil is . . . well, concepts. Then we'll never learn how the soul is worked on. Then for intellectuals there will be discourse or jargon, while for the public there will be ever more jazzed-up fantasy. In fact, the two are blending now. The big public is picking up the jargon to add to its fantasies. . . ."

"You're going too fast for me," said Spangler. "So you decided to let everybody have it, and force everybody to undergo the facts in some form."

"To recover the world that is buried under the debris of false description or nonexperience."

"It wasn't the material in your pieces that gave me trouble," said Spangler. "Some of that was damned interesting. It was the way you put the facts that was hard to take. Maybe it was your attitude that was intolerable. A modest journalist would have said that he was working up some stuff about Chicago. In the old days he would have said the city was his beat. But you're saying, 'I was assigned to it,' which makes it like a visionary project, or the voice of God saying, 'Write this up, as follows.' Now, believe it or not, you didn't sound much different forty years ago. When I read *Harper's* I was hearing echoes from our youth."

Echoes of youth implied that little or no progress had been made. But Corde was not bothered by this. Spangler, the world-communicator, was a maker of discourse (increasing the debris of false description). Twice weekly, readers all over the U.S. picked up their fresh thick newspapers and turned to Spangler's column to tune up their thinking on world affairs, to correct their pitch. Dewey was quoted often by *Le Monde* and *The Economist,* so why should he be bothered by the opinions of his adolescent sidekick? He had every reason to be confident, relaxing in the plate-glass warmth of the Intercontinental. In the café you saw about you East German trade representatives, members of Chinese missions, costumed, turbaned Nigerian ladies—and as a final bonus two old buddies from Chicago, one of them a figure of international stature. And Corde wondered whether he wasn't being interviewed by Dewey. Interviews were Dewey's great strength. Pressing for true answers, he fixed you with a hard eye, he was in control. "How seriously should I take you?" was his big unspoken question. But this was more than an interview. Spangler was testing whether his old pal was the real thing. Corde had written about Vico and Hegel like a humanist-professor-intellectual. And Spangler, although he had risen so high, gone so far, wanted to rise higher still. Above the Walter Lippmann bracket to which he aspired there was the André Malraux bracket. There you breathed a different air altogether, reviewing with De Gaulle the whole history of mankind, doing Napoleon, Richelieu, Charlemagne, Caesar, touching on the way Christianity and Buddhism, the arts of ancient China, the astronomy of Egypt's priesthood, the Bhagavad Gita. Chicago origins need be no hindrance. A man could pitch himself beyond the Lippmann category, if he hit upon the right combination of forces.

An odd silence came over Spangler. Corde thought, I'm unjust. I'm being too satirical. I'm going to miss something about the man while I gratify my taste for wicked comment.

The impression Spangler now gave Corde was that of a man in a control tower monitoring unusually heavy traffic. He said, "We were boys together, and you may think, Good old Dewey has worked his way to the top and stepped on quite a few fingers and even faces en route; now he wants to enjoy a sentimental hour. And since I was a little creep who turned into a big-time oracle, you may be amused. As much as you can be amused on the day of this funeral, which seems to upset you so much. But what would you say to taking stock, or doing an inventory?" He was agitated, and Corde, too, was anything but calm.

He gave Dewey plenty of time. He himself was under the influence of—well, of Scotch whiskey and of strong coffee odors; also of the methyl blue of sharp winter flashing from the beveled corners of the plate glass, the streaming threads of orange, the colors of the spectrum, quivering with heat on the table. Then for some reason, with no feeling of abruptness, he became curiously absorbed in Dewey: blue eyes, puffy lids, tortoise-shell beard, arms crossed over his fat chest, fingers tucked into armpits, his skin scraped and mottled where the beard was trimmed, the warm air of his breathing, his personal odors, a sort of doughnut fragrance, slightly stale—the whole human Spangler was delivered to Corde in the glass-warmed winter light with clairvoyant effect. He saw now that Spangler was downslanted in spirit. The slight wave of his hair, which had always had an upward tendency, apparently had reversed itself. And he used dye, that was perfectly plain. But this was a mere observation and no judgment. *Let* him touch up his hair. Seeing him so actual, vanities were dissipated, you were in no position to judge, and there was no need for judging. Spangler's rays were turned downwards, and his look openly confessed it. He had been a kook, but certainly no coward. Maybe on this death day Corde was receiving secret guidance in seeing life. Perhaps at this very moment the flames were finishing Valeria, and therefore it was especially important to think what a human being really was. What wise contemporaries had to say about this amounted to very little.

"Where would you like to begin?"

"We already have begun," said Spangler, softening his tone. All he wanted, probably, was to feel secure in ordinary human dealings. With an old pal, this should be possible. As a distinguished person, he couldn't afford to take chances, come off looking foolish. "Let's look at the curve of your career, for a minute. You started with a bang, describing Stalin, Churchill, Truman, Attlee. You actually *saw* those guys! But then you settled down on the *Herald Tribune* doing lighter cultural features, very good, no special world perspective. All of a sudden, in your mid-forties, you head back to Chicago and turn into a professor. Well, of course America is where the real action is. This is terrible news to have to tell humankind, but what else is there to say? The action *is* at home! And so you go back." Spangler was earnestly controlling his face and the effort itself had a distorting effect. He was looking almost lewd, but the source of the intensity was mental. "You're back to America, a prof and a dean. Is it a kind of retirement? You're reading books, talking to academics, trying to get the right handle on things, I presume. Then all at once it's: Bam! Here is how things look. Is there any salvation for this order? The harsh things of the soul, what do we do about them in America? You hit Chicago with everything you've got. Mostly, it turns out, you're partial to two black men. One runs a cold-turkey rehabilitation center for heroin addicts and the other is warmly human to derelicts and criminals in County Jail. Everybody else is only trying to contain this doomed population of blacks—the underclass."

"Or to hustle it opportunistically, politically."

"You made that plain enough," said Spangler. "It was when you got apocalyptic about it that you lost me: the dragon coming out of the abyss, the sun turning black like sackcloth, the heavens rolled up like a scroll, Death on his ashen horse. Wow! You sounded like the Reverend Jones of Jonestown. You give yourself the luxury of crying out about doom, and next thing you know you're up to your own neck in squalor. So unless your purpose was to get the discussion into a better key, I can't see what you gained. Actually, I think you were sore as hell with your academic colleagues, because they hadn't found the right key to play all this in. Isn't that what they were supposed to do—and why they got so many privileges?"

Corde lowered his large round head towards the brilliant and twisting prismatic colors of the table, putting up his hand to stop his unbalanced eyeglasses from dropping, and said, rumbling, "I admit some disappointment there. . . . My late brother-in-law, Zaehner, used to tease me about academic life. He would say a professor with tenure is like a woman on welfare with ten illegitimate kids. They're both set for life, never again have to work." Corde immediately began to regret saying this. It was mischievous. And he had forgotten that they were no longer boys in Lincoln Park. There was a gap in judgment here. They were men now—journalists, at that, quick to see an opening. But Dewey, laughing hard (turned on, ignited), was showing his sharp teeth and putting the heels of his hands to his sides just as he used to do forty years before.

"That's great, Albert, just great. Was Elfrida's husband such a wit? I didn't realize it."

"Her late husband."

"I heard you the first time. He passed away?"

"Three, four years ago. My sister has just remarried."

"Pretty woman, Elfrida. I made a pass at her once. I suppose she told you."

"Yes."

"But you never mentioned it—that's because you were brought up an American gentleman. If I had had that kind of information on you, I would have baited you. You used to say that your people were Pullman car Americans. Not quite accurate. They didn't take an upper berth; they traveled in a drawing room. And wasn't your mother's father governor of the Virgin Islands, or was it the Philippines? You see, you had better breeding than me. So when I propositioned your pretty sister she laughed at me. I *was* a preposterous kid. But I told her preposterous kids were the most uninhibited sex partners. Still, I couldn't get her serious attention. You might not have liked it if she had taken up with me—it would have been quite a test of your breeding to be an uncle to a child of mine. But she snubbed me. Serves her right that her boy is such a twerp and nuisance—what's eating him, anyway?"

Corde lifted his shoulders. "Search me."

"Oh, come on, Albert. . . . It isn't like you not to take a view. Don't deprive an old friend of your interpretation."

"I was saying just a while ago that you couldn't even mention your only sister without broaching all the big social questions."

"Whom did Elfrida marry this time?"

"A judge."

"That'll go down big with her radical son. But since he gives his mother so many legal headaches . . ."

". . . She made an aspirin marriage."

Spangler warmly blinked at him, approving. "Do you say things like that among academic friends? . . . I didn't criticize you for becoming a prof, Albert. I've pushed you about it mainly from curiosity. I myself have thought it would be nice to retire to an academic setting eventually. I never got to go to college. But it shouldn't be too hard, with my record in public life, to become a fellow somewhere."

"You ought to be able to name your own spot, Dewey, like Hubert Humphrey or Dean Rusk."

Spangler received this with a flush of self-congratulation, but he also inclined his head in thanks. Corde thought, I'm not full of rancor and envy, and it pleases him. My mental attitudes, he says, haven't changed in four decades, but then neither have the personal ones, and it may be a pleasant surprise. He may inspire satirical thoughts, but I don't feel like sniping. I have no impulse to pick on him. If he's a fat little obnoxious bastard, which is what I think *he* thinks he is, it doesn't matter, because I evidently love him as I used to do. I can't take it back. I must be immature that way. Affections like this probably seem grotesque to a wordly and psychoanalyzed old party like Dewey.

"I may ask you for advice on universities one of these days, although to judge by your attitudes you may not be the party to turn to."

"When I went off to Dartmouth after my mother

died—and I was mourning more than I realized—I had wonderful teachers whom I never forgot, and I read Plato with them, and the poets."

"Yeah, yeah—Chapman's Homer, realms of gold. And that's what you wanted to come back to, more of the same—culture and civilization, the stronghold of humanism. Stupid to expect it. Nevertheless, such a setting would be nice for the declining years, if I have any."

"Why, aren't you well? You look okay."

"I seem more or less normal, I suppose. I guess I can tell you this, although it would hurt me if it got around. But you have too many headaches of your own to start gossiping about me. I went to Chicago to have surgery. Diverticulitis."

"Is that serious? Isn't it what Eisenhower had?"

"It's serious enough for me to be wearing the bag. Do you want to see it?"

"Not particularly."

Dewey showed it to him anyway, impulsively pulling out his shirt. Yes, there was the square plastic envelope. Something dark and warm was inside. Corde's teeth were on edge.

"I'll be back in surgery by and by. They'll try to hook me up again. There's more to see. I have a flap of flesh here."

"I'll take your word for it. What is there to hook up?"

"Two ends of the intestine. The doctors can't promise success."

So this was why Spangler had gone out of his way, had sent his car twice, had made time for Corde in a busy schedule, had come to the crematorium. He's not a man for funerals. He was wrecked, sick, his insides were uncoupled. He stared at Corde. His acquired controls were turned off and the double ducking mannerism returned, as if he could not bring his chin to rest. His expression was angry. But he pushed his shirttail back matter-of-factly.

"They'll sew you together. You'll forget all about it by summer." I'll take you back to Woolworth's lunch counter and buy you a roast-beef-and-white-gravy sandwich.

"Don't talk like a jerk. You're a horse's ass, Albert."

The creature of flesh and blood going through the mill—only one possible outcome. That was Spangler's message. What are you trying to give me! He was flushed, the heat rushing into his blue eyes. His look was fiercely sarcastic. Well, they were on a human footing, at least. Spangler said, "In this condition, what woman will sleep with me?"

"That's a thought. But if it's that important . . ."

"If it's that important, I can get lists of ladies with the same trouble. Or else there are kinky broads enough. Masses of female masochists." He was softening. "Or maybe you think elder-statesmanship has calmed me down and I can't be the horny little bastard I was. You wouldn't be completely wrong. I've had my innings. Well, the bag is depressing, it throws a shadow on my self-image. Otherwise I'm in good health enough. Remember, I never had cavities in my teeth, nor any other complaints until this one, if you don't count complaints of the psyche or character. I can tell how you thought of me, how you *formulated* me, Albert—a near psychopath who was saved by becoming a shaper of public opinion. Sometimes, when driving up to the White House to be received by Bugs Bunny himself, I would get weird, deep tingles in the nervous system. I would think of you and some laconic wisecrack you might make in your basso profundo. But with all this your feeling is that I'm not so bad for a comic monster, sort of sweet, in fact. But now, to use a gangland expression, death has me fingered."

Corde said, "That's not such a bad résumé." What he felt was a compression inside, a stirring in certain of his organs; sadness, then faintness, something like "fatedness" and lastly immense pity. This flow of feeling occurred quite slowly. It took its time. It wouldn't do to show the pity. Spangler would be offended, and quite rightly.

"I have to confess to you, there *was* one bit in your articles that agitated me, Albert. It was the patch about your talk with the Public Defender in the case of the rapist who kept the woman in his trunk and killed her. After he killed her he hid the body under trash in a vacant lot. And then you shifted into that Vico of yours. I got sore, I thought what a fucking time to get pedantic! I cursed you for it. But then I saw why you were doing it."

"It was about the human customs that are observed everywhere. And if not, why not. . . ."

"I know what it was about. I don't need your help. Children born outside the law and abandoned by parents can be eaten by dogs. It must be happening in places like Uganda now. The army of liberators who chased out Idi made plenty of babies. Eaten by dogs. Or brought up without humanity. Nobody teaching the young language, human usages or religion, they will go back to the great ancient forest and be like the wild beasts of Orpheus. None of the great compacts of the human race respected. Bestial venery, feral wanderings, incest, and the dead left unburied. Not that we have any great forests to go back to. There was Jonestown in the Guyana jungle, where they put on public displays of racially mixed cunnilingus as a declaration of equality, and where some cannibalism seems to have occurred, and finally the tub of Kool-Aid poison. But that wasn't the ancient forest, it was the city. . . ."

Corde had pulled his hat and coat towards him.

Spangler said, "We still have so much to talk about."

"You'll be taking off this evening?"

"Back to Paris. Well, this has been an interesting hour. I haven't maintained such a long relationship with anybody else. It would have brought us a lot closer together if you had been an analysand. Believe it or not. But in spite of the barrier, I can't tell you how curious it's been. You were hell-bent from the beginning to unfold your special sense of life. You were blocked. I saw it and I didn't predict much. Then, all of a sudden, it all pours out. There's a passionate but also a cockamamy flowering. You still haven't had a complete deliverance. . . ." Spangler waited for an answer, but Corde was silent, looking over the tops of his glasses into the street, at the first signs of dusk. Spangler said, "I see you've checked out on me. How long do you expect to stay here?"

"I want to leave as soon as we're able. Get my wife out."

"I'll call you from abroad if I see any news. Anything else I can do?"

"Not unless you want to smuggle out a couple of Tanti Gigi's featherbeds, or a few valuable Macedonian heirlooms," Corde said.

14

Gigi struggled in the vestibule with a stepladder, much beyond her strength to haul. She wanted the high storage bins opened. Corde took over. You wouldn't have believed how spacious those bins were. They contained boxes and boxes of stuff. "All this was kept for Minna," said Gigi, and she was determined that Minna should have a full inventory, every last doily and cake fork accounted for. Since condolence calls were taken in the dining room, and the parlor was not private enough, the boxes were opened in Minna's

room. So out came old letters, diaries, Turkish trays in
beaten metal, damask linens, tongs and snuffers, a
cut-glass fruit dish, a fifteenth-century treatise in Latin,
printed in Germany, a monastic accounts book in
Greek sewn with waxed thread which was snarled into
lumps, a small Gallé vase, a box of table silver, carved
screens, prints and drawings, and also coins and trin-
kets. No article of real value could leave the country.
Everything had to be appraised and taxed. "National
treasures" would be confiscated. Now and then Minna
came in and looked at these relics, Gigi identifying the
photographs. "This is our great-uncle Boulent, who
was a trigonometry teacher in Thessalonike." Corde
was fascinated by the objects that came out of the
boxes. Gigi made Oriental gestures to express their
value, circling and stirring with her finger. She wrote on
a piece of paper, "I shall show which objects *must* reach
Chicago." She then tore up the note and put a match to
it in the ashtray. With top-secret significance, she
touched the Gallé vase. Next, the cut-glass fruit dish. It
was diamond-shaped and narrow and Corde didn't
himself much like it, a foolish elaborate object, but that
was neither here nor there. She put her finger also on a
small Roman landscape in watercolors. "Yes, but how
do we pull this off?" said Corde. Gigi tapped him on
the breast. She had great confidence in him. Wasn't he
a dean? Didn't he contribute to national magazines?
The Ambassador sent for him, limousines came to the
door.

Corde persuaded Minna to come out into the air for
half an hour. Helping her into her fleece-lined brown
leather coat, he was aware of her thinness—the *structural* Minna, what you would see on X-ray film, came
through. In the sunlight her face was as white as
meringue. A small hollow had formed just below her
underlip. That was where the grief control seemed
concentrated. He couldn't help but think of his own
mother, the wasted mummy look of her last days, the
big furious stare she would turn on you. He told Minna,

"I hope Gigi doesn't get too serious about the relics she's collected."

"My mother hid them away, and I don't want those bastards to take them."

"We may have to pay to get them out."

"The appraisal will be unreal. And with what money?"

"I'll come up with the money. What I really wanted to talk about was going home."

"I can't, right away."

"We'd better, for all kinds of reasons. There isn't much of December left. The new term starts soon. Besides, there's the time at Mount Palomar they're going to reserve for you."

Corde knew what he was doing. Professionally Minna was superconscientious. Nothing was allowed to interfere with duties. Mostly it amused him that this beautiful and elegant woman should behave like a schoolgirl, with satchel and pencil box. When she was getting ready to set out for the day, he sometimes joked with her. "Got your compass and protractor? Your apple for teacher?" Together with her big fragrant purse, a bag of scientific books and papers was slung over her shoulder—ten times more stuff than she needed. But occasionally the gold-star-pupil bit did get him down, and she was cross with him, interpreting his irritation as disrespect for her profession. It had nothing to do with that. She put in a ten-hour day, never missed a visiting lecturer, a departmental seminar. Her tutorials, rehearsed far into the night, must have been like concerts. What he minded was her fanatical absorption. He often had dinner waiting for her, and towards seven o'clock began to listen for the sound of the key in the lock. A lady wrapped up in astronomy going about Chicago after dark? She gave him (it was absurd!) wifely anxieties. But now (manipulative, but it was justifiable) he was using the astronom͏ back to Chicago.

"Of course we've got to leave," she said.

to make sure first that Gigi is protected. This isn't even her legal address. The apartment is in Mother's name. Can I let the old girl be put out in the street?"

"It's not a matter of streets. I assumed anyway that we'd bring her to the States."

"I'm glad you assumed it, but that takes time."

"If there's a lease in Valeria's name, you must have inherited it."

"Who knows what kind of law they have here. I need to talk to a lawyer."

"Whatever it may cost—fees, payoffs—that part is easy. Isn't there a lawyer in the family?"

"More than one."

"It's all going to take months. Let somebody dependable take charge right away. We can't—you can't do it."

"In good time," she said. She didn't want him to push, she was resentful.

"As soon as possible. I don't think you should stay. Also I can see that Gigi is winding up to make a big deal out of the glassware, coins, icons, Latin books. . . ."

"It was against the law. Those objects should have been declared. My mother hid them for me."

"Hundreds of thousands of people are hiding glassware, or watches like my Christmas present."

"Maybe, but it's still risky. Mother understood how to do things like this. Gigi will never manage. I'm afraid she'll get into trouble. Besides, Gigi sees herself carrying out Valeria's wishes. She wants me to see everything so she can be in the clear. So there can't be recriminations later. She feels responsible."

"All right. Yes. I can see that. I don't think you care all that much about these items. You don't want the enemy to get them. I assume the officials grab the valuable ones for themselves. As for Gigi's outwitting them, that's just fantasy. And she wants *me* to get the relics out. That's more fantasy."

"Are you sure your journalist friend doesn't travel on a diplomatic passport?"

"We've already gone into that. He couldn't. Newspapermen can't be government agents. Compromising. Terrible idea, especially for a superstar. He might as well be working for the CIA. You can see that."

"He might have good advice, though, if he's as smart as I gather he is."

They walked silent for a while. The street was gray. The piled earthquake rubble smelled moldy, even though refrigerating December checked the decay. Corde found himself looking for the rat silhouettes in the street, flattened like weathercocks by traffic.

He had counted on the good effects of air; his purpose had been to get Minna away from the telephone. A thankless role, the solicitous sensible husband. He was accused of manipulating her. He read this in her brown eyes, plain enough. To invoke the new term and Mount Palomar *was* manipulative, but the aim was to bring her home. His helpfulness rejected, he felt a touch resentful. She was unjust to him. But then, look—"unjust"! Such childish pedantry was a sign that he, too, was dog tired.

She said, "What were you and your friend Spangler talking about yesterday?"

"I think our theme was which of us had done the right thing during the last forty years. Or if either of us had done anything right. We . . ."

But Minna didn't let him continue. She said, "I don't really want to talk about him."

"Let's not, then."

"Albert, I feel absolutely torn to pieces."

"Of course. You are."

"Can you help me to deal with this a little? You're an impartial person, sometimes, and a pretty good psychologist. You won't be judgmental if I tell you. I wake up in the night, and everything good in my life seems to have leaked away. It's not just temporary. I feel as if it can never come back. It's black in the room, and even blacker and worse outside. It goes on and on and on, out there. I'm mourning my mother but I also feel

terrible things about her. I'm horribly angry. Can you
tell me . . . ?"

What an innocent person! She did stars; human
matters were her husband's field. Some division of
labor! And swamped with death he was supposed to
bail out with a kitchen cup of psychology. His round
face crowned with felt hat looked down into her face,
which was not only as white as meringue but as finely
lined (December daylight was unsparing). What was
the case? Her loved and admired mother (how could
you not admire an omnipotent Roman matron) had
assigned her daughter, for safety, to the physical
universe—not exactly the *mysterium tremendum;* that
was religion. But science! Science would save her from
evil. The old woman protected Minna from the police
state. She endured ostracism, she fought the officials,
and she finally got her daughter out of the country. But
this powerful protection was gone. And now Valeria's
disappearance had to be accounted for. Where was the
strength on which Minna had always depended? In
short, mortal weakness, perplexity, grief—the whole
human claim. Minna hadn't made the moves frequently
made by scientists to disown this claim: "Don't bother
me with this ephemeral stuff—wives, kids, diapers,
death." She was too innocent for that. So she turned to
her husband for help. She loved him. And as soon as
she asked for help the strength drained out of him. But
he had only himself to blame for that, because he *had*
taken human matters for his province. Neither more
nor less. He was justified to Minna the scientist as
Albert the human husband. He said, "I may not be
able to tell you much."

"But you think about these things all the time. I
watch you doing it."

"Then let's see . . . Why do you suppose you feel so
angry?"

"On the plane I was frightened that we mightn't get
here in time. But the truth is that I didn't actually
believe she was going to die."

"I follow that. You thought Valeria had all the strength there was. I mentioned in London that she was falling down."

"I remember. But I couldn't take it in. You'll say this is crazy, but—this is a confession—my mother gave me her word that she'd live to be ninety."

"How could anybody do that?"

"Don't ask me—I'll tell you what happened. The one time my mother came to the U.S., we went to see Pablo Casals at Marlboro, ninety years old, rehearsing an orchestra. We were both terribly impressed, especially Mother. Here was this ancient man, he was shrunk together in a single piece, no waist and no neck. He had to sit down to conduct. He scolded. But how strong he still was in music. If you understand me. Now, there was a girl in the orchestra who played the clarinet, and she was about nineteen. He stopped the music and said to her, 'Can't you get more life into it?' Then Mother and I looked at each other. And when we were leaving the shed—that outdoor hall—she said, 'Why shouldn't I do that, too—live to be his age?' It was put as a joke, but it was serious underneath."

"It would have been better to keep it a joke. But you took it as a promise."

She nodded. "I see I must have."

"So when I warned you that she was slipping, you brushed it off. Your mother kept her word."

He was about to say, "That's like believing in magic," but he refrained. For one thing, everybody followed magical practices of some sort—he could identify a few of his own. And then, too, you didn't reveal to such a woman how cleverly you observed her. She was as intelligent—phenomenally intelligent—as she was childlike. The boundaries between intellect and the rest meandered so intricately that you could never guess when you were about to trespass, when words addressed to the child might be intercepted by a mind more powerful than yours. So the Dean stared at his wife. It was incomprehensible that Valeria should give

such a daughter the sort of promise (about death!) you
made to a kid, and that the learned daughter should
hold her to it. This was Alice in Wonderland: "Drink
Me." Mature, highly serious women entering into such
an agreement. And it had twelve years more to run.
During this time Minna was to get on with her astronomy, equally safe from the decadent West and the
decadent East. But Minna now told all, this was a
confession. Ah, the poor things, poor ladies! They
made him think of one of Rilke's letters: *"Je suis un
enfant qui ne voudrait autour que des enfances encore
plus adultes."* The mother, in this case the more adult
child, promised not to desert her daughter, and this
promise was also to have kept Valeria alive. But the
best she could do was to hang in there until Minna
arrived from Chicago.

"I wasn't old enough to feel it when my father died. I
was sad because everybody else was. But my mother's
death is really horrible—being a corpse, and cremated,
and tomorrow the cemetery. I can't accept it. And it's
even worse to be angry, it's horrible. Not like a grown
woman. I feel vicious." White, pinched, Minna was
scarcely breathing, and her outraged eyes went back
and forth across his face. He put his arm about her
waist, but the gesture had to be withdrawn. She didn't
want it. She stood too rigid. He then tried to warm his
hand in the square pocket of his overcoat.

He said, "I remember being sore, too, feeling abandoned when my own mother died. I was just an
adolescent, of course. But . . . I'm not the wise psychologist type. Psychology is out of my line. I even
dislike it."

What he was thinking was that Minna's demand was
for Valeria. She wanted her mother, and it was impossible to replace Valeria. That was beyond him, beyond
any husband. True he had gotten into the habit of
attempting whatever Minna needed. He no longer
asked whether this suited him, whether he was risking
his dignity by pushing a cart in the supermarket,

reading recipes, peeling potatoes. Magic practices, yes. But minor ones. But he was no magician; far from it. What he had to offer was active sympathy. Active sympathy should be enough. Why wasn't it! There was a touch of anger in him over this, but the anger was even worse than the inadequacy. He understood, in form, what he should do. The heart of the trouble was in the *form*.

Minna was saying, "All these days we haven't had time to talk. I realize that you're very upset, too, and brooding in the room. I used to think you didn't mind sitting, being by yourself, that you were naturally a quiet person."

"Ready to become a stay-at-home."

"In spite of what people said about you."

"What people said. You listen too much. They said I had raised a lot of hell. Much they know."

"I'm not criticizing, Albert, just reflecting."

Minna marrying Dean Corde: a superclear mind had made a dreamer's match.

She said, "You turned out to be a much more emotional and strange person than I ever expected."

He accepted this, nodding his head. But he wasn't nodding wisely, he was nodding from ignorance. You couldn't fathom Minna's conceptions of strange and normal because she was so astronomical. The hours she spent with you, dear heart, were hours among the galaxies. But she came back from space. There was her mother, and there was her husband to come back for. It was something like Eros and Psyche in reverse. Picturing himself as Psyche, Corde agreed that it was probably better for Eros not to turn on the light. (The Dean was only now discovering how many important things he had neglected to think about.) He was certainly not the man she had supposed she was marrying. Luckily she hadn't made a serious mistake. She had chosen a husband who intended to love her, meant to love her. Yes, she took some pride in having given the marriage due consideration. The truth was that she had done the right thing in spite of it. We knew all kinds of things but not the ones we needed most to know. Modern achievements, the Dean believed, jets, skyscrapers, high technology, were a tremendous drain on intelligence, more particularly on powers of judgment and most of all on private judgment. You could see it in every face, how the depleted wits fought their losing battle with death. Faces told you this. He had learned this from his own face, and he confirmed the discovery by daily observations.

He wasn't merely sorry for his wife, he was horrified. It wasn't only that she was white and drawn but that her features were set in anger, and a kind of accusation. Her mouth was drawn down at one corner and the contraction gave her an expression of face he had learned to dread. He decided, I'd damn well better get her out of here. I never saw anybody go down so fast. This is ruining her.

She thought he was nodding in agreement, and he did agree about being deceptively quiet. He was quiet because he had made so many bad mistakes; he had his work cut out for him, thinking them over. That was the quiet part. He was also misleadingly domestic. She had never noticed how many household duties he took on—the groceries, cooking, vacuuming, washing windows, making beds. He did all this by way of encouraging or conjuring her to change her ways. Let's have a household. Let's not eat frozen TV dinners. But she herself was misleading. It was because people said such things about the wicked Dean that she was attracted to him. She wanted to marry a wickedly experienced but faithful man, a reformed SOB, a chastened chaser, now a gentle husband; and she got what she wanted, all the benefits of his oddity and then some. Earlier women, her unknown rivals, had been defeated. She could believe that she had reformed him. He was even a husband who grieved when she was grieving. He felt like a pity-weirdo. Everything moved him, came back to him amplified, disproportionate, moved him too much, reached him too loudly, was accompanied by overtones of anger. There was some sort of struggle going on. She said she wasn't criticizing, only reflecting, but he couldn't believe that. *You're* supposed to know —*you* tell me. That was how he interpreted the contracted corner of her mouth.

"So you were angry with your mother?" She went back to that.

"It's supposed to be normal, not a sign that there's no love but just the reverse. But I guess the clinicians would say it wasn't the kind of love we'd feel if we were everything we should be. Well, that's standard psychiatry." To himself he added, That's what bothers me about it.

Now what was the position? The position was that Corde had accepted responsibility for keeping his wife posted on sublunary matters. She did boundless space, his beat was terra firma. A crazy assignment, but he enjoyed it most of the time. He liked the fact that she, who had grown up in a Communist country, should have to be told by her American husband who Dzerzhinsky was, or Zinoviev. He had done his homework in Paris while writing on Tsvetayeva. He had done a piece also on Boris Souvarine, so he could describe postrevolutionary Russia. What, never heard of Zinoviev and Kamenev? Nobody had told her about the Moscow trials. "You'll have to fill me in." She wondered whether her father had been aware of Stalin's crimes. She even began to look into Corde's books and to ask, "Who was this Madame Kollontai?" Or, "Tell me about Chicherin." He would say, "Why clutter your mind?" However, it was pleasant at dinner to draw Chicherin for her or to explain what Harry Hopkins had done or describe the members of the brain trust. She was beautifully innocent, a classic case. She also laughed at jokes too old to be told to anybody else. She adored jokes. And when she asked him for the spellings or definitions of words and he gave them in his deep voice without raising his goggled face from the newspa-

per, she would say, "You're my walking, talking reference book. I don't need to touch a dictionary." But
grief, death, these were not your ordinary sublunary
subjects. Here he was no authority. Minna was critical,
she was angry. What was the point of telling him now
that he was not the husband she had thought she was
marrying? Was she referring to his Chicago pieces and
the fulminations they had touched off? She disliked
noise, disorder, notoriety, any publicity. Was this what
she referred to? Only a remote possibility, but it all had
to be considered, for now that Valeria was dead and she
had only him, Corde, to depend upon, total revaluation
was inevitable. So, then, who was this man? What have
we here? He tried, himself, to see what we had. An
elderly person, extensively bald, not well proportioned
(Mason was contemptuous of his legs), sexually disrep-
utable, counter, spare and strange maybe, but not in
the complimentary sense. And then there was the
moral side of things to consider. And the mental, too.
Besides, Valeria had had a different sort of husband in
mind for her daughter, a younger man, a physicist or
chemist, with whom she would have had more in
common. Somewhat painful, all this. Although Valeria
had changed her opinion; she had come around. And
what would a chemist son-in-law have told her on her
deathbed—something more scientific, positive, intelligent?

Anyway he was now being reviewed *da capo* by his
wife, whom death had put in a rage. He had to submit
to it. But since she was going over him so closely, as if
seeing him as she had never seen him before, it might
be worthwhile to say something useful, or enlightening.
What else was there to do in the circumstances? Speak
up!

Here goes, however mistaken, was what he said to
himself.

She was, in fact, asking him a question just then:
"What does that mean, 'If we were everything we
should be'?"

"As matters are, people feel free to plug in and plug out," he said. "Whatever it is, or whoever it is, contact can be cut at will. They can pull out the plug when they've had enough of it, or of him, or of her. It's an easy option. It's the most seductive one. You learn to keep your humanity to yourself, the one who appreciates it best."

"I see. . . ."

What was it that she saw? She was far from pleased with what he said.

"Of course you see. It's the position of autonomy and detachment, a kind of sovereignty we're all schooled in. The sovereignty of atoms—that is, of human beings who see themselves as atoms of intelligent separateness. But all that has been said over and over. Like, how schizoid the modern personality is. The atrophy of feelings. The whole bit. There's what's-his-name—Fairbairn. And Jung before him comparing the civilized psyche to a tapeworm. Identical segments, on and on. Crazy and also boring, forever and ever. This goes back to the first axiom of nihilism—the highest values losing their value."

"Why do you think you should tell me this now, Albert?"

"It might be useful to take an overall view. Then you mightn't blame yourself too much for not feeling as you should about Valeria."

"What comfort is it to hear that everybody is some kind of schizophrenic tapeworm? Why bring me out in the cold to tell me this? For my own good, I suppose."

It was no ordinary outburst. She was tigerish, glittering with rage. Her altered face, all bones, turned against him.

"This might not have been the moment," he said.

"I tell you how horrible my mother's death is, and the way you comfort me is to say everything is monstrous. You make me a speech. And it's a speech I've heard more than once."

"It wasn't what you needed. I shouldn't have. The

only excuse is that I'm convinced it's central. That's where the real struggle for existence is. But you're right. A lecture . . . it was out of place."

"You lecture me. You lecture. I could make *you* these speeches now. You even put it into your *Harper's* article, about Plato's Cave, and the Antichrist."

He made a gesture of self-defense—it was minimal. He said, "That's not quite it. There's an old book by Stead called *If Christ Came to Chicago,* and what I said was that Chicago looked as if the Antichrist already had descended on it."

"I tell you you lecture about plugs and tapeworms and those sovereign, or whatever it is, human atoms, and how capitalism is the best because it fits this emptiness best, and is politically the safest, for horrible reasons, and so on. I'm tired of hearing it."

"I wasn't aware that you were following so closely. I didn't realize that I said so much about it. I'll stop it."

"I heard you all right, Albert. Against my will. I don't want to hear more of it today."

"Yes, yes, I was wrong."

Her rage now began to fade. The glitter passed off. She said, "It's probably your kind of affection. Besides . . . now you couldn't do much anyway."

"Yes, that was the general idea, but obtuse."

Now she relented altogether. She said, "I understand you're in an emotional state yourself, and you haven't had anybody to talk to except your pal the journalist, and that probably wasn't very satisfactory."

"I suppose we'd better go home. Walking is unpleasant at this time of the evening."

Subdued by his failure with her, he considered how he might do better. It was worse than nothing to be so elementary on such a subject, to misjudge his wife's feelings, to sound like a high-class educated dummy. Academic baby talk. Either you went into it with the full power of your mind or you let it alone.

They had walked as far as the boulevard when they turned back. Lecturing, speechifying, emotional states, she said. Spangler had used different terms—crisis, catastrophe, apocalypse. They concluded, each from his own standpoint, that he was seriously off base, out of line. Naturally, he suspected this himself. He half agreed with Mason senior—almost half. Men like Mason senior went to business. Business was law, engineering, advertising, insurance, banking, merchandising, stockbroking, politicking. Mason senior was proud of his strength in the La Salle Street jungle. Bunk, thought contentious Corde. Those were not animals fighting honorably for survival, they were money maniacs, they were deeply perverted, corrupt. No jungle, more like a garbage dump. Leave Darwin out of this. But—calming himself—these Mason types belonged fully to the life of the country, spoke its language, thought its thoughts, did its work. If he, Corde, was different, the difference wasn't altogether to his credit. So Mason senior believed. Corde's answer was that he made no claim to be different. He was like everybody else, but not as everybody else conceived it. His own sense of the way things were had a strong claim on him, and he thought that if he sacrificed that sense—its truth—he sacrificed himself. Chicago was the material habitat of this sense of his, which was, in turn, the source of his description of Chicago. Did this signify that he did not belong to the life of the country? Not if the spirit of the times was in us by nature. We all belonged. Something very wrong here. He pursued the matter further, probably still feeling the painful reverberations of his obtuseness with his wife. To belong fully to the life of the country gave one strength, but why should these others, in their strength, demand that one's own sense of existence (poetry, if you like) be dismissed with contempt? Because they were, after all, *not* strong? A tempting answer, but perhaps too easy. A critical lady looking at one of Whistler's paintings said, "I don't see things as you do." The artist said, "No, ma'am, but don't you wish you could?" A delicious snub but again too easy. The struggle was not

the artist's struggle with the vulgar. That was pure
nineteenth century. Things were now far worse than
that.

Corde thought that he wasn't advanced enough to be
the artist of this singular demanding sense of his. In fact
he had always tried to set it aside, but it was *there,* he
couldn't get rid of it, and as he grew older it gained
strength and he had to give ground. It seemed to have
come into the world with him. What, for example, did
he know about Dewey Spangler? Well, he knew his
eyes, his teeth, his arms, the form of his body, its
doughnut odor; the beard was new but that was knowledge at first sight. That vividness of beard, nostrils,
breath, tone, was real knowledge. Knowledge? It was
even captivity. In the same way he knew his sister
Elfrida, the narrow dark head, the estuary hips, the
feminized fragrance of tobacco mixed with skin odors.
In the case of a Maxie Detillion the vividness was
unwanted, repugnant, but nothing could be done, it
was there nevertheless, impossible to fend off. With
Minna the reality was even more intimate—fingernails,
cheeks, breasts, even the imprint of stockings and of
shoe straps on the insteps of her dear feet when she was
undressing. Himself, too, he knew with a variant of the
same oddity—as, for instance, the eyes and other holes
and openings of his head, the countersunk entrance of
his ears and the avidity expressed by the dilation of his
Huguenot-Irish nostrils, the face that started at the
base of the hairy throat and rose, open, to the top of his
crown. Plus all the curiosities and passions that went
with being Albert Corde. This organic, constitutional,
sensory oddity, in which Albert Corde's soul had a
lifelong freehold, must be grasped as knowledge. He
wondered what reality was if it wasn't this, or what you
were "losing" by death, if not this. If it was only the
literal world that was taken from you the loss was not
great. Literal! What you didn't pass through your soul
didn't even exist, that was what made the literal literal.
Thus he had taken it upon himself to pass Chicago

through his own soul. A mass of data, terrible, murderous. It was no easy matter to put such things through. But there was no other way for reality to happen. Reality didn't exist "out there." It began to be real only when the soul found its underlying truth. In generalities there was no coherence—none. The generality-mind, the habit of mind that governed the world, had no force of coherence, it was dissociative. It divided because it was, itself, divided. Hence the schizophrenia, which was moral and aesthetic as well as analytical. Then along came Albert Corde in diffident persistence, but wildly turned on, putting himself on record. "But don't you see . . . !" He couldn't help summarizing to himself what he should have said to Minna.

He would moreover have said (they were now rising in the small china-closet elevator—there was no harm in these unspoken ideas, and when all this was over she might be willing to let her husband tell her his thoughts), he would have told Minna, "I imagine, sometimes, that if a film could be made of one's life, every other frame would be death. It goes so fast we're not aware of it. Destruction and resurrection in alternate beats of being, but speed makes it seem continuous. But you see, kid, with ordinary consciousness you can't even begin to know what's happening."

15

Minna couldn't go to the cemetery next morning; she was sick. Nothing by halves, she was violently sick. She could keep nothing on her stomach, not even a cup of tea, and she had woman trouble. Something like a grenade went off within the system. Gigi moved Corde out of the bedroom. She said he would sleep in the "drawing room," where the bulky, peeling leather armchairs were. Well, all right. The old woman took total charge, changing linens, putting soiled things to soak in a tub. Two doctors, a team, came to the house before ten o'clock. They were the ones assigned to the diplomatic corps. "They will charge a lot, but others will not have the drugs," Gigi said. Corde stood by. The physicians were a lady and a gentleman, working together. The lady turned Minna over, the gentleman gave her a shot. You had to admire their professionalism, their dexterity with a needle.

"Can't we put the cemetery off till tomorrow?" Corde asked.

A preposterous question. The announcement was already in the papers.

Vlada Voynich volunteered to sit with Minna. So Corde and Gigi together with one of the feeble old uncles were driven to the cemetery by Traian in the Dacia. Once more slammed within tin doors, and the motor roaring under your feet. It looked like melancholy sunny weather—low winter beams coming through cold haze, the prevailing light russet. As a rule Corde avoided cemeteries and never went near the graves of his parents. He said it was just as easy for your dead to visit you, only by now he would have to hire a hall.

He did not realize that the Dacia had already been to the crematorium and that Traian had picked up the canister of ashes. The Dean failed therefore to understand why Tanti Gigi was doubled up, weeping, in the seat behind him. He reached back to give her comfort. She took his hand and held it. All he could see, half turning, was that Uncle Teo, bolt upright in the corner, preferred to stare at the street with big gray eyes as if to dissociate himself from her keening. Her white head was pushed against the back of the seat. Same old woman who had changed Minna's sheets so efficiently

only a while ago, who had shown him cheerful box
camera snapshots last night—young Gigi, a high-
fashion doll of the twenties in a short dress, leaning
against a lion in Trafalgar Square, waving to the folks in
Bucharest. Corde didn't learn until Traian had parked
the car beside the iron stakes of the cemetery fence that
Gigi had been bent double over the tin cylinder of
Valeria's ashes. She was pressing it to herself under the
coat. But when he helped her to the sidewalk and she
came bowed through the door, black shawl slipping
from her head, she gave him the long can to hold. He
waited until her small feet, the turned heels of scuffed
shoes, found the pavement securely; and her sloping
shoulders found the fit of the coat again—that heavy-
looking light coat of synthetic fur (its realism continued
to shock him). Her dark purple long bagging mourner's
dress overhung her low shoes. Then her cardiac patient's face (her face was full of illness just then) told
him that she wanted the cylinder back. And now he
identified the object in his hand. The air was cold, but
the can was warm. Passing it to her, he heard the sound
of larger fragments, bone perhaps, or dental pieces.
Perhaps they weren't even Valeria's. Who could tell
what the crematorium workers shoveled up.

They went first to the office, where the usual exchange of official forms took place. Fees to be paid,
cigarettes to be handed over. Inside the gates, a gang of
cemetery beggars waited, more Oriental than European. Then you remembered again that Istanbul was very
close, Cairo just over the water. For contrast with the
beggars there were the family friends trying to look
decorous in their dated Parisian or Viennese suits,
shoes, dresses. Standing between beggars and friends
was the Greek Orthodox priest. Cousin Dincutza said
that he was personally acquainted with Valeria, used to
call on her occasionally. The priest was stout, strong;
he was sourly masculine, bearded, sallow, sullen; the
hem of his rusty cassock was unstitched and coming
down. There was a separate committee of sharp, henny

ladies. Perhaps it was the black clothing that made them look so very ancient. But if they were old Dincutza types, Corde was for them. Cousin Dincutza was wonderful now. She took total charge of him at the cemetery, protective, advisory. And he greatly needed her advice. This conspicuous foreigner, the man of the family here, was a bit lost. (All the real business, of course, was done by Traian.) And with her jutty teeth, whispering in rudimentary French, Dincutza instructed him continually. As they were setting out from the office she motioned him to go forward and take Gigi's arm.

So they set off in a group. They walked through the cemetery. It was dense with stones and obelisks. The newer monuments were protected from the weather by heavy plastic sheets fastened with belts and ropes, and rattling in the wind. In Chicago, middle-class families covered their furniture with this material; here it was the obelisks and their fresh gilt inscriptions that were protected. No melancholy pleasant winter sunshine now, the weather again turned dark, windy. At the Raresh grave more mourners were waiting.

Considering the season, the color of the grass was surprisingly fresh. Could there be some special source of warmth underneath? There were tapers in large numbers, leaning every which way. Some were sheltered in lanterns but the gusts came down on the rest. The old cousins had seated themselves on benches, and the gypsy beggars crowded up behind—a wild lot, but that was customary, so no special notice was taken of their demented behavior. Dincutza observed (he must have looked rotten, in need of her support) how well Valeria had kept this plot, with *quelle dévotion* flowers were planted. The autumn ones, small asters, had survived the early snow. Now the priest got the service under way. Efficient and gruff, he spoke, sang. Now and then a howl came out. Troubles of his own, obviously. Priests were not pampered in this part of the world. He looked, Corde thought, like a big-bellied

tramp in his country boots. In the scuffles of the wind
the tapers blew out. Where they fell, there were
patches of soot in the grass. Old women rekindled
them. Corde shivered because he had respectfully
removed his hat while the priest chanted. Dincutza
made gestures ordering him to put it on again. Bless the
old girl. When the hair was thin you lost heat through
the top of the skull. This was elderly knowledge. She
had it. She understood.

Now came the traditional cake, white and creamy,
huge, swimming loosely and quivering on its platter.
The beggars went for it. This was their main course.
Dincutza politely offered Corde a taste, but he wanted
no part of this death sweet. Anyway, the beggars were
helping themselves with their hands. By now the gusts
had overcome the last of the tapers, which had tumbled
together in the black-spotted grass. It was time to
install Valeria's ashes in the waiting socket of the
tombstone. This, as you faced the monument, was on
the left side. There would be only Valeria and Dr.
Raresh here. From all sides a rude rattle of plastics in
the wind, the lashed obelisks, those short Cleopatra's
needles—there was little open space, the paths were
exceedingly narrow.

A cemetery workman pulled out the disk that sealed
the socket in the granite and Gigi surrendered Valeria's
ashes to him. Corde, on Dincutza's instructions, was
holding her up. So Gigi, sobbing, gave up the metal
cylinder and the workman tried to push it into the
opening.

Regulations must have changed since the stone was
raised. The cylinder was too large. Uncle Teo and
others moved in to examine the difficulty. There was
just a shade of difference in the dimensions and if only
a few chips of granite were knocked away from the
opening the tube might slide in. On instructions from
Uncle Teo and the cousins, the workman applied his
chisel, tapped once or twice and then swung his hammer widely—two, three blows. Fragments sprang from

the back of the monument, and then the material
around the socket crumbled. This was not granite, it
was cement. The rounded shoulder of the monument
came off, slid down. Gigi did not faint away but she
slumped against Corde. He held her up and a space was
cleared for her on the bench. Now the lashed sheets of
plastic over the surrounding obelisks clattered hard as if
to give it away that it was not solid marble they were
protecting but a facade. At the core of each obelisk
there was cement. Conferring together, Traian and the
relatives decided to deposit the cylinder overnight in
the ossuary. The socket could be widened, the damage
would be repaired by tomorrow.

Then the entire party walked very slowly along the
grave-bordered footpath to the principal avenue. Again
the line of beggars holding out their hands. The cylinder was left at the low stone building (ossuary? charnel
house?), deposited in a box. Then everyone returned to
the office by the gate.

The rest of the business was left to solid Traian in his
zooty raw tan leather jacket. He went in to arrange for
the repairs. The old colleagues and cousins separated
quickly, for it now began to rain. Umbrellas were
opened.

And suddenly the inner significance of the event (old
friends paying last respects, a mourning sister) disappeared. Weather took over, nothing but cloud and rain,
gloom over the dark green, old people finding shelter,
the priest in his hobo boots striding over gravel,
hurrying through the big gates. Corde, feeling empty,
guided Gigi to the car. Traian trotted around to open
the doors and reattach the windshield wipers. He then
turned on the ignition and made a wide U-turn in the
vast wet avenue, brown with machine fumes. Corde
became aware how much distress had accumulated in
him only when the car passed Valeria's mourners, the
graveside group, at the tram stop. Dincutza stood
among them. Then he said to Tanti Gigi, "Let's back up

and take Dincutza home with us. Please tell Traian.
. . . We can squeeze her into the back."

"Oh, my dear, what a kind thought, but we have not
the space."

"It could be done."

It couldn't. And this was not the time to press Gigi.
And by now they were already blocks beyond the tram
stop. But it gave him a hard pang. Gigi said, "We are
all well accustomed to the trams, Albert. Everybody,
but everybody, rides them. And although the steps are
too high for elderly passengers, the service, furthermore, is excellent." But Corde was sick at heart, all the
same. A grind of two hours, perhaps, on the trolley car.
Eighty-year-old Dincutza had looked after him. He
went home in style while she waited in the rain. There
must in addition be a special kind of fatigue—cemetery
fatigue—felt by people who were aware that they
would soon be back to stay. He could anticipate that
himself.

Minna was asleep when they returned, and Vlada
offered him a drink. He took more than one. He filled
his glass several times—for the chill, for the cement, for
the dark stone, bone, charnel smell, and for Cousin
Dincutza. The fermented plum liquor made him smell
like a still.

White and full-faced—dark lipstick, dyed hair, wide
bosom, bunchy hips—Vlada looked at him with sympathy. "Getting a little thick for you?" she said.

"Getting? It's been all along. How is Minna?"

"Not too well. Before she fell asleep, she wanted to
talk about all the things that had to be done yet."

"What is she planning?"

"Not she, so much. Tanti Gigi. Important projects."

If he had encouraged her, Vlada might have made
satirical comments about Tanti Gigi. There were hints
of that, he saw them, but he kept her honest. She said,
"I came to sit in the study when Minna went to sleep,
because the telephone had been ringing. I think they

gave her Demerol, so she isn't likely to hear it. Poor
Minna, she's never had to take this much. . . ."

"Nothing like this, no."

"She forgot what Eastern Europe was like. With her
mother's protection, she may never have known it as
the rest of us did. As Americans, even if the place is
bugged, we can speak freely here. Valeria had plenty of
trouble, of course, they almost destroyed her, but she
was exceptionally strong and well connected."

"Why shouldn't her mother have protected her?"
said Corde.

"Why, of course, it was natural," said Vlada. "And
people here all are dying to send their gifted children to
the West. A mad desire to get out. What would Minna
have amounted to if she had stayed? After it became
clear that she wasn't coming back, the Minister of
Education called Valeria in. He was a tough old
Stalinist. Valeria asked him, 'What were *you* prepared
to do for her?' She said, 'My daughter knows how her
mother was treated here.' But you've heard this before.
Well, here we are, Albert—what?—five thousand, six
thousand miles from Chicago? . . . By the way, there
was a call for you, earlier, from Paris. A man named
Spangler. Is that the columnist? Is he a friend of yours?
He said he'd call back within the hour."

"Yes, it is the famous Spangler. Well, well. He must
have news for me."

"He didn't tell me anything. I said you'd be back
soon from the cemetery."

"There must be a result in the case. He wouldn't call
me otherwise. He should have told you something. Just
like Spangler. . . ."

"Why don't we chat. It'll help you to bear the
suspense," said Vlada. "I always hear good things from
you when you let yourself go."

"If peculiar."

"All the better when they are. I realize you haven't
decided yet about Beech."

"I haven't been able to think about lead. Lead is

heavy and I'm feeling light. But I haven't forgotten, it's one of the things I keep at the back of my mind. I still haven't got it clear what Beech expects."

"You think he'll expect total agreement with his views, and that would make you his mouthpiece?"

"He's the scientist. His views would be sound. Mine would only be impressions."

"Why should that enter into it?" said Vlada. "I don't see why there should be a conflict if you limit yourself to reporting."

Corde said, "He takes an apocalyptic view of the poisoning of the earth. If I didn't accept his picture we might not get any where. Let's give it a quick inspection: First man conquers nature, and then he learns that conquered nature has lost its purity and he's very upset by this loss. But it's not science that's to blame, it's technocrats and politicians. They've misused science. Yes, I see this is an unfair simplification. I admire the man. But I suspect that if I didn't buy his apocalypse he'd be annoyed, even wounded."

"But your articles had apocalyptic emotions in them," said Vlada. "That's just what got him."

"You can't hitch these two apocalypses together. Doesn't he believe he can straighten me out? Something like, 'I can give the man the real reason for this anarchy he reported. It's lead poisoning, lead insult to the brain.' My friend Spangler was very sharp with me about catastrophes. He told me I went too far, being poetical, mentioning the Antichrist. He's dead against the whole Antichrist business. It's too theological and Moral Majority for his taste. Besides, he's a journalist with a following of millions, masses of people who depend on the press to keep them in balance (what else have they got?). I wouldn't be surprised if he believed that it was up to spokesmen like him—maybe primarily to himself alone—to ensure stability, to put down disorder with his own behind. Fat little Dewey Spangler, as long as he sits tight and bears down with his backside he can suppress evil and save us from anarchy.

All he has to do is say all the right things while he prevents the wrong ones from being spoken."

As if to hear better, Vlada moved nearer on the damaged brocade sofa, her cup in her lap. This heavy woman, and pale, eyes large and dark—she was as intelligent as she was stout. Her hair, parted evenly down the center in two symmetrical waves, suggested that the fundamental method of her character was to balance everything out, and that she kept a mysterious, ingenious equilibrium, her fat figure and her balanced thoughts being counterparts. Obviously she wanted to draw him out. She took only tea. The *pálinca* was for him, to drive away the cemetery drizzle and also to make him talk. She said, "You seem to think I have nothing but Beech on my mind. It's not so. I'm interested in what you've seen over here, and what effect it's had on your state."

"I'm in a state?"

"Your state of mind as an American in a place like this."

Yes, Vlada did often ask for his American opinions. She hadn't herself been naturalized for more than five or six years. To her he was an American American. She sometimes led the conversation around to such subjects as Abolition, the Civil War, Mormonism. Not long ago in Chicago, the ladies had had him talking through dinner and until a late hour about buffalo hunters, frontier fighters, Bowie knives, Indian wars. Minna, too, found this wonderfully entertaining, exotic.

"So you want my American standpoint. I wonder if there is such a thing. Maybe I'm not the American you ought to ask."

"Your personal interpretation, then."

He reflected that he had made a speech to Minna in the street yesterday; it hadn't turned out well. That failure (crushing failure of sensitivity) was a stimulant. He wanted to do better, to try again. Vlada was receptive. He was tempted to talk. Her aim was to help him to work off tensions and reduce the anxiety of waiting. He said, "I don't know about interpretations. What about impressions instead, or maybe improvisation. Have you ever read about the Italian *improvvisatori,* mostly from Naples, who used to entertain audiences two hundred years ago? You'd suggest a theme, and they'd give an inspired recitation. Where would you like me to begin? I could start with the little sofa we're sitting on. It's the Orient. But I think you're going to ask about Valeria's death, and what I was thinking when I saw the Colonel."

"What about the Colonel?"

"He was teaching us a lesson. I think a little of it was meant for me."

"What was this lesson?"

"What was the lesson? Well, they set the pain level for you over here. The government has the power to set it. Everybody has to understand this monopoly and be prepared to accept it. At home, in the West, it's different. America is never going to take an open position on the pain level, because it's a pleasure society, a pleasure society which likes to think of itself as a tenderness society. A tender liberal society has to find soft ways to institutionalize harshness and smooth it over compatibly with progress, buoyancy. So that with us when people are merciless, when they kill, we explain that it's because they're disadvantaged, or have lead poisoning, or come from a backward section of the country, or need psychological treatment. Over here the position was scarcely concealed that such and such numbers of people were going to be expended. In Russia, for the building of socialism, that policy was set by Lenin from the first. He would have allowed millions to die in the early famines. More would have died in the early years if the kindly Red Cross and Herbert Hoover hadn't distributed food. Even with us, conservative capitalism has to temper or conceal its position that classic conditions of competition will bring suffering and death—American conservatism has its own difficulties with the pain level. Suppose the public expense of kidney dialysis is ninety thousand dollars a year in a clinic that keeps six or seven dim, unproductive lives going—will we let these old folks watch the television for another year yet?"

"On the other side, it's brutality," said Vlada.

"On the other side, it's the archaic standard, Oriental and despotic, affliction accepted as the ground of existence, its real basis. By that standard we're unformed, we Americans. What do we think the fundamentals are, anyway—the human truth! And this fucking Colonel was running us through the Brief Course, a refresher for Minna and an introduction for me, the representative of the rival superpower with his unformed character. I've heard Europeans say that the American character doesn't even exist yet. It's still kicking in the womb. The French, the Germans, they know a little more about the archaic pain-level standard. But they live now as we do, comfortably. Only they've had it. They had the trenches in the first war, and the bombing of cities in the second, and the camps. They'd like to retire from history for a while. They're on holiday. They've been on holiday since they cleared away the wreckage in 1945. I don't blame them. I only observe that it prevents rigorous positions from being taken. In that respect they share the American condition. Life is highly enjoyable and there's great reluctance to focus clearly on a pain level. And when a brutal action is necessary—well, think of the scene of our withdrawal from Saigon."

"I thought when you were talking about your friend Spangler that you were going to be a little more amusing."

"When we've worn ourselves out with our soft nihilism, the Russians would like to arrive with their hard nihilism. They feel humanly superior. Even the Russian dissidents, especially the right wing, take the high tone with us. They say, 'We haven't got justice or personal freedom but we do have warmth, humanity, brotherhood, and our afflictions have given us some

character. All you can offer us is supermarkets.'
Whereas the best defense that liberal democracy can
make goes like this: 'True, we're short on charisma and
fraternal love, although you have it in debased forms,
don't kid yourselves about that. What we do have in the
West is a kind of rational citizens' courage which you
don't understand in the least. At our best we can be
patient, we keep our heads in crisis, we can be decent in
a cold steady way. Don't underestimate us.'"

"Do you buy this?"

"No."

"Why don't you?"

"I don't think you can be managerial and noble at the
same time. Do you think those Chicago articles are
about rational citizens' courage?"

"I somehow expected your inspired recitation would
have something to do with Chicago."

Corde said, "You're right. Let me try that now. Here
in Bucharest I've been thinking about those articles.
Why did I write them? It was late in life for me to act up
and sail up the Chicago River to make such a bristling
gunboat attack. I even seem to have thought readers
would be grateful for this, another sign of immaturity.
In middle age I came back to Chicago to make a new
start. Ten years later, I may have to do it again. It's like
inexhaustible adolescence, a new start every few years.
And at the outset I didn't intend to be provoking. I
started out in all innocence. I took a light tone. I even
thought it might be fun. Like quoting Matthew Arnold
about the stockyards in 1884: 'Pigsticking? No, I
haven't gone to see the pigsticking.' I wasn't looking for
trouble. No sermons to preach about the death of cities
or the collapse of civilization. I'm too much of a
Chicagoan to feel up to that. Not for me, dear God, to
work all this out! I sympathize up to a point with the
objections of my friend Spangler. He accused me of
abyssifying and catastrophizing. We have a weakness in
America for this. Partly it's been first-class show business. We've been brought up for generations on Cecil

B. De Mille's 'special effects'—the Sign of the Cross,
lions and Christian martyrs, the destruction of Sodom,
the last days of Pompeii. This poor make-believe,
however, is a dangerous distraction. Because this *is* a
time of the breaking of nations. It's all true. Now,
Spangler pointed out that you begin with the abyss and
end up with Jones of Jonestown, where death was
mixed up with 'special effects.' But it doesn't seem to
me that *I* was being histrionic. I didn't want to demon-
strate or remonstrate or advocate or prophesy. I most
certainly did not intend to set myself up as *the* spokesman of the sufferer. But perhaps Spangler's main
charge against me was that I was guilty of poetry. And I
don't know exactly what to make of that. He himself
was keen on poetry in his youth. He's now a spokesman, though, and poets never really were liked in
America. Benjamin Franklin said better one good
schoolmaster than twenty poets. That's why when we
have most need of the imagination we have only
'special effects' and histrionics. But for a fellow like me,
the real temptation of abyssifying is to hope that the
approach of the 'last days' might be liberating, might
compel us to reconsider deeply, earnestly. In these last
days we have a right and even a duty to purge our
understanding. In the general weakening of authority,
the authority of the ruling forms of thought also is
reduced, those forms which have done much to bring us
into despair and into the abyss. I don't need to mind
them anymore. For science there can be no good or
evil. But I personally think about virtue, about vice. I
feel free to. Released, perhaps, by all the crashing.
And in fact everybody has come under the spell of 'last
days.' Isn't that what the anarchy of Chicago means?
Doesn't it have a philosophical character? Think of a
beautiful black chick who spends days with a razor
hollowing out a copy of *Ivanhoe* for her desperate
lover. Think how symbolic his actions are when he fires
a shot into the floor of Judge Makowski's courtroom.
He rushes out, they kill him. He dies with histrionic

flash. Shot in the head, the head he was probably stoned out of, he leaves us a message. And what's the message? . . . 'You better be more rigorous, man! You better think about the first and last things.'" The telephone was about to ring. It gave its preliminary chirrup.

"Maybe what I've been saying proves that I myself suffer from 'insult.'"

The phone rang and he took the call. "You may have heard already, or am I the first?" said Dewey.

"The first what?"

"Then I am the first. The jury found that man of yours guilty, and he got a sixteen-year sentence. You have a victory."

"How did you hear this?"

"From my office in Washington. Is it exciting? I had my people alerted and they phoned me just a while ago at the Meurice. Do you feel good about it?"

"Sixteen years. I feel worked up."

"Well, it went as you wanted it. I bet your cousin Detillion is disappointed."

"I wonder. Win or lose, it was bound to improve his reputation. Chicago is still more his scene than it is mine. Dewey, listen, I'm grateful to you for taking the trouble. I'm thankful for your call."

"We had a couple of memorable talks," said Spangler. "After forty years, to find out how much you still have in common with a friend is damn important. I hope to stay in touch now."

Corde returned to Vlada, sitting beside her on the orange brocade sofa with the Oriental inlaid back, behind them the drizzling city and in the next room his sick wife, but mercifully, warmly sleeping, her large eyes closed, his pretty lady, lately so ravaged.

"I gather that you are the winner," said Vlada.

"It went as I wanted it. As I suppose I did. . . ."

"That at least is over."

"Going back will be a little simpler now."

"Simpler—you're referring to the college?"

"Partly."

"Was it only the man, or the woman also?"

"She gets a separate bench trial, and with plea bargaining—that's how it was explained to me—she'll get about eight years."

"So . . . there's your justice."

"Nothing comes out neat and even. But those two cost the boy his life. I don't take much stock in the punishment, but the alternative was that they would go scot-free. It's true I used clout and special privileges to nail them. It's true that nobody will change, the jails stink and nothing significant has been added. In jail, out of jail, Lucas Ebry and Riggie Hines are exactly the same. There are millions more where they come from —not attached to life, and nobody can suggest how to attach them. Now listen, Vlada, Minna and I have got to get out of here. If she's going to be really sick."

"Whether it's sickness or mourning . . ."

"In any case, I'll take no chances with Communist hospitals, and I won't wait until she's too sick to travel. Either Zurich or Frankfurt would be a short flight."

"There's your phone again," said Vlada.

It was Miss Porson, speaking from his office. "The man has been sentenced."

"A friend just called from Paris with the news."

"The Provost said I should tell you how well it came out, from his point of view."

"I'm sure he's glad it's over."

"And he sent a message to the poor darling—how is she? The Provost has been in touch with the observatory and she has—you both have—accommodations at Palomar next month, the fifteenth and the sixteenth."

"Now there's a help," said Corde.

"Now then, did Dr. Voynich give you the news about your sister and the Judge?"

"Dr. Voynich is sitting here with me. Of course I've heard about the marriage."

"How nice." Miss Porson had chatted her way to the commanding heights of gossip. "I talked to your sister

just now, wondering whether she would have a message
for you, and before I could congratulate her she told
me that her son had taken off."

"He's gone somewhere?"

"I'm just coming to that. He's been angry. Very
angry."

"Over the marriage or the verdict?"

"He's left the country."

"Where did he go—how does she know that?"

"He charged his ticket to her account. He went to
her travel agent, and he's now in Mexico, so far as she
knows. She didn't discuss it with me, but he's under
bond, isn't he?"

"He may have gone to have his sulks in some nice
tropical place."

Corde said this not because he believed it but in
order to move the conversation to another subject.
Mason had little interest in sunny holidays. Already, at
the age of twelve, he couldn't have cared less about the
porgies and the flounders. Let them stay where they
were. Let Uncle Albert, his leg laid open by rows of
barnacles, join the fishes in the drink—him with his
abstracted look, falling into the sea. Corde was in no
mood to chat with Miss Porson and speculate about his
unhappy sister on the transatlantic telephone. Miss
Porson with her good white hair and her calamine-
colored Alexander Woollcott face was warmly sympathetic, but he didn't at all care to bandy civilities with
her.

"There's somebody who wants to say hello, Dean.
Lydia Lester is standing here."

"Oh! Let me talk to her," said Corde.

Not much was said.

"Well, it's over."

"I'm sorry I had to leave during the trial."

"I understand that. I'm sorry about your wife . . .
your mother-in-law."

Slender, nervously pretty, Lydia Lester had long hair
to shield her from the world, reticent long hands, pink

lips. From the bad side of the tracks unwanted reality had descended on her (how the tracks meandered now!). And which way would she go? Back to maidenliness, he expected. "What are your plans?" he said. She mentioned none. He said he was coming back soon and hoped she would have dinner with them. He did not ask to speak to Miss Porson again, but put the phone down lightly, giving her no time to cut in.

"Do I understand from the conversation that your nephew has taken off?" said Vlada.

"Letting his mother have it because she married without his consent. His new stepfather is political enough to get the case against him dismissed and recover the bond—about five thousand bucks, I think. So Mason has gone to Central America to look over the revolutionary options. Intimidation of witnesses is no big deal, a mere college boy scaring black men who have criminal records. But there is one piece of good news, an open date at the Palomar Observatory."

"Minna won't want to miss that," Vlada said.

"Got any practical advice?"

"Take her away as soon as you can. I have another week here, and I can lend a hand with Gigi. They won't force her out of the apartment; that's not hard to take care of, it's done all the time. And as they'd say in Chicago, the authorities won't make waves. It's nothing to them that you're a dean, but it counts that you're a journalist. Also that you're connected with the Ambassador and with the famous columnist Mr. Spangler. They won't bother your old Tanti Gigi. You be nice to them now and they'll be nice to you, and forget the bygones. Are you so eager to get home, yourself?"

"It's not as if we were going back to order, beauty, calm and peace."

She said, "Still, you'll be glad to see Lake Michigan from your window again, I'm sure of that."

16

For some weeks it had been impossible to give the world his full attention—he had been too busy, absorbed, unsteady, unbalanced. But now, thanks be to God, the world began to edge back again, to reveal itself. On the plane when he held his wife's thin hand, she was too ill and bitter to be aware of his touch; she shut him out. But he was minutely aware of things, and the source of this awareness was in his equilibrium, a very extensive kind of composure. Not that this composure didn't have tight areas, crawl spaces, narrow and painful corners where longtime miseries rankled and to which there was no easy access, but this rankling—sometimes an electric prickling in a circle around his heart—couldn't be separated from his sense of improvement, of coming into his own. And in Chicago, when he brought Minna to be examined by Dr. Tyche, he wondered whether the doctor, glancing twice at him—a significant double take—wouldn't order *him* to the hospital, too.

No, it was Minna who was hospitalized at Wesleyan for tests and observation. Careful, judicious old Dr. Tyche said he would not care to offer a diagnosis before the laboratory results were in. A tactful man, he did not intend to discuss Minna's illness with the Dean, but he perfectly understood her state—she was so tormented that it was better to be sick. Let it be a medical problem. On the second day, Tyche was able to tell her that she was anemic, underweight, dehydrated, deficient in potassium. She was helped into a wheelchair by

313

the nurse, X-rays of her chest were taken, she was
examined by specialists, given shots. She slept a great
deal and her husband, who came twice daily, sometimes studied her—even lying on her side, she appeared
purposive, going forward, the black hair spread about
her, and in profile her large, female sleeping eye
painfully severe under the lid, as if she were getting
stern lessons in her sleep. He was driving back and
forth along the lakefront afternoon and evening, bringing glycerin and rose water for her hands, nail scissors,
plastic tubes of shampoo, scientific papers she wasn't
yet able to read. Irritable, she found fault with him, and
sometimes he was wounded—that is, the old self would
have been wounded.

The habits he had acquired in Eastern Europe were
curiously binding, he found. He did not make full use
of the double bed but slept on its edge as if he had been
laid there like a yardstick. Mornings he sat in his chair
just as he had sat in Minna's old-country room. Vlada
had been right; he was glad to see the lake from his
window and have the freshwater ocean for company.
At his back the city, unquiet, the slum and its armies
just over the way: blacks, Koreans, East Indians,
Chippewas, Thais and hillbillies, squad cars, ambu-
lances, firefighters, thrift shops, drug hustlers, lousy
bars, alley filth. In the elevator, Mrs. Morford had told
him that she was waiting her turn in the butcher shop
when a young man put his hand into her coat pocket.
She said, "What are you doing?" and he answered,
"What do you *think* I'm doing?" Mr. Vinck, the cop on
the fifth floor, was burglarized and his collection of
handguns was taken. Teams of thieves ripped off the
wheels of cars in the building garage and left them
sitting on bricks. The elevators were vandalized, swasti-
kas scratched into the hard metal of the walls and the
numbered buttons pried out of the panels. Old people
like herself, said Mrs. Morford, her eyes sadly downcast, lived behind locked doors. And, thought Corde-

(oh, so widely read, what was the good of it), if the good bourgeois of the nineteenth century could loll and dream in his overfurnished Biedermeier coziness, if his drawing room was like a box in the theater of the world, Mrs. Morford on her inflation-shrunk pension, among all the comforts of home, was shut in like a birdie in a cage.

He didn't go to the college; the thought of it repelled him. That would be a bad scene. He wasn't ready for Alec Witt and he didn't notify Miss Porson of his return. He planned to telephone his sister on New Year's Day. To congratulate her wouldn't be too hard, but he preferred to postpone talking to her about Mason. He drove out once to try to find the building where Rick Lester had been killed. He knew the block but not the address. The buildings were all Chicago six-flats in any case, heavy brick, beginning to bow with age, the courtyards miry and gathering litter. It was into one of these courtyards that Lester had fallen. Corde put to himself the question Mason had stuck him with about Lester's death—did it matter so much? Was it King David crying out over Absalom, was it Lear fumbling with Cordelia's button? There was a heavy death traffic which called perhaps for a revision of views. "Can't go through it on the old iambic pentameter," was how Corde formulated it. Must modernize.

But at home he sat usually with his back to the decayed city view. From his corner window he could see the Loop and its famous towers, but he looked directly downward at the working of the water, on bright days a clear green, easing its mass onto the beaches, white. The waters bathing the waters in sun, and every drop having its own corpuscle of light, the light meantime resembling the splash of heavy raindrops on paved surfaces—the whole sky clear, clear but tense. On days of heavy weather you felt the shock of the waves and heard their concussion through the building. Under low clouds you might have been look-

ing at Hudson's Bay and when the floes came close you
wouldn't have been surprised to see a polar bear. Only
you didn't smell brine, you smelled pungent ozone, the
inland-water raw-potato odor. But there was plenty of
emptiness, as much as you needed to define yourself
against, as American souls seem to do. Cities (this had
been impressed on Corde when he pored over Blake—
Spangler had not stopped him by kidding him about
it)—cities were moods, emotional states, for the most
part collective distortions, where human beings thrived
and suffered, where they invested their souls in pains
and pleasures, taking these pleasures and pains as
proofs of reality. Thus "Cain's city built with murder,"
and other cities built with Mystery, or Pride, all of them
emotional conditions and great centers of delusion and
bondage, death. It seemed to Corde that he had made
an effort to find out what Chicago, U.S.A., was built
with. His motive—to follow this through—came out of
what was eternal in man. What mood was this city? The
experience, puzzle, torment of a lifetime demanded
interpretation. At least he was beginning to understand
why he had written those articles. Nobody was much
affected by them, unless it was himself. So here was the
emptiness before him, water; and there was the filling
of emptiness behind him, the slums.

Anyway, he slept on the edge of the bed, in a
provisional position, feeling something of a stranger in
these most familiar surroundings, made his coffee, read
the papers, had the waves for company. He did not go
in for African violets again; they would only die while
he and Minna were at Mount Palomar and visiting
colleagues at La Jolla and in the Bay Area. He threw
out the dead plants and kept the potting soil in a plastic
bag at the bottom of the broom closet, along with shoe
polish and floor wax. He went out to the greenhouse on
Peterson Road opposite the cemetery and bought a red
azalea for Minna's room, a small tree, the finest to be
had. This offering, like almost all his offerings, was
problematic. In her present condition she was hard to

please. Human contact was repugnant to her unless its intent was to heal.

Nevertheless he made the lakefront trip twice daily, and he deliberately confined his conversation with Minna to ordinary subjects. He hadn't washed the car because dust made it less noticeable to car thieves. He had telephoned the laundry. Mail had accumulated in the receiving room, but he hadn't brought it upstairs; he'd wait until the second of January and then have Miss Porson open and sort it. For old times' sake he had stopped at the Lincoln Park Zoo on the way to the hospital, not to look at the animals but to see whether the Viking ship was still there. A team of Norwegians had rowed it across the Atlantic ninety years ago and it had been preserved near the waterfowl pond, where he and Dewey Spangler had had their ignorant arguments about Plato. He was sure that there had been Viking shields hung decoratively along the gunwales. If they had been mere ornaments they had rotted away, but some of the great oars were still there, laid under the ship.

He said, "Will you be starting up your dancing lessons again when we get back from California?"

"You never liked me to go."

"On the contrary, I liked it very much when you came home full of color, lively, pretty. Is there another astronomer in the world who can tap-dance?"

She said, "What about you and your club—have you gone swimming there?"

No, he didn't go to the club. Certain passages in his articles showed why he was wise to absent himself.

In the locker room I tune in on the conversation of a new member (Nick? Jimmy?). Naked, he holds before him a Bacchic belly from which, however, he appears to get no Bacchic pleasure. He is rather gloomy, shortish, curly-haired with large sideburns, hanging red cheeks, springing whiskers. A regretful eye tells you that this vital prosperity is not his fault, is unwanted, does not ensure Nick's happiness. His business? He runs a girlie nightclub in one of the suburbs. Wrapped in a towel, he is one of those useful members who like to give advice. A young executive comes, the black-bearded type with chic eyeglasses, a long slender turtleneck, an attaché case. As he undresses he asks Nick for suggestions. One of the men in his office is being married next week, and the boys want to give him a final stag party. "We're thinking of one of the Rush Street joints." Nick warns him, "You're asking for a rip-off. As soon as a fellow comes in they make him buy a fifty-dollar bottle of stinking champagne. Why don't you fellows rent a good hotel suite. Have dinner served, and if you hire a couple of girls to put on a show, it'll be a nicer evening and much cheaper. You'll get more mileage from the girls on a private arrange-ment, and it's undignified for professional people to go to Rush Street and be hustled like conventioneers and eat and drink a lot of crap." He warns another member not to patronize the barbershop next door to the club. "They charge you ten bucks for a lousy job—force you to have a shampoo. You just washed your hair in the shower, didn't you? Why should he wash it again and sock you ten bucks, plus a two-dollar tip, and still you'll come out looking like an Eskimo woman chewed on your hairline with her teeth." Nick knows every con there is and he is keen to protect the dignity of the members.

And this one, about another member, a young lawyer, who explained on the telephone why he had to miss an appointment with me at the club.

As he speaks I hear a sort of glad misery or cheerful desperation, his happiness at being where the action is: "I had to go to a closing. My associate prepared the documents while I was out of town, and he screwed up. I had to straighten it out. The first six months the seller was not supposed to get a share of the net from my client, and they dropped this clause from the contract. When I arrived and saw what was going on I said, No way. It wouldn't have been more than fifteen thou, but I wasn't going to let my guy get fucked even that much. The deal was over a restaurant where your average check runs thirty or forty bucks per capita. Not that my client is the type who would keep straight books. But in the meantime, what happens? The cops descend on the restaurant and bust it on account of the liquor license. It's that crazy new captain on Chicago Avenue. He has a special hard-on for the place, because somebody told him it's supposed to be Sinatra's favorite when he's in town, where his whole entourage goes, and that's big business, because when the word is out that you might see Sinatra there's always a crowd of yokels sitting waiting for a glimpse. All that crowd of yokels are on junk and the Chicago Avenue captain has a thing about dopies. He couldn't close the place, the management is entitled to a hearing, but it didn't do business much good when a dozen cops with helmets and riot equipment broke in, like 1968. They did it twice and scared hell out of the diners. There was only me to take care of all this, and it was one of those days. I'm so sorry I stiffed you"—stood you up. All this in a voice that trembles with electrical excitement. The big time. I leave the club and wait at the bank of elevators. The lake wind bellows and rages in the shafts, those long wild gullets. . . .

Corde knew better than to tell Minna why he might be uncomfortable at the club, discreetly avoiding mentioning his articles to her, the troubles he had brought on himself. He saw how it was, undisguised, when she looked at him—the blank of death. Her mother's death had taught her death. Triviality was insupportable to her. Her judgment was rigorous, angry. She wanted no part of his journalism, articles, squalor. Suburban pimps or smart-ass lawyers beneath contempt and the great hordes, even of the doomed, of no concern to her, nor the city of destruction, nor its assaults, arsons, prisons and deaths. And wiping out all fond memories, for the present at least, adopting the universe as a standard.

"I think I should have a talk with Dr. Tyche."

"I wonder if I didn't do the wrong thing by coming back now. I worry about Gigi."

"You were in no condition to help her. Gigi is all right, don't worry about Gigi. And you're better off here, at Wesleyan with Dr. Tyche."

"He's an angelic old man."

"That's exactly what he is. I had him in mind."

"I suppose you were right."

"To insist?"

"To take over when you did."

She had her doubts about Corde's good intentions. About her mother there were no doubts; she came from her womb and they were bound by true bonds. She had no doubts about Dr. Tyche, whose small old face was gentle and healthy. Age and devotion to patients had refined his goodness. But Corde—she loved him but he was suspect. And so he should be. We were a bad lot. For a complex monster like her husband, goodness might be just a mood, and love simply an investment that looked good for the moment. Today you bought Xerox. Next month, if it didn't work out, you sold it. It was an uncomfortable sort of judgment, but Corde was beginning to realize that this was how he wanted to be judged. Minna gave him a true reflection of his entire self. The intention was to recognize yourself for what you (pitiably, preposterously) were. Then whatever good you found, if any, would also be yours. Corde bought that. He wasn't looking for accommodation, comfort.

He had a very short talk with Dr. Tyche in one of the high corners of the hospital—to the south the mighty towers of the city, to the west collapse and devastation.

"What's her condition, really, Doctor?"

"Well, a serious trauma."

"Her mother promised to live a decade yet."

"I see. It's a broken promise, too. Well, the death of a parent does things like that to people."

"Yes, can turn us childish. I've heard, Doc, that in

the crucial days of the female cycle a woman can have edema of the brain, and irrational fits? . . ."

The doctor was too canny to answer this, and smiled it away. You didn't give out medical opinions which might later be quoted in disputes. "When you get the curse your brain swells. The doctor told me that!" Tyche would only say, "The iron and potassium levels are very low, and the whole system weakened."

"Will she be able to go to Mount Palomar?"

"She asks me that every day. I don't see why she shouldn't."

Corde drove home, comforted. The weather was bright, keen blue, an afternoon of January thaw. His car had been parked in the sun, so he didn't need to turn the heater on. At home he set a kitchen chair out on the porch. It was mild enough to sit there, on the lee side of the flat. The light was the light of warmer seasons, not of deep winter. It came up from his own harmonies as well as down from above. The lake was steady, nothing but windless water before him. He had to look through the rods of his sixteenth-story porch, an interference of no great importance. Whatever you desired would be measured out through human devices. Did the bars remind you of jail? They also kept you from falling to your death. Besides, he presently felt himself being carried over the water and into the distant colors. Here in the Midwest there sometimes occurred the blues of Italian landscapes and he passed through them, very close to the borders of sense, as if he could do perfectly well without the help of his eyes, seeing what you didn't need human organs to see but experiencing as freedom and also as joy what the mortal person, seated there in his coat and gloves, otherwise recorded as colors, spaces, weights. This was different. It was like being poured out to the horizon, like a great expansion. What if death should be like this, the soul finding an exit. The porch rail was his figure for the hither side. The rest, beyond it, drew you constantly as the completion of your reality.

17

The Cordes, after Minna was discharged from the hospital, attended a party given by Judge Sorokin's brother and his wife. Corde tried to get out of it. He said to Elfrida, through whom the invitation came, "Parties? No. Too tiring." But Elfrida answered, "Don't impose your unsocial habits on her. You're a fusspot, Albert. You want to keep her in a gloomy room and fuss over her. She's naturally a cheerful person and needs to get out. If it were an evening affair it might strain her, but this is only a brunch in lively company." Corde got the message: Elfrida recommended Minna to follow her own example. Grieving daughters like pained mothers should behave with female gallantry. "And I haven't seen Minna at all," said Elfrida. "For that matter, I haven't seen you, Albert, and you're going west soon. Are you on leave, by the way?"

"I'm taking care of Minna. The college thinks I couldn't make better use of my time."

"My brother-in-law and his wife won't bore you, I promise."

"What is he?"

"Ellis Sorokin? Engineering consultants, cybernetics —he runs a big company. His wife is a computer wizard. Or witch. She's a very pretty woman, and fashionable, and a horsewoman. You'd never believe computers were her line."

"Let me talk to Minna about this."

"No brush-off, mind you," said Elfrida.

"I'll get back to you, Elfrida. I can't tell Minna that I've accepted for her, you know that."

"There you're right. She has a mind of her own."

Minna said, "Yes, I'd like to go. I want to see Elfrida. I love her really. And don't you see, Albert, she wants her family to be represented at this party. The new in-laws. And at a time when Mason is being so lousy to her. If we don't attend she'll feel let down." Minna's motives were wholly feminine. But you would be ill-advised to mention your insights to her. Don't be smart. Make no speeches.

"If you think you're up to this," said Corde, deep-voiced.

"If I run out of steam I can leave early."

For the occasion, Minna curled her hair, wore a red knitted suit with a white trim, a mermaid brooch that had been Valeria's, and Valeria's rings, the ones that had been sawed from her fingers—Corde had just brought them back from the jeweler. He himself, never one for soft raiment, looked like a dean on Sunday. He had left his best suit in the old country, together with shirts, sweaters and socks. Minna had rubbed some color into her cheeks. She still looked pinched but her skin was smoother, the hard dints of grief under her lower lip were going. Some would say that this was the will to live, or the natural resilience of the organism. Well, perhaps, but Corde would have said that she had work to do. There was that zone of star formation waiting for her. Minna did not talk much to her husband about stars; he lacked the physics for it. Perhaps she didn't care to discover how ignorant he was of what concerned her most. To try to work the subject up would have been a mistake. He would have pestered her with half-baked, layman's questions, involving her in tedious explanations impossible for him to follow. So he let that alone. But if she would live for the sake of her stars, he didn't ask for more. She, from her side, was clever, too. She let him tell her about Clemenceau or Chicherin or Jefferson or Lenin so that she could exclaim, "Really, I am *so* dumb!" They were even, then, a dumb matching a dumb. Now, that was intelligent, and strategic, and sympathetically graceful. You might love a woman for her tactfulness alone.

At Ellis Sorokin's Lakeshore Drive high-rise apartment building, a Negro took your car in the garage, a Mexican in green uniform was your doorman, and then you rose in a silent elevator to the altitudes of power. When you got out on the fortieth floor you looked as an equal at the Hancock Tower, "Big John," and at the sugar-cube sparkle of the Standard Oil Building—on all the supershapes of the Loop, in which, perhaps, some sense of common worship was concentrated. The windows of the Sorokin apartment descended nearly to the floor, but though you were so high, you didn't really need to feel that you might fall, and you enjoyed the safe sense of danger.

The Judge's brother resembled him—the same firm, smooth head, tanned creased face and thin mouth and black eyes, a touch of the Indian or the Tartar there. His wife was blond and elegant. Her color was fresh. She had money to spend and—why not?—she spent it, in her innocence, on high fashion. Her elegance was not intimidating, she didn't lay it on you oppressively. Wandering slowly over the ceiling there were green balloons, dozens of them, each one tied with lace ribbon, as expensive as possible. "And what a lot of work," said Corde. The young woman for all her wealth and computer witchery was greatly pleased. "I put in hours and hours blowing them up. But it's a very important occasion, you know."

Corde would have guessed a party for the newlyweds. Not at all; it was the dog's birthday party. Champagne, sturgeon, lobster, Russian eggs for starters, and lunch to follow. The dog was black, huge, gentle—a Great Dane. You were introduced to him in his circular wicker bed, almost a divan, where he lay indolent. Touching, Corde thought as he bent down to stroke the soft animal. The dog sighed under his hand. Wrapped and ribboned birthday presents were stacked beside his bed, and there were congratulatory telegrams.

Elfrida looked somewhat nervous and worn, yes, but also she was deliciously swarthy, discernibly a bride. Her arms, still fine, were heavily braceleted and she carried, as always, the mixed feminine fragrance of perfume and tobacco—almost rank but in the end a good pungency. She embraced Minna, and her brother (no grudges there), and Corde shook the Judge's hand—a rude hand, and all of a piece, as though the fingers were incapable of separate action (outdoor men sometimes have this iron sort of handshake). Congratulations! The bearded Judge was all friendliness. He gave Corde reassuring masculine signals: everything under control, not to worry.

It was a small party. One of the couples owned a Great Dane from the same litter, so there was a relationship. The husband carried color photos of the dog in his wallet and showed them at the table. These were all church people. The Sorokins, too. Episcopal. Their minister was present. Also a classy old woman, a grande dame, very old (her wrists and ankles appeared lymphatic, and her sleeves were adapted to these swellings at the wrist). Very lively, she was obviously devoted to the worldly minister—*he* knew his way around. The grande dame was a connoisseur of miniature reproductions and knew all the most important collections of Lilliputian rooms. She remembered that the celebrated Mrs. Thorne had commissioned a tiny Jackson Pollock, but it didn't please her and she sent it back. "Imagine what it must be worth now!" Corde could be social enough, when it was necessary. It helped to fondle the Great Dane when the animal came nudging and sighing. What to do with all this animal nature, seemed to be the burden of the dog's groans.

He was groomed like a show horse, your stroking told you that—the texture of the short coat, the velvet of the great jowls.

The guests were served chicken Kiev at a glass dining table which was set on a pedestal of contorted wood, something like the trunk of a forest giant flown from the Congo.

Corde had one of the better views: the parks, the winter meadows of drab green cut into geometrical shapes like baize, the big trees like shrubs, the lake too remote to be water, the black-brazen mills at the Indiana end, fizzing out their gray gases.

The birthday tapers when they were lighted reminded Corde of the tapers in the grass before the Raresh grave, and the rings on Minna's fingers made him think of the raspberry grains of blood that had been wiped from them. Then everybody sang "Happy Birthday, Dear Dolphie." Yes, decadence, of course, Corde supposed, though he was almost certainly the only one who supposed it. An all-but-derelict civilization? And the dog, if he represented the Great Beast of the Apocalypse, was also the pal of the Sorokins', on whom the blond wife doted. For her, Corde would have been glad to think, there was no catastrophe and nothing was corrupt, and all living creatures—all!— were equal in her cheerful American heart. She now began to unwrap the great dog's birthday gifts— biscuits, playthings and mock bones, all the carefully packaged products of the billion-dollar pet industry. To oblige his mistress, who stooped with it in her hand, the animal unwillingly licked one of the glazed bones. A high-ranking uncle in the National Guard sent a five-star dog collar, the authentic insignia of a General of the Armies.

And then the balloons, which were of the shade of green poured into the Chicago River on Saint Patrick's Day, were gathered up and set loose from the porches, everybody at play, the clergyman, too, and the aged grande dame, her brittle hair scarfed up in Gucci silk holding these toys by the bands of suggestive lace. On the fortieth floor you were already in the lower stratum of the upper air, out in the naked wind. The balloons, released over the rail, were snatched straight up, out of sight in a vertical updraft, and then they reappeared in flight and you saw them by the dozen spotted over the sky and driven apart, far out over the lake, towards the dark sky-wall where the mills stood. With Sorokin's field glasses you could follow them awhile yet, and then you couldn't see them anymore. The wind had boomed them into Michigan.

Elfrida admitted to Corde, quietly, that Minna wasn't looking well. "You weren't exaggerating. If you're going to California, you should arrange a long weekend in Santa Barbara, rest in one of those good hotels."

Minna was thanking the hostess, in her full, elaborate style—she was strong on etiquette. "We'll be going," said Corde. He kissed his sister with a quick sense of flying through a zone of familiar warmth. She pressed her long cheek to his circular one. "You did right, Elfrida," he said.

"There is the Mason problem, still," said the Judge. "Where is he now?"

"Down in Nicaragua, the last we heard. He telephoned his mother, but wouldn't say what he was doing or where he was going. He's not ready to forgive her."

"For bringing a white child into the world?" said Corde. "Or however he interprets the primal curse? But I don't think that self-injury is a need of his character."

"That's what his psychiatrist used to say to me," said Elfrida.

"But I wonder," said Corde, "whether he's still in touch with Cousin Maxie."

"Ah, that's just it," said the Judge. "It would give a new publicity boost to old Detillion. But he hasn't put out any statements. And we'll have to wait for the hearing before we can be sure that Mason intended to jump bail."

"Our Uncle Harold was with the Marines who chased out Sandino in the twenties," said Corde.

Elfrida said, "I doubt that Mason was ever told that fact." She now gave the conversation a different turn. "You never said, Albert, that you had met Dewey Spangler overseas."

"No. It never occurred to me to say. How did you hear about it?"

"How did you *not* hear?" said Elfrida. "Haven't you seen the papers?"

"No. We canceled before Christmas and delivery hasn't started again."

"And didn't anybody call you about it? It's unnatural."

"I keep the phones unplugged. I don't want Minna disturbed. She's had enough of telephones."

"I'm astonished. I would have expected somebody, a colleague from the college or a neighbor in the building, to knock at your door."

"Why, what is it in the papers that's so extraordinary?"

"A column by our old friend Dewey, where he lets himself go. How you met behind the iron curtain, the boyhood friendship, Lakeview High, your wife's predicament. I got more information from that little mug than from you."

"I don't know the man myself," said the Judge. "I only hear from Elfrida how he used to be when you were youngsters. I follow his column from time to time, but this article is kind of a departure, unusually personal."

"How personal?" Corde asked Elfrida.

"A certain amount of reminiscence," said Elfrida. "Pretty brief but packed tight, and really pretty curious —full of observations about American society and culture, and Albert Corde of Chicago as a phenomenon. What would you call it—a short study, a personal memoir, and if you ask me, also a love letter. Not in such good taste, either."

Corde's heart sank. He experienced also a kind of vascular tightening in the legs, like a man who gets to his feet too quickly, momentarily paralyzed.

"We've upset Albert," said Elfrida to her husband. "When the pink turns up on the cheekbones and his lips press together, he's worried or hurt. I didn't find anything so harmful in what Dewey wrote, Albert. Overblown. Pretentious. Here and there he actually slipped into poetry, and I don't think he has a real gift for that kind of thing."

"He said something similar about my articles in *Harper's*," said Corde.

"Oh, what a comparison!" said Elfrida. "But the worst I'd feel in your place is privacy shock. And with Detillion at work we've all been conditioned or immunized to that. Well, Albert, wait at least until you've read him. It isn't so bad. In my opinion, he wanted to join forces with you."

"You've got a copy, haven't you." Corde stated rather than asked this.

"We talked it over before coming," said the Judge, "and decided that on the off chance you had missed it, it was better you should see it, just in case you had to protect yourself."

"But Elfrida was just saying it wasn't so bad."

She was opening her alligator purse. "You certainly could do without this," she said. "Although comparatively it's minor." As she handed him the folded paper she shone her look upon him, but what really—*really!*—her eyes were saying he couldn't have told you.

18

At home, he gave Minna a cup of tea. Then she said she would lie down and read something—what did he recommend? She always consulted him about reading matter. He knew her simple, old-fashioned tastes. Tanti Gigi, from whom she had learned English at the age of ten years, had given her poems to learn by heart: "The Little Black Boy," "The Sick Rose." He said, "I'll give you Blake's Songs. The two contrary states of the human soul. I was reading Blake while you were at Wesleyan."

"And what will you do with the rest of your afternoon?"

"Go over a few items on my desk."

He withdrew to his corner and unfolded Dewey Spangler's double column of print. It was headed "A Tale of Two Cities."

Corde didn't find it poetic. It was written in Spangler's dependable expository prose for the busy reader. It began with a brief nostalgic paragraph: meeting an old friend who had been his rival in Miss Gumbeener's class at Lakeview. In two sentences he did the friendship. Corde described the whole event as an exhibition match—*Monstre Gai* versus *Ennuyeux Sentimental,* five rounds of boxing. The *Ennuyeux* won the first round. Dewey got off to a clumsy start, speaking of "relationships difficult to form with people in public life." He didn't need to mention Kissinger and Nelson Rockefeller, or make them sound like characters out of Plutarch. But he recovered a little towards the end of the paragraph, evoking the friendship of two "inordinately bookish high school kids." He spoke of his gifted pal Albert Corde, "even then a mysterious individual," who later made a considerable reputation in the International *Herald Tribune,* eventually becoming Professor and Dean Corde. The Dean never intended to mystify anybody, but mystify he did, with his mysterious character. One wonders what effect Deep Analysis might have had on such a person, but Albert Corde was inexplicably hostile towards Psychoanalysis. It will portray the man at one stroke to record what he once said about it. "Psychoanalysis pretends to investigate the Unconscious. The Unconscious by definition is what you aren't conscious of. But the Analysts already know what's in it. They should, because they put it all in beforehand. It's like an Easter Egg hunt. You hide the eggs and then you find 'em. That's on the up and up. But Analysis ain't." Dewey went on, "With an attitude like this my old friend therefore remained mysterious.

"As personal idiosyncrasy this warranted no objection, but not long ago Dean Corde went public and wrote two mystifying articles about the City of Chicago, puzzling and disturbing many readers."

Albert Corde, Spangler wrote, had made his debut as a journalist with the only literate firsthand account of the Potsdam Conference. This Dartmouth junior, a GI who had enlisted and served in France and Germany, happened to be in Potsdam and wrote a brilliant piece for *The New Yorker.* He saw Stalin in an armchair as plain as you and me; he saw Churchill's fall from power and watched Harry Truman play poker and drink whiskey. Of course he was only a kid, with no background in history or world politics. Corde was then twenty-two years of age, but his remarkable account of this conference, which had such dark consequences for the world, has been unjustifiably neglected by the anthologist professors and is forgotten. From the first, the Dean's talent was for observation, not for generalization and synthesis (he lacked Spangler's intellectual

grand mastery), and he was wise to stay away from
international politics.

But just picture it—the two friends from Lakeview
High School meeting in a Communist capital during the
dismal days of late December. In the hospital, an old
woman dying; and in Chicago a jury trial. The Dean
had become involved in a disagreeable matter involving
the death of a student. There was unpleasant infighting.
This was hardly as important as it appeared to a
hypersensitive man. "To a friend seasoned in modern
politics, covering the world scene in depth for twenty-
five years—riot, terrorism, massacre, the strategies of
power—Professor Corde's personal distress seemed
exaggerated. Temperamentally, he was tender-minded,
incapable of grasping the full implications of world
transformation, the growth of a new technology for
managing human affairs, the new factors, the analytical
paradigms which guide the decisions of authority in all
postindustrial societies." The Dean was a delicate spirit,
a genuinely reflective person. This was why he gave up
journalism and took cover in the academy. Coming out
again to have a look at the present sociopolitical scene,
he went into shock. His particular brand of humanism
could not prepare him for what he saw in the streets
and skyscrapers. Here was a clear opening (Dewey
became very grand in this next passage) for the revival
of a humanistic outlook. "Underdefinition of the criteria by which men are defined opened an opportunity to
Humanists to introduce their models, as against Eco-
nomic Man, Psychological Man and other typologies.
But the Dean has no bent for such enterprises. He is
not a man for models, he is a sensitive and emotional
private observer. Trained urbanologists regarded his
Chicago articles as excessively emotional."

These "paradigms" and the "underdefinition of the
criteria" were Malraux thrusts, Hegelian world history
in an updated American form. Who among Spangler's
colleagues in Washington or New York could handle

such concepts—Reston, Kraft, Alsop in his best days? And what of Walter Lippmann himself?

We were getting into deeper waters now, and Corde's heart took on a monitory heaviness. Warning: Anything can happen here.

The trained urbanologists had found the articles too emotional. "This was predictable in a personality of so rare a type, appalled by the transformation of his native city. For Corde is attached to Chicago by strong feelings and the physical and human destruction he describes in *Harper's* fills him with pain. As a fellow Chicagoan and an old friend I can testify to this. But it should be added that even in his youth Albert Corde, the son of a wealthy and privileged family, did not know the Chicago in which the rest of us were growing up. It takes the most American of all American cities to create this native son who is as unlike his fellow Americans as he can be. When your correspondent and his old friend met for a drink in Bucharest, the Dean repeated the amusing remark an elderly English traveler had once made to him: 'I suppose there's nothing too rum to be true.' I apply this to the Dean himself. He is an American almost too rum to be recognized as such by his fellow citizens. This was why it was hard for them to follow his argument."

As he read this, the Dean discovered that he almost stopped breathing. What a smart little monster Dewey was, and what a keen schemer, and how rivalrous. He disposed of the Dean by describing him as an unwitting alien. How cleverly he got rid of him. Corde had to admit that Dewey had put his finger on an important fact. In touch with the Sadats and the Kissingers, the Brezhnevs and the Nixons, interpreting them to the world, Dewey was a master of the public forms of discourse. If you were going to be a communicator, you had to know the passwords, the code words, you had to signify your acceptance of the prevailing standards. You could say nothing publicly, not if you expected to

be taken seriously, without the right clearance. The
Dean's problem had been one of language. Nobody will
buy what you're selling—not in those words. They
don't even know what your product *is*.

"Professor Corde," Dewey went on, "is very hard on
journalism, on the mass media. His charge is that they
fail to deal with the moral, emotional, imaginative life,
in short, the *true* life of human beings, and that their
great power prevents people from having access to this
true life. What we call 'information' he would charac-
terize as delusion. He does not say this in so many
words, but in his recent sketches he tries to outline
creatively the right way to apprehend public questions.
If he emphasizes strongly the sufferings of urban populations, especially in the ghettos, it is because he thinks
that public discussion is threadbare, that this is either
the cause or the effect of blindness (or both the cause
and effect) and that our cultural poverty has the same
root as the frantic and criminal life of our once great
cities. He blames the communications industry for this.
It breeds hysteria and misunderstanding. He also
blames the universities. Academics have made no
effort to lead the public. The intellectuals have been
incapable of clarifying our principal problems and of
depicting democracy to itself in this time of agonized
struggle. Reading Dean Corde one is reminded of
certain pages of Ortega y Gasset's *The Rebellion of the
Masses* (incorrectly translated as *The Revolt*) and also
of passages in André Malraux's memorable conversations with General de Gaulle, and of the final work of
Malraux's dying days. . . .

"But if the Dean is hard on the media he is even
more bitter about the academics. The media are part of
corporate America. They are part of the problem,
hence their 'impartiality' is meaningless. But the universities are a deep disappointment to him. I gather
from his conversation that he thinks academics are not
different from other Americans, they are dominated by
the same consensus and ruled by public opinion. They

were not set apart, with all their privileges, to be like everybody else but to be *different*. If they could not accept difference they could not make the contribution to culture that society needed. The challenge to the Humanists was the challenge to produce new models.

"I am not," Dewey astonishingly wrote, "an admirer of Jean Jacques Rousseau. I would not agree with Immanuel Kant that he was a great man. He did, however, understand that the challenge of modern egalitarian societies would be the creation of high human types, such individuals as would satisfy the human need for stature and love of the beautiful. This would not be elitism in the ordinary acceptance of the term but generosity and love of humankind, the exact opposite of snobbery and false superiority. I assume that this was why my friend Albert Corde gave up a quite successful career in journalism to become a professor. His hopes disappointed, he went out to investigate the surrounding city, and he will forgive me for saying that he went slightly mad. It wasn't only the collapse of urban America that got him but what Julien Benda called the treason of the intellectuals. . . ."

Oh, fuck you, Dewey, and your Julien Benda! Corde, knuckling his eyes, smarting with sweat, read on. There wasn't much left, thank God.

"Dean Corde must have offended his colleagues deeply. They should have been irradiating American society with humanistic culture, and in the Dean's book they are failures and phonies. That's what his articles reveal. I wonder whether my dear old friend realizes this. I am not sure that he has a good idea of what they were up against, the magnitude of the challenge facing them. Who would, who could make high human types of the business community, the engineers, the politicians and the scientists? What system of higher education could conceivably have succeeded? But Dean Corde is unforgiving. Philistinism is his accusation. Philistine by origin, humanistic academics were drawn magnetically back again to the philistine core of American society. What should have been an elite of the intellect became instead an elite of influence and comforts. The cities decayed. The professors couldn't have prevented that, but they could have told us (as the Dean himself somewhat wildly tries to do) what the human meaning of this decay was and what it augured for civilization. Scholars who were supposed to represent the old greatness didn't put up a fight for it. They gave in to the great emptiness. And 'from the emptiness come whirlwinds of insanity,' he writes.

"A little coaching in *realpolitik* would have done the Dean no harm. It was too bad that he was carried away by an earnestness too great for his capacities, because he is a very witty man. In conversation he was charming and amusing about politics and the law in Chicago. When he wasn't sailing in the clouds with Vico and Hegel he was extremely funny. He made some memorable remarks about the varieties of public welfare in the United States. There are high welfare categories as well as low ones. Some professors work hard, said the Dean. Most of them do. But a professor when he gets tenure doesn't *have* to do anything. A tenured professor and a welfare mother with eight kids have much in common. . . ."

The damage that these sentences would do was as clear as the print itself. By a process of instantaneous translation, Corde read them with the eyes of Alec Witt, the Provost. He thought, Dewey has done it to me. Alec Witt has got me now, convicted out of my own mouth. Of course I could try to say that I was only quoting, that this was Mason senior speaking, but Witt isn't going to listen to explanations, nor will he care what actually was said. The trouble is all in the nuances. Oh, the nuances! Dewey and I never did get our nuances together, not in forty years. And the college won't care to hear about the nuances. And here's the progress I've made with the Provost. At first I was suspect, and presently I was distrusted and afterwards disliked. Finally by my own sincere efforts I

worked my way down into the lowest category—
contempt. And then, "The man is a disaster." And
finally, "The sonofabitch is a traitor." Yes, Dewey's
done it to me this time. This was the Dewey who never
had a college education letting us all have it. And at the
same time wanting to draw close. And to take me in his
embrace. And hoping to soar far beyond Walter Lippmann. And this is something like the letter he wrote
from New York when we were kids, when Uncle
Harold, that old goon, jimmied open the drawer and
read aloud to the family what Dewey had written, and
gave Mother so much pain. That was winter, too, but
this is more mean-looking; now the wind is from the
north, with rain, and harsh water.

19

Corde did not speak of this to Minna until they had left
the Los Angeles airport in the Budget Rent-a-Car. He
thought it would be easier to talk in open country. Here
at any rate the sun was shining. He had counted on
some help from the climate. And from astronomy, of
course. Whatever, technically, she was thinking was
wonderfully good for her. On the plane she had
actually chatted with him about the birth of stars from
gas clouds, the embryonic form of these suns, their
infrared rays and the radio waves they emitted, the past
of our own sun, its future. She had mentioned something called FU Orionis. He never bothered her with
questions about hydrogen, helium, lithium. He remembered the wise Egyptian who had told Cleopatra, "In
Nature's book of infinite secrecy, a little I can read,"

but she was making such excellent progress that he kept this to himself, although as a rule she liked him to quote her quotes.

When the foothills began he told her what Spangler had written—briefed her quite fully on the consequences. He said, "I didn't want to molest you with all this."

"I see. . . . I wouldn't have been able to do that, keep all that to myself. It was very masculine of you. But stupid! I'm your wife. I'm *supposed* to be told."

"I couldn't predict how you'd take it. Of course, I'm very glad. . . . So then, Dewey really screwed me. It wasn't me that made that crack about professors and welfare mothers . . . Zaehner, poor man."

"Ah, yes, it was Zaehner. But you did quote."

"It was all distorted. Much of the rest I didn't say, either. Although here and there he got me right. But how could he not know what such a column would do to me. Forty years of *almost* communication . . ."

"And not even forty years is enough? But that's not news to you, either. And why did you talk so openly to him?"

"There's the whole thing—having people to talk to. To be able to say what you mean, mean what you say. Truthfully, it did occur to me at the Intercontinental that Dewey was interviewing me. But I figured it was nothing more than his professional habit."

"If you actually sensed that he was doing an interview, why did you talk?"

"I only said that it had the format of an interview. It didn't cross my mind that I was opening my heart to the press."

"I must read the article. I will, when we get to Palomar. I can understand why you would talk. Talking was about the only desire you had a chance to satisfy, over there."

"Yes, and it was the day of the funeral. Besides, I always did love Dewey. And partly I was affected also by the exotic place, so far from home that somehow it all seemed off the record. I never expected to account to Alec Witt for all that. . . ."

"Alec let you have it."

"Not shouting, of course; that's not his style. His style is to go after you in short rushes. Each one of them is pleasant. But then you begin to see where he's maneuvered you. He hasn't ever been rude to me. He's never been anything except considerate. But there's a grinning glow. And finally at the kill there's a great radiance. He told me I could always say what I liked and say it publicly. Academic freedom protected me. I was, however, involved in a contradiction which, surely, an intelligent man like me couldn't overlook. A tenured professor had no obligations to the institution except minimal adherence to its rules, but the responsibilities of an officer of the administration, once you had accepted them, limited your options. I had made the administration *very* unhappy. While everybody was deeply sympathetic to me, people who had sacrificed for the college, and so on, given their best energies, fought for liberal education as well as for the very survival of the institution, were *deeply* wounded. He beat on my soul good and hard. He could have been singing *Exsultate, Jubilate* as he kicked hell out of me. His task was to make sure of my resignation without serious offense to you, or blocking any effort I might make to take you away. He executed this like a kind of angel. He bound me while he hit me."

"Then you told him that you would resign as dean?"

"Yes," said Corde. "I told him that. My purpose in going to his office was to tell him. As for you, it was a rule with me not to meddle, I assured him. To find out how you felt he'd have to talk to you."

"That was right," said Minna. "But how disagreeable for you, Albert."

"Not so bad. I'm not much hurt. It's not my game. I wasn't meant to be a dean. I didn't say that to the Provost. I said I was resigning and it wasn't necessary to discuss the motives, but that I did want to say what a valuable institution the college was for the city, along with Northwestern and the University of Chicago, and how important it was for young people learning about painting and poetry, reading history, classics, the sciences, to have libraries and fine instruction. These islands, how badly the country needs them. I almost said, 'If only to counterbalance the S.M. establishments.'"

"What are those?"

"The sadomasochistic shops, where people now go as if to the beauty parlor—with virtually the same carefree attitude."

"You have a really endearing character, but you do somehow work in such strange things," said Minna.

"But I didn't say. I *almost*. I only told him I was grateful to the college. I told him no lies, and I wasn't perverse. Anyway, he wasn't really listening. He accepted my resignation letter and passed to another subject—Beech. Did I intend to write an article about Beech? I said that I guessed I would do more writing."

"Along the lines of the *Harper's* pieces?"

"Oh, absolutely. Why not?"

She said, having thought about this for some miles, "It won't be a restful life."

"I won't do articles like the Chicago ones unless I'm stirred in the same peculiar way. That doesn't happen often. I'm quiet enough as a rule. I don't like controversy. I'm good enough at my trade."

"But how are you going to practice it?"

"We'll have to see what happens. Dewey said I had quite a successful career in journalism. I'll take it up again, as quietly as I can."

"Now will you tell me about Beech?"

"I spent a long afternoon with him."

"The best people in Geophysics swear by him."

"I like the man."

"And you've decided to do the article? Wouldn't that be a good way to start over?"

"I arranged to help him with it. Those lead conclusions are his, not mine. *Something* deadly is happening. I'm with him to that extent. So I'll advise him about language only. Then I won't have to agree ignorantly."

She took his hand from the steering wheel, pressed it, kept it in her lap. She said, presently, "We aren't too far from the Indian mission. We can stop there and take a break."

"The trip is tiring you. We didn't make smart arrangements. We should have flown in yesterday and rested overnight in Los Angeles. I can stand that place for about ten hours."

The mission was in a sheltered, warm zone. Corde and Minna looked into the handicrafts shop—beads, turquoise, arrowheads, gloves in the dim showcases, clusters of moccasins gathering dust in the corners. Then they sat in the inner court. "Five minutes in the sun?" said Minna. She followed her schedule. The heavy arches of the cloister formed a small square. In the foreground, flowers; behind the whitewashed arches, darkness, but tranquil darkness.

Corde said, "You know what? It threw Dewey Spangler into a frenzy of happiness to have such crushing wonderful things to say. It put him right on the summits. And best of all, he could blame the mischief on me. He was so delirious that he couldn't think what it might do to his pal. Maybe it was the cuts in his intestines that put him in such a state."

"I wouldn't think any more about him," said Minna.

When they returned to the rental car, Corde reluctant, dragging (but realistically, how long could they stay seated in a mission garden choked with flowers?), Minna said, "Valeria had a high opinion of you, Albert." Her head was down; she clipped the seat belt into place. "She trusted you."

"You think so?"

"What you told her last of all was what she wanted most of all to hear."

No more was said of this. Corde was moved. His wife, unskilled in human dealings, was offering him support from her own main source. What came through Minna's words was that she was alone in the world; and with him; she did have him, with all his troubling oddities; and he had her.

Minna now began to talk about the chances for a clear night. Here on the lower slopes the sun was shining, and that was promising, but conditions changed very rapidly here. When it was cloudy, the dome didn't open. She said that several times.

"I'm sending up prayers for optimum weather," he said. "But I read here and there that the new robots out in space transmit fantastic information, pictures you can't get from the ground."

"That's mostly true. But there's something I need from the two-hundred-inch telescope."

"Even that, I understand, you can see on the TV monitors in the control room."

"Won't do," said Minna. "I have to have the plates."

"You aren't going to sit up there, in the eye of the telescope, or the cage, or whatever it's called? I hope not."

"I've done it a hundred times."

"But this time?"

"I think yes."

"Can't you send up somebody with instructions?"

"No. Last time one of the smart young people made the fine corrections for me, and the results were unusable."

"But you aren't well enough, Minna."

"No? I am, though."

Interference was out of the question. The professional line! How severe she was, drawing it. How he presented himself at the barrier, petitioning. For her own good. It amused them both—each in his own way. "You've lost too much weight," was all that he found to say.

"I'll be wearing the insulated suit. And they keep the cage warmer now than in the old days."

At five thousand feet there was snow on the ground,

a thin cover over the huge raw clearing around the dome.

"No clouds at all," said Minna. "We're lucking out. Now, if no fog develops . . ."

To his great relief, she got the weather she wanted, and while she was getting herself ready, talking to colleagues, he explored the enormous dark emptiness of the dome, passing under the gray barrel of the great telescope and hearing the stir of the machines that operated it. He was warmly dressed, he had brought his parka from Chicago. One of the younger assistants in the observatory was assigned to keep him company. "Let's inspect the layout. Have you ever seen it before?"

"Not this particular dome, and never any of them with a guide."

The tall young man, bearded, had the air of a ski instructor, and he talked about right ascension, mirrors, refractions, spectrum analysis. "I can't follow," Corde said at last. They stopped in midfloor, a vast, unlighted, icy, scientific Cimmerian gloom. The hugeness of the dome referred you—far past mosques or churches, Saint Paul's, Saint Peter's—to the real scale of the night. We built as big as we could build for the purpose of investigating the *real* bigness. The dome's interior was segmented by curved beams. Corde had never been inside an empty space so huge. The floor was endless to cross. Despite his sweaters, coat, double socks, parka, he was cold on the encircling catwalk. They stepped out on the outer gallery—light steel spongework underfoot; you could see through it. The snow extended to the edge of the enormous clearing. He went inside again.

If you came for a look at astral space it was appropriate that you should have a taste of the cold *out there*, its power to cancel everything merely human. That he understood so little of the tall young man's lingo made no difference; he went on talking, but Corde several times refused to go to the rooms below where you could

sip coffee, read magazines, practice billiard shots.
Minna had said when she was leaving him, "It looks
now as if they're sure to open by and by. I'll send for
you."

Her messenger found Corde and his guide on the
catwalk. Dr. Corde was going to the cage, and would
he like to ride up, too? Yes, he did, of course.

He ran down eagerly. The junior colleague who had
been guiding him was coming along to help Minna
install herself in the eye of the huge instrument. She
was wearing the tight-fitting suit. As she went into the
open lift, Corde following, he asked again, "You're
sure you can take the cold?"

"Don't fuss over me. I'll come down if I can't, my
dear."

True, he was foolishly fussing. She had lost her
natural insulation. Temporarily emaciated. Permanently excited. She said to the stooping, bearded young
man, "My husband has never been up."

"Never?" He pressed the switch and they began to
rise.

The lift was attached to one of the structural arches.
It didn't go straight up; it followed a curved course.
Except in one low corner of the interior, there was no
light. And now the vast dome rumbled. Something
parted, began to slide above them. Segments of the
curved surface opened quickly and let in the sky—first
a clear piercing slice. All at once there was only the lift,
moving along the arch. The interior was abolished
altogether—no interior—nothing but the open, freezing heavens. If this present motion were to go on, you
would travel straight out. You would go up into the
stars. He could make out the edges of the open dome
still. And because there was a dome, and the cold was
so absolute, he came inevitably back to the crematorium, *that* rounded top and its huge circular floor, the
feet of stiffs sticking through the curtains, the blasting
heat underneath where they were disposed of, the
killing cold when you returned and thought your head

was being split by an ax. But that dome never opened. You could pass through only as smoke.

This Mount Palomar coldness was not to be compared to the cold of the death house. Here the living heavens looked as if they would take you in. Another sort of rehearsal, thought Corde. The sky was tense with stars, but not so tense as he was, in his breast. Everything overhead was in equilibrium, kept in place by mutual tensions. What was it that *his* tensions kept in place?

And what he saw with his eyes was not even the real heavens. No, only white marks, bright vibrations, clouds of sky roe, tokens of the real thing, only as much as could be taken in through the distortions of the atmosphere. Through these distortions you saw objects, forms, partial realities. The rest was to be felt. And it wasn't only that you felt, but that you were drawn to feel and to penetrate further, as if you were being informed that what was spread over you had to do with your existence, down to the very blood and the crystal forms inside your bones. Rocks, trees, animals, men and women, these also drew you to penetrate further, under the distortions (comparable to the atmospheric ones, shadows within shadows), to find their real being with your own. This was the sense in which you were drawn.

Once, in the Mediterranean, coming topside from a C-class cabin, the uric smells and the breath of the bilges, every hellish little up-to-date convenience there below to mock your insomnia—then seeing the morning sun on the tilted sea. Free! The grip of every sickness within you disengaged by this pouring out. You couldn't tell which was out of plumb, the ship, or yourself, or the sea aslant—but free! It didn't matter, since you were free! It was like that also when you approached the stars as steadily as this.

The lift stopped and his wife, in the sort of thermal suit she wore, smiled at him. Perhaps his parka amused her. They had reached the top of the telescope. She climbed down into the pit of it, into the cage filled with technical apparatus—gauges, panels glowing, keys to press, wires. The stooped assistant got in with her to help her to hook up. The young man was quick. Agile, he climbed again into the lift. She waved to her husband, cheerful, and closed herself in. She was Corde's representative among those bright things so thick and close.

Corde said, "She'll be all right, I suppose. She's not too long out of the hospital."

The young man pressed the switch for the descent. "Never saw the sky like this, did you?"

"No. I was told how cold it would be. It *is* damn cold."

"Does that really get you, do you really mind it all that much?"

They were traveling slowly in the hooked path of their beam towards the big circle of the floor.

"The cold? Yes. But I almost think I mind coming down more."